***Everybody loves Stella Cameron!***

"Stella Cameron leaves you breathless, satisfied . . . and hungry for the next time!"

—Elizabeth Lowell

"Sizzling, sexy, and sensational!"

—Jayne Ann Krentz

"Stella Cameron writes an exciting, fast-paced and very sensual novel—just the kind of book I love."

—Linda Lael Miller

"Stella Cameron works magic with our hearts and casts a seductive spell."

—Katherine Stone

"Stella Cameron's books are filled with wit, grace and sizzling sensuality."

—Anne Stuart

"Her narrative is rich, her style distinct, and her characters wonderfully wicked."

—*Publishers Weekly*

"Stunning!"

—*Romantic Times*

"Dazzling and refreshing!"

—*Affaire de Coeur*

***Turn the page and discover for yourself the incomparable magic of Stella Cameron!***

**He'd wanted her for as long as he could remember . . .**

"We never got a chance to dance together before," Sebastian said into her ear.

She followed him across the floor, despite backless sandals and her own hesitancy, burying her face in his chest when the last notes were played. When they stopped and he tilted her face up to his, a smattering of applause broke out. He kissed her nose, then the corner of her mouth.

Laughter joined the applause.

"You haven't changed," Bliss said. "You were always wild."

"I'd prefer to think of myself as spontaneous," Sebastian replied.

"Stop it. Why are you doing this to me?"

"I want to be with you. I'll take it any way I can get it."

"You must think I'm an idiot. You left me. You stayed away nearly half of our lifetimes. Now you'll do anything you have to to be with me? Please, credit me with a little intelligence."

"I couldn't be here any sooner." Those were dangerous words, words he couldn't afford to have probed too deeply. "Forgive me."

"Forgive you. Forgive you? Sebastian, I've got to get on with my life and *forget* you. I have forgotten you."

"No you haven't. I can see it in your eyes. You haven't forgotten any more than I have." He held her a little closer. "Those months with you were the best months of my life. I remember every one of them—every day. If I could change things, I would. If I could turn the clock back, I would."

Bliss fought it, but the truth came out. "So would I."

*Also by Stella Cameron:*

SHEER PLEASURES
PURE DELIGHTS
BREATHLESS
ONLY BY YOUR TOUCH
HIS MAGIC TOUCH
FASCINATION
CHARMED
BRIDE

*Forthcoming Books:*

BELOVED (In September, 1996)
GUILTY PLEASURES (In March, 1997)

# TRUE BLISS

STELLA CAMERON

ZEBRA BOOKS
KENSINGTON PUBLISHING CORP.

ZEBRA BOOKS are published by

Kensington Publishing Corp.
850 Third Avenue
New York, NY 10022



First Printing: August, 1996
10 9 8 7 6 5 4 3 2 1

Printed in the United States of America

*For Maureen Walters,*
*with affection.*

# Prologue

Sebastian Plato was bad news.

Dark hair the wrong side of too long fell toward narrowed eyes the color of green glass; broken green glass. Glittering green glass. His tan was the kind Seattleites weren't supposed to have—a tan from the sun. The visible edges of his teeth were very white. His mouth had smiling corners. Corners that lied. Sebastian Plato didn't laugh. His green glass eyes didn't grow warm—ever.

*Stay away from that boy,* every "nice" kid's parents warned. *He's trouble.*

Bliss Winters whistled softly and focused on a worn silver belt buckle fashioned in the shape of a coiled snake. The snake's tail wound into a lazy S.

The belt was a school legend. Bliss swallowed, and whistled some more. Her dry mouth and throat produced no sound.

Did Sebastian Plato really do the things they said he did with that belt?

Bliss sat a little straighter in her cafeteria chair, and frowned at her sandwich. If he did those things, why did the girls who talked about them act as if they were sorry for those who hadn't experienced . . . whatever? She glanced up at six feet or so of stomach-twisting *bad news.*

Sebastian Plato stared right back. And the legs of the chair opposite Bliss's squeaked as he pulled it aside.

Her heart broke into a tarantella rhythm.

Whistling wasn't an option anymore.

He sat down.

The chair squealed some more as he scooted his long legs under the table.

Bliss eyed her sandwich.

Sebastian Plato had big hands, very big—and tanned like his face. Long fingers, blunt at the tips. They rested on the tabletop and drummed lightly. Tap, tap, tap, tap, tap. Then the other hand. Then just the index finger of the right hand while the left curled into a fist, a fist with a pale scar across the knuckles.

Nonchalance, she told herself. Play it cool.

She wasn't Morris and Kitten Winters's only child for nothing. Haughty nonchalance subdued the opponent every time. Sebastian Plato definitely fell into what Bliss's parents regarded as "an opponent," one of those who didn't equal their social status.

Bliss rested an elbow on the table and aimed a corner of her sandwich at her mouth.

"What d'you call a dachshund sitting on a rabbit in January? . . . In Minnesota?"

The sandwich missed Bliss's target. She glanced around the high-school cafeteria. He was talking to her. Really talking to her. He had to be. The room had emptied and they were the only two people at this table.

He tilted his chair onto its back two legs and jiggled. The lazy S, slung low over a flat stomach, glistened. "So, what's the answer? What d'you call it?" he asked.

She set down the sandwich and pushed her glasses back up her nose. "I don't know."

"A chilly dog on a bun."

"A . . ." She frowned. He must be making fun of her. Of course he was making fun of her. Why else would he be hanging around?

"A chilly dog on a bun!" He grinned and his green eyes narrowed some more. "Get it?"

Bliss looked over her shoulder, then back at the wild boy she'd heard other girls call, "dishy." "I get it," she told him. Wild, dishy, dangerous boys didn't seek out dull, ordinary girls. "What's the point?"

Sebastian let the front legs of his chair hit the tiled floor with a thud. "No point," he said airily. "An ice-breaker is all. Just making conversation, Chilly Winters. Get it? Ice-breaker? Chilly—"

"Very funny."

He crossed his arms on the table and rested his chin on top. His hair slid even farther forward. He regarded her from its shadow. "Best I could do," he muttered. "Y'know why they call you Chilly, don't you?"

"I think I've figured it out." She wasn't like them, or interested in being like them, and she didn't say much—that made them think she was cold.

Bliss picked up her sandwich again and peered at the contents; rapidly drying tuna, and wilted lettuce.

"You bring your lunch every day, don't you?" Sebastian asked.

Why would he care? "Yes."

"Because the food they sell around here isn't good enough?"

"I'd rather eat the food around here," she said before she could stop herself.

He considered before saying, "What's it like to be rich the way you are?"

"What's it like for you to be—" She closed her mouth and lowered her eyes.

"To be what?" he said. He reached across the table, tapped the back of her hand. "Look at me. What's it like to be what? More than a year older than every other senior because you dropped out of school for a year? A guy with a reputation for being *dangerous?* A guy they say deals in drugs and totes guns?"

"Do you?" This time she clapped a hand over her mouth.

"Absolutely." Sebastian blew upward at his wavy, black hair. "You've seen me flashing my piece, haven't you? And you've gotta get sick of me trying to sell you coke."

"Yes." Bliss laughed a little. "Really sick of it." Maybe it was all lies. At least he could joke about himself.

"Your dad's a senator. And you're rich."

Same old questions. Same old curiosity. Same old assumptions that it was great to be the daughter of Senator Morris Winters and his wife, Kitten. "My folks are rich," Bliss said, resigned.

"What's that like?"

"The truth?"

"Yeah." He scrunched down and laced his hands behind his neck.

"I've never been the daughter of poor people, so I've never known anything else. My mother doesn't want me to eat school food because she doesn't want me to get fat."

"Mrs. Morris Winters, pres of the PTA." With his hands still behind his neck, Sebastian slipped slowly sideways. He spent a long time peering under the table at Bliss before jerking himself up to his former position. "She's got some imagination, hasn't she? Your mother?"

Bliss's face throbbed with heat. "You're rude."

"One more thing people say about me. You'd have to eat a helluva lot of school lunches just to reach well-covered."

Bliss took a large bite out of the horrible sandwich the family housekeeper, Mrs. Lymer, had made. She chewed ferociously.

"I like the way you look," Sebastian said.

Bliss's jaws missed a beat, then she kept on chewing.

"Why are you in a public school?"

She swallowed with difficulty. "I like being here."

"I didn't ask if you liked it. I asked why."

Because Daddy thought it looked good to his constituents. "My parents believe in public education."

"But not in public education lunches?"

"No." He was quick. Sharp, quick, big, self-confident—a dish. And dangerous. She heard the other kids whisper about him. When Sebastian showed up, the whispering stopped.

"You must be the only student in the history of the school to have a ball field named after her old man. At least in his lifetime."

Scrambling out of her chair and fleeing the room wasn't a choice she could make. Not dignified. Morris and Kitten Winters' first family law: A Winters must always be dignified.

"Didn't it embarrass you to have your dear old dad buy a new stadium for the school?"

She folded her arms.

"I watched you when he gave that dedication speech."

Bliss looked at the table.

"I watch you every time he gives a speech. Some of the kids think he's great. Some of the girls think he's sexy."

"Have you finished?"

"Nope. We're the voice of the world, right? The kids? The world the way it's going to be? Morris Winters' way?"

"It embarrasses me," she said. Let him sneer at her for being honest. All the other kids sneered, why not Sebastian, too? "All of it. The stupid field. And every time he comes here, it embarrasses me."

"I know."

Blinking didn't stop her eyes from stinging.

"When your dad talks, you look like you want to disappear—or die."

Bliss met his stare.

"It stinks to feel like dirt, doesn't it?" he said. "I watch you all the time, Chilly. I've wanted to talk to you for weeks."

Another girl strolled toward the table. She ignored Bliss and said, "Hi, Sebastian." Crystal Moore was captain of the cheerleading squad, and drop-dead gorgeous.

Sebastian looked at her and Bliss almost turned away when he made a visual run from long, shimmering red hair over the type of body he would never refer to as less than "well-covered."

"You going to the game tonight?" Crystal asked. "There's a party afterward."

"There's always a party afterward," Sebastian said without cracking a smile.

Crystal wrapped her arms around her books. She spared Bliss a curiously spiteful glance before focusing the power of her violet eyes back on Sebastian. "See you there, then."

He watched Crystal walk away.

Bliss watched Sebastian.

"Like I was saying"—he turned to her once more—"I've wanted to talk to you, Chilly."

"My name is Bliss."

He spread his long fingers on the scuffed, beige tabletop. "Okay. I like Bliss. I wanted to talk to you, Bliss. I like you, too—Bliss the girl."

"You don't know me."

"I told you. I've watched you for weeks."

Her tummy made a roll.

"You're different."

"No kidding!" She snorted.

"In a good way. Have you always lived in Seattle?"

"Yes." Bliss rapidly stuffed the remains of her lunch into Mrs. Lymer's brown sack. "I'd better get going."

"Why? You've got an open period."

She stopped in the act of getting up. "How do you know?"

"I looked up your schedule."

Her next breath stuck on top of the last bite of sandwich. She dropped back into the seat. "I don't understand." They said he . . . They said he forced himself on girls. The fast girls said he didn't have to force himself. Bliss's palms sweated.

"You don't understand a guy liking a girl?"

"Well . . ." She'd never had a boyfriend, never been on a date—unless you counted the awful, awkward social pairings her mother had arranged.

"You think I'm on the make, don't you?"

She felt the horrifying burn of tears in her eyes. "I'm not sure what to think. We've never even spoken to each other before, but now you tell me you know all this stuff about me. You've been watching me. Of course you're not on the make, but I don't know . . . I don't know why you'd watch me."

"That's one reason." He dipped his head to look into her face. "You come right out and say what you think. Everyone else around here worries about the impression they make before they speak. So they don't say anything real."

Bliss had never felt so flustered—or so jumpy—in her life. She said, "I'm clumsy. Socially inept."

"Sounds like something you've been told."

"It is." And she couldn't imagine why she was repeating such personal information to bad boy, Sebastian Plato.

"Your folks?"

Bliss puffed up her cheeks. "I guess." It was too late to take back everything she'd said.

"I know how that can be. Something else we have in common. Not living up to family expectations."

She almost told him they had nothing in common. But they did. They were both different, different from all the kids they went to school with, and different from what their parents wanted them to be.

"I'm not the way people say I am." Sebastian's lips came together in a straight line. His lean cheeks moved as he set his teeth.

"Why are you telling me this?"

"Because I want you to know the truth."

"Why?"

"I've told you," he said. "I like you."

Her skin prickled. "You don't know me," she reminded him for the second time.

"I want to. You won't want to know me because we're from different . . . Well, you know what I mean. But I wish it wasn't that way. It took a lot of guts—or maybe stupidity—for me to do this. To talk to you."

"Someone dared you."

He screwed up his face. "Huh?"

Bliss made two fists in her lap. "Someone bet you wouldn't come and talk to me."

"Shit!"

She turned her head away. "You wouldn't be here just because you wanted to be. I don't care. You can go and tell them you did it now. Or are they around somewhere, watching?"

"You're like me."

Bliss wasn't sure she'd heard him correctly. "I beg your pardon?" she said. She looked at him again and got the crazy notion he could read her mind.

Amazingly, he extended a hand, palm up, on top of the table. "Shit. You really are like me, aren't you?"

"I hate it when people swear."

"Yeah. Okay. Put your hand on mine."

Bliss studied his broad palm, his wiggling fingers.

"Come on. There's nobody watching. And no bet. Why would there be? I don't have any friends in the school. I don't fit in—same as you."

"Crystal Moore wants to be your friend."

"Crystal Moore wants to be everyone's friend—if she can use them somehow. Don't ask me why she thinks she can use me. Give me your hand."

Lifting her shoulders a little, half-expecting whoops of laughter, Bliss put her hand on his. He easily closed his grip around her wrist.

No one laughed.

She trembled inside.

"You're seventeen," he said.

Bliss nodded. He seemed to know everything about her.

"You drive your own car. Shiny new cream BMW."

"And you drive a black Ford pickup." Her color heightened once more.

"You do know I'm alive." Sebastian grinned afresh. "You do care."

"You drive fast. It would be hard to miss you."

"Most people don't seem to have any trouble."

"They all watch you," she said, liking the way his fingers felt too much. "I hear other kids talking about you." No boy had ever held her hand before. No boy even spoke to her. About her, in whispers, but not to her.

"I know they talk about me," Sebastian said, echoing her thoughts again. "And I know what they say."

Bliss relaxed a little. "I really ought to go."

"I wish you'd stay. For a while?"

"Are the things they say about you true? Don't kid around this time. Tell me."

"You won't believe me, but no."

Bliss tilted her head. "They say I'm stuck up. They laugh because I'm . . . well, because . . ."

"Because you're not one of their clones. Matching the pack is everything around here. I don't match either. We've got that in common—for different reasons. That kind of makes us the same, doesn't it?"

She couldn't help smiling at him. "I guess. Why did you drop out?"

His clasp tightened. "Family thing. I thought I was proving something. It was dumb."

"You're back now," she said, feeling sorry for him, for the anger she saw in the sharply drawn lines of his face. "It's no big deal."

Sebastian looked into her eyes. "I've never done this before."

She wasn't sure what he meant.

"I mean . . . I've never felt I wanted to get to know a girl the way I want to know you."

Bliss resisted the temptation to make another check for spies.

"Say something." He settled his free hand on top of hers. "You let me hold your hand. You can't totally hate me."

"I don't! I like you." She couldn't believe she'd said it.

Sebastian's smile widened. The smile showed strong, square teeth, and made gold flecks glitter in his green eyes. "That's cool. Gee, I can't believe . . . Hey, d'you want to take in a movie?"

Bliss's mind went blank.

"I don't know what's showing. Don't go to movies much."

"I can't." But she wanted to. Bliss dragged her teeth over her bottom lip. "My folks—"

"Sure." He grimaced and released her hand. "It was a dumb idea anyway."

"My folks don't let me go anywhere unless it's somewhere they set up," she told him in a rush. "I'd like to go to the movies with you. I really would. But—"

"You mean it?"

She nodded emphatically.

This time his smile spread slowly. Bliss felt her own smile in response—and a ripple of excitement.

"You're free this period every day."

Bliss swallowed. "Yes."

"We could kind of make this our time . . . Lunch and the fifth period. If you want to."

She didn't trust herself to say anything.

"We could go somewhere. Maybe to the library. The Seattle Public Library. We could study together."

Bliss laughed.

His grin became wry. "Sounds out of character, huh? I pull down pretty good grades. They'd be even better if I put some effort in."

"You look different when you smile. I didn't think you ever did that."

"Never had much reason." He wasn't smiling now. "You could consider it a service project—helping big, bad, Sebastian improve himself—at the library."

"I don't know."

"You're afraid people will see us together and start talking."

"No. I go to the library. There's almost never anyone from school there."

He dipped his head to look at her again. She liked the way he did that. "So, Bliss, will you come tomorrow?"

"I shouldn't."

"You can drive your car and I'll use my wheels?"

"I don't know."

"What's to lose? We'll hardly even be able to talk. We'd get shushed."

"I guess you're right." Why shouldn't she choose her own friends? Why shouldn't she do some of the things other girls did?

"Tomorrow then?" He frowned a little, and she saw his throat jerk. "Public library?"

"Yes."

* * *

Twelve weeks today.

Every day for twelve weeks—except for weekends and school vacations—they'd met during lunch and the fifth period. Mostly they went to the library, but they'd also gone to a little beach park occasionally. Today was cold, especially for May. They'd be at the library again.

There wasn't time to go to his locker. Sebastian slung his gym bag over his shoulder and made a dash for the parking lot.

As always, the crowd in the corridor parted to make way for him. They didn't know him, but they'd singled him out for a lousy rap he hadn't earned—unless keeping to himself was a sin.

He had to get to the lot before Bliss drove away.

Bliss, Bliss, Bliss. He could close his eyes and see her face. Hell, he saw her face every moment, awake and asleep. How could all these jerks have missed what a babe she was, how terrific-looking she was?

His good luck they had missed the signs, not that any of them was her type.

And he was?

Yeah, he was. Bliss said so, and it was true.

He shoved open an orange door leading from a corridor beside the little theater to athletic fields and the parking lots.

The sky was a pale, steel gray—clear, swept free of clouds by the steady wind that bent soldier-precise lines of firs between parking strips.

Wearing her puffy red parka, Bliss hurried toward her car.

"Hold up." Sebastian ran down the steps from the back of the building. "Hey, Bliss! Wait for me!"

She heard him and spun around, and stood still.

He knew, even before he drew close enough to see, that she'd be frowning, that she'd be worried something was wrong. They had an agreement never to draw attention to their relationship, not at school, not anywhere.

Sebastian broke into a run, lowered his head and pounded toward her.

"What is it?" He heard the panic in her voice. "Sebastian! What's happened?"

He reached her, caught her around the waist and lifted her off the ground. Into her neck he said, "Have I told you what a terrific kisser you are?"

She held absolutely still for a moment, then pummeled his shoulders with her fists. "You rotten, evil person. You low, wormy, sneaky, critter. You—"

"Ooh, I hate it when people swear."

Bliss thumped him again. "I didn't swear. You frightened me. And if someone sees us like this we'll never hear the last of it. Let me down. Now. D'you hear me? Let me down."

He dropped her as suddenly as he'd picked her up and she let out a strangled, "Oomph!" before grabbing at his sweatshirt to steady herself.

Sebastian held her hands against his chest. "First you don't want me to touch you. Then, when I let you go, you maul me. What's a guy to think?"

She drew her hands away as if they burned, but she smiled that sweet, soft smile that lighted up her blue eyes. He'd never known another girl with dark red hair and blue eyes. If the rest of those morons had taken the time to check behind her glasses, they'd have found out what they were missing.

"I'm going to make you wear sunglasses all the time, Bliss. Dark sunglasses. Very dark."

"Huh?" The palm of her right hand slid beneath his hair to feel his forehead. "Are you sick?"

"Nope. Ain't got no whee-heels," he sang, mimicking the heartbroken voice of a country singer. "Ain't got no whee-heels. I'd go to the lib-brar-ree wi' my girl, but I ain't got no whee-heels."

The crunch of approaching footsteps on gravel injected a shred of caution into his up mood. Smoothing his expression he looked over his shoulder and saw Chuck Rubber—who actually thought his name was macho!—and Crystal Moore. Pausing every few steps to perform mouth-to-mouth with enough suction to syphon a fifty-gallon tank empty in about a second, they bore down on Bliss and Sebastian. Sebastian looked at Bliss and put a finger to his lips.

"Hey, you two," he said cheerfully. "Don't suppose you've got jumper cables?"

Chuck—the school's prize running back—leered at Sebastian and said, "Some of us don't need jumper cables, Plato." He gave Bliss far too long a look. "Hi, there, Chilly, baby. This guy putting the make on you?"

Sebastian took a step toward Rubber, only to experience a jab of pain when Bliss "accidentally," stomped on his foot.

"I've got cables," she said, sounding out of breath. "I expect that's what you were going to ask me about, Sebastian."

He read the plea in her eyes. "Yeah. Yeah, that was it." There wasn't time for these idiots anyway. "I'd appreciate borrowing them."

"Sure." Bliss turned on her heel and walked rapidly toward the BMW.

"Run along," Rubber said. "When the little rich girl calls, the big poor boy follows."

Crystal must finally have felt the approach of danger. She wrapped both hands through Chuck Rubber's arm and pulled. "Come on, Chuck," she wheedled. "You promised we'd have some fun. *Come* on."

Rubber looked down into her violet eyes, and lower, and Sebastian decided against any close examination of the guy's bodily reactions. He could almost feel the pressure inside Rubber's fly.

"Here they are," Bliss called. "I think."

Pawing mindlessly, Crystal and Chuck trotted away, climbed steps to another strip of cars, and hurried out of sight.

"That's enough time wasted," Sebastian said. "Let's go."

Bliss made him hide in the back seat while they drove from the campus. Once on the city streets, he sat up and leaned over her shoulder. "Hey, sweetheart. Don't drive so fast. I scare easily."

"Don't joke around. That was too close back there. Where's your truck?"

Sebastian whistled soundlessly before saying, "In the shop."

"How did you get to school?"

"Bus."

She laughed. "School bus? That must have been something. It's a wonder they let you on."

"Not the school bus, smarty. Metro bus."

The drive to the library took only minutes and, unbelievably, a parking space opened up as they arrived.

For the first time, Sebastian walked up the steps and into the building at Bliss's side. He felt waves of anxiety coming from her.

"Loosen up," he told her. "Nobody's taking any notice of us."

"I wouldn't care if they did. I'd *like* it if they did, except for the row I'd face if someone told my folks they saw me here with a guy."

Sebastian didn't tell her what he thought of her parents. "Newspapers. I need to look up something in yesterday's *New York Times*."

"Really?"

"Really. I'll tell you about it."

As soon as she was seated, with her books spread before her, Sebastian got his newspaper and sat opposite. He opened the paper, held it up, shook it a couple of times, and let it drop on top of the book Bliss was reading. He pored over a small article at the bottom of a page.

"Psst!"

"Hmm?" He controlled his desire to grin.

"Psssst!" Bliss hissed. "Sebastian."

Several, "Shushes," sounded around them.

Sebastian continued to read. He reached under the paper and sought Bliss's fingers. When he looked up, she was staring at him.

He smiled at her. God, he loved her. He really loved her.

Gradually her lips parted and her eyes widened.

Sebastian withdrew his hand, shook the paper mightily and folded it. "Ready to go?"

Her mouth remained open. "Sebastian!"

"Shush!"

She sent the irritated man to her right a dazed glance.

Sebastian got up, went around the table, and sat beside her. He put his mouth close to her ear and whispered, "Well, what d'you say?"

"How . . . I mean, where did you get it? Oh, Sebastian, I don't know what to say."

On the ring finger of her left hand he'd placed a simple gold band with three small but pretty diamonds at its center. From his pocket he took the box. Flipping it open, he showed her what was inside. "This is the match. The wedding ring."

Tears slid silently down her cheeks.

"Hey." He rubbed them away with a thumb. "Did I make you unhappy?"

"No. Happy."

"Then you will marry me?"

"I want to."

"Listen. I know we'll have to wait till you're eighteen. That's about a month, right?"

She nodded. "My folks will—"

"Flip. Yeah, I know. So you won't be able to wear the ring when they might see it. I got this, too." He produced the gold chain he'd bought. "You'll only wear the ring on your finger when we're together—until we're married. You can put it on this around your neck for the rest of the time. Okay?"

He heard her swallow.

"I'm going to work, and go to college. Study business. We'll make it fine. Your folks will come around once we're married."

Bliss rested the ring against her lips and swiveled in her seat to face him. "Either they'll come around or they won't have a daughter. I get to choose who's most important in my life and I choose you."

He wanted to yell. Instead he hugged her—and ignored the tuts and shushes.

"Sebastian, I know I'm not supposed to ask, but how did you manage to buy the ring?"

"I stole it."

She jerked away, her mouth opening again.

He shook his head and chuckled. "No, I didn't. I bought it. And you shouldn't ask. We'd better get back to school before we're late. When we're in the car I'll put the chain on for you."

A little unsteady, Bliss got to her feet and started pushing her unread books back in her bag. She paused and looked at him. "What's wrong with the truck?"

He shrugged and returned the paper.

When he returned, Bliss caught his sleeve. "You always fix your own truck."

"Not this time." He offered her a downturned grimace. "Don't think the old jalopy's going to recover at all. Terminal, so the people in the shop said."

"Oh, Sebastian, you fibber. You sold it, didn't you?"

He took the book she held and tucked it into her bag. "We really have to hurry."

"Didn't you?" Her pointed chin jutted toward him. "You sold your truck."

Lies didn't belong between people who intended to spend a lifetime together. "It was old. It's good for me to walk more anyway."

"You sold that truck you love to buy the rings. Admit it."

Sebastian kissed the ring on her finger and looked into her eyes. "I sold the truck to buy rings for the girl I love more than anything in the world."

Evening hadn't taken all the sting out of the day's sultry late-June heat. Bliss wiped the back of a hand over her damp brow and opened the car window a crack.

Ahead of her, across Western Avenue, the homeless people

drifted into Victor Steinbrueck Park to stake their overnight claims to grassy beds with a water view. A few couples and families remained, stretching their Saturday outings.

The sun had begun to slide lower over Seattle's Elliott Bay. Already, on the far side of the bay, the Olympic Mountains showed in black outline against a sky turned the color of molten lava and ribbed with trailing scarves of purple cloud.

Bliss clutched the wheel and straightened her arms. This was the night. The night and the time. Tonight she and Sebastian would leave Seattle and they wouldn't come back until it was too late for anyone to challenge their marriage.

Marriage. They were going to be married. The ring she so loved, but had been forced to hide in the weeks since Sebastian gave it to her, was on her finger now. The few possessions she'd absolutely had to bring—not enough to be difficult to get out of the house without comment—were in the trunk.

She was frightened, but she wouldn't change a thing about what she was determined to do.

The clock on the dash was fast. Bliss always set it ten minutes ahead so she wouldn't be late. The clock showed 9:15 when it was only 9:05.

Silly habits.

Conforming was a habit. Not that she was ever likely to be wild.

And running away to get married without her parents' knowledge wasn't wild?

It was wild. Wonderfully wild. Bliss leaned her head against the rest and closed her eyes. As soon as school was out she and Sebastian had known they couldn't wait. As long as there'd been at least their daily meetings to look forward, they could bear the hours in between. With summer ahead and the threat of long separations, they'd decided to go to Reno.

"Excuse me, miss."

Bliss jumped so hard she banged her elbow on the door. She stared into the dusk-shadowed face of a motorcycle policeman.

He raised his helmet visor. "Something wrong, miss?"

"No! I mean, no. I'm waiting to pick someone up."

"You're sure? You've been here a long time."

She glanced at the clock again. Sebastian was twenty minutes late. But he had to rely on buses from his parents' home in Ballard. He'd chosen this spot for its anonymity and because they both knew exactly where it was. "I'm sure, officer," Bliss said, smiling. "It's okay, isn't it? To park here?"

"Yes, miss. Just making sure everything was okay. Good night, then."

"Good night." Bliss watched him start his cycle and make a slow U-turn to join another officer on the opposite side of the street. The two men looked toward her and she aimed her eyes straight ahead.

Sebastian wasn't close to his parents. He didn't say much, but he had told her that. And he was adopted, grateful for having been adopted, but not grateful that he'd never lived up to his father's expectations. He had a sister, Maryan, to whom he seemed close. Maryan was two years older, and the biological child of the Platos, who'd been unable to have more children after she was born. Sebastian had been selected to be the son they couldn't have.

He should be here by now.

A transient shuffled along the sidewalk. Swathed in a ragged plaid blanket, his sandy hair matted, he swayed for a moment, nearly lost his balance, then staggered against the side of Bliss's car.

She sat very still, praying he couldn't see her in the swiftly thickening darkness.

Tapping on the passenger window sent her heart flying. She leaned across the seat to open the door for Sebastian—and looked into the vacant, slow-blinking eyes of the man in the blanket.

Bliss pressed her fingers to her mouth, trapped a scream in her throat. She was jumpy, stupid. The poor thing couldn't open a locked door. And he was obviously too drunk to know what he was doing anyway. She pressed her head back again and squeezed her eyes shut

With her right hand, she covered her left and felt the coolness of the gold band, the shapes of the diamonds. Sebastian had sold his beloved truck to buy the ring, and then spent the rest of the school year catching buses.

When she opened her eyes again, the man was gone . . . And it was 9:45. Darkness had fallen completely. Streetlights cast a pale glow over the road and the park. Lights inside Angelica's café illuminated diners, and customers laughing in the bar.

Bliss wiped her palms on her jeans. She was shaking.

Where was Sebastian?

"Are you Bliss?"

She jumped again, this time at the sound of a woman's voice whispering her name urgently. Bliss glanced out of her window at a young woman with short, brown hair brushed forward in spikes around an angular face and said, "I'm Bliss. Who are you?"

The woman rubbed at the space between thin, arched brows. "Sebastian asked me to come."

Bliss's stomach fell sickeningly. "Who are you?" she repeated.

"Maryan Plato. Sebastian's sister. I've got to talk to you."

The shaking in Bliss's hands spread over her body. "Get in," she said, watching the other woman's loose-limbed walk as she went immediately to the passenger door. Bliss let her in and watched while she settled herself in the seat. "Has something happened to Sebastian?"

Maryan Plato leaned forward and gripped the dashboard with large hands. "I was afraid I wouldn't be able to find you. I promised Sebastian, see."

Bliss could scarcely breathe. "Is he sick?"

Maryan shook her head.

"What then? Tell me where he is. I'll go to him."

Maryan shook her head again.

"Tell me!" Bliss couldn't stop her voice from scaling upward.

"He had to get out of town."

"Out—" Bliss couldn't clear her brain enough to understand.

She almost blurted out that she knew Sebastian was leaving town, with her. "What do you mean?"

"He asked me to tell you he was sorry, but you've got to forget him."

"No," Bliss whispered. "I don't believe you. He didn't tell anyone about us. Neither of us did."

"Something happened."

"What?" Bliss almost screamed. "Please. You're frightening me."

"He . . . He's in trouble. He had to get out quickly."

"Without telling me? He wouldn't do that. I would have helped him."

Maryan turned to Bliss. "You can't help him. He's got to help himself now—and her. He's got to make it right."

Bliss shook her head. "Stop it! Stop it, do you hear me?"

"Listen to me." Maryan's big hands gripped Bliss's arms. "Calm down and listen. I can't change what's happened and neither can you."

"We're going to be married," Bliss said brokenly.

Maryan stared.

"He's coming to meet me and we're going to leave Seattle and get married."

"Jesus," Maryan said, half-under her breath. "He didn't tell me you thought *that*. I was supposed to say he couldn't make the date. Are you sure about the—"

"Of course I'm sure." Bliss held up her left hand. "We're engaged. We've been engaged for more than a month."

"Damn." Releasing Bliss, Maryan made fists and pounded her jean-clad thighs. "How could he have been so stupid? No wonder he did everything he could to get out of it."

Every mouthful of air Bliss swallowed made a choking sound.

"Okay." Maryan took a visibly deep breath and held it. "Okay, I'm just going to say it and we're both going to get on with our lives. Sebastian's in trouble."

"But—"

"He had to leave town in a hurry or face prosecution."

"Sebastian never did anything—"

"He left with a girl called Crystal Moore."

She was going to be sick. "He couldn't have. How do I know you're Sebastian's sister?"

The other woman turned dark eyes on her. "How many people knew you were coming here to meet him tonight?"

"Just Sebastian."

"Uh-huh." She switched on the dome light, reached into her pocket and took out a thin wallet. Opening it, she showed Bliss a picture of herself on a driver's license and pointed to the name, "Plato, Maryan, M. Is that good enough?"

"Why would Sebastian leave town with Crystal Moore? He hated her."

Maryan snorted. "Evidently he didn't hate everything about her. Her father's some sort of religious fanatic. Either she had to get out of town, too, or her dear, pious father was going to kill her."

"But, I don't . . . Oh, please tell me this is a joke."

"Some joke. At least Sebastian had the decency to do the right thing. He took her away to keep her safe from her crazy father. She's pregnant."

"He wouldn't do this to me."

"Oh, wise up. He told me about your cute little after-lunch meetings. He's a big boy. What do you think he did with all his nights."

Her throat felt squeezed and twisted. "He's good. He's not the way the others think he is."

"He's a red-blooded man. And he got a girl pregnant."

*"No!"*

"Yes. And now he's trying to make it right. Go home to Mommy and Daddy."

*"No!* I want Sebastian."

"You can't have him. He's finally done something right. He's left Seattle with the girl he raped."

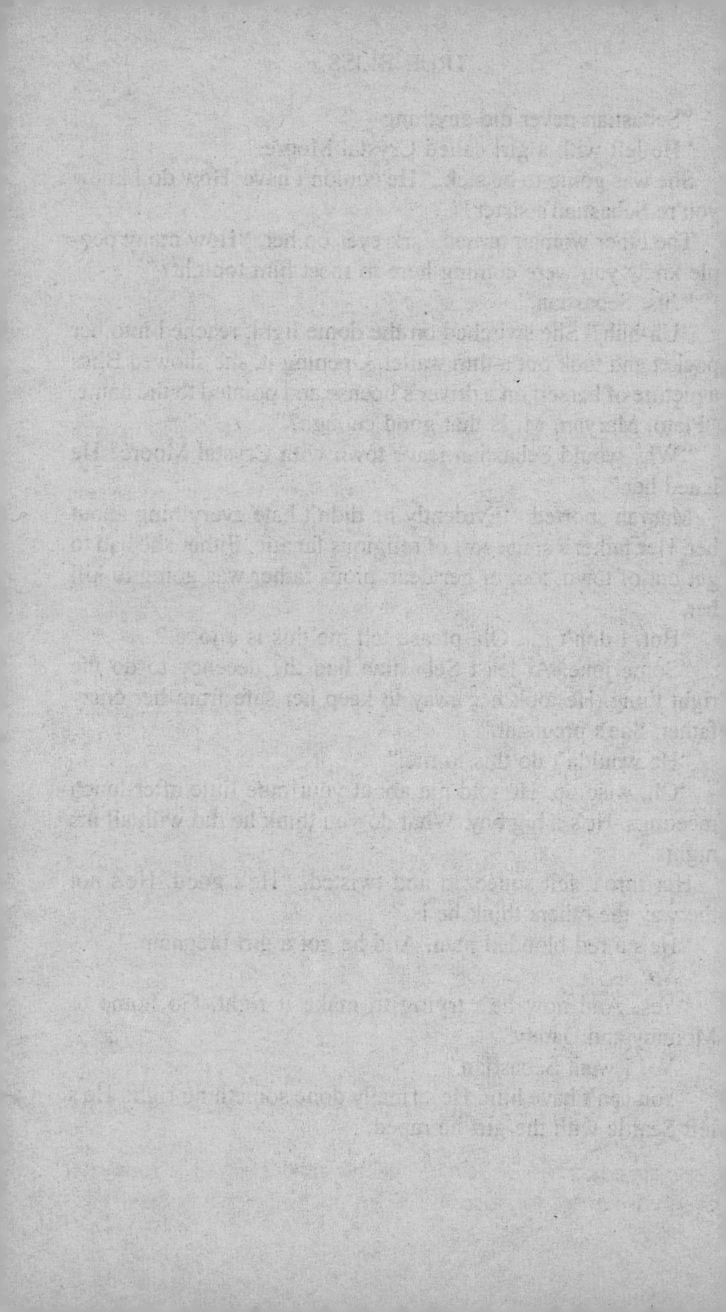

# One

"When I was growing up, this was a one-horse town populated with tight-asses." Sebastian Plato looked down from his new thirty-second floor offices onto the sun-drenched streets of Bellevue. Bumper-to-bumper midday traffic wound sluggishly between sleek glass buildings in shades of blue, rose, gunmetal gray. "It's still populated with tight-asses. Probably tighter. Doesn't anyone own anything but a Mercedes or a Lexus here? Or at least a car that didn't just come off the lot?"

"You can't tell the makes of cars from this height, Sebby."

He crooked a finger at Zoya, a still spectacular ex-supermodel who kept Raptor Vision, the modeling and talent-agency division of Raptor Enterprises, where he wanted it—on top. "I know the cars they're driving down there," Sebastian told her. "Come here and look at this place."

"I've already seen it. We should be deciding how you'll deal with Maryan when she gets here."

"Leave Maryan to me."

"She's due, Sebby."

"Don't sweat it. Get over here."

Zoya was almost as tall as Sebastian, with her waist-length black hair slicked severely back and arranged in a mass of braided loops. Her face was all sharply boned, exotic flamboyance. She stood beside him and said, "You don't drive a Merc or a Lexus."

"I'm not from Bellevue," he reminded her in a tone that warned her not to raise the worn-out topic of his less-than-traditional taste in personal vehicles. He pointed beyond the buildings of Bellevue, to the breadth of bordering Lake Washington and the soaring glass and concrete towers of downtown Seattle in the distance. "When I was a kid we stayed over there. Wouldn't come to the eastside on a bet. We called this place the burbs, and laughed at people who lived here."

"Childish." Zoya never tempered her opinions with tact.

Unperturbed, Sebastian said, "As I told you, we were children then. Children are childish."

"But you're still disdainful of Bellevue."

He shrugged. "Why would you live here when you can live in the middle of things?"

"A good question," Zoya remarked. "One wonders why Sebastian Plato, big city dweller, would choose to buy a house here."

"I was speaking in generalities. I want to be close to the office."

"Next question," Zoya said. Her thick lashes lowered over eyes almost as black as her hair. "Why would this man choose to open a branch of Vision here, rather than in Seattle?"

"Statement," Sebastian said curtly. "I have my reasons." And he didn't intend to study them too closely.

"Maryan still doesn't—"

"Maryan will have to accept my decision in this. I know she still doesn't think we should have started operations in the Seattle area. The subject isn't open for discussion. It's a natural step. Natural, and overdue." And the first expansion that had filled him with enough confusion to mess with his sleep.

"I can't disagree with that," Zoya said. "Too bad we've got this other business to contend with."

Sebastian turned from the window and prowled his office. Didn't have his stamp on it yet. Probably never would since he didn't expect to be here long.

Or did he?

Damn, he hadn't been this unsure of himself in ten years—not since he'd founded his fledgling Raptor Enterprises on swagger, bullshit, and other men's money.

He sat on his rosewood desk and planted his feet on the burgundy leather chair. Those men had taken smart flyers on him. They'd made back their investments several times over.

Zoya's soft, white silk dress swished as she swept up a press release. "Will you meet with this O'Leary woman?"

"No."

"No?" She leaned over the back of the chair and swung the paper between finger and thumb. "Of course you'll meet her. She and her group are accusing us of luring kids into sin and death. Big seller topics. We'll get media coverage. It'll be great for us. Best PR money didn't buy."

"I don't like burgundy. This chair can go. And the rugs."

"Fuck the rugs," Zoya said succinctly. "And the chair. Dammit, Sebastian, this is business. And it's not like you to be coy."

He reached to whip the paper from her fingers, and tossed it on the desk. "Leave it to me. I'll deal with it."

"Maryan's plane is probably getting in from Chicago as we speak. She'll wonder why you aren't snapping up this opportunity."

"No, she won't," Sebastian said shortly.

"Your sister never passed up a promotional opportunity."

"Maryan won't question passing up this one." They couldn't afford too much publicity here. Not unless he wanted his past spread all over the papers.

"But—"

"Drop it, there's a love."

One of Zoya's many skills was a nose for the right moment to switch topics. She returned to the windows that wrapped around three sides of Sebastian's office. "Wait till Maryan finds out you've bought that house in— What's the place called?"

"Medina."

"Yes, Medina. We all thought you only intended to come out here for the opening."

"You presumed. I may move my headquarters here."

Stunned summed up Zoya's expression nicely.

"New York's great," Sebastian said. "It'll be a great place to visit frequently."

"You aren't telling me you intend to live in—*Medina* permanently."

"More successful men than I am do." Sebastian stuck his hands in his trouser pockets. "The suburbs are good places for families."

"You don't have a family," she pointed out.

"At my age it's time to think about settling down."

Zoya laughed her deep, smoky-toned laugh. "Thirty-five? Just. True, you are approaching dotage, my love. But you are joking, aren't you? You don't really plan to be here longer than it takes to make sure we overcome the current little unpleasantness, do you?"

He ignored the question.

"This is me. Zoya. I'm on your side forever, remember? I don't know much about your pre-Raptor days, but aren't you the man who left Seattle right out of high school, the man who said he was never coming back?"

"Things change." And some things didn't change nearly enough—or soon enough.

"How many years ago was that? Sixteen? Seventeen?"

"Fifteen. I sat out a year."

Zoya turned sharply. "Sat out of high school? Were you sick?"

He didn't owe her explanations, but what the hell. "Sick of trying to live up to expectations. I thought I was showing my old man I was master of my own fate. It's history."

A buzzer sounded on his intercom. Sebastian pressed a button and said, "Plato."

"Is there even the vaguest possibility that you told a Mr. Nose he could come to see you, Mr. Plato? Surely not."

"Wait." Sebastian cut off the line to his secretary's office. "Where did you find that guy, Zoya?"

"Hmm?" She raised her perfectly arched brows.

"My *secretary.* Mr. Tight-ass himself, William whatever his name is?"

"Namsuk," Zoya told him. "William Namsuk. He's very qualified. Secretaries aren't all thirty-six double D's with panty allergies."

Sebastian knew when to grin. He grinned at Zoya now. "Not nice, my love. And I haven't earned *that* kind of reputation."

She shrugged and went back to watching a jet traverse a transparently blue July sky. "William's Bellevue to the eyeballs. Born here. Grew up here. Went to grade school here. He did go to the University of Washington, so he has been out of town, at least as far as Seattle."

"As I said, Mr. Tight-ass himself. Only answers to William—don't call him Bill. Is it even vaguely possible I told a Mr. Nose he could come to see me? *Surely* not."

"Did you?"

Sebastian flipped the intercom switch again. "Hey, Bill. Send in Mr. Nose."

"Shame on you," Zoya said when Sebastian cut the connection again. "Still a mean little boy inside that handsome hulk, hm?"

He couldn't refute the jibe. And right now he didn't care.

The door opened to admit a rumpled little man in khaki. Lean, blond and good-looking, William Namsuk paused long enough to aim a disdainful glance at Sebastian, then closed the door behind the newcomer.

Patting his numerous pockets, Nose shambled across the room. "That guy out there's gonna hurt hisself," he said. "He's so uptight he's gonna choke t'death."

Sebastian avoided Zoya's eyes. "I wasn't expecting you, Mr.—"

"Nose. Just call me, Nose." A guffaw revealed tobacco-stained teeth. "My old lady reckons that with a moniker like mine I should 'ave been one of them wine sniffers. I tell 'er I'm very good at what I do sniff, thank you very much."

"Sit down," Sebastian said. "Don't let me keep you, Zoya. I'll get back to you on this." He tapped the press release.

"Oh, I can wait, darling." Her voice dripped with amused curiosity. "I'll just look out the window until you're finished with, er, *Nose.*"

He had to get her out of the room before Nose said something Sebastian didn't want to share with anyone—yet.

"Ashtray?" Nose asked. He located a mangled pack of Camels in a sagging pocket over his left thigh, extracted a bent cigarette, and clamped it between his teeth.

"Sebastian?" Zoya made as if to rush at Nose. Smoking wasn't part of her regimen for perfect bodies.

"Leave this to me." Sebastian caught her arm and ushered her gently, but firmly from the room. He gave her his best attempt at a conspiratorial grimace, murmured, "Boyhood acquaintance. Good heart, but always a bit disturbed," and closed the door on her, *"Oh!"*

Nose had lowered his scrawny frame into a black lacquer chair shaped like a tall, springy Z, with an apparently unsupported burgundy leather seat. With a grimy thumb, he produced a flame from his lighter and set fire to shreds of tobacco drizzling from his cigarette.

Sebastian stuck his hands in his pockets and strolled to lean against the edge of his desk. "From now on you're someone I knew when I was a kid."

Nose took a deep drag, exhaled slowly and squinted at Sebastian through the smoke. "Sure. Old buddies, right?"

"Someone I knew when I was a kid. Vaguely. You heard I was back in the area and came looking for some sort of job."

"Anything you say." The cigarette bobbed. "In other words, you don't want anyone to know about our business?"

"Right."

"Always fancied a nice office in a ritzy building like this."

"Yeah. How—"

"What're you offerin'? Need someone to take the place of that nancy boy out there?"

Rolling in his lips, Sebastian contained a chuckle. "Sure. You'd fit right in. How are your keyboard skills?"

Nose waggled his fingers. "Just turned down the Seattle Symphony." He removed the cigarette, flicked ash into the zen garden on the desk, and unbuttoned a big pocket on his right thigh. "I've got most of what you're looking for." A brown envelope, bent in half, came into view.

"Did you verify the answer to the big question?"

" 'Course. That was the simple part. You already had it right."

"I thought I did." And he'd made some giant decisions based on being almost sure he was right. "I wanted absolute verification." He couldn't go forward without being certain—and even now, even being certain, he still had to question why he was rushing toward the craziest, most impulsive move he'd ever made.

Nose studied him impassively. "Your verification is here." He tapped the envelope, then held it out. "D'you know what you're messing around with here?"

Did he? "Maybe. Maybe not. Why don't you tell me?" He took the envelope.

"Powerful people."

Mildly confused, Sebastian frowned. "I'm powerful people, too." Not that he saw the connection between powerful people and his business in Washington State.

"These powerful people don't let anything get in their way." Nose sniffed, and ground the Camel out among the precisely placed rocks in the formerly perfectly raked sand in the zen garden. "Nothing ever proved, you understand. But from where I'm lookin' it begins to look like anyone who gets in their way takes a long hike."

Sebastian crossed his feet and leaned toward the other man. "What are you talking about? What does . . . Sorry, Nose, I think of myself as sharp, but you're leaving me in the dark here."

"Ain't so difficult to understand. The person you're interested in has connections to people in high places. Those people in high places always get what they want. Maybe it don't matter, but seems to me that if you was to get in their way, or mess with something—or someone—of theirs, you might end up like some others have."

"And how is that?" Sebastian asked softly.

Nose's sad, brown eyes shifted beneath shaggy, dun-colored brows. "I dunno for sure. But I haven't been able to verify their recent whereabouts. Or any whereabouts at all."

Small hairs rose along the length of Sebastian's spine. "I'm not paying you to have an imagination."

"Imagination? Not me, old buddy—old vague acquaintance, that is. Not a shred of imagination in this body. Ask anyone. They'll tell you. Nose ain't got no imagination. Anyway, I'll leave you to look over that little lot."

"Okay. Okay, yeah, do that." The envelope was bulky.

"You want me to keep digging?"

A metal butterfly clasp held the envelope shut, but the flap wasn't stuck closed. "Is there anything else to dig for?"

"Oh, sure. Always is. But it's up to you. Say the word and we'll call this a done job."

"No." He had no right to be digging up other people's business. But he would dig anyway. "No, if there's more, find it. Stay on top of it. Okay?"

"You've got it. I'll be in touch." Nose opened the door.

Maryan came in as the private investigator went out. She said nothing while she watched Nose leave.

"Who was that?" She wrinkled her straight nose. "He looks like a bum."

"Some sort of computer type." He'd have to be careful or he'd be telling lies he didn't have to tell. "You know what slick dressers those guys are."

Maryan glared. She let her well-worn briefcase slip from her fingers and thump on the carpet. "That dog of yours makes an ugly front office statement."

"Beater likes watching people come and go."

"He's an ugly mutt."

Sebastian smirked. "You're right. That's part of his charm."

"He doesn't like me."

Time to change the subject. Sebastian jutted his chin in what he hoped was a playful way and waved. "Hi, Sis. Good flight?"

"Lousy flight. Lousy town. When I saw Mt. Rainier, I thought I was going to throw up. Everything's so goddamn clean here it makes me want to spit on the sidewalks."

"You don't like it here."

"And you've got a goddamn lousy sense of humor."

Sebastian smiled thinly. "I do try. And I didn't ask you to come to Seattle."

"Someone's got to see what the fuck you're up to." She marched around his desk and threw her tall, thin body into his chair. Her badly crushed, red linen suit might as well be burned. Her short brown hair with its silver streak at one temple was gelled back and did nothing to soften the unhappy lines around her eyes and mouth.

Sebastian knew a twinge of guilt. "You worry too much, Sis. And you look beat. Kick your shoes off. How about a—"

"Gin. Over ice. No vermouth."

He made the decision that this was one time not to mention that she drank too much. "Coming up." A freestanding, cylindrical pillar of steel contained the bar. A single finger's pressure, and it spread open, jawlike, from an invisible seam.

"When I finally realized how far you were taking things here I knew I'd better find a way to get us out, and quickly. What d'you think you're playing at?"

Maryan had always been there for him. "Knock it off, Sis, there's a good girl." She'd come through when he'd been a lost kid of not even twenty and there'd been no one else to turn to. Without her he'd have had a harder time making it through college and through more rough times than he wanted to remember.

"Is it true?" Her voice assumed the brittle quality she rarely used on Sebastian.

Slowly, he poured gin into an etched crystal glass.

"Is it?" She coughed. "Hurry with that, will you?"

Sebastian brought her the gin. "Sounds like you picked up a bug on the plane."

"We ought to be expanding the airline."

Sometimes his adoptive sister's propensity for subject-hopping irritated Sebastian. "The airline's on target and in good hands." He believed in as much autonomy as possible for the men and women who ran the essentially separate divisions of Raptor.

Maryan closed her eyes and drank.

"I'm going to have a car brought around for you. It'll take you to my place. Sleep till tomorrow. You look as if you need it."

Her dark gray eyes snapped open again. "I asked you a question."

"You're pushing, Maryan. I don't like it when you push, you know that."

She bared her small teeth. "I want this place closed down. I want it closed and I want us out of this town—out of this state—*now.*"

He tolerated a great deal for the sake of a lot of old times. "If you want to turn right around and fly out, be my guest. Don't try to tell me what to do." Willing his temper under control, he tossed ice cubes in a glass and covered them with water from a pitcher. "You don't even sound rational."

"Don't tell me I'm irrational."

"Then don't *be* irrational. This project's been underway for more than a year. Is it rational to sail in and demand we pack up and walk away?"

"After what I found out today, yes."

Sebastian didn't bite at her lure. "Even if backing out wouldn't cost us millions, I wouldn't do it. I know you don't like Washington. I do. I'm staying here, Maryan. Get used to it."

She coughed, sputtered, and wiped the back of a hand over her lips. "Staying? What do you mean, staying?"

"As in I intend to live here again. I like it here."

"Since when?" She set the glass on the desk and gripped the arms of the chair. "You hated it. You know you did."

"I didn't always hate it," he told her quietly. "There was a time when I thought Seattle was the most special city on earth."

When Maryan was really angry, her gray eyes became the color of old silver. They were old silver now. "I followed you out of Seattle. I left everything behind to follow you, to help you make a new beginning when you didn't have anyone else. I've always been there for you."

"I'm grateful for that." Losing his cool would only cause one of their rare, ugly scenes. "But we have lives to live now. We have for a very long time. I don't need babying. And I am the boss, Maryan. I am Raptor Enterprises."

"I'm your partner."

"One of my partners. One of my junior partners." And, although she had a good mind, they both knew she would never have risen to the position he'd made for her if she hadn't been his sister.

"I gave up my own life for you!"

"Please—"

"I asked you a question. Is it true?"

"Is what—"

"Don't bullshit me, Seb. You've bought a house right here on the eastside, haven't you?"

"The grapevine's been busy."

"Oh . . ." She flapped a hand. "Of course I'd find out if you bought a house. You detested the eastside."

"When I was a kid, for God's sake."

"I know about Hole Point, you know."

Sebastian stood quite still. He leveled a stare into his sister's cold eyes and raised the water to his lips.

"I know! *She's* there. She owns the place. And you drive right through Medina to get to it." Her big-knuckled finger shook when she pointed it at him. "You lied when you said you weren't coming here because of her. You lied, dammit!"

The door flew open and banged against the only wall in the room. A bronzed, bleached, musclebound man strode toward the desk. "Sweetie? Maryan, sweetie? What's going on in here?"

"Hi, Ron," Sebastian said. He put down his glass. For once

he was delighted to see Maryan's latest, and, at a two-year tenure, longest-surviving lover.

Ron York ignored Sebastian. "I heard you scream, pet."

"I told you to wait outside for me." Ron's "pet" glowered at him. "Get out."

"Is he picking on you again?" Twenty-five to Maryan's thirty-eight, Ron hovered over his cushy meal-ticket and cast an accusing stare at Sebastian.

"She's overwrought," Sebastian said pleasantly. "Good thing you showed up, Ron. I've got to pop out. I'll have William arrange for a car to take you to my house."

"Don't you leave me like this," Maryan shrieked. "Don't you dare."

He winked at Ron, swept up the press release, and headed for William's office. "You'll love the house, Ron. Olympic-size pool. Sauna. Full weight room. The works."

Ron's carefully assumed air of umbrage softened.

"William," Sebastian called as he slipped through the doorway. "My sister and her friend are exhausted from their trip. Make sure—"

"Leave it to me, Mr. Plato," William said, cutting Sebastian off. Already on his feet, the secretary moved between his employer and the scene in the inner office. In a low voice William said, "Don't give this another thought. You have another appointment, don't you?"

"Yes," Sebastian said, pleasantly amazed at William's smooth authority. The guy liked challenge! Sebastian liked people who liked challenge. "Yes, you're right. I have another appointment."

Beater, the "ugly front-office statement," levered his part Doberman, part English sheepdog body off the polished slate and fell in at his master's heel.

Finally closed inside his private elevator, Sebastian allowed himself to soak up a few moments of blissful peace before reaching into Nose's envelope and extracting the contents.

He scanned the first sheet of paper, his gaze shifting rapidly over essential facts. Thirty-two. Owner-director of Hole Point, a colony for artists in any medium. Former professor in the Women's Studies Department at the University of Washington. Undergraduate degree from Georgetown. Master's, Georgetown. Doctorate, Harvard.

The elevator came to a gentle stop and the doors to the foyer of the building slid silently open. Sebastian nodded to the doorman and walked outside into a hot, airless afternoon. He preferred to drive himself, in his vehicle of choice—a black Ford pickup. The current model stood at the curb. When Beater had lumbered into the back, Sebastian got into the cab, started the engine and turned on the air-conditioning.

A second sheet of paper contained, in black-and-white terms, the facts he'd hoped would be confirmed. Unmarried. Unmarried now, and never married before.

Euphoria might be inappropriate under the circumstances, but he felt it anyway—until he remembered Maryan.

Why had she chosen today to show up?

Sonuvabitch! Something had to give with her. The drugs and booze, the sex—always with much younger men, the tantrums that grew wilder. She needed to go into a treatment center—another treatment center.

He slammed the steering wheel. Last time she'd promised she wouldn't backslide. And he'd been fool enough to believe it.

Later. Today was too important to louse up with Maryan's sick obsessions.

Beneath the second sheet of paper lay a photograph.

*Bliss.*

Sebastian's gut smacked together. This was the first time he'd seen her as anything but the serious-faced seventeen-year-old in the snapshots he locked in a fireproof safe wherever his present home happened to be.

Red-brown hair, parted slightly off-center, fell sleek and straight, to curve toward a pointed chin. The face was a little thinner than he remembered, but he did remember it—perfectly.

He glanced away, through the side window, at a group of teenage advertisements for Banana Republic. The kids laughed as they crossed the street, tossed their expensively cut hair, tugged on the sleeves of cotton sweaters tied about their waists.

Fifteen years. Fifteen years ago he'd been a teenager—almost twenty it was true, but still a teenager.

The woman in the picture stared at him with beautiful, honest, dark-blue eyes. Her lips were parted, just a little, in a faint smile. Turned from the camera slightly, her expression showed a hint of self-consciousness. He rested a forefinger on the mouth, outlined the jaw, and got the fleeting impression he felt her soft warmth. And his belly grew even tighter, so tight his next breath wasn't easy.

Successful, smart men who had outrun a past that would finish many, kept on running. They didn't turn back and risk opening old wounds that had healed too many years ago to open on their own. Fresh wounds could only be deliberately inflicted now.

He slid the papers back into the envelope, but left the photograph on top and set them all on the seat beside him.

Just a friendly visit. A friendly visit from an old friend who was newly returned to the area. Sebastian checked his wing mirror and maneuvered into the flow of traffic. They were both grown-ups now. More than grown-ups. They'd lived a lot of years and traveled a lot of miles—they were different people entirely. Surely she'd be glad to see him.

His shirt stuck to his back. For God's sake, he'd never managed to put her out of his mind and now he intended to try to force some sort of reunion. He intended to get her to pick up what he'd walked away from *fifteen years ago.*

Maybe this was some sort of slow-moving senility. Or a crazed fixation.

He turned a corner onto NE 8th Street and drove west.

Hell, he wasn't a maniac with an obsession. Unless not being able to fall out of love with a woman was a manic obsession.

If she'd forgotten him, she'd have married, wouldn't she?

Shoot, he was a bad joke. A man who could make himself believe he'd remained the love of a woman's life even after he'd betrayed her.

So she could tell him to get lost. No big deal. All he'd have to do was figure out what to do about the millions he'd spent setting up shop while he catered to his delusion.

A light turned red ahead and he applied the brakes.

Maturity had made her more beautiful. Still quiet—he could tell that by the tilt of her head, the shyness in her eyes—but lovely.

They could love again. Or at least, try. He could tell her how it had all happened, explain the desperation that had driven him away from her when he'd wanted, more than anything, to be with her forever.

He stopped Zoya's damned press release from sliding onto the floor and read the brief announcement: "Women of Today (WOT), headed by activist Prue O'Leary, has declared its intention to force the new Bellevue branch of Raptor Vision to back out of its proposed Washington State venture. In response to questioning, O'Leary states that a committee is preparing a public exposé of the New York based conglomerate's modeling and talent agencies. The committee will be spearheaded by respected local academic and patron of the arts, Bliss Winters."

No coherent thoughts formed.

From somewhere, horns blared.

It was a joke. The timing couldn't work out like this. It was Zoya's idea of a joke.

Zoya didn't joke, didn't know how. Until today, Zoya had never even heard of Bliss Winters.

# Two

"If we start now," Polly Crow said, pointing at her sister with a flour-caked rolling pin, "we can avoid all kinds of silly stuff later on."

Fabiola Crow, Polly's twin, flipped her long, blond mane. "I don't care. I'm not trekking all over this place dropping bricks in toilet tanks."

It was going to be a long, hot summer.

Bliss rolled her chair away from the computer where she was trying to work on her accounts. She looked across the kitchen table into the unblinking, brown eyes of Spike, the Crows' shaggy, oversized mutt. Bliss wiggled her eyebrows. The dog's response was to bare her teeth in what the twins insisted was a smile. Its effect on Bliss was invariably an urge to hide any bare skin.

"Bliss," Fabiola said, posing dramatically—Fabiola aspired to being an actress and a model. "Bliss, are you listening to me?"

"Always," Bliss said, deadpan. As referee-in-chief to the Crows she listened a lot.

"She wants me to go around the Point stuffing bricks in all the cabin toilets to cut down on water usage."

Polly hummed the alto part of the "Hallelujah Chorus," pausing to conduct episodes of silence for the intervening parts. Cook, and a marvelous cook for those residents of Hole Point who chose to take meals at the main lodge, Polly also sang in small clubs around Seattle.

"We definitely need to curb expenses," Bliss said.

"Cut the utilities," Polly told her promptly. "Conserve water and we'll be doing our part to help with the shortage. *And* we'll save money."

"There isn't a shortage yet," Fabiola said loudly. "But ten bricks in ten loos won't stop one from coming."

Polly banged the rolling pin down. "That's exactly the attitude that's landed this country in the kind of mess we're going to leave for our children to inherit." She smacked her hands together, sending flour in all directions. "People like you who insist they can't make a difference. Using everything up. Not a bit of consideration for the mess the next generation's going to be faced with. *And,* we've got to cut expenses at the Point. Bliss just said so."

Spike reared onto her back legs, rested her front paws and long muzzle on the table, and curled her top lip.

Bliss curled her top lip in response.

Spike growled.

"Polly doesn't give a rat's ass about saving money," Fabiola said, smoothing skimpy denim shorts over shapely hips. "She's turned into a rabid conservationist."

"Speaking of rabid," Bliss said mildly. "Could you please get this animal's head off the table? The health department would close us down."

Polly picked up where she'd paused in the "Hallelujah Chorus," finished with a flourish, and segued into a gum-numbing rendition of "America the Beautiful."

"She wants us to recycle bath water," Fabiola said. The only housekeeper in history—Bliss was certain—with two-inch-long crimson nails, Fabiola made the word "recycle" sound like a disease.

Bliss ignored the argument that had been waged for several days. Relief must be imminent. The Crow sisters would soon move on to a new dispute.

Bliss said, "Cutting utilities isn't going to do it, I'm afraid." If she had time she'd panic about the state of finances at Hole Point. "Insisting people pay rent on time might be more useful."

"Now you're talking," Fabiola said. She slapped down a pile

of clean sheets and hitched a long, slender, tanned thigh on the edge of the table. "Affordable doesn't mean free, Bliss. This joint is sagging at the seams and it's because there are a lot of so-called *artistes* in residence who think the world should support them."

"Oh, we shouldn't be that harsh," Bliss said. "My mission here is to provide people with a peaceful, inexpensive place to pursue their talent. Those talents are a gift to the world and they're less and less revered."

"Excuse me while I puke," Fabiola said, rolling her eyes. "Of course we mustn't risk interrupting the flow of genius by mentioning anything as vulgar as money. Perish the thought that the odd commercial enterprise might be useful and pay the rent. Hole Point is a refuge for these people. You make it possible for them to do whatever they're doing, but you're giving up everything for it. That's not right. You've helped Pol and me by not charging us rent at all, but we do try to pay back."

"This place would fall down without you two," Bliss said, considering Spike's potential reaction to a teensy poke of a toe under the table. "You more than pay your way. And you're right. I'm going to have to be firm and talk to the others—some of the others—about being timely with their payments."

"Good." Fabiola grinned her approval. "And we've got to look into filling up the rest of the cabins. This is the lowest occupancy we've had."

Bliss murmured agreement. "True. But it's summer and we have to expect some turnover. And it takes time to check new people out. The wrong tenant can upset things for everyone. We've already proved that."

"Boy, have we?" A red nail claimed Fabiola's attention. "That Lennox Rood is a piece of work. God's good gift to women, or so he thinks. Certainly expected you to throw yourself into his arms. Shows we never should bend the rules and let men in. Men cause trouble every time."

"Let's leave Lennox out of this," Bliss said. "He's not so bad. He made some wrong assumptions. Anyone can do that." And she'd rather not think about fighting off good old Lennox when he'd decided to wow her with his sexual creativity.

Fabiola watched Bliss speculatively.

"Yes, they can," Bliss said. "We all imagine things sometimes."

"Sure. I bet you always imagine it's a great idea to hide in someone's shower. Naked."

"Oh, Fab!"

Fabiola ignored the protest in Bliss's tone. "Surprise!" With a finger on top of her head, Fabiola wiggled and twirled. "Hop in here for a wet wall job, you lucky woman."

"You're terrible." Bliss shook her head and laughed. "It was awful."

"It was horrible," Polly said. "I heard you scream."

"I was shocked," Bliss protested, still giggling. "He looked so silly. And so mad when—when I laughed."

"Uh-huh. I still say it's a good thing you weren't alone here the way good old Lennox thought you were." Fabiola never gave up a point easily.

"Good thing," Polly agreed, sliding a berry pie into the oven. She ran water into the large mixing bowl she'd used, and washed her hands before washing the bowl.

"No reason you can't save that for the coffee when you've finished cleaning the bowl," Fabiola remarked. "Waste not, want not."

"I have a son," Polly said grimly. "I don't want my Bobby blaming me because he's going to be deprived of the natural joys he's got a right to."

"For crying out loud!" Fabiola threw wide her arms. "Bobby's only five, and *I* don't have any children—thank God."

"Your children thank him, too."

"Polly, you can be so—"

"What are you going to say to Prue?" Polly asked, turning her back on her sister. "She called three times this morning."

"Nothing," Bliss said shortly, but her stomach clenched so hard she opened her mouth to breathe. Life as the daughter of difficult parents had taught her to avoid issues too hurtful to confront. "I'll deal with Prue later."

"We read the piece in the paper," Polly said. Wiping her hands, she moved to her sister's side. "We didn't know you were on some committee."

"I'm not." Prue had violated every confidence Bliss entrusted to her. "What they printed is a mistake."

Fabiola set the linens on a counter and pulled a chair up to the table. "It says you're the chairperson."

Dragging another chair, Polly approached. "We think it's very interesting. All this corruption stuff."

"I don't," Bliss muttered. How had she managed to convince herself she was over Sebastian Plato? "I think it's disgusting. But it's nothing to do with me."

Polly crossed her arms on the table and rested her chin on top. Her blue eyes took on a contemplative light. "We weren't going to bring this up, were we, Fab?"

"No. We won't if Bliss doesn't want us to."

"I don't." She felt sick, and too hot. "No, I can't talk about it."

"Polly and I are women of the world, you know. We've lived."

Bliss wiped sweating palms on her pants and raised her eyes to the level of a row of empty wine bottles of questionable vintages ranged along the plate rack that surrounded the big kitchen. Each bottleneck contained the remains of a candle.

"Every one of those is a notch," Fabiola announced, following Bliss's gaze. "Each one is a testimony to passion. Nights of ecstasy. Isn't that so, Pol?"

"Too true," Polly agreed, but she didn't look at the bottles.

"I remember every man to go with every bottle," Fabiola continued. "I used to be wild, but I had my standards and my rules."

"One bottle per man," Bliss commented. They weren't going to stop talking about the newspaper article, and Sebastian. Taking off her metal-rimmed glasses, she polished the fogged lenses on the tail of her loose shirt. "One candle per customer."

"They were *not* customers," Fabiola said.

"Just an expression," Bliss told her. She was the boss around here and she could just get up and walk out. *We never walk away from an argument.* Bliss's father had made very sure that his lifelong instructions played loud and clear, and right on cue.

"I never wanted a long-term thing." Fabiola sniffed and pointed to a tall, dark green bottle with very little candle left, but a great deal of globby old wax running in congealed rivulets down its length. "He was the best of the lot. You should have seen him. His eyes were—"

"The same color as that bottle," Bliss finished for her. "Is there a reason for bringing this up now?" She was afraid she knew the answer.

"We don't want you to think you're the only one . . . That is, we don't want you to feel embarrassed about having a secret past. We want you to know we're not shocked."

Bliss opened her mouth, but couldn't decide what to say.

Polly reached to clasp Bliss's hand. "What Fab means is that we're glad you've known passion, too. We're glad you're not a repressed prude after all. And we want you to be proud of your womanhood, not ashamed of it."

"I am *not* ashamed of my womanhood!" Bliss snatched her hand away and stood up. They didn't know her. No one had ever really known her—except Sebastian. "Since when have I had the reputation for being a repressed prude?"

Fabiola stood up too and said, "Since always. We all thought you didn't even know what it was for."

*"It?"* Words failed Bliss a second time.

"Fab's right," Polly agreed. "I mean, you've never seemed interested in men as long as we've known you. When Lennox came on to you, you freaked. Now we find out you've had this torrid affair with this fabulous man who took advantage of you and dumped you. I mean, it just goes to show how you can never be sure—"

"Stop!" Bliss waved her hands. "Stop right now. Where is this coming from? How have you shifted from my being chairperson—which I'm not—of some action committee, to my having had a torrid affair? And been taken advantage of? And then been dropped?"

Polly moistened her lips. "We've upset her, Fab."

"Oh, how astute of you," Bliss muttered.

"A woman's body is made for love," Fabiola said. She pointed at Bliss's blue shirt, a castoff left behind by a previous tenant, and her purple terry-cloth pedal pushers. "You try to make yourself invisible in all those horrible clothes you wear, but underneath them beats a passionate heart. And your flesh sings with lust at the sight of a great pair of male buns, just the way mine does—and Polly's."

"Used to," Polly amended. "I'm a mother."

"Gosh, darn it!" Bliss sat down again—hard. "I'm sorry. I never swear. But you're making me so angry."

"You didn't swear," Fabiola said. "You're so squeaky clean and pure, it's a bit painful. Or that's what we thought."

"Okay." She didn't swear, and she didn't lose her temper. Years of watching her father do both had made her hate it when people lost control. "I'm going to be very calm. And you're going to be very calm. Fabiola, what is it you've heard about me—apart from the committee thing?"

"We already know you don't exactly hit it off with your parents."

Bliss screwed up her face. "What does that have to do with this?"

"If you got along with them, you wouldn't do this dumb thing of trying to make this place pay for itself."

Polly said, "That's right, Fab. If she trusted them to love her regardless, she'd just admit it can't be done and say she needs to go into her trust fund. And that would be that."

"And that's not under discussion here," Bliss said, feeling colder inside by the second. "Don't try to change the subject."

"All right." Polly sent her sister a warning glare. "You let me do the talking. The reason you're going to be chairperson of this committee is because Prue O'Leary's friend's daughter's friend got lured to New York and ended up dead in some porno movie maker's studio."

Bliss rubbed her eyes.

"You're not to cry, Bliss. Men aren't worth it."

"Shut up, Fab. She's upset. She can cry if she wants to. Anyway, the man who did the luring is opening up a place just like the one Prue's friend's daughter's friend went to. Right here. In Bellevue. Almost on our doorstep. And you're going to help close it down and run him out of town."

Bliss shook her head wearily. She should have made herself read the newspaper article. "From what I was told, a branch of Raptor Vision is opening in Bellevue. The man who owns Raptor Vision doesn't—as far as I know—make pornographic movies."

"No, but—"

"And he wasn't the person involved in the death of this poor girl."

Fabiola shook her head. "Not directly, but—"

"In fact, the girl made up her own mind to go to New York because she had some idea of becoming a model. Then she got involved in the terrible situation that cost her life."

"Yes," Polly said, signaling for Fabiola to be quiet. "Prue's afraid that if there's a big-time New York modeling agency here they'll exploit more kids the way they exploited Prue's friend's—"

"Friend's daughter," Bliss interrupted. "I don't think we should pursue this without some sane consideration of the truth involved."

"Oh, Bliss." Fabiola's eyes glistened. "You loved this Sebastian, didn't you?"

Sebastian. Sebastian who in Bliss's mind was forever twenty, and tall, and tanned, and letting go of her hand as if he'd stop breathing until he could hold it again. Sebstian who had said, *"Tonight,"* and then left town . . . and Bliss.

"It wasn't the friend's daughter," Polly said hurriedly, sounding anxious. "It was the friend's daughter's friend. Prue told the papers you've got *privileged* knowledge about this man, Bliss.

This Sebastian Plato. The one with the airline, and the advertising agency, and everything. Now, since the paper says he was brought up in Seattle and went to the same high school at the same time as you, it makes sense, doesn't it?"

"Does it?" Bliss struggled with a ridiculous urge to cry. After all these years. And over something that had been a stupid teenage piece of nonsense.

"He was expelled for raping a girl. Prue told us."

Bliss curled her fingernails into her palms. "School was already out for the summer."

The silence that followed stretched far too long.

Fabiola got up, came around the table, and draped an arm over Bliss's shoulders. "Oh, you poor, dear thing. You're so gentle. How could the beast have done that to you?"

"Sebastian wasn't expelled. School was over. We'd graduated. And I wasn't the girl he . . ." She gently removed Fabiola's arm and scooted back to the computer in its niche beside the refrigerator. "I was just his girlfriend. The only part you've got right is that he dropped me when he left town. I haven't seen him since. I don't know anything about his life or his business since then, and I don't care, either. I'm not chairing a committee to oust him. I'm furious with Prue for telling the press I am. And I'm going to call up the papers and have them print a retraction saying it was a mistake. Would you both be kind enough to get back to work?"

She stared at her spreadsheet until the numbers ran together. The twins' sandals scuffed on the worn tile floor and the door to the terrace opened. A heated breeze scurried against Bliss's back, ruffled strands of hair that had worked loose of the rubber band at her nape.

Sebastian Plato. Darn him anyway, she had outgrown the need to cry at the thought of him a very long time ago. Bliss settled a hand on her neck and bowed her head. She wasn't crying at the thought of him now, only at the thought of how much he'd hurt the girl she'd once been.

A wet nose nuzzled her elbow and she jumped. Spike pushed her gray-and-white head onto Bliss's lap and sighed.

"Auntie Bliss?" Bobby Crow's young voice wasn't the welcome interruption it usually was. "I've found someone for us. Because we need more people. Auntie Bliss, I said we're not full up."

She scratched Spike's ears and pushed her gently away. Arranging a smile, she scooted her chair around to face tow-headed Bobby. "New residents have to apply . . ." Bobby held a man's hand, a tall man's hand.

Bliss flinched. Bigger, his body the mature body of a powerfully built man rather than that of a boy about to become that man; nevertheless, she'd have known Sebastian Plato anywhere.

# Three

She'd have known him anywhere.

Blood pounded in her head. Even seated, she felt too far from the floor.

"Mom said we need more people," Bobby said, glancing anxiously at Polly, who stood beside Fabiola. The twins, who hadn't made it outside, gaped at Sebastian. "Didn't you, Mom?" Bobby persisted.

Polly cleared her throat and removed the apron from her brilliantly striped cotton caftan. "That's what I said." She and Fabiola exchanged *wow!* glances and raised their eyebrows. Their attention instantly snapped to Bliss.

They knew who he was. She could tell they knew, and that they were gauging her reaction to him.

Bobby settled his free hand on top of Sebastian's and looked up, way, way up at him.

Sebastian looked at Bliss. He looked at her as he had once before—the first time they'd met. Serious, assessing, insolent—only now the insolence blended with total confidence.

She flinched again. Across the room she felt him, felt the force of him like successive blows—one, two. Had there been a sound it would have been an *oomph* as air rushed from her lungs at the first punch. The second connected with her belly, her womb, the muscles in her thighs. Cold, hot, numb, the pain of returning blood. Weakness.

He spread the long fingers of his free hand over his flat belly and Bliss remembered a belt buckle in the shape of a silver S, a silver snake. The belt he wore today was of soft black leather, with a leather-covered buckle. Below the buckle his well-worn jeans faded to paler shades in places. One of those places was the more noticeable because Sebastian Plato had something he couldn't entirely control. That was old news. Bliss made herself look at bleached-out denim over his thighs—safer that way.

"Mom wants Auntie Fab to put bricks in the loos," Bobby said, bracing one sneakered foot on top of the other and swinging on Sebastian's arm. "I bet you'd put your own brick in." He regarded Sebastian with obvious awe.

Fifteen years.

His lips parted, but he didn't appear to know the words to say, anymore than Bliss knew them. The eyes were just as green as she remembered, the mouth just as fascinating.

No. The eyes were greener, the mouth more fascinating, the slanted angles of his dramatic face more ferociously commanding for the addition of fifteen years of living lines.

Bliss pushed at the strands of hair that hung around her face. Her glasses needed cleaning again. Oh, God, she had on the old blue shirt and purple pedal pushers Fabiola had rightly criticized.

Not that it mattered. Sebastian couldn't have come here because he was drawn to what had once been between them. A childish thing.

"You'd put your own brick in the loo, wouldn't you?" Bobby asked, sounding almost fretful. His elfin features had pinched. A little sponge for atmosphere, so his mother said of him, and she was right. "Auntie Bliss, he would. Is it all right? Auntie Bliss?"

"Of course it's all right, Bobby," she said, smiling at him. "Thank you for taking care of things for me."

"Thanks, Bobby," Sebastian said.

Blow three.

The voice was the same.

No. Not the same, the same, but quieter? Yes, a quieter, darker version of the boy's voice, the boy overcoming so much with sheer bravado. A quiet, firm, confident yet kind voice now. The dearest voice in the world.

Oh, damn, oh, damn, oh, damn. She'd prayed for him to come back, for the whole despicable story to be a lie. Then, when he hadn't come back, and the story only grew worse, she'd prayed never to see him again.

His small finger hooked under his belt. He was hard. He was hard and staring at her, and knowing she had to see his reaction to her. She almost turned away. Whatever or whoever was turning him on couldn't be her. She needed to remember he was "a red-blooded American male." He probably walked around constantly ready for sex.

Fabiola cleared her throat.

Bliss managed to smile at her. "If you could do that for me, Fabiola, I'd be grateful." Please don't let Fabiola ask what Bliss was talking about.

"No problem," Fabiola said, as if she understood perfectly. "We'll find a way, won't we Pol?"

"You've got it," Polly said, nodding gravely. "It'll take—ooh, a long time, I should think, shouldn't you, Fab?"

"Ooh, probably hours. But we'll come through for you, Bliss. See you later." She and Polly turned in unison and all but jammed in the doorway in their hurry to leave. Spike bounded across the room to follow.

"Hey, Bobby," Sebastian said, when the sisters were gone. "Do you suppose you could keep an eye on my truck?"

"Why?"

"Oh, just in case."

"Why?"

Sebastian smiled at the child. "You're a wise man. Never do anything you're not sure of. My dog, Beater. He's in the back and he gets nervous if he's left for long."

"You shouldn't leave dogs in cars. They can hydrate."

"De—" Sebastian pressed his lips together briefly. "You're right, but he's okay for a few minutes. And he's not shut in. He just doesn't like anyone getting close to my truck when I'm not there. Would you watch, and come and tell me if anyone goes near?"

Bobby considered. "No one comes around in the afternoons. They're working. I'm not allowed to bother any of them. They're *artists,* y'know. They paint and write and stuff. There's one lady who's with Vic. She makes pots n'stuff. He's a painter. I'm not allowed to go there at all because the lady's his—alive. She's—"

"Vic's life model," Bliss said, aware of warmth in her cheeks. She couldn't make herself think of what to do or say next.

"That's interesting," Sebastian told Bobby. "I need to speak to Bliss and I worry about Beater. Would you watch him, please?"

Bobby released Sebastian's hand and said gravely, "Okay. I'll tell you if anyone comes." His thin, tanned legs bore him rapidly from the kitchen, to the terrace, and out of sight.

Sebastian closed the door quietly and faced Bliss. His arms hung at his sides. She watched him make fists, brace his legs apart, breathe deeply enough to stretch his shirt over his heavily muscled chest and shoulders.

She wouldn't allow herself to look away.

He crossed the room and stood on the opposite side of the kitchen table, looking down at her. No hint of gray showed in his dark, wavy hair, or in the hair that showed at the open neck of his denim shirt. She had to lower her face. The kid who had once dropped out of school for a year still favored jeans that fitted every inch, but the inches were more solid, even more impossible to avoid staring at—repeatedly.

She felt him duck his head. She closed her eyes and her heart turned. He'd always done that, ducked his head to make her look at him.

The only sound in the room came from a box fan jammed into an open window.

Bliss smelled Sebastian, a clean smell, simple soap and laundered denim.

He touched her.

The tips of his fingers settled just beneath her jaw. His thumb moved lightly over her cheek. When Bliss opened her eyes, his were on the skin he stroked. The corners of his mouth twisted downward. Bitterness? Anger? A thin, white scar marred the upper bow of his mouth on the right side.

Once she'd known everything about him, or thought she did. Now she knew nothing—nothing of his life since the afternoon before he'd left Seattle.

"Fifteen years," he said.

She couldn't speak.

His eyes flickered to hers. "I'm sorry."

Tears? Why now? How could they come now? And how could he turn up after all this time and say, simply, "I'm sorry," when it was too late for sorry.

"Sounds asinine." He kept stroking her cheek, back and forth. "Not enough. Nothing would be enough, would it?"

Bliss fought the tears and opened her mouth to breathe.

Sebastian's thumb shifted to her bottom lip. "What a mess. What a bloody awful mess. I've wanted to come to you ever since."

If she answered, she'd break down.

"The early years were hell. Then I thought it was too late. Then I felt I had to try to prove I was worth something before trying to put it all back together."

She began to tremble, then to shudder.

"I was a fool and I knew it. I know it now. A fool for letting it all happen in the first place—having to leave. Thinking I had to leave. And then I was sure it was too late. You'd have your own life. Be married to someone else."

*Why didn't you call, or write? Just to let me know how you were, that you were okay? At least in those first weeks when I wanted to go to sleep and never wake up because I was afraid you were dead. I couldn't believe you'd leave me like that unless you were dead. I wanted to be with you, so I didn't want to live anymore.*

"You never married," Sebastian said. "I couldn't believe

my . . . I couldn't believe it at first. Say something, Bliss. Please."

She pushed herself to the back of her chair, pulling away from his touch. "You look well." Inane.

"So do you. You're so beautiful it hurts." He raised his face to the ceiling. "I sound like an idiot. But it's true. You don't look any different."

"Yes. No different except for those fifteen years, huh?" Now she sounded angry. She mustn't let him know how she'd counted those years, how she'd pored over photographs of him in business journals, and over articles about his ventures.

"You're angry with me."

"No!" *Yes.* Yes, she was angry. She was insanely angry. He'd messed up her life.

"I don't blame you. You've got every right to be angry. Vengeful, even."

"I'm not angry. And I'm not vengeful. I'm not . . . anything anymore. I'm happy."

"Are you?"

"Yes. Yes, I am, of course I am. I'm doing things that matter to me. I'm making a difference, even if it's only small."

"Why aren't you married?"

"Not everyone wants to be married."

"You did. And I wanted to be."

"And you are," she reminded him, shifting in the seat, so desperate, so confused she couldn't sit still. "How's your wife? How many children do you have now?"

"Bliss—"

"No." She couldn't stand this, not for another instant. He overwhelmed her. And he shouldn't be here, had no right to walk in here. "I want you to go away. I don't know why you're here at all."

"Don't you?"

"No. Oh, no, no, I don't."

"I had to come."

"You didn't have to come before." She raised her chin. The

burning in her eyes didn't matter anymore, or the wetness on her cheeks. What he saw, what he thought, didn't matter anymore. "You left me without a word—except from your sister. And you never as much as sent me a note."

He came rapidly around the table. "You were hurting, Bliss."

"You're right. I was hurting. How could I not be hurting when I loved—" She massaged her brow—"I loved you. I was going to run away and marry you. God, I hate this. I never wanted you to see how you'd hurt me. How can you come back now? Why have you come back? Drat! It's unbelievable."

"I was trapped. I couldn't get out of it and I didn't want to make things worse by prolonging things for you."

Bliss shook her head. "Forget it. It's all been over forever now. I don't care anymore. I'm just crying out of some maudlin empathy for the person I used to be. It hurt then. It doesn't hurt anymore."

"It never stopped hurting for me."

She dropped her hands into her lap and stared at him. "How can you lie like that?"

"I'm not lying."

"No? Look at you." Didn't he know she could see his sexual reaction to what was happening between them? Passion, even passionate anger, turned him on. She flushed and her heart raced. "Sebastian Plato, success story. You've got it all, old friend. If you'd been upset about walking away from what we had, you'd have tried to let me know. You'd have tried to help me understand. And don't tell me you've lived with a broken heart for fifteen years and just now decided to come and tell me. I don't believe you."

"Of course you don't." He stood over her. His leg touched her knee. She felt him above her. She felt his heat. The sting of her own arousal disgusted and frightened her. He told her, "How do I make you believe I came back to Washington because of you?"

"Don't make me laugh!" She tilted back her head to see his

face. "What would make you think I'm the kind of fool who'd buy that drivel?"

"Oh, I know you're no fool, Dr. Winters."

He'd researched her pretty thoroughly.

"I went along thinking you must have a comfortable life with someone else," he said. "Then . . . Hell, I don't know what made me do it. I guess I got low enough, lonely enough—empty enough. I just started trying to find out what you'd done with yourself. I couldn't find any record of a marriage. I couldn't believe it. A woman like you never married?"

"Women—not all women need a man to make them feel complete."

"You do."

Bliss's vision blurred. She took off her glasses and set them down.

"I remember how you came alive with me. You loved me, Bliss. And I loved you."

Past tense. What would he say if she told him she'd never stopped loving him, that she considered herself sick because she didn't think she would ever stop loving him?

"What do you want, Sebastian?"

He made no sudden moves. She was aware of the slow descent of his big hands onto her shoulders, of his looping his fingers around her neck and raising her chin with his thumbs until she could either lower her eyelids, or stare into his eyes—so close the gold flecks glittered.

Bliss stared into his eyes.

He bent over her. His mouth settled on her forehead, just rested there, then he kissed her softly and she heard a small, broken sound from deep in his throat.

The next kiss found her lips.

Not the same. The same man, the same falling, sweetly drowning sensations, but a different time and place. Once kisses had been enough. Kisses and touches, and the promise of more to come had been enough. They weren't enough now—they were too much, too much to endure when they tore into her, laid her open, whipped to burning reality the hundreds of days and nights of settling for the loss of him.

Sebastian found her hands and drew them around his neck. He lifted her to her feet and surrounded her, held her so tightly she couldn't breathe. But she didn't want to breathe. She only wanted these kisses, these sensations.

They struggled against each other, pressed closer, passed their hands greedily over each other's body. The time fled away. They were teenagers and they were adults. All at once, all blending. The heat of their youth became the fire of their adult coming together.

*You are not a teenager.*

Bliss's lungs burned. She gasped, and pushed at Sebastian. He held her even more firmly. His heavy erection probed her belly. His thighs flanked hers, trapped hers.

She drove her fists into his shoulders and turned her head away.

He released her so abruptly she toppled into the chair. Just as quickly, she was on her feet again and putting distance between them.

"I'm sorry," he muttered. "I shouldn't have done that."

Bliss reached the sinks and put her hands behind her to brace her shaky weight. "No. Neither should I."

"I didn't come here to kiss you."

"Of course not."

"At least . . ." He sat in the chair she'd vacated and buried his face in his hands. "I wanted to kiss you when I saw you. I want to kiss you again, now. And that's not all I want."

*Revelation.*

"Why are you here? Really here?"

"To see you. I told you. I came to Washington, to Bellevue, to see you. Some crazy notion made me decide to come here and mend fences."

"Crazy," she agreed, wanting to believe him.

"I'm not married, Bliss."

She bit into her swollen bottom lip.

"I haven't been for years."

She shouldn't be glad, but she was.

"No one wanted me to come here. I did it anyway."

Surely he didn't expect her to believe he'd done so because of her. "This area's very different from what it was when we were kids."

"Uh-huh. Actually it's been a natural expansion for me for a long time, but I've kept away."

She frowned.

"I stayed out of the Northwest because . . . It seemed best. Then I decided I wanted to prove I wasn't the punk all those people thought I was."

"The people where you lived? The people we went to school with?"

"Yeah. All of them."

"So you're setting up shop here."

"Not because of them anymore. Oh, I want to prove myself, but that's not the main reason. I wanted to see if there was a chance for you and me, Bliss."

Her blood stood still, and her heart.

"Now I know there is. I felt it. When I kissed you, I felt it. You still feel something for me."

She still felt something for him? Was that any way to describe all that raging, pent-up sexual and emotional hunger he'd unleashed?

He smiled at her, the lopsided smile she'd never been able to erase from her memory. "You may be a little thinner, Bliss."

"You're bigger." She looked at the holes in the toes of her sneakers. "I'm a lot older."

"You're thirty-two. Perfect age. I'm thirty-five. Not so bad, huh?"

"This is too much."

"I know. But we're going to work our way through it. I used to love how fragile you felt in my arms. Made me feel protective. Funny, I never wanted that with anyone else—not before or since."

"You're"—she needed to show him she wasn't still an innocent kid—"You're aroused."

He gave a short, hard laugh. "That obvious, huh? Yeah, I am. All it took was one look at you. Does that offend you?"

She tried to appear unmoved. "It happens."

He was silent for a moment. "Not to me. Not like this. But I guess you have the same effect on every man."

Bliss tugged on the horrible shirt. "I haven't noticed."

"Zoya showed me the press release."

*Zoya.* Bliss glanced at him. "Press release?" Zoya was the model, the gorgeous creature who was the figurehead for Sebastian's modeling and talent agencies.

"The most recent of a number that have appeared, evidently. About WOT. Women of Today."

"Oh, that."

"You never used to be a joiner."

"I'm not a joiner now." How would they handle it? How would they deal with everything that had happened since they were last together? Could they?

"The release says you're the chairperson for the action committee that intends to make sure Raptor Vision never opens its doors in Bellevue."

Stillness enveloped Bliss. She studied Sebastian. He was serious now—business serious. "How long have you been back?"

"A couple of weeks. I've bought a house in Medina."

Almost all routes to Hole Point ran through Medina. "So we're neighbors." And despite his urgent need to see her again, he'd waited two weeks to come here.

Sebastian's slashing brows drew together. "Five minutes from your gate to mine. That's all hogwash, isn't it? The stuff in the papers? You won't be leading a bunch of bra burners in a revolt against me?"

She picked up a glass, filled it with water from the faucet, and drank. Her thoughts jumbled. Sebastian had never been conniving. He wouldn't show up here, kiss her silly, then use her reaction to that kiss to make her back off from throwing any obstacles in his professional path.

He hadn't been conniving? Had he?

She'd never believed he was a rapist, but he hadn't contacted her to deny it—and he'd left town with Crystal, the girl he was reported to have raped and made pregnant.

"Hey, Bliss?" She heard him get up and approach. He set an elbow on the counter beside the sink and looked into her face. "Chilly?" He gave a little laugh.

Through the windows, afternoon sunlight shimmered over Lake Washington. Bliss stared at it. She'd come to love her little estate on the water, her haven with the quiet souls who came to find a peaceful place to work.

"They got it wrong, didn't they? Someone printed your name by mistake because you used to belong to this ball-breakers' group—when you were teaching at the university, maybe?"

Bliss looked at him and felt again the force of disbelief that he was here, that he stood so close he almost touched her. He had touched her. How he'd touched her. He'd kissed her and she'd kissed him back. They'd held each other.

"Bliss, say something." Hardness replaced question in his eyes, in the set of his commanding features. "I can't believe you'd be small-minded enough to let these people use you. Not out of spite, or something."

"You . . . Sebastian, you came here because of a press release, didn't you?"

"I was coming here before I saw the press release."

"Were you?"

"Yes."

"Why should I believe you?"

He stood up sharply. "Because I don't tell lies, dammit."

"Don't you?" Bliss drew herself up, too. "Forgive me if I feel like laughing at that statement."

"I'm damned." He stepped away, shoved his hands in his pockets, turned away, then back again. "I don't know what to say to you. You are chairing the silly little committee. You are trying to get back at me. Shit!"

Bliss put the glass in the sink.

"Oh, I'm *sorry,*" he said. "I forgot. You don't like bad language, do you?"

"No."

"Forgive me. I'll try to do better."

"I don't like liars or cheats, either."

"God— No one calls me a liar or a cheat."

"Because you're so successful you've been able to buy respectability." She leveled a steady gaze at him. "Have you been able to buy new memories for people, too. Have they all forgotten you raped your wife—before you married her?"

Beneath his tan he paled.

Bliss rubbed her eyes. "You'd better go."

"Amazing," Sebastian said softly. "You've been waiting for an opportunity to say that to me. All this time you've been waiting. And drying up inside while you waited."

The words smarted. Bliss locked her knees and felt her skin turn cold. "Have you finished?"

"Almost. A normal woman would have made a life for herself by now instead of waiting around for an opportunity to strike back for something that happened when she was a kid."

"Are you suggesting you don't think I've had a life without you?"

"Well, have you?"

"My life isn't your business. It might have been once, but not now. You made it clear you didn't want it to be. Please send Bobby in to me."

He hesitated, then she saw him make up his mind. "Okay. Fine."

"We like the gate kept closed. Perhaps you'd take the time to get out of your car and see to that as you leave."

Sebastian opened the door. "I'll do that. Nice to see you again."

"Yes, very nice."

"Bliss"—he paused in the doorway—"I don't advise you to lead an attack on me."

"Oh. Why's that? What would you do, shoot me?"

"Don't say stupid things. I wouldn't harm you physically, but I'd make you look a damn fool in front of all these people who think you're such hot shit."

"So long, Sebastian."

"Lady professor still carrying a torch for childhood sweetheart."

"How . . . Get out!"

"Leading a vendetta against him because she never got over being spurned."

Bliss turned her back on him.

"Jealous because he left town with someone else on the night when he was supposed to take her to Reno to get married. Mad as hell because she thinks he fucked her over—or because he didn't. Sorry about that."

She covered her mouth.

"Don't do it, Chilly. I'll cut you to ribbons."

"Oh, no you won't." She rounded on him, her heart pounding. "I'm going to do the cutting. The shredding. With the help of my committee."

# Four

He could get used to this. Oh, yes, this was the life Ron York had been born for. He stood on the terrace of good old Sebastian's newly acquired lakefront home and sipped a vodka martini.

Stretched on a chaise beside the pool, wearing a sleek swimsuit in her signature color—red, Maryan sighted Ron and waved.

He waved back. She was okay. Bearable. And she was his ticket to all this. In the two years since she'd picked him up in a Greenwich Village club, he'd learned a great deal. Most importantly, he'd learned he was never going back to being blond, blue-eyed Ronnie who earned his pretties as a fat man's butt boy.

The paper-thin platinum Piaget on his left wrist told him it was almost four. Sun polished the waters of Lake Washington and turned the surface of Sebastian's oval pool a blinding shade of turquoise.

"Ronnie! Ronnie, where's my drinkie?"

She drank too much, but that made it easier for him. Maryan was as sexually demanding drunk as sober, but she tired faster.

"Ronnie?" Her voice grew petulant.

He raised his own glass and called, "Just a minute, luv. I'll be right there," before going back into the plant-filled conservatory where a wet bar nestled in an alcove. Three cubes of ice and gin to the rim. That ought to see her on the way to nighty-night land in no time. At least he could hope. There was always the danger that he'd let her get too drunk before she got her jollies. Maryan would fuck till she got it off, even if they were both in pain by that time. The secret was to cut off the booze before she was entirely numb, stick it to her like a steam hammer, then top her off with an industrial-strength nightcap.

Ron sighed and looked at himself in the mirror behind the bar. Not a millimeter of fat anywhere. And he looked great in these surroundings, great against the trappings of wealth.

Sebastian had fantastic taste.

And Ron had figured out what everyone else seemed to have missed; Sebastian Plato spent most of his spare time alone and his name hadn't been linked to a woman's for years, not seriously.

Ron smiled as he stepped gingerly over rough granite tiles between the terrace and poolside. The tiles were hot on the soles of his bare feet. There were other things around here that might be hot. Deliciously hot. Like cool, distant, powerful Sebastian, on a long, warm night. Ron shivered at the thought.

"What kept you?" Maryan asked when he sat on a chaise beside hers and held out the gin. Her voice was already slurred from the three gins she'd knocked back since they arrived. "I missed you, Ronnie." She dipped a forefinger in her gin, sucked it, and tucked the finger inside the crotch of his yellow bikini swimsuit.

"Careful, luv." Ron hardened despite himself. Another of his talents—he knew what he preferred, but he was always ready for sex, however it came.

Maryan wriggled her finger.

Ron almost dropped his glass. "Maryan! We wouldn't want to shock your brother's housekeeper."

Maryan blinked very slowly. "Don't give a flying fuck what his housekeeper thinks. Anyway, haven't seen the woman. I'm not even sure she's here. Mmm, Ronnie, you are such a big boy." She bared her gritted teeth and pulled him free of the trunks.

"Luvvie!" Ron giggled and glanced over his shoulder at the house. "Maybe we should go in and take a nap." Maybe they should go in and she should take a nap. The sooner he got her naked and did whatever she decided she wanted this time, the sooner she'd be snoring and he'd be free for a few hours.

Maryan squeezed. She held her tongue between her teeth and squeezed hard. "I want to do it out here. Let the old bag watch if she's around. Do her good. Maybe she'll give her husband a treat later. Take off your suit."

"God." At least there were no other houses close enough to overlook them. "What if Sebastian comes back?"

"She won't say anything to him. He always chooses staff with no ears or eyes. Likes his privacy."

Ron didn't have to be told that. "I meant, what if Sebastian sees us? . . . Well, you know?" Maybe that wouldn't be such a bad idea. A better idea might be to get rid of Maryan and do a little skinny dipping in the pool until big, bad Sebastian showed up.

"Stand up, Ron."

He looked at her, and down at himself. "I *can't,* luvvie."

"Stand *up.*"

He felt flushed. "No, Maryan. Give me that towel. Come on, let's go inside."

She increased the pressure on his prick. "Do as I tell you, there's a good boy. Maryan makes sure you have a lovely life, doesn't she? Always? And she doesn't ask much in return. But she does like her few little pleasures."

What the hell—let 'em all look. Ron set down his drink. He stood up and Maryan pulled on his most sensitive flesh until she could study it from below with smiling relish.

"I'm a con . . ." She paused and swallowed from her glass. "A connoisseur. I pick these flawlessly." She ran her thumb over the tip of his penis. Her throaty chuckle became a gurgle of glee. She smacked his flank and watched him spring even harder.

"We need to talk," he told her, using another little trick: dis-association. "You were right when you said we'd have our work cut out here if we couldn't get Sebastian to leave quickly. From what I saw today—and from this place—I'd say he's digging in pretty good."

"Not now." Maryan slapped him again.

Ron flinched. "Inside, my love." Even a man of his single-minded powers was human. "I've been thinking. We've got to be very careful to protect your interests." To protect his own interests.

"Mmm. You do a wonderful job of dealing with my interests."

"I read that local newspaper article. That's the woman, isn't it? The one heading the damned committee against us. That's the woman you think he may have come here to pick up with again?"

"Fuck me, Ronnie?" She plucked at red lace ribbon that closed her suit between her breasts.

"Concentrate. We've got a lot riding on this. Bliss her name is. Some professor? God, think of it." He'd thought about it and decided he recognized one of his own. Sebastian was bisexual. But a confused bisexual rather than sure of himself like Ron was. That could be changed, but if Sebastian started playing around with some old girlfriend who made him feel guilty, Ron's plans might be in danger. That wasn't going to be allowed to happen.

"Ronnie!" Maryan wailed. "You're ignoring me."

"I'm not ignoring you. I want you to . . . I want to help you figure out a way to make sure Sebastian doesn't do anything we'd regret."

Maryan's next stinging blow snapped Ron's control. He reached for her glass but she clung to it, laughing and slopping gin. When he made a grab for the drink, she dunked her fingers in it and rubbed the cold booze over his penis.

He yelled and started to shrivel, and he grasped both of her wrists.

"Oooh!" Maryan shrieked. "So forceful. I can't have you ruining your big, strong image with that little apology for a cock, can I. We wouldn't want people talking about you being a friggin' little freak."

"That's enough." He began to yank her to her feet.

Her mouth, closing over him, made him forget what he needed to do.

# Five

His dear sister was giving her lover a blow job.

By Sebastian's pool.

In broad daylight, in full view of anyone who happened to stroll by.

He threw the envelope on his bed and turned his back on the vision of Maryan staggering while she and Ronnie-baby helped her out of her swimsuit.

He should be grateful the housekeeper didn't live in and that he'd told her he wouldn't be eating dinner at home. As long as none of the gardeners or the pool crew turned up, the show outside would play to an empty house—an all but empty house.

But he didn't like it. He didn't like it one damn bit and he was going to kick Ron's ass out of town and drag Maryan off to some upscale drying-out tank.

"Sebastian! Sebastian, are you here?" Zoya's distinctive tones sounded from the foyer downstairs.

Grabbing up the shoe he'd already shed, he ran onto the open upstairs balcony, took the stairs two at a time, and skidded to a halt in front of his open-mouthed Head of Operations for Raptor Vision.

"Hi, Zoya. I thought you had dinner plans."

"I did." She frowned at him. "That was before I got a call from some reporter on a fact-finding mission."

Sebastian glanced toward the open-sided sitting room. A glass wall separated it from the conservatory. The downward angle toward the pool, together with the screening plants in the conservatory, cut off any view of the coupling couple.

"This has been a hell of a day, Sebby."

"Mm." He calculated what it would take to get Zoya out of the house without making her suspicious. "What did you say?"

"I said, this has been a hell of a day."

"Yeah. Yeah, you're right. I want you to go home, make yourself a long, cold drink, and put your feet up. Don't give the job another thought till tomorrow." Smiling at her, he took her elbow and started toward the still-open front doors.

Zoya went several steps before planting her elegant feet. "I came to talk to you."

"You're tired and overwrought."

"Overwrought, my ass. I don't get overwrought. Pissed, maybe, when you suddenly start behaving like someone I never knew, but not overwrought. Can we sit down, maybe. The long, cold drink does sound good."

"Oh, sure. Which paper did you say called?"

"Out of L.A., I think."

He squinted. "L.A., huh?" A distant laugh floated on the early evening air. At least it wasn't getting too cold out there. "Amazing how these guys follow you around."

"This wasn't a guy. Do you have a diet Coke?"

"Of course. What did she want to know?"

"Who?"

"The reporter. The one from L.A."

Zoya glanced toward the living room.

Sebastian managed to walk her another step toward the front door.

Carrying a squeaky, orange spider in his mouth, Beater lumbered from the direction of the kitchens. He deposited the spider at Sebastian's feet, sat down, and panted.

Sebastian looked at the spider. So did Zoya. He laughed. "This mutt thinks he's a little puppy. Loves to play." He bent to retrieve the spider and threw it back in the direction from which Beater had come. "Fetch, boy!"

Beater sank to the floor and closed his eyes.

A shriek sounded, and a splash. Thank God. They'd decided to take a swim. "Will you look at that?" Sebastian said, indicating the dog. "Never does what I tell him."

"Maybe it's an authority problem. But I am looking."

Sebastian glanced at her, then at Beater—and his own feet. One brown boat shoe. One bare foot. He chuckled self-consciously. "I was just starting to get changed when you arrived."

"Figured as much." Her attention went to the hand that still held her elbow. And his other shoe. The sole had left dusty tracks on her white silk sleeve.

"Hell!" Sebastian jerked his hand away and dropped the shoe. "Hell, I'm sorry. I don't know what's with me. Distracted or something, I guess. Look at that." He shoved his foot into the shoe and slapped at Zoya's sleeve. "You'd better get right home and soak that in some water before it stains."

"You don't soak silk in water."

"Oh. Brush it, then."

"What is the matter with you, Sebastian Plato?" She glared at him. "Forget my dress. Forget the damn dog and his damn rubber spider. I came here because we've got trouble. Huge trouble, boss. And I think you know what I'm talking about."

He was afraid he might.

"Why didn't you come clean with me?" She flicked at the dust on her sleeve. "If I'd known what we were really looking at here I'd have brought Phil in. You should have brought Phil in. We hire a troubleshooter to deal with things like this."

"I didn't think—"

"Hell! If I'd known, I'd have dug my heels in and refused to let you come here at all."

Sebastian shoved his hands in his pockets. A dull pain niggled behind his eyes. "It isn't up to you to tell me where I go, and when. I'd like to be on my own, Zoya. Do you mind?"

"I know you'd like to be on your own. That much is obvious. Although I'm not sure exactly why. And I've got a lot riding on what happens here, too. I've got money in this one."

Her tone irked him. "Your idea, not mine. You wanted a piece of the action. I gave it to you because you convinced me you deserved the opportunity. End of story."

Zoya wiggled the heavy gold chain at her neck and said, "Is it true you were engaged to this Bliss Winters?"

Oh, shit.

"Is it?"

"We were kids." And his weeks with her were the best part of his entire life.

"Kids who intended to take off for Reno and get married?"

For Bliss's sake he had to take the heat out of this. "Someone's getting carried away."

"Someone sure is. Look, I'm exhausted. Can we sit down?"

"Sure. Who did you say this reporter is?"

"I didn't. But I think she's on the right track. Your *kid* thing with the professor is messing us up. It could mess us up big time if any of the mud she's slinging sticks to Vision. It was bad enough when that poor girl died—"

"Wasn't it just today you told me to respond to the O'Leary woman? Didn't you say something about sin and death being the kind of buzzwords that are good publicity?"

Zoya snorted. "Not if you're the one directly connected to the sin and death."

"I'm not, for God's sake. What are you—"

"At least the sin."

"I live like a monk." This was over the top. "I work. I work. And I work."

"You don't have to live like a monk," she said quietly. "We've discussed that."

He avoided her beautiful eyes and wished he didn't know what she was talking about. Zoya had made it clear that she'd like to be more than a business colleague. Sebastian couldn't feel what she wanted him to feel.

"Okay," she continued briskly. "We've got a problem and we've got to deal with it. Whatever happened between you and Bliss Winters happened a very long time ago. Evidently the woman's a big brain and prominent in society here. She's not going to want this childhood trash dug up. You'll have to go and see her."

Yeah, he might have to do that—again.

"Yes, that's it. Get in touch with her and arrange a meeting."

He'd behaved like an idiot, like a nasty, spiteful punk kid. He'd come on to her. Then he'd threatened her.

But she'd threatened him right back.

"Give her a call," Zoya said, her high, smooth brow drawn into rare creases of concentration. "Tell her you'd like to get together. For old times sake."

"Original."

"Don't be snide. It doesn't look good on you, and you aren't good at it."

"Right." Things were too quiet outside. "I'll get right on it. As soon as you leave."

"Are you trying to get rid of me?"

"I told you I had a headache."

Beater started to snore gently.

Zoya gave the dog a disgusted look. "Call the professor while I'm here. I want to know what she says."

"I can't do that." He massaged his temples. "I mean, I'm not ready. I've got to think for a bit."

"There's no need to think. Just do it. I'll tell you what to say."

Women. Right now they were the pain behind his eyes.

"Whatever you do, don't ruffle her feathers. She's smart, so the first thing she'll think is that you're trying to manipulate her."

Zoya had that right, the concept. The tense was wrong. Bliss already thought he was trying to manipulate her.

"Are you hearing me, Sebby?"

"Yes, I'm hearing you."

"Good. These academicians are elitist, remember. And they think they know everything."

"That's because they do know everything."

She snorted again. "About something or other. The point is

you've got to flatter her. Tell her how impressed you are with her accomplishments."

"And she isn't going to see through this?"

"No! They fall for the groveling reverence every time."

"How many academicians have you known intimately?"

Zoya thought for a moment. "My father had a friend who worked at Duke."

"What was his subject?"

She cleared her throat. "Basketball. He was a coach."

Sebastian was too uptight to grin. "Leave this to me, okay? I agree we've got a problem and I'll deal with it."

"Play to her ego."

"I'll do that."

"Be respectful." She didn't appear to notice the return of his hand to her elbow, or the slight pressure he applied there. "Admiring. Tell her she's the only professor you know."

"She is." And he'd already blown the admiring respect thing.

"Offer to do something for her favorite cause."

"I'll think about it."

"We could work all this out together." She tried to turn toward the living room. Sebastian turned her back. "I want to help you, Sebby. And I want to help me. I'm worried. I should have listened to Maryan. She said coming here was a bad idea."

"And I decided coming here was a good idea." He still did, but he hated the way he'd handled Bliss so far.

She was wonderful.

He'd remembered her eyes just as they really were. Bluer than any he'd ever seen.

"Endow a chair."

"What?"

Zoya flapped her free arm. "Endow a chair. I've heard how you do that. Five hundred grand or so and they put your name on a chair or something. You could say you want to do it for her. Put her name on the chair. In big letters."

"I don't think that's exactly how it works. And I think we're getting ahead of ourselves here. Sweetheart, I'm going to have to beg you to let me go and lie down."

She rounded on him and peered into his face. "You poor darling. You are sick, aren't you? Lie down at once and I'll get you a cold drink."

A cold drink obsession, that's what she had. "I'll be fine."

"I insist."

"You could have a good idea about the chair thing."

"You think so? You could offer a scholarship or two as well." Beater rolled onto his considerable back and continued snoring with all four long legs crooked in the air. Zoya shook her head and added, "A teen center might counteract this gossip about us and the dead girl. Why don't you ask Professor Winters to help you set up a teen center?"

*Professor Winters?* His Bliss had become a professor. Unbelievable.

"For underprivileged kids."

He concentrated on Zoya. He didn't always like her.

She smiled brilliantly. "I know you're thinking I'm a calculating bitch, but I really do believe it would do you good to get involved with some civic work."

Splashes and laughter resumed.

Sebastian closed his eyes.

"Where are Maryan and the slime?"

The slime was Zoya's term of endearment for Ron. "They went out," he said. It wasn't a complete lie.

"I worry about you," Zoya said. "You look tired."

"I'll be okay. A good night's sleep will set me up. I think I'll go right to bed now."

"Okay, okay. I can take a hint."

Finally. He smiled wanly and put a hand at her waist. "Thanks, sweetheart. I'd like to be a good host, but I've got too much on my mind. I need to unwind—on my own."

"But you will think about my suggestions?"

"I will."

"And you won't charge in there without discussing it with me?"

He winced.

"What's the matter?"

"Nothing." He wished he hadn't already "charged in there." "It's just the headache." Not that he'd have missed that kiss. From what he'd felt, Bliss wouldn't have missed it either. He intended to bank on that.

A high-pitched but definitely male whoop split the air. Coming this way. Sebastian hurried Zoya to the door. "Drive carefully."

"Sebastian?"

"Would it be okay if I called you later?" he asked. "After I've had a chance to do some thinking?"

"Of course, but—"

"Thanks."

"Where did you say Maryan and Ron had gone."

"Oh"—he cast about for something brilliant but came up empty—"They're out enjoying the sights I guess."

Zoya grew still and stiff. "Yes. The sights."

He swung around to see what she was looking at.

Maryan and Ron stood on the priceless Aubusson rug in the living room, dripping. Staring at Sebastian and Zoya, and dripping. And giggling.

They were both naked, except for the red lace bow that decorated Ron's tube steak.

Sebastian turned off the air-conditioning and rolled down his window. The air felt good. When he concentrated really hard on his destination, the memory of the scene at the house didn't shine quite so vividly before him.

"He won the ribbon!" Maryan had squealed, patting that ribbon, and falling against Ron. "First fucking prize!"

Zoya had laughed. She'd still been laughing when she left.

No amount of concentration would completely wipe that little picture out. He'd already been to Hole Point, found that Bliss was out, and been given a great deal of help on where to find her by the leggy blond, Fabiola.

He still couldn't shake the image of his sister and that red bow.

Bliss had gone to some guy's gallery show at a store in Bellevue Square Mall. Sebastian drove past the mall on his way to the office each day, but he'd never been inside. Following Fabiola's directions, he made a turn from Bellevue Way onto a drive leading to a multistory car park. By the time he'd parked, and walked through an upper floor of Nordstrom's, he wasn't so sure he'd made the right decision in trying to talk to Bliss again so soon after the first fiasco.

A guy at the grand piano in the department store played "Sunflower" and Sebastian breathed a little deeper, a little easier while he let the music flow over him. He passed women in velvet hair bands, silk scarves and sensible flat shoes drinking lattes at little wrought-iron tables. All so smart, so sure of themselves.

The burbs.

He jogged down an escalator and strode between potted palms and shoppers. These people paid as much for their baby strollers as he'd been paid for the sale of his beloved first Ford truck.

The thought stopped him.

As much as he'd paid for Bliss's rings. Shit, how had he made such a mess of his life? Some people would laugh at him for even thinking his life was a mess, but it was. Oh, he had money, lots of money—more money than any man needed. But he didn't have the one thing he'd wanted more than anything; Bliss Winters as his wife.

A girl wearing black lipstick, and with rings in everything, including the tongue she held between her teeth, stared at him. With her arms crossed over a middle left bare between a short, breast-hugging top, and the waist of ragged jeans, she made a slow circle around Sebastian. Shades of New York City. He should feel right at home in the company of a looney.

He smiled politely and set off again, briskly.

Then he saw Bliss. Wearing an ankle-length black dress that flapped, and with her hair loose, she entered an art gallery.

Sebastian eyed a bench in the middle of the mall, but with a perfect view of the shop door. *Coward.* No, he wasn't a coward, he was being thoughtful. He'd wait patiently until she came out rather than interrupt her visit with her friend.

Her friend.

*"Lennox is a painter,"* Fabiola had said. *"Or some people think he is."* Sebastian didn't think Fabiola sounded as if she liked Lennox, but that could have been wishful thinking.

*"I* don't like you, Lennox," Sebastian murmured, taking small pleasure in his own perverseness.

From his vantage point on the bench, he watched Bliss walk slowly back and forth between the gallery walls. She studied each painting carefully, with intense concentration.

Daubs of color. No form. Sebastian could see that much without getting an inch closer. Give him a good landscape any day.

Better yet, black and white photographs. A man knew where he was with a photograph.

An athletically built man separated from a group inside the gallery and tapped Bliss's shoulder.

Sebastian leaned forward.

Bliss turned and smiled.

The guy put his arms around her.

Sebastian stood up. Damn the guy's nerve, putting the make on Bliss. She wasn't returning the embrace.

Sebastian started toward the shop door—and caught Bliss's eye through the window. She frowned and shook her head, just once. The message was implicit. *Don't interfere.*

He held up his palms, forced a toothy smile, and backed away, all the way away to the bench where he sat down again.

It had to be Lennox. What kind of a name was Lennox? Oh, Len-nox! A name that went just fine with a man who wore a navy blue blazer with brass buttons, and white duck pants, at eight in the evening. A name for a man who blew his perfect brown hair dry and sprayed it.

Not the kind of man for Bliss. Elegant in her simple way. One of a kind. He rubbed his palms over his thighs. In the now of Sebastian Plato, women wore only couturier, right down to the red lace bows . . . He shoved the image of the bow aside again.

On the day when he'd first found the guts to talk to her, Bliss had told him she ate lunches from home because her mother didn't want her to get fat. Looking at her now, at her slender body in the too-big dress, he remembered needling her by looking under the table. Sebastian smiled.

If there were a way to throw her over his shoulder and take her home to his bed he'd probably die of happiness. Yeah, he'd die a happy man. All she'd have to do was lie there and let him hold her, let him bury his face in her hair, feel her breath against his neck, her head on his shoulder.

Sebastian shuddered all the way to his toes inside their deck shoes.

He looked toward the upper floor of the mall. He ought to

leave. He'd managed to stay away for fifteen years! And now he couldn't be objective about anything when it related to Bliss.

Lennox slipped an arm around her waist and turned her toward one of his daubs. He pointed, made shapes in the air, bent over Bliss and smiled adoringly at her.

He whispered something in her ear. She eased away.

Sebastian smiled. Maybe Lennox would take the hint. Bliss didn't want any part of him.

A stream of shoppers passed in front of the shop. The crowds were thick, the noise too.

He stood up to see better. Lennox stared unseeingly toward him, his hands sunk deep in his pockets. His expression was? . . . Speculative? Not glad, or sad, but speculative. He wandered outside the shop and scanned the crowds.

There weren't many people in the gallery.

Bliss wasn't in the gallery anymore!

In the space of a few moments she'd managed to leave unnoticed, and had deliberately given him the slip. *"She goes up to the second floor of Nordy's to buy a cookie for Bobby, then catches the bus back."* Sebastian broke into a run and scoured the upper gallery—and saw a slim woman in black hurrying toward the entrance to Nordstrom's.

"Thank you, Fabiola," he said aloud, running flat out, dodging strollers, and mommas, and daddies, and the sleek groups of women with velvet hair bands. "Thank you! Excuse me, ladies!"

They just stood there and stared at him while he ran by. He'd never understand why women would do that, just stare at a man when he went by. Like they'd never seen a man running before.

He caught Bliss as she drew level with the black grand piano inside the store. He caught her by the arm and swung her around. "Hey, there, old buddy. I thought that was you I saw."

She blinked rapidly behind her wire-rimmed glasses and said, "Why are you here?" very softly.

He ducked his head until she raised her chin. The pianist tripped smoothly from "Masquerade" into a conveniently rich rendition of "Samba Beach." "What did you say?" Sebastian mouthed at Bliss.

Her teeth sank into her bottom lip, just as he remembered them doing so often—usually when he wanted to kiss her, and she was afraid someone would see. "Want to dance?" He drew her into his arms so fast she had no chance to resist.

"We never got a chance to dance before," he said into her ear, and thanked his good fortune that dancing was something he'd learned to do very well along the way.

At first she stumbled over his feet, but, despite her hesitancy—and backless sandals, and amid chuckles from onlookers, she followed him into the short samba, burying her face in his chest by the time the last notes were played.

When they stopped, and he tilted her scarlet face up to his, a smattering of applause broke out. Sebastian kissed her pink nose, then the corner of her mouth.

Laughter joined the applause.

"You haven't changed," Bliss said. "You were always wild."

"I'd prefer to think of myself as spontaneous."

"Stop it. Why are you doing this to me?"

"I want to be with you. I'll take it any way I can get it."

"You must think I'm an idiot. You've stayed away almost half of our lifetimes. Now you'll do anything you have to, to be with me? Please. Give me some credit for a little intelligence."

"I couldn't be here any sooner." Those were dangerous words, words that he couldn't afford to have probed too deeply.

Bliss looked at him quizzically.

"You want some coffee?" he asked her hastily.

"I want to go home."

"How about my home." *Red bows.* "I mean, how about I take you to your home."

"I came alone. I'll go home alone."

"It's getting dark out there."

"I'm a big girl."

He held her away and studied her baggy, black cotton dress

l the way to slim ankles and narrow bare feet in brown Birken-ocks. "No, you're not."

"What?"

"You're not a big girl. You're little. You always were."

She drew herself up. "I'm five-eight in my . . . Oh, for crying ut loud." Furtively, she checked around. "I suppose there's omeone watching, right? Someone who'll say I'm spurned or omething. They'll say I let you dance with me willingly enough nd that will supposedly prove I'm besotted with you."

*Déjà vu* all but winded Sebastian. "That's one of the first iings you ever said to me. When I talked to you in the school afeteria. You thought I was doing it on a bet and someone ould hop out and laugh."

The corners of her mouth jerked—down. She was struggling gainst tears.

"Hey, I'm sorry." Very firmly, he wrapped an arm around er shoulders and led her through the store and outside. A little ar served coffee drinks and snacks. He sat Bliss at one of the on tables on the balcony overlooking NE 8th Street. "Sit here. Vould you like some coffee?"

She shook her head. "A cookie. One of the shortbreads with ink frosting."

*For the boy.* Sebastian nodded and went for the cookie, never aking his eyes off Bliss until he returned. "Here you go." He ut the white bag on the table in front of her and sat down. Please hear me out, okay?"

"I don't cry," she said, staring at her lap. "Twice today you've nade me want to cry."

Earlier she'd done more than want to cry. "All I'm asking ou to do is listen to me."

"I'm so tired, I could sleep right here."

"Not too tired to come and see lover boy." He clamped her vrist to the table, stopping her from leaping up. "I don't believe said that. Forgive me."

"Forgive you. Forgive you? Sebastian, I've got to get on with ny life and *forget* you. I have forgotten you."

"No you haven't. I saw it in your eyes this afternoon. You haven't forgotten anymore than I have."

"Thanks for getting the cookie." She curled her fingers over the bag. "I don't want to talk to anyone. You're here because you want me to squelch this action committee for you."

That would be nice. "I'm here because I want to be."

"I'm not good at conflict."

"Who's the guy?"

Her fine brows rose. "Guy?"

"Don't kid around, Bliss. You aren't good at that, either. The snazzy dude in boating gear."

"Snazzy." A smile put light back into her dark blue eyes. "Is that a word in current usage?"

"Must be. I just used it. Lennox. Who is he?"

"How do you know his . . . You went to the Point."

"Don't blame Fabiola. She knows I'm a friend of yours so she told me how to find you."

"You used to be a friend of mine."

"I still am. At least, I want to be. Who's good old Lennox?"

"A friend." Bliss made to get up.

Sebastian scraped his chair beside hers and put a hand on her arm. "Don't leave me. I really need you, Bliss."

She sat down slowly. "You do know this is bizarre, don't you? Showing up a lifetime after you left me sitting in a car in downtown Seattle waiting for you to take me away to get married?"

It hurt him to think about that night. "If I could change it, I would. If I could turn the clock back, I would."

Bliss looked at his hand where it rested on her wrist and said, "So would I," so quietly he wondered if he'd misheard.

Sebastian gripped her a little harder and averted his face. "They were the best months of my life. The months we had. I remember every one of them—every day."

She didn't respond, but neither did she attempt to move.

"This afternoon. After I left you. I couldn't believe I'd said those things to you. To you, of all people. I hate myself for that. I'm every kind of a fool, Bliss."

"You're not a fool. You never were."

How little she knew about him, really knew about him. He'd made a mistake. Many mistakes, but one gigantic mistake that he'd never be able to erase, not completely. And he hoped he never had to tell her about it.

"It's getting late," Bliss said. "Bobby will be waiting for his cookie."

"How old is he?"

"Five."

He looked at her. "We'd have had children by now."

For a moment she stared back at him. Then her face crumpled before she covered it with her free hand.

"Oh, no." Almost roughly, he pulled her toward him, wrapped her tightly in his arms. "My mouth is on a suicide mission. A thought comes into my head and, blap, it's out."

She struggled, but he wouldn't let her go.

"I'm going to take you home now."

Bliss shook her head. She pushed on his chest until he released her. "I'm going to catch—" A bus pulled into the stop on the opposite side of the street, picked up a single passenger, and pulled out again. "I'm going to catch the bus."

"The one that just left?"

She shrugged. "There'll be another one. I'll wait here for a few minutes then go down. You don't have to stay."

"Bobby will be waiting for his cookie."

The faintest of smiles flitted over her features. "Big, quick, wild, Sebastian. Some things never change."

"And for these things, we are grateful," he told her, leaning a little closer. "They all said I was crazy to come here."

"Why?"

"To Bellevue. They said if I was going to expand into the Northwest it should be to Seattle or Portland."

"Oh." She tucked the cookie bag into a pocket in her dress. Her arms were bare and she hunched her shoulders.

"Cold?"

"No." But she shivered. "Why didn't you go to Portland or Seattle."

"Because Bellevue's closer to you."

Just as he'd visualized a thousand times, she took off her glasses and set them on the table while she pressed a finger and thumb into her closed eyes.

Sebastian settled a hand carefully on top of her head, stroked her hair slowly, slipped his fingers to rest on her nape.

"You want me to believe you found out I live near Bellevue, then decided to spend a fortune setting up a branch of your modeling agency here? Oh, Sebastian. You never used to be a liar. At least, I didn't think you were."

"I'm not," he told her, rubbing the back of her tensed neck. "And you've got it right. That's exactly what I did. It started when I made a few simple inquiries and found out you weren't married. I just kept on thinking about you. Couldn't stop. Now I'm here."

She shook her head again.

"You are cold. And I'm going to drive you home."

Retrieving her glasses, sniffing and searching through her pockets, she started to get up. Sebastian pulled out a handkerchief and pressed it into her hand. She used it to wipe her eyes and blow her nose. She went to give it back, but laughed and put it into a pocket. "Thanks. I'll send it back to you."

"You don't know where I live." Yet.

"To your office. I'll find the address."

Very firmly, Sebastian took her left hand in his. "I'm going your way. Can we stop talking about it and let me get you back to your nest?"

He saw her make up her mind. "Okay. Thanks. I probably shouldn't let you, but I'm tired. Exhausted, actually. So I'll accept."

Nordstrom's was beginning to close. They hurried through the store to the garage where Sebastian had parked.

As they approached the Ford, Bliss stopped walking.

"What is it?" Sebastian asked.

"That's not yours."

He frowned, then realized what she was asking. "Oh. Yes, it is mine. I never drive anything else. Never will."

She went silently to the passenger side and waited for him to open the door. Gathering her dress in one hand, she climbed in. Sebastian caught a glimpse of pale, graceful legs all the way to smooth thighs. He slammed the door harder than he intended and walked around the hood, making a great deal of fiddling with his keys.

To lie with her in his arms. Naked.

He turned his back on the truck and ground his teeth. They'd been friends, then sweethearts. Funny, old-fashioned word. They'd never been lovers. The kisses had aroused him, the kisses and the touches. But there had never been any question of expecting more until they had married. This afternoon Sebastian had known the unbridled wanting of a man for a woman—for the first time with Bliss.

It was all a jumble. Teenagers, adults, the old warm yearning and certainty they'd one day have it all, and now his longing that was a poignant thing wrapped up in heated desire.

Sebastian took in a big breath and got into the cab. He didn't trust himself to look at her. Neither of them spoke until he'd waited for a break in traffic on NE 8th and headed toward the lake.

"What happened that night? That day? When you left me? Just the day before everything was okay."

He barely stopped himself from braking. Of course she wanted to know. He'd been ready for her to ask, had thought about what he'd say.

"It's a fair question, isn't it?" she said.

"Maryan—"

"Your sister came and told me to go home. She told me . . . She told me you'd left Seattle with Crystal Moore."

"That was true."

"Yes. It was weeks before I could bring myself to believe it, but I had to. Everyone I saw made a point of telling me how sorry they were."

"Shit."

"Mm. I didn't realize they knew about us, but they did."

He hadn't realized either. "How did they know?"

"You didn't tell them?"

Sebastian glanced at her. "Why would I, anymore than you?"

"Because it was all a joke."

He yanked the wheel and screeched to a halt at the side of the road. "A joke? You're going to have to spell that one out for me."

"We can't stop here."

"I can stop anywhere I damn well please."

Her hands went to her cheeks. "Don't shout. I will not talk to anyone who shouts at me."

Sebastian made fists on his thighs and said, "I'm sorry. I don't like shouting, either. But, Bliss? What do you mean, a joke?"

"I don't know. I thought . . . When other kids started laughing at me I decided you'd made a fool of me for some reason."

"Let me get this straight." Swiveling in his seat, Sebastian inclined his head to see her more clearly. "What we had was a joke. Is that what you're saying? I strung you along so I could make a fool of you with other people? Bliss, I'm the guy they hated, remember?"

"Maybe that's how you thought you'd get them to stop hating you. They hated me more, so you . . . Oh, drop it. We're too old for this now. I'd appreciate the ride home."

"What we had was as real to me as it was to you. I never doubted it was real to you. If I hadn't . . . If things had gone right for once, we'd have been married. And we'd still be married. I'm more sure of that than anything else in my life."

"Please take me home."

"Not until you admit your theory's a load of crap."

"I hate it when you—"

"All right!" He held up his hands. "I'm sorry I swore, okay?

I went through hell after that night. It was no joke. Take it from me."

"I went through hell, too."

"And I'm sorry for that, my love."

"I'm not your love."

He dropped his head forward and crossed his arms tightly.

"I'm going to get out and walk," Bliss said.

Sebastian said, "Don't do that. I'll only follow you." He'd been naive to think she wouldn't want to know every little detail.

"You didn't just lead me on because someone else thought it would be funny?"

"No." The next breath pained him. "Maryan told you I had to leave."

"She told me you sent her to say you'd had to take Crystal away."

He had to be so careful what he said. It had to be the truth, but not too much of it. "That's what I told her to say."

"You'd been seeing me in the daytime, but we couldn't meet at night because of my parents."

"There's no way to change what happened."

"You were a red-blooded boy. Man. I was the daytime diversion. You got restless at night. That's more or less what Maryan told me."

Nice touch, Sis. "Did she?"

"I really want to go home."

"Okay." He faced the road again and schooled himself to drive off at a steady pace. "It wasn't the way Maryan made it sound. I wasn't running around at night."

"Crystal was pregnant."

Why had he thought, even for a second, that Bliss would somehow, by some miraculous means, not have heard that part of the story?

"Her father's a religious fanatic," he said, keeping his eyes on the road. "She seemed one way to all of us when she was in school. Sure of herself—snippy. She was a scared kid really.

At home she was threatened every day. If she ever brought what old man Moore called 'shame' on his household, she'd die."

Bliss made a small, distressed sound.

"They didn't know she was a cheerleader. Someone bought the uniform for her—don't ask me how that worked. But she used to keep her stuff at school and tell her folks she was working late on the newspaper. When the squad practiced—or there was a game."

"It's tough trying to live up to parents' rules and expectations," Bliss said, almost as if she didn't know she'd spoken at all. "Why is it so tough?"

Sebastian cut through quiet residential streets on his way to Hole Point, but he drove more slowly than necessary. "I don't think it has to be that way," he said. "If people didn't become parents accidentally, or just because they think it's what's expected of them, or for a load of other lousy reasons, then kids would have at least one certainty to build on."

Bliss turned toward him. "What would it be?"

"That they were wanted. Simply that. That they were wanted for themselves, and as extensions of their parents' love for each other."

When Bliss didn't answer he glanced at her. "What? What are you thinking?"

She'd leaned the side of her head against the rest and was staring at him. "We know a lot about each other, don't we?"

His grin was bitter in the gloom. "You could say that. We know a lot about where we came from. The type of people. What they expected of us. What we were supposed to provide for them."

"I didn't live up to my parents' expectations," Bliss said.

He laughed. "How can you say that? You're a fantastic woman. Fantastically accomplished and a wonderful person."

It was Bliss's turn to laugh—with no humor in that laugh. "Thank you. Isn't life weird? If we'd ended up together, I probably wouldn't have pursued an academic career and I guess I wouldn't have regretted it. Who knows what I'd have done. I do know it wouldn't have pleased my folks.

"But what I have done doesn't please them, either. I've never been what they wanted. Oh, forgive me, I'm sounding maudlin, and I hate that."

"You've got a right."

"No, I don't. I've got a good life. And your folks should be thrilled with you. Your dad wanted a son who would do all the things he thought he should have done himself and you've accomplished that."

"He's dead. They both are."

"Oh, I'm—"

"Don't say you're sorry. I wish I was, and that makes me feel as bad as I probably am. I made him pay for not being proud of me when I was growing up."

They reached the driveway to Hole Point sooner than he would have liked. "Just about there," he said.

"Thanks. I'll hop out here."

"Please don't, Bliss."

Lights showed in the kitchen windows of the lodge and, a little beyond the building, a lantern glowed on the wall outside the door of the closest cabin. Sebastian let out a slow breath and waited.

She cleared her throat. "What do you want? From me?"

How could she do anything else but wonder. "A chance. I want a chance with you." He killed the engine and turned to face her. "Another chance."

"Didn't you marry Crystal?"

"You really haven't made any attempt to find out about me, have you?"

The soft pressure of her fingers on his jaw shocked him. "Of course I have. I've read articles about you. I know all about Raptor and its ingenious founder. I've checked for any mention of you over the years. Do you believe me?"

He covered her hand on his face. "I don't know."

"I've got copies of them all."

Sebastian drew her palm over his mouth.

"There was never any mention of your private life—except

for the fact that you wouldn't discuss it and didn't grant personal interviews."

He closed his eyes and kissed her palm.

With her free hand, she touched his closed eyes. "Did you marry Crystal?"

"Yes," he murmured. "But we're divorced."

"And the baby?"

"I'd rather not talk about it."

"The poor child's one of those accidents you were talking about, right?"

"Past tense."

In the darkness, he felt her apprehension. Then she reached for him, framed his face and brought his brow to rest on hers. "Dead," she whispered. "I never even gave such a thing a thought. I'm sorry. We can be so selfish when we're unhappy."

His instant flare of joy was wrong, but he caught at it gladly. If she was unhappy it had to be because of him and she wouldn't be unhappy because of him if he didn't mean anything to her.

"You did the right thing," she told him. "You married Crystal because she was carrying your child. And because you wouldn't allow her to face whatever her father might do to her if you didn't."

"Bliss." Cautious, braced for her to flee at any second, he stroked her bare arms. "I don't expect everything to be perfect. Not immediately. Not ever, really. Perfect isn't something I've ever aspired too, just whatever success is. This time it's success with you."

"I don't understand. Success with me? You make me sound like a business venture."

He laughed shortly. "That's probably because business ventures are the only kind I've had any experience with lately. I mean I want to be successful with you. Not—no, not the way that sounds. I don't mean I'm trying to get you into bed." Oh, happy day—but one step at a time, and for all the right reasons.

When she didn't say anything, he looked at her. "What are you thinking?"

"I can't put it into words." In the almost-darkness her eyes were huge. "I . . . Dealing with this sort of thing is pretty much outside my experience now."

Her lips glistened a little, and her teeth. The risen moon sketched the curve of a high cheekbone and the line of her pointed chin.

"Now? Does that mean you've had a lurid past?"

"Oh, yes, very lurid. I was always a fast female."

He laughed, and she joined him. The slackened tension was a relief. The relief didn't last. "There isn't anything we can accomplish, Sebastian. Even if we really wanted something together, it's too late. You agree with that, don't you?"

"No."

She caught at one side of his collar and tugged lightly. "I'm not going to lead some vendetta against you. It's not my style."

"That's not why I'm here. I've told you the truth, Bliss. I want a chance for us to start over." But he hadn't said it, not that bluntly, until now.

Bliss's eyes met his slowly. "You've got to be joking. How could such a thing possibly happen. We don't know each other anymore."

"Don't we?"

"I . . . I don't know you."

"Yes, you do. I'm the same person I was when you were ready to run away and marry me."

"How can you be?"

Not caring about the console that separated them, Sebastian leaned toward her. He pulled her closer, wrapped her in his arms, caught her hair in one hand and drew it together behind her neck. "Try me out. See if I'm not the same."

If he could see her more clearly, he knew she'd be blushing. She swallowed and he heard her throat click.

"Go on. Kiss me, my old friend. Take your time with this one. Remember where we were with kisses by the time we'd decided they weren't going to keep on being a whole meal for very long?"

"Sebastian," she said, a note of awkwardness in her voice. But she lowered her eyes and brought her lips to his. "This feels so strange. How can something feel strange and familiar at the same time?"

"Because it's familiar but you didn't expect it to happen, so it's strange."

"You always did have an explanation for everything." Her breath was sweet and warm on his lips.

*Not the whole meal for very long.* Well, they'd been the hors d'oevres of his experimental love, the entrée of his blossoming love, and they'd ended up being a phantom dessert when he should have been having the real, whole enchilada.

Bliss kissed him. He let her set the pace, held himself in check when his drive blasted to full, pressing need. He could so easily let his mouth signal the message of his desire, his hands make the nature of his quest clear.

She kissed him gently, her lips barely parted. Gradually her arms encircled his neck and she absorbed his weight. And her mouth opened. As if she thought he might not be sure, she coaxed him with her tongue, pausing a second here, a second there, gathering purpose as he responded. The balance was delicate. He gauged her need to build confidence, to build trust. Push her, even the tiniest bit now, and he might frighten her into retreat.

Her breasts were an inflaming pressure against his chest. Still he kept his arms around her. This was not a wedding night, only a reprisal of their first passionate kisses. What had happened earlier that day didn't count—reflex action, nothing more, at least as far as Bliss was concerned.

The passage of her long, cool fingers from his face, to his neck, to his shoulders—inside his shirt, all but stopped his heart. His erection surged against his fly.

Sebastian centered his concentration on her mouth. This was her show. She must let him know when she was ready for him to respond in other ways.

The hair on his chest, the skin over his collarbones, the rock-hard muscle of his shoulders beneath his shirt—she fingered each inch with tentative curiosity.

At last she drew a breath's distance away from him, her eyes still lowered.

"You're a great kisser," he murmured.

They both laughed.

"You were a very able student." And he was more than ready to turn her into a graduate student—with him. He'd already steeled himself not to think about the other men who must have gone past the kissing stage with her, the first man to make love to her.

That man should have been him. "I'd like to start over. I know you've said that's ridiculous, but you can't say the feelings aren't there."

"I can't say that, no."

He dared to hope. "I don't care how long it takes to get back what we had." Now he was lying. "Yes, I do care. I'd love to take you home to bed right now."

"Sebastian, don't."

"No. I'm just being honest." Brushing his fingers from her arm to the soft rise of her breast was the most natural move in the world.

She didn't stop him.

Sebastian flattened his hand over her breast, surrounded it through the dress.

Bliss breathed in sharply and her back arched. She felt it too, the pent-up sexual need. Her nipple hardened beneath his palm.

The pressure inside his jeans took his breath away. Almost savagely, he buried his face in her neck and hugged her again. This time there would be no wrong moves.

"You're going to give us another chance, aren't you?" he said against her soft, sweet-smelling skin.

He held his breath in the silence.

"What will that mean?" she asked.

So careful. And he couldn't blame her. "It'll mean we decide to go forward together. As slowly as you want."

"You mean we start all over."

He couldn't make himself laugh. "I don't think it'll be quite like that. We're not exactly the same people we were the first time. But I mean we decide we have something together that we want. And we go after it. And this time no one gets in the way."

She made circles on his chest, on top of his shirt. With each circle, she passed over a nipple. He resisted the urge to start undressing her. Clearly she was preoccupied and didn't know how aroused he was. "I need to think about it," she said.

*God.* "I won't rush you." *But I'm dying right now.*

Inclining her head, she studied him, or what little she must be able to see of him. And the circling finger descended over his ribs, his hip, to his leg. She looked down and watched the languid smoothing of her own fingertips on his thigh.

Control. Control was everything now.

"You are too . . . too everything, Sebastian. You were so stunning when we first met. I couldn't believe you'd want to even look at me. Now you're . . . Well"—she shook her head—"you just are, that's all." Spreading her fingers, she gripped the heavy muscle on top of his thigh. "Your legs always fascinated me."

If she'd kicked his gut it wouldn't have contracted with more force. "Your legs always fascinated me," he told her. But if he actually touched them it would be all over.

"I'd better get inside. The twins and Bobby will be in their bungalow by now, but I need to sleep." She chuckled a little. "Or to try to sleep."

With supreme effort, Sebastian drew himself up. He straightened in his seat and turned on the dome light. "I'm going to write down my phone numbers for you."

"Why?"

"Just because"—he looked at her, at her swollen mouth and glittering eyes—"because I want to know you can reach me if the urge moves you. And I want you to set the pace, my love. You call me, okay? Call me anytime—day or night—and I'll come for you."

He took out his wallet and pulled out a card with his Bellevue business number on it. He turned the card over and found a pen to write down his Medina number. Snapping the wallet shut, he handed her the card.

When he offered it to her, she hesitated, grew rigid.

Sebastian frowned. "What is it?" She didn't take the card, so he put it into her hand and closed her fingers. "Bliss? What's the matter?"

"Nothing." With a sudden flurry, she threw open the door and jumped out.

"Bliss!" He shot from his seat and started to follow her. "Bliss, what's wrong?"

"Nothing." Her voice broke and she coughed. "Nothing. I don't know what came over me. Forget it, okay? Just forget it."

She ran toward the gate, opened it and immediately closed it behind her.

Sebastian walked rapidly after her.

Bliss swung back. "Good night. Thanks for the lift home."

"Bliss?"

"Don't follow me. Forget me. I'm no threat to you."

Stunned, he watched her hurry away in the direction of the lodge. Something had happened. In that instant when he'd given her his card, something had changed.

He took another step toward the gate. Forget her? She was no threat to him?

"Fine," he said through his teeth. "Oh, just absolutely, goddamn terrific. I give up. Have it your way."

# Seven

In full flight, with the sound of Sebastian's roaring engine at her back, Bliss fell, panting, against the front door to the lodge. She felt for the crack between logs in the wall, found the key, and let herself in.

Once inside she ran to the kitchen to make sure the twins and Bobby had gone home. Empty. They'd gone to the bungalow they shared. Fabiola and Polly had each other, and Bobby. They didn't have to adopt strangers and turn them into some sort of hodge-podge family, just to feel needed. By the age of thirty-two, most people had figured out how to cope with reality and make their own place within that reality.

*"Street smarts, Bliss. That's the best analogy for what you don't have. Some things you can't learn from books. You don't know the score—not in any game that counts. And when you're faced with the truth, you're shocked."*

How many years ago had her father barked those words at her from the other side of his mahogany desk in the beautiful house where Bliss had grown up, the house that had never really been her home? A lot of years, yet she could be hearing them now. She'd listened to her father, and tried not to see her mother's satisfaction as she watched the man she worshipped put down the efforts of the daughter she resented.

Whenever she messed up big-time, Bliss heard her father's voice delivering one of his lectures. Tonight she'd messed up big-time—again.

She would not wallow in self-pity.

Bliss took the bag containing Bobby's "pink" cookie and set it on the table. Sebastian had said they'd be parents by now if they'd stayed together.

They never would be together, so why indulge in melodramatic longings for what might have been?

*"Some women don't have to try to prove they're as good as men to find a place in this world," Kitten Winters said. "Your father wouldn't have wanted a woman who thought she knew more than he did, would you, Morris?"*

Of all the horrible times to start thinking about her parents. She knew she'd never done anything to please them and it shouldn't matter anymore.

*"With our connections you could have the kind of marriage other girls dream of," Morris Winters said. "The schooling's a good thing. But a college professorship? I don't think so, missy. What I need from you now is a match with some good strings attached. Loyalty. Dedication to whatever will do us the most good. That's what it's all about. An alliance worth something to a family with a plan. This family. You're pretty enough. We could do quite well with you."*

Mommy and Daddy dreamed of the White House and Bliss had never been even the minor asset they'd hoped for. She'd finally stood up to them and declared her independence. In public they spoke as if their pride in her was boundless. In private they contacted her only with requests and warnings, and to inform her of plans for "family" occasions. For the five years since she'd decided to dedicate herself to the community at Hole Point her mother had made it her mission to try to "socialize" and "civilize" Bliss again. Kitten's call demanding an explanation for her daughter's name being linked with Sebastian's, and Raptor Vision, should have come by now.

Bliss poured lemonade from a jug in the refrigerator into a tall glass. She left the kitchen and trailed back through the great room the residents frequently used. She didn't bother to put on any lights. After five years in the home her father's sister had left her, she didn't need more than moonlight to see her way.

*"She might be salvageable with some help," Kitten said. "Cut that frightful hair and learn how to put on makeup. Throw out every item of clothing you own. Let me see to getting you into something that'll draw attention away from aspects we don't want to accentuate. Contact lenses, too."*

Her mother had steadfastly refused to consider contacts when Bliss was growing up. Eventually she hadn't wanted them herself anymore. After Sebastian.

A great, painful rush of emotion blossomed.

Street smarts. That had been what started her thinking about her parents. Daddy had been right about that, she had no street smarts. If she did she wouldn't be reduced to babbling idiocy by a small thing that should be accepted as part of life.

No, she shouldn't consider Sebastian's ridiculous suggestion that they reopen the past. What an idiot she'd been to get carried away by that fairy tale, even for a moment. But neither should she fall apart because she realized he carried a condom in his wallet.

Her face blazed. "Fool, fool, fool."

A narrow balcony ran the length of the second floor above the great room. Once there had been three small bedrooms opening off that balcony. The walls between the bedrooms had been removed to turn the entire second floor into Bliss's own retreat.

Sebastian couldn't have had any idea why she'd suddenly dashed away from him.

She went into what she called her library, a book-lined area at one end of the big, open-beamed bedroom suite.

Of course he carried a condom. All men carried condoms.

"No street smarts. No darn basic know-how." And she was considered a know-it-all feminist!

She didn't have the vaguest idea whether or not most men carried condoms in their wallets. If they didn't, they ought to.

That's right. Standing in the middle of the room, with a glass of lemonade in her hand, and frowning through the moonwashed gloom, Bliss felt furious with herself. Sebastian was a responsible male in a world where more people should be responsible.

She didn't want to be alone anymore.

Yesterday it had all been okay. Today, tonight, the peace she'd learned to find comfortable was all churning, all confusion—and emptiness.

Where there had once been three dormer windows, one in each of the original bedrooms, three French doors now accessed a roof garden at the back of the lodge. The center pair of doors stood open. A breeze ruffled the pages of an open book on the table beside Bliss's favorite chair.

She walked through the current of cool air to the foot of her bed and kicked off her sandals. Beneath her bare feet, the old, smooth cedar floor still held remnants of the day's warmth.

The brass footrail of her bed glimmered. Silence pleased Bliss—usually. The night silence was absolute now, and she didn't like it. This solitude, this silence, was the sum of her life's efforts. Not a soul in the world thought of her as the center of their existence.

So what? Relationships equaled entanglements with the threat of misery when they ended. She'd been there and she wasn't going back.

She took off her glasses and put them on the chest at the foot of the bed.

A click startled her.

One of the doors swinging shut.

Bliss turned. Sure enough, one of the open doors had closed. The second had begun to shut, too.

Had begun to shut. No, to . . . It moved slowly over the rag rug Bliss's great-grandmother had made. The door inched to meet its mate as if someone were trying to close it very quietly.

The arcing flip of her heart sickened Bliss.

She made her legs work, kept her eyes on the door while she edged to the bedside lamp and flipped it on. She switched on the lamp, and knocked her late aunt's little Steuben bell over.

It gave a dull, scraping clang as she set it upright again beside her lemonade.

The door handle rotated, and was still. The moonlight should have illuminated anyone standing outside. No silhouette showed through the panes, but there had to be someone out there.

Bliss looked around for a weapon and grabbed the only thing she could reach, her wooden-backed hairbrush.

Obviously she'd been robbed. The best course was to give the intruder enough time to get away, then call the police.

The old stereo was still on its shelf in the central, sitting area of the suite. Her collection of antique silver buttons and buttonhooks rested on the velvet tray beneath the glass top of the map table. More than a dozen crystal bells lined a high shelf, and jade figurines, another legacy from her aunt, crowded a tall curio cabinet.

Her gaze sought, and found, every item of value.

Bliss's legs trembled. She locked her knees, but her muscles still quaked. She could hardly call the police and tell them she thought someone had closed her doors but nothing seemed to be missing and she hadn't seen an intruder.

She rose to her toes and crept across the room. Putting on the light had been a stupid move. If there was someone out there, they'd see if she picked up the phone.

When Bliss opened the door closest to her bed, the immediate current of air felt almost good. If she weren't scared, it would feel great. "Who's out there?" she shouted, feeling foolish.

The high, white moon flooded the entire terrace. Big wooden flower boxes flanked the low railings that surrounded the three open sides of the terrace. The scent of the roses Bliss raised was sweet, and mingled mysteriously with the vanilla essence of blue and white woodruff nestled beneath the shrubs.

Darn her stupid imagination anyway. There wasn't a soul out here, nor had there been. The other doors must have caught a cross current and banged shut.

Not banged. Closed softly, the handle released—softly.

She hunched her shoulders and walked to the top of the flight of steps that led to the enclosed garden outside the kitchens. "Is there anyone down there?"

No movement but for the rustle of breeze through willow branches.

From the lake came the sound of a vessel slipping through the night under motor. A bird cried once, then no more.

She must concentrate on getting back to normal. There was absolutely nothing wrong with the way she'd chosen to live. All this upheaval she felt could be set at the feet of Sebastian Plato and his unbelievable intrusion into her well-ordered routine.

A click sounded behind Bliss.

She jumped and spun around. "Who's there?" She wasn't alone. There was another presence. Bliss felt it.

The stairs. If she ran down the stairs, she could get away and make a dash for the closest cabin.

The cabin was empty and had no phone. None of the cabins had phones.

The light in her bedroom went out.

Bliss backed into a flower box and cried out as rough wood gouged her calves.

A tinkling chime sounded. Aunt Blanche's Steuben bell? Someone was ringing the bell?

"Send him away, Bliss." A high, thin female voice issued from inside. "He'll spoil everything if you don't send him away."

The cold slick of fear over her skin quickly came and went. A stupid trick. That was it—enough. Pursing her lips, Bliss started back toward the bedroom.

And the doors closed the instant she reached for a handle.

Inches away, on the other side of the door, a flat, white face shone. No features. No body.

Bliss screamed.

The face disappeared.

Bliss spun away and dashed for the steps. Her bare feet pounded on wood until they slapped against the concrete flagstones in the kitchen gardens. Even if the door to the kitchens weren't locked at night, going into the house was out of the question.

She tore open the gate, and collided with a very solid body.

# Eight

The first blow landed across the bridge of his nose. Sebastian yowled. He made a grab, but missed the weapon.

The second blow connected with his windpipe. Gasping, he grappled with Bliss. He knew it was Bliss. He could smell her. Dammit, he could *see* her.

"Shit! What's the matter with—ouch!" Blow number three cracked the knuckles on his left hand. "Stop it. Bliss! Stop it, now." Swiping at the blood he already tasted on his upper lip, he grasped her and spun her around, clamped her back to his chest, and hauled her feet off the ground.

Trapped against his body, she resorted to pounding his shins with her heels.

"Bliss, it's Sebastian." He danced to avoid her pointy little heels. *"Bliss!"*

She grew first rigidly still, then limp—she sagged in his arms.

Oh, great. Now she'd passed out.

"Sebastian?"

"What the— What is going on here? Why are you trying to beat the crap out of me."

*"Don't* talk like that."

She was on the verge of hysteria but still managed to lecture him about his language. "Answer me."

"Put me down."

"So you can beat me with your baseball bat again?"

In a very small voice she said, "I don't have a baseball bat."

"Whatever you're hitting me with. What's happened here?" Apart from wind in the trees, nothing else shifted. The lodge was in darkness.

"I had a little problem."

"No kidding." If she wasn't scared out of her wits, she was giving a great impersonation of someone who was. "Is there any reason why we shouldn't go into the lodge."

"Yes!" She clung to his arms now. "I mean, no, of course not. Why are you here? Why are you sneaking around back here?"

"Sneaking around?" He'd laugh, only he recoiled from the thought of what laughing would do to his nose, and his throat. "I wasn't sneaking. I knocked on the front door. Then I heard you shouting and came to see what was going on. And you screamed. Believe it or not, I was worried about you."

"I'd like to stand, please."

"Oh"—he'd forgotten that her feet still swung above the ground—"yeah. You're not going to haul off with the weapon again, are you?"

"No." She sounded strange.

Sebastian set her down. "You were scared, Bliss. When you ran into me, you thought I was a threat."

"Forget it."

Gingerly, he touched his nose. "That may take a while. If you don't mind I'd like a washcloth and some water."

She faced him. "Why?"

"To clean the blood off my face. I wouldn't want to frighten anyone else tonight."

After a pause she said, "Blood?" and her voice rose. "Where? What's bleeding?"

"My nose. You hit it."

"Oh. Oh, no. Well"—she spun away, and back again—"the kitchen door's locked. We'll go in the front."

Catching his hand, she sped around the lodge, towing him at a trot. Outside the front door, she scrabbled along the log wall, muttering as she did so.

"Now what?" His nose was swelling.

"Can't find the key. We always keep it here."

He glanced past her and into the dim interior of the lodge. "The door's open." It hadn't been when he'd knocked but he wasn't going to mention that yet.

Once again he felt a rigid stillness in her. "She came out this way."

"I beg your pardon?"

"She . . . Oh, nothing. I guess I didn't close it properly when I got home."

Either there was something she wasn't telling him, something that had frightened her badly, or she needed psychiatric help. This wasn't the Chilly Winters of old.

Sebastian passed her and turned on the first light-switch he located. Lights glowed in amber-colored sconces on the log walls of a big room decorated in comfortably worn mountain-rustic.

He looked back at Bliss.

She hovered on the threshold, her chin thrust forward, and she peered into the room as if she expected something large and unpleasant to leap at her.

"Okay, that's enough pussy-footing around here." With his help, she entered the room more quickly than she might have chosen. When she bumped into him and rested her free hand on his chest, Sebastian applied a foot to the door and slammed it shut. "Spill it. What happened after you got in here? I drove around for, oh, no more than fifteen minutes before I knew I had to come back and make you talk to me."

"You didn't have to," she muttered, her eyes still roving rapidly over her surroundings. "I don't scare easily. I'm fine."

"So fine you leap out at innocent people and bloody their noses with sticks."

She looked at him fully then. The way her mouth fell slowly open brought him a measure of grim satisfaction. "Sebastian! Oh, I'm sorry. Oh, dear, you're bleeding."

"I already said I was."

"Come with me." She hauled him behind her up a flight of

stairs and into a long room that evidently served as her living quarters. Some sort of study, became a sitting area in the middle of the room, then, finally, a bedroom. Bliss marched him past the bed and into a bathroom with the same log walls as the rest of the building. "Sit on the toilet. No, sit on the edge of the bath. No, the toilet. It's safer."

"Safer?"

"You must be light-headed. I don't want you to fall in the tub."

"I'm not light-headed." But he sat on the toilet gratefully enough. "What did you hit me with?"

She held up a wooden-backed hair brush.

Sebastian squinted. "No. You hit me with something bigger than that."

"It was the best thing I could find." She sounded aggrieved.

He *felt* aggrieved. "Thank God you didn't get your hands on a poker. Or a knife."

She took a washcloth from a drawer in a wicker chest and soaked it with cold water. "I heard something in the garden so I went out to check."

"You went out from where? The kitchen door's locked."

She dabbed at his nose. Sebastian winced and drew a hissing breath through his teeth.

"I was up here."

"Up here? And you picked up a hairbrush and ran outside and down to the garden. You didn't keep the doors shut and make a telephone call for some help?"

"No." Her hand hovered in midair. She leaned to look into the bedroom, then popped back into the bathroom again. "The lamp was already back on," she said vaguely, and slapped the cloth back on his nose.

"Ow!"

"Oh, Sebastian. You poor thing." Her touch grew gentle once more.

"You just said the lamp was on again."

"Forget it."

"You've suggested that already. I'm not forgetting a thing here tonight."

Bliss lifted his right hand and arranged his fingers on top of the washcloth. "Just keep it there. The bleeding's stopped. Cold is what it needs to keep the swelling down. Now I'm going to try to explain why I'm behaving like a madwoman."

"That would be a relief."

"And when I've finished, you'll be sure I am a madwoman."

He smiled slightly. "No wonder," he said.

She looked at him closely.

Her eyes were unforgettable. They also didn't do a great job in the practical applications department. "You aren't wearing your glasses. No wonder you're wandering around bashing people you mistake for murdering fiends on the rampage."

"Can you make it into the other room?" Her expression showed no amusement.

Sebastian got up. He didn't make an attempt to stop her from threading an arm around his waist and helping him to a comfortable chair near the middle of three French doors. He considered, and discarded the idea of tipping her onto his lap when he sat down.

She dropped to the floor and sat close to his feet.

He held the cloth over his nose, sank back, and closed his eyes. When she didn't attempt to say anything, he lifted his eyelids a fraction and looked down on her bowed head. "Ready to talk about it?"

"I don't know how to begin."

"Maybe the point when you suddenly ran away from me without any warning would be good."

"I was going to call and apologize for that."

"Great. Now you don't have to call. You can tell me in person."

Her face shot up. "I don't have to apologize. What I decide to do at any given time is my own business."

"Hey." He signaled for peace. "You were the one who said she wanted to say sorry. But forget it. Sorry isn't high on my list of necessities."

"I was spooked," she said. "I suddenly realized that what you were suggesting was out of the question. And I was embarrassed that I'd responded to you the way I did. Okay?"

"Only responded? As I remember, right before you led the retreat, you were leading the band."

Her eyes blazed. So did her face. "I've explained why I decided to stop what was happening."

"Fair enough." Not fair enough, but he'd return to the point after he'd got her to explain the rest of her behavior. "I've already told you I came back here because I couldn't let you go like that—not without trying to find out why. And you know why I went to the back of the lodge. Now it's your turn, Chill."

"No one calls me that anymore."

If he couldn't find a way to not only warm her up, but keep her warm, the nickname was going to become all too appropriate. "Why don't you tell me why you turned into a hairbrush-wielding dervish?"

"Either someone tried to scare me badly tonight, or there was a ghost hanging around in this room when I got home."

As casually as possible, Sebastian removed the cloth from his face. "I assume you're joking about the ghost. Do you mean someone was in the house waiting for you?"

She focused on him again, rose to her knees, and took his left hand in both of hers. "Your knuckles. Oh, my. Oh, darn it. I hit your knuckles, too, didn't I?"

He sighed and settled a brave expression on his battered face. "Don't give it another thought. It hardly hurts at all anymore."

"Good."

So much for masculine bravery bringing out the protective urges in women. "I'd better check this place out."

Bliss shook her head. "No need."

"You're probably right. But I ought to make sure."

"There's no one here anymore."

Sebastian considered her serious face before saying, "How can you be sure of that?"

"I just am. I'm used to being here on my own. If there was anyone here, I'd feel it."

"And you felt someone here earlier?"

"Yes. We don't have to talk about it anymore, do we?"

"Not if you don't want to."

She laced her hands in her lap. "I don't."

"This is an interesting room."

"My aunt died here."

He dropped the washcloth.

Bliss picked it up, folded it again, and replaced it on his nose. "Some years ago. My father's sister. She was a lot older than him and a bit strange, but we liked each other."

Sebastian glanced at the simple brass bed with its white chenille spread. "That's not the bed?"

Bliss looked at it, too, and frowned. "Oh, no. No, Auntie Blanche didn't die in that bed. I bought that one. Her bed used to be there." She pointed at the location of Sebastian's chair.

He overcame the urge to get up.

"When this was three bedrooms she slept in the middle one. Do you believe in ghosts?"

Sebastian smiled slightly. This girl—this woman of his had gone off on conversational tangents from the day they'd met. "No, my love, I don't believe in ghosts."

"Auntie Blanche used to ring the bell when she wanted something."

"Really?" Sebastian said. In this light, her hair was more red than brown. Her eyes were navy blue, and distant.

Bliss grinned, and was once again the seventeen-year-old he'd fallen in love with. "She was over eighty when she died," she said. "A demon, really. She liked being up here and making everyone come over and run around after her. I was the one who loved to come. It was better here than at home."

He met her eyes and she looked away. "When we were kids you made me want"—he leaned forward and offered her his hand—"you made me want to be the best I could be."

"I know."

They'd never needed to fill in all the blanks. So often they hadn't had to say a word to be understood. "Come on," he said, wiggling his fingers. "Hold my hand."

Bliss looked at it. "You did that in the cafeteria."

"That first day. Yes, I know. And you finally put your hand in mine."

She put her hand in his now and he closed his fingers around her slight palm and wrist.

"Think there's anyone watching?" He pulled her a little nearer. "To make sure I earn my bet?"

Bliss held her bottom lip in her teeth.

"Maybe Auntie Blanche?"

She tried, unsuccessfully, to pull her hand away. "You are dreadful, Sebastian. Always were. Always will be."

"Can't argue with that. At least, I *was* dreadful, but I'm not anymore. You live here alone?"

"Yes."

"I thought maybe the two blondes and the little boy shared the place with you."

"No. They use the bungalow that belonged to my grandparents. It's closer to the water."

"But you have tenants or something here."

"Not in the lodge. There are ten cabins on the property."

"Big place."

"Uh-huh. Unfortunately we're short of tenants at the moment, but we'll fill up again come fall. We always lose people in the summer."

"Has there been anyone special for you since? . . ." He looked at the ceiling. "Sorry. One more thing I shouldn't have said."

"Do you care?"

Sebastian couldn't meet her eyes. "Yeah. I care a lot. I know I've got no right, but logic and feelings don't always have much to do with each other."

"They never have anything to do with each other."

He did look at her then, and at their joined hands. "We could try starting from right now. This minute. Pretend we met for the first time tonight."

"No, we couldn't."

"No." But he felt a flicker of hope. "We can't because we've already shared so much. I'm glad we have. Not the bad stuff, but the best parts."

"Sometimes they were all I had."

Her words were a blow, and a caress. "I prayed I hadn't made it too hard on you, but I did, didn't I?" Sebastian asked.

Bliss scooted nearer. She settled her free hand on his knee and rested her cheek on top. "Not hard the way you mean. Sure it wasn't easy dealing with what some people said. But the hardest part was the way you . . . You just disappeared. One minute I was so happy I could hardly bear it. The next minute I was so broken up I thought I would die. And there was no one to ask. No one to ask what had happened. There were all the rumors, but nothing definite. I never met your folks, so I couldn't try to ask them. I didn't even know exactly where you lived and there wasn't anything in the phone book."

"My father didn't believe in listed telephone numbers. If someone ought to be able to reach you, they'd know your number because you gave it to them." He stroked her hair. Each time he raised his hand, soft strands clung to his skin—threads of red silk. "I want you, Bliss. I've never stopped wanting you."

"I'm not the girl you left behind."

Very carefully, he bent to kiss the back of her neck.

She buried her face against his thigh, rubbed the long line of muscle from his knee to his groin and back.

Sebastian was instantly hard. He held still.

"Why can't I resist you?" she asked.

"Because I'm a lucky bastard."

"Don't!" She raised her face to glare at him. "Why must you?—"

"Tell the truth?" He chuckled at her horrified expression. "See? I haven't really changed. I still can't help saying things just to shock you. Bliss, can I stay with you tonight?"

Her face grew even paler than usual, her eyes even bigger and darker.

"Just to make sure you're safe," he added hurriedly. "You go to bed. I'll sit here and keep watch."

An instant wash of pink covered her cheeks. "You mean you don't want to sleep with me?"

For a second Sebastian's mind went blank.

"Oh, darn," she said. "Why do I always make such a fool of myself? I'm fine, really I am. Thanks for being concerned, but I don't need you to stay."

"I want to sleep with you."

"Oh." The tip of her tongue curled upward over her top lip. A small but visible shudder shook her. "Oh, I see."

Geez, how had he managed to botch this so badly?

"You mean go to bed with me, right?"

"Well, yes. Yes, I want to go to bed with you." *First prize in the romance stakes, Plato.*

Bliss got awkwardly to her feet and stood in front of him. "I'm not really good at this."

Somewhere between asking to stay with her for the night—as if he wanted to borrow a quarter for a phone call—and pointing out, oh, so subtly, that, yes, he wanted to go to bed with her, this had not gone well.

She was frowning as if with deep concentration. "I'm not a complete novice. It's just that I've been pretty much tied up with making a go of this place in recent years. There hasn't been any time for—well, for the other."

"The other?"

The black dress might be loose, but the soft fabric settled intimately over her breasts. "You know. Men." Her bare feet were elegant, and her ankles.

"Men. Yes, of course." The fewer of those she'd had time for, the better. Not, of course, that he believed in double standards. "You've been busy, hm?" He braced an elbow on the arm of the chair.

"Very. I'm trying to make a go of it here without having to

ask my parents to release my trust fund. Daddy tied it up until I'm thirty-five. My parents still think I'm going through some sort of adolescent rebellion."

He didn't say he hoped good old Morris Winters hadn't found a way of spending her trust fund on his political campaigns.

"I don't want the money at all. I'm going to make it without it. I am," she said.

"I believe you."

"Should I take my dress off?"

Sebastian's elbow slipped off the arm of the chair.

She frowned again. "I feel funny."

He felt funny, too. "Come here." He might have made a mess of this so far. There was no reason to keep on making a mess. "Come on. I want to kiss you."

"Before I take my dress off?"

Sebastian got to his feet and pulled her into his arms. She'd feel what she'd already done to him, but evidently she wasn't in the mood to be leisurely.

Bliss wrapped her arms tightly around his waist and pressed her face to his shoulder. She was shaking! "What's wrong?" he asked her, rubbing her back, grimacing at the strength of his erection. "Why are you trembling?"

"Cold," she muttered.

It had to be eighty degrees in this room. "We'd better get you into bed."

She shook harder.

"Do you think you're getting sick?"

"No. Don't stop holding me. I think I need . . . Oh, the tension's too much. I need a release."

She needed a release? Sebastian caressed her shoulders, the tops of her bare arms. "Me too, love. I've waited so long for this."

Bliss extracted her arms and smoothed his chest. She concentrated while she unbuttoned his shirt. "I'm not going to think any farther than right now."

The desperation he heard excited Sebastian. He could scarcely believe his luck. She was as aroused as he was. "Right now's enough," he told her. "For now."

"Does your head ache?" Bliss studied his nose closely.

Sebastian took advantage of the opportunity to kiss her. He discarded finesse. The pounding pressure building in his gut wasn't interested in finesse. Her mouth opened and her tongue met his. Their faces moved, slanted, their tongues reached for more.

Her spine was long, her waist small, her bottom rounded just the way he wanted it to be rounded. And she didn't even flinch when he urged her pelvis against his and ground their hips together.

She wanted release. He wanted release. They were going to get it. The trembling that overtook him came without warning. He flexed his jaw and fought for control. Wherever he touched her, she seemed to burn him. He couldn't let her go, couldn't stop if the lodge fell down around them.

"Sebastian?"

"Yes, oh, yes." He pushed a thigh between hers, pulled her dress up around her hips, allowed himself the luxury of a study of her very long, very smooth legs—all the way up to skimpy, orange lace and satin panties. Her buttocks tensed beneath his hands. The riding motion of her body on his thigh almost sent him over the edge.

Bliss's head fell back. She made incoherent sounds and clutched at his shoulders beneath his shirt. Her fingernails scraped his skin. He squeezed his eyes shut and enjoyed the pain.

"It feels so . . . so . . ."

Sebastian didn't ask her to finish the thought. He grasped her firm little bottom, smoothed the warm cleft through satin and lace, and kissed her throat.

Her skin was soft. He flicked his tongue beneath the neck of her dress and over the swell of a breast.

Bliss pushed away from him. Still trembling under his skin, Sebastian opened his eyes. He breathed through his mouth to steady his heart. "What?" he asked her. "What, sweetheart?"

She spread the fingers of her right hand on his bared chest. "You are so marvelous. I can't believe we're here, like this."

"Oh, believe it, love." He made a grab for her but she evaded him. "Bliss, honey, I'm dying. I need you."

"Yes, of course."

*Yes, of course?* She'd always had an oddly old-fashioned way of putting things. "Come to me. Come to me now."

Keeping her eyes on his, she crossed her arms in front of her, took handfuls of the black dress and pulled it over her head. She tossed it aside.

Sebastian's legs almost buckled.

Her hands went behind her, to the clasp of the wispy orange lace and satin bra that matched her panties.

"Wait," he told her, taking his fill of the way she looked. Long and lithe, gently flaring hips, the smallest of rises at her belly, the thrust of her mound and the suggestion of dark hair through lace. "We ought to do this together."

She dropped her arms.

Sebastian shed his shirt, then removed his jeans and shoes in one motion. When he stood naked before her, her lips parted and remained parted. Her eyes passed over him, lingering at points she couldn't possibly miss—and she swallowed.

"You need me," she whispered.

"You noticed." His attempt at a laugh didn't work. "I think we need each other. We've waited too long for this." But tonight the wait wasn't important, only being with her was important.

Bliss came toward him and he gasped with shock as she closed a hand around him. Watching his face, she stroked with a delicacy that winded him. "Oh, sweet lady. Oh, my sweet lady." Failing her tonight was out of the question. "Just a minute, Bliss. Slower, okay, love? I'm only human."

She released him at once.

Sebastian covered her uptilted breasts, dipped under the tops of low bra cups to graze her stiffened nipples.

"I feel so wonderful," she told him, almost as if she might cry. "Open, Sebastian. I feel open. Inside and outside. I never knew this was what I was waiting for. It couldn't be like this with anyone else."

"No." Following his fingers with his tongue, he bared a dark pink bud and made a wet circle without touching the urgent center. She cried out and moved, tried to thrust herself into his mouth. He smiled and brushed his beard-rough cheek over the tip of her nipple instead. "I want you to feel this all the way to your spine, my love. All the way to your womb."

"Sebastian," she moaned. "Please."

While she begged, she performed her own torture, finding and holding his penis again, cupping a hand under the weight of him and squeezing.

Unbidden, his hips began to move. "I don't think you'd better do that," he told her, hissing through his teeth. "Not if you want me to last as long as I want to last—with you."

"How long will that be?"

He paused an instant and looked at her, but her eyes were closed as she made a finger map of his male assets. "We got out of sync here, honey. I'm naked."

Her eyes opened at once. She released him and her hands went behind her back once more. The hook on her bra parted and she shrugged her shoulders forward, shedding the garment, spilling her wonderful breasts. Dropping the bra, she braced herself against Sebastian's waist while she pulled down her panties. She raised one leg to pull a foot free, then raised the other leg.

He couldn't resist the opportunity to slip his fingers between her vulnerable folds. The full flesh there met his touch, and the slippery evidence of how ready she was.

Bliss almost fell. Her foot hit the floor with a thud and her knees sagged. Sebastian worked the place that rendered her helpless, and relished the jut of her hips and the weak moans of pleasure she uttered.

When she started to pulse he withdrew his fingers and tipped her back over an arm. She clutched at him, but when he closed his teeth and lips on a nipple she let go. She let go and held her breast to his mouth. Shifting, she silently begged for the same sucking at her other nipple. Sebastian obliged and reached between her legs again at the same time.

Bliss sobbed. Standing on tiptoe, she contracted strong little muscles around his fingers and he felt the spasms break. Her eyes opened, fixed on his, and her color rose. "Foreplay," she whispered, breathless.

She was one of a kind. "Foreplay," he agreed. "Great hors d'oeuvres. I want to taste you."

She frowned, but he smiled and dropped to his knees in time to complete her climax. Holding her open with his thumbs, he gripped her groins and worked her the rest of the way, exulting in her shriek when release came.

The next instant, her knees joined his on the floor. "Incredible," she said. "Incredible, Sebastian. What do you like best?"

His shy little friend had come a long way. "I like everything. With you, I want it all."

She made to hold him again, but he stopped her, and kissed her instead. "You have a great mouth," he told her. "Use it on me, please. I'd like that."

He wasn't used to telling a woman what he wanted. He wasn't used to being asked what he wanted. But he could get used to it.

Bliss bowed over him. With the tip of her tongue, she touched the tip of his penis—quickly. He gasped, and reached over her back to smooth her buttocks.

"Is that what you want?" she asked.

He fought for control. "You're a witch. Great start, witch."

Her tongue curled around, and those straight little teeth tested as if to see just how hard he was. "Harder by the second," he said. "About to explode."

She kissed him there, many small, feathery kisses, and she stroked the insides of his thighs. "Good?" she asked.

"Damn good. I mean, very good." He groaned. "Take me in your mouth, Bliss. All the way in. Oh, yeah."

The warm, wet inside of her lips slid over him so slowly his hips rose. Just as slowly, she reversed the process, only to manage to draw him in again, almost to the hilt.

Sebastian played with her swollen breasts. "I think we'd better move on," he told her. "I want to be inside you before this is over."

Her mouth left him aching. "Here?" she said. "Or the bed?"

He'd get used to her matter-of-fact approach. He already liked it. "I think I'd like that comfortable chair of yours."

She frowned, but followed where he led, to the chair, to sit astride his hips. He flipped the end of his penis through damp, dark red curls and the folds they hid.

Bliss shuddered, mightily this time. He tilted her over him to press a nipple into his mouth while he fondled the other breast. He nudged at the entrance to her passage, eased just inside and felt her clamp tightly around him.

He inched a little farther.

"Sebastian?"

"My turn to tease," he said. And she'd never know how much it was costing him.

"You've forgotten something."

The next restrained thrust took him deeper. The sensation was electric, through his testicles, up into his belly.

Bliss used her toes against the floor to make his task more difficult. She lifted away from him.

He laughed and started to pull her down on him.

"You've forgotten something, Sebastian."

The trembling under his skin, became a shudder. He couldn't keep this up. "What, sweetheart? I haven't forgotten anything."

"The condom."

*The condom?* He clasped her waist. "Condom?"

"I think it's wonderful you're so responsible."

"What the hell? . . . Oh, wow. Bliss, honey, I didn't even think. What's wrong with me?"

"Passion," she said, her brow furrowing. "The throes of passion made you forget."

He hadn't forgotten. It didn't matter, not with Bliss. He wanted them to have a child. "I want—" God, what was he thinking about. "Oxymoron," he muttered. How far ahead of himself could one man get?

"Oxymoron?"

"Me, and thinking. At the moment, anyway. Oh, forget it." He sat her on the end of his knees. "Bliss, you must think I'm a dolt."

"No. It's okay. Your wallet's in your jeans, isn't it?"

Wallet? He wetted his dry lips. "Yes. Why?"

"Well." She shrugged and lowered her eyes. "You're prepared. Shall I get it for you?"

He couldn't imagine what she was talking about.

"It was stupid of me. But that's why I ran away earlier. I saw the condom in your wallet and I kind of lost it." She peeked at him. "Stupid, right. Obviously a man like you is prepared for . . . Well, for certain things."

Sebastian narrowed his eyes. "What things."

She blushed. "You know. Making love."

"The condom in my wallet."

"I saw it. The shape of it. I'm not a complete ninny. I know what I'm seeing when a man has a condom in his wallet."

"I see." He lifted her to stand on the floor and swept up his jeans. Still sitting down—the safest place for the moment—he produced his wallet and studied it. "Ah. Yes, I see what you mean. I should be more careful."

"No," she said anxiously. "No, not at all. I'm very impressed when people show responsibility. There isn't enough of it in this world."

Sebastian fingered the fine, soft black leather. "Not particularly flattering." He deliberately bared his private parts—still very much on parade and ready to march. "But they say perception is everything."

"I don't understand."

He flipped open his wallet and removed the packet he always carried there. This he put into Bliss's palm. "I carry it for good luck."

Her expression went from cautious curiosity to pink embarrassment, to pale anxiety. "Oh, Sebastian."

"Oh, Sebastian is right." An abrupt urge to laugh began to

lessen his need for other things. "See what I mean by not being very flattering?"

She opened the packet and took out a gold ring.

"Never could bear to be parted from it," he told her. "I always hoped I'd finally get to put that wedding ring on your finger one day."

"Oh, Sebastian."

Finally he'd robbed her of original words. "And you thought it was a condom. Size-four-and-a-half and it was still loose on that skinny finger of yours."

# Nine

Bliss pushed up onto her elbows. She tucked the top sheet firmly around her body and leaned forward to peer across the room. With the footrest of her threadbare old recliner up, and the back stretched as flat as possible, Sebastian slept.

Clamping the sheet under her arms, she crawled to the bottom of the bed and retrieved her glasses from the cedar chest.

The night before she'd closed the thin white draperies she kept drawn back from the French doors during the day. Gray-blue dawn pierced the light fabric to dust the room with shades of shadow. She didn't check the clock, but sensed it couldn't be much later than five in the morning.

Bliss pushed at her hair and sat on her heels.

Sebastian's chin rested on his shoulder. He wore his jeans—unsnapped at the waist—but no shirt or shoes.

She crossed her arms beneath her breasts and settled more comfortably to watch him.

The ring in its plastic pouch had been replaced in his wallet. Even while fresh tears of emotion prickled her eyes, she felt again the deep embarrassment of the previous night. He'd always carried the ring—to remind him of her. Or so he said. And she'd looked at the outline of that very small ring and thought . . . She set her lips in a straight line. So she wasn't a woman of vast sexual experience. So what? It had been a simple mistake.

*"Oh, yeah. A very simple little mistake,"* Sebastian had said, while he settled himself in the chair. *"Something tells me there's*

*an educational gap here. We need to do some talking just so I know what I'm up against."*

And he'd insisted she go to bed while he slept in the chair. *"Because I'll feel better if I know you're safe. If I went home, I'd only be calling you all night to make sure."*

But he'd resisted sharing the bed. *"That really wouldn't be a good idea. Don't worry about it, love. We'll get around to making sure you're ready for me."* Surely not the words of a man capable of rape? Yet she'd accused him of raping Crystal and he'd retaliated with anger rather than a denial.

Last night he'd absolutely refused to enter into any further discussion about making love with her. And he'd gone to sleep in minutes—seconds. And she'd been awake for hours. As soon as he woke up they'd be discussing a lot of things. She knew what she wanted now and she knew he wanted it too. Sex didn't have to mean anything but that—sex. They were both grown-ups. Why shouldn't they enjoy each other with no strings attached?

Because he probably didn't want to, that's why. Either he was keeping tabs on her to make sure she didn't interfere with his business, or . . . Could he really have been longing for her all these years?

Bliss studied the way his thick, dark lashes shifted a little. His lean face carried its dramatic lines into sleep. The slightest parting of his wide, clearcut mouth showed a hint of white teeth. A day and a night's growth of very dark beard accentuated his sharply defined jaw and the vertical lines beneath his cheekbones. She hadn't asked him about that scar on his mouth.

He stirred and laced his hands on top of his flat belly. The hair on his chest—and elsewhere—was black, too.

Bliss registered the sound of a car engine in the lane leading to the gate. Vic Taylor, the artist who'd been a Hole Point resident since Bliss opened the colony, often spent nights away and returned early in the morning.

Vic and his potter model, Liberty Lovejoy, were Polly's least favorite tenants but, as Bliss often pointed out, they paid their rent most of the time.

Sebastian had to be uncomfortable, or he would be when he woke up. Bliss climbed from the bed and pulled on her blue terry-cloth robe. Moving quickly and quietly, she gathered the clothing she'd discarded the night before and stowed it out of sight.

"Sebastian?" She bent over him. "Sebastian, I want you to go to bed properly for a few hours."

He smiled in his sleep and rolled his face away.

She walked to the other side of the chair. "Sebastian." Gently, she stroked his cheek. "Come on. Let me get you into bed."

"Sounds good," he said, so clearly she jumped. He trapped her hand against his face. "Mmm. Just a minute."

Bliss kissed his lips.

Sebastian's arm snaked around her shoulders and he almost jerked her off her feet. "Stop it!" she said. Giggling, she scrambled to retain her balance. "I want you to stretch out on my bed. If you don't, your back won't be worth anything."

"You come with me," he mumbled, his eyes barely opening as she applied a foot to the chair and brought him sharply to a sitting position. "C'mon, love. We gotta do that again."

"I don't think we did it in the first place," Bliss muttered.

"Mmm." With an arm draped around her shoulders, he got to his feet and crossed meekly to fall onto the bed—and drag her down on top of him. "Mmm." He slipped a hand inside the robe to fondle her breasts.

Instant thrill became instant arousal. "I thought we had to talk," she said into his ear.

With his palm, he made circles on a nipple. His eyes were tightly shut again, but his grin grew wider. He deserted her breasts long enough to ease one of her hands down inside his jeans.

Hard and heavy and hot. Bliss dug deeper and filled her fingers. He was already performing a sleepy inventory of her breasts again, then dipping down between her legs and drawing all those tiny, electric muscles to tingling alert.

"Take your clothes off," he said.

Bliss ignored him and set about kissing any of the many spots of bare skin she could find. He was the only true addiction she'd ever known.

"Time for our chat." Sebastian sounded wide awake now.

Lifting her head, she looked down into his narrowed green eyes and felt her stomach drop away, and other places inside her grow tight with tension.

In the distance she heard a rapping on the front door.

"Who's that?" Sebastian said, lifting her to sit on his belly with a knee either side of him. "Does that feel good?" He pushed a hand between his naked belly and her naked bottom.

Bliss bit her lip and gasped.

He nodded. "I'll take that as a yes. Why, oh why did it have to take so long for me to get back to you?"

The knocking downstairs became louder and more insistent.

"Go away!" Sebastian shouted.

She pressed a hand over his mouth. "Hush. It's probably Vic come to talk about the latest row. He'll go away."

"Vic, huh?" Her robe parted company with her shoulders and Sebastian contrived to rise up and kiss her breasts. "Beautiful," he muttered. "You're getting wet, love. Nope. You are wet. We'd better have that talk."

Nervousness flittered in her stomach.

Battering more closely described the assault on the front door now. "If I don't go down, he'll think something's going on in here."

"It is," Sebastian said. "Who's Vic?" He tipped her flat on top of him and kissed her deeply.

Being drunk must feel like this. Bliss fought free and leaped to the floor. "Don't!" she warned when he would have come after her. "You stay right there while I go down and deal with this."

"No way." He swung his feet to the rug beside the bed. "The only man who looks at you like that is me."

Bliss scooped up his ankles and hauled them back on top of the mattress. She didn't point out that all this possessiveness was very newly found. "Stay put. I mean it. I've been managing my life for a long time." Very firmly, she pulled the robe back on and belted it. "Vic isn't interested in me as anything but a landlady and occasional confessor. I'll let you know when the coast's clear."

Without giving him a chance to argue, Bliss left the room and ran downstairs. "Coming," she called, opening the door and shielding her eyes from the rush of early morning light into the dim great room.

"Oh, look at you!" Kitten Winters marched into the lodge. "For goodness' sake, close the door before anyone sees you. You're an absolute fright."

Bliss bowed her head and took several deep breaths while she gently closed the front door. "Good morning, Mother. Nice of you to drop by." Please, please let her say whatever unpleasant things were on her mind and leave—quickly.

"I'm not dropping by. I never drop by unannounced."

"Really?"

Bliss trailed past her mother and continued on into the kitchen where she plugged in the coffee maker.

Kitten Winters wore a lightweight pink knit suit with a double row of buttons down the jacket that pronounced it a Chanel creation. Her quilted pink leather purse and shoes made the same statement. At—Bliss glanced at the blue and white Delft clock over the stove—at five-fifteen in the morning, Kitten's bleached hair curved from hairline to nape with not a hair out of place. Her pink velvet headband scarcely made a dent in the careful teasing job.

"You're looking yummy, Mother."

"Why is it that what would be a compliment from anyone else, sounds like an insult from you?"

"Would you like a cup of coffee?" Please say no.

"I should think so. Because of you I hardly got a wink of sleep last night. You can thank me that it isn't your father who's here. He wouldn't be as calm and kind as I am."

Bliss got out two mugs and set them on the counter. "It certainly is early," she said. "Much too early for you to come here shouting and insulting me."

"Ooh, Bliss," Kitten said, folding into a chair like a rag doll and cupping her face in a tragic pose that made sure her perfect makeup suffered no damage. "How can you talk to me the way you do? After all I've done for you. You take, and take, and give nothing in return."

"Mother—"

"All that education. All the opportunities we've given you. And what have we asked in return? A little consideration, that's all. You know your father's planning to run for the presidency. These are very important times for him, dear. You and I have to be selfless. We've got to put his good before our own."

"You mean the good of the nation before our own, don't you?" Bliss asked mildly.

Kitten's hands became fists on her knees. "This nation will get a great man if it gets your father, a better man than any nation deserves."

"As you say."

"Sebastian Plato. That's why I'm here. There's no point in tiptoeing around. We're horrified at what's being suggested. My God, Bliss. Your father was at the Hunt Club last night and Walter DeFunk asked if you were still having an affair with that *Plato fella.* Can you imagine your father's embarrassment?"

Bliss barely stopped herself from dropping a glass mug. *"Still* having an affair?"

"Oh, I knew it." Kitten leaped up. "I just knew it. You did become involved with him at that horrible school you insisted upon attending."

Resisting the urge to throw the mug, Bliss set it down on the nearest counter. "You and Daddy chose the schools I went to for your own purposes."

"How can you?—"

"I can because it's true. You both decided it would look good to Daddy's constituents if his daughter went to public schools. It gave him a chance to be president of the booster club and embarrass me with his big gifts and speeches. And you played lady of the manor with the PTA."

Kitten tapped a pump on the floor. "You are so ungrateful."

"Let's stop this now," Bliss said. "What I do with my life is absolutely none of your business. Do you still want coffee?"

Kitten flapped a hand. "I don't care anymore. The idea. A daughter of mine being sexually active in high school."

"I wasn't sexually active in high school. And I'm the only daughter you have—as far as I know."

The pink purse hit the table and slid. Bliss stopped it from falling off.

"You are the biggest disappointment of our lives."

"I know, Mother."

"You've wasted all that education you insisted on." She gestured vaguely. "This excuse for some sort of good work. Den mother to any so-called artist who can't earn a living. You're doing it to embarrass Morris and me. And now I find out you were involved with some dreadful boy behind our backs."

Bliss wasn't going to lie.

"Weren't you?" Kitten pushed.

"Sebastian Plato was my friend when we were in school. He was a very dear friend. I suppose you do know who he is now, don't you, Mother?"

"Certainly I know. He's a man involved in practices your dear father opposes. Bliss, your father's presidential platform will pivot on his fight against the corruption of our young people."

"Mother, this is all completely uncalled for. You have no idea what you're talking about and neither, apparently, does Daddy."

"How dare you question your father!"

As usual, there could never be any hope of a sane discussion with Kitten Winters if her husband's views were an issue. "I'm sorry," Bliss said. "Forgive me if I've done anything to disturb either you or Daddy. You have nothing to fear from me. Please tell him that."

"Give me that coffee." From the choke in Mother's voice, tears were imminent. "Why do you always have to hurt us?"

Bliss poured coffee and set it on the table. "I would never intentionally hurt you."

"But you sought out this boy, this person who was of an entirely different . . . Well, his background isn't the same as ours."

"Mother—"

"Do you deny you're having an affair with him now?"

"Yes!" She felt her color rise and turned away to pour coffee for herself. She hadn't lied. They weren't having an affair—yet. "Would you like cream?"

"You know I don't take cream. And neither should you. Even if you don't worry about your arteries, you should certainly keep an eye on those hips."

Bliss smiled into her mug.

"Did I say something humorous?"

"Not really. How is Daddy?"

Kitten sniffed. She retrieved her purse and produced a tissue. "Morris is a wonder. The things he's had to endure would break most men."

Anxiety sobered Bliss. "Daddy isn't well?"

Blowing her nose loudly, Kitten shook her head. "You don't understand, do you? His health is perfect. Another amazing thing considering the worry you bring upon him. This Plato man is all over the papers. If you—"

"Sebastian and I are not having an affair." Peace, at least for the moment, was all Bliss cared about.

"Well, then, that's a good thing. I do wish you'd stop all this silliness and let your father and me guide you, Bliss. Do you remember that delightful young Chester King?"

Some things would never change. "You mean the man Dede—I forget what her other name was—but she married him didn't she?"

"They're divorced," Kitten said, with more than a hint of satisfaction.

Bliss knew all about Chester King, and the reason his wife had divorced him.

"The man's worth a fortune. And his connections!" She pressed her hands together and glanced heavenward. "He knows *everyone,* Bliss. And he likes you."

"Liked. I haven't seen him in years." Heavy footsteps, clomping over the wooden floors in the great room, panicked Bliss.

Kitten was too engrossed in her current topic to notice any impending intrusion. "Chester mentioned you to Morris just the other day. Asked how you are and what you're doing."

Bliss could imagine how that conversation went. No doubt she had been elevated to the status of Mother Theresa with sex appeal.

"Bliss—"

Female crying drowned out Kitten Winters. Not Sebastian, but Vic Taylor—resident painter—came into the kitchen. He grasped Liberty Lovejoy's wrist firmly in a tanned hand.

Bliss didn't dare look at her mother.

"H—h—he doesn't love me!" Liberty's pale green eyes were puffy and red-rimmed. "All I am to him is a—a—a *thing.* I'm an *object.*"

"She threatened me with the Hole again," Vic said, referring to the source of the estate's name. A precipitous hole through treacherous rock dropped to an inaccessible space that filled with lake water. Vic stuffed Liberty onto a chair, but kept his hold on her. "I can't let the silly bitch out of my sight."

Of all the mornings for this to happen, it had to happen on the one when her mother was present. "You know I don't like it when you use that sort of language, Vic."

"Oh, fuck the bloody language, Bliss. I'm in trouble here. I need this . . . I need her, but I need her without swollen eyes and a snotty nose. You know I can't work in the presence of ugliness."

Liberty howled afresh.

From the corner of her vision, Bliss saw Kitten rise carefully from her chair and withdraw into the computer alcove.

Naked to the waist, shirts were out of the question—they hampered his creativity, Vic spread his legs inside tight, black leather pants with long fringes at the side seams. His black, lizard cowboy boots had tooled silver toe caps.

"You heard him," Liberty said. "He needs me, but only for his own selfish purposes."

"My purposes usually suit you very well, my little love nymph," Vic said. "You adore seeing your spectacular pair of . . . You like the way I paint you. You like *everything* about the way I paint you."

Bliss sent out a silent plea for Vic to stop right there. If he went into the more exotic aspects of his painting techniques in front of Mother they'd better hope a Medic 1 unit was already parked outside.

"Listen up, children," Bliss said, lapsing into Vic's preferred mode of dialogue. "We've got to put the art first. Liberty's art, too. You have your pottery, Liberty. It's important. And so is Vic's painting."

Vic beamed and nodded knowingly at Liberty. Of average height and muscular, he had an all-over tan and made sure as many people as possible saw its entirety.

Liberty tossed back the luxurious dark brown waves that reached her waist, and cried afresh. At least she was fully clothed, a rare occurrence.

"Liberty," Bliss said. "Please try to be calm." They must all get out of here before Sebastian decided to put in an appearance. He wouldn't do that.

"She thinks I'm in love with someone else," Vic said to Bliss. A black bow restrained his long gray hair at his nape. His eyes were a shade lighter than his hair. "She can't seem to grasp the very simple fact that my art is everything. I don't have *time* to love a woman, not in the way she wants my love—although I do understand, of course."

Kitten made a small, strangled sound and Vic turned around to stare. He said, "Good morning. What's this, Bliss? Avon calling?"

"This is Kitten Winters," Bliss said firmly. "My mother." Enough was enough.

"You don't say? I didn't know anyone still had one. Tell this . . . Tell our friend here that if she kills herself, she'll be replaced."

Liberty popped up and slapped him.

"Oh!" Kitten slumped against the refrigerator. "Bliss, who *are* these dreadful people?"

His feet bare, as was his chest—all the way to his still unsnapped, and partially unzipped jeans, Sebastian was already inside the kitchen before Bliss was aware of his approach.

Liberty was the second to see him. Her mouth made a luscious O and she whistled. "Will you look what Bliss has got, Victor? My, my, they do say still waters run deep."

Bliss wrapped her robe very firmly about her and yanked the belt tight—and caught her mother's eye. If Kitten's amazed stare wasn't funny, it would definitely be insulting. Her mother, Bliss realized, had never made the jump from being parent to a child, to being parent to an adult—especially an adult who might be of interest to the kind of man who presently surveyed this assembly with glittering green eyes.

She tried to flash him silent warnings to say nothing.

Sebastian stared at her, his eyes narrowing in concentration.

Bliss shook her head.

"You are a secretive one, Bliss," Liberty said, studying Sebastian from various angles. "We ought to ask him over, Victor. Don't you think he'd make a perfect Adam?"

Bliss didn't even want to consider what Liberty might mean. "Mother, I'm sorry this isn't a good time for us to talk. Why don't we have lunch one day next week?" She pried Kitty from her ineffectual hiding place. "I'll call you later when things aren't so busy around here."

Kitty drove the elegant heels of her little pink shoes into the worn linoleum. She pointed at Sebastian. "Was that man upstairs, Bliss?"

Vic motioned for Liberty to be silent and stepped between Sebastian and Kitten. "He came with us," he said, casting Bliss a conspiratorial look.

"He did not," Kitten declared. "You've been here. You and

that woman came together. I know that man just came downstairs. And the only room up there is yours, Bliss."

Sebastian crossed his arms and raised his brows at Bliss.

"That's right," she said, taking a firm hold of Kitten's elbow. "I'll tell you all about it later. Don't worry, Mother. I'm a big girl."

Kitten wouldn't budge. "If you're, well, involved with someone, we want to know. Your father will want to make inquiries. For your own good, Bliss, you know that. You're well—simplistic in some ways. You forget you're a woman of means."

"Thank you for caring," Bliss said, desperate now. "Tell Father I'll be over this afternoon."

"Hah! Now I know you're trying to get rid of me."

What was the first clue? "Never, Mother. It's just that—"

"Who are you? How long have you known my daughter."

Bliss gave up. She picked up her coffee and drained the mug.

"Come along," Kitten said. "Answer me."

"I've known your daughter since she was seventeen—that's fifteen years, Mrs. Winters. The name's Plato. Sebastian Plato."

# Ten

Hard to tell with Willy boy, Ron decided, lounging in the anteroom to Sebastian's office and watching William Namsuck, official watchdog.

Ron supported an elbow on one arm of a putty-colored leather loveseat and rested his head. If William was picking up any vibes, he hid it well.

"He must have called in," Ron said when he couldn't stand the uninterrupted sound of William's keyboard a moment longer.

"No."

Little shit. An hour alone with him and the tune would change. Since he'd had the money and the trappings, Ron hadn't met one of his own kind who couldn't somehow be persuaded he was in love for a night—or five minutes.

But he liked to be desired. He liked to be the pursued rather than the pursuer. "Did Mr. Plato come back here last night?"

William glanced at him.

Ron inclined his head, parted his lips and curled his tongue over his top teeth.

"I haven't seen Mr. Plato since he left for his appointment yesterday," William said, and went back to pounding his keyboard.

Not a hint of pink showed on his slim face. No flicker to show he'd recognized a signal. Bored and peeved, Ron pushed to his feet. More to the point, he was goddamn angry.

"When does Zoya get in?"

"I'm sure she is in," William said without looking up this time. "Her office is on the floor below this. The photographic studios are there, and that's where prospective clients are interviewed."

Ron considered his options. One option he didn't have was to cool his heels while Sebastian played around with some woman Maryan believed could ruin everything. "I'll go down and see Zoya. Let me know the instant Sebastian arrives."

William didn't answer.

Blood pumped too hard at Ron's temples. He strode to the desk and leaned over until William raised his face. "Listen, friend," Ron said. "If you want to keep this job, you'll jump when I ask for something. Got that?"

"I'm not at all sure I have."

Ron bent closer. "Ms. Plato is Mr. Plato's partner."

"I'm aware of that."

"And Ms. Plato is *my* partner. Am I making more sense now?"

Putting distance between them, William pushed his chair back from his desk. "When Mr. Plato arrives, I'll tell him you'd like to see him and that you're with Zoya. Will that be all?"

"For now." *Fucker.* "Yes, for now." *But don't turn your cute little ass on me if it's not for sale.*

He took the stairs rather than the elevator. Trips with Maryan had a way of interfering with his exercise schedule.

The next floor down seethed quietly. Men and women came and went along a corridor where thick gray carpet swallowed their footsteps. Most of the faces and bodies in sight were a testimony to careful selection, selection for maximum impact.

Ron eyed the talent. Impressive. He pushed through glass doors into a large reception area where obvious seekers after fame and fortune struck arrogant poses, or shrank self-consciously in chairs around the room.

A middle-aged brunette held court here. She didn't reciprocate when Ron wished her a good day. "Sign in over there and take a seat," she told him. "Got a portfolio?"

"No," Ron told her deliberately. "You're new."

She did look straight at him then. "I beg your pardon?"

"I said you must be new to Raptor Vision. I'm Ron York—from the New York offices. Is Zoya inside?" He indicated double doors behind her desk.

Suspicion clung to her expression. "Who did you say you were?"

"Ron York," he said clearly. "I'll show myself in."

"You can't—"

"Watch me," he said, marching to the doors and entering without knocking. He shut himself inside and flipped the lock.

Outfitted in a shiny black exercise halter and briefs, Zoya stood at a bar that ran the length of one mirrored wall. She spared him a glance that radiated dislike and turned her back on him. Effortlessly raising one leg, she straightened it on top of the bar, bent sideways to grasp her toe and layered her upper body on the leg.

No one knew exactly how old she was. Ron had tried the math and mid to late thirties was the closest he could come. But she could be ten years older. Grudgingly, he was forced to admit she was fabulous.

He walked behind her and stood so close she wouldn't be able to lower her leg without bumping into him. "Where's Sebastian?"

She swiveled her torso to bring her face to her ankle. "Where's Maryan?"

"It's only nine-thirty in the morning."

"Hangover?"

He ran his forefinger along the underside of her raised leg. "We all have our weaknesses."

She didn't miss a beat. "Don't we, though?"

"Maryan thinks this Northwest venture is important to you."

"Does she?"

"She thinks you've got to make a go of it here."

Zoya gripped her ankle with both hands. "I want to make a go of Vision wherever we open."

Ron slipped a hand under her arm and inside the halter to cup her breast.

She gripped her toe and pulled.

"Maybe Swiss Spas won't renew your contract," Ron suggested. Zoya was the famous face behind the preferred skin products of the rich-and-afraid-of-aging. There was talk that she might be dropped from the next campaign.

"Your concern is touching, Ron," she said, as if he hadn't pushed his other hand inside her pants.

He pinched her pointed nipple between two of his fingers. She was hard all over. If he had to be with a woman, at least the hard kind didn't disgust him. Maryan was thin, but her tits were big and they needed a lift.

When Zoya turned on him, she was so fast Ron tripped and fell. She stood over him, her legs spread at the level of his hips. "Make your point."

He rose to his elbows and got up with as much dignity as he could manage. Zoya was instantly in his face, backing him across her huge teak and navy-blue leather office.

"We've all got too much to lose here," he said, smoothing his hair. "You can't afford to have Sebastian do anything stupid. Neither can Maryan or I."

"Translation?"

"After our little gathering last night—after you'd gone—he left. I got up early to look for him. I don't think he came home. Where would he go unless it was to see this woman Maryan's scared shitless about?"

Zoya rested a long fingernail on his mouth. She narrowed her eyes. "Which woman would that be?"

He hesitated. If Zoya really didn't know, he couldn't risk enlightening her without Maryan's say-so. "Don't play dumb with me."

"Dumb?" She arched her long, high eyebrows. "Ronny boy, if you want to share information with me, you've got to have something to share. You don't give. I don't give."

"Look"—he wetted his lips—"we could agree to keep each other informed of anything that might be important."

"You and Maryan are afraid of something here in Seattle. Maybe I'm afraid of something, too, but I haven't realized it. Why don't you tell me what you're afraid of and I'll decide if I think it's anything we ought to worry about."

"I asked you," he said. She wasn't afraid of him. She felt she had the upper hand. Ron didn't like that. "You tell me. I can be trusted not to speak out of turn."

"Can you?" She backed him all the way to her desk. "I think we'll have to prove how cooperative you can be." In a fluid motion, she stripped the halter over her head and dropped it on a chair.

Ron looked at her high, sharp breasts. She laughed deep in her throat, put her hands on her hips and swayed just enough to make her flesh bounce. "Suck me, Ron."

He swallowed.

Zoya reached between his legs and squeezed. "You need help here, baby. Suck what I'm offering. Should do the job."

"Why are you doing this?"

She laughed again. "You've made it pretty clear you wanted a little fun. I'm just obliging."

"Maryan wouldn't like—"

"Maryan won't know. And you started it." She knew how to use her hands. He hardened despite himself. "That's the way, lover. Sex is good for us. And don't tell me you prefer the hoops that drunken cow puts you through."

Ron knew danger when it stared him in the eye. "Maryan's okay."

"Sure she's okay." With deft fingers, the tall model unbuckled his belt, unhooked and unzipped his olive green slacks, and sent them around his ankles. "Oh, my. Black next to a man's skin always turns me on."

He stopped himself from saying she didn't need turning on anymore than she already was.

She dispensed with the "black next to his skin" as only a

woman with a great deal of practice could. "Will you look at that?" Smiling, she draped the front of his shirt to frame his prick.

"Like what you see?" he asked, barely parting his lips.

"Well, I think this treatment suits it better than red ribbons." Calmly, she took off her briefs and sat on the edge of the desk with her legs spread. "Let's see how it works. Make it fast. I've got a lot of people waiting to see me out there."

Ron balled his hands into fists.

"Want to hit me?" Her smile turned down. "Come on. Try."

She was dangerous. Only absolute confidence would allow her to do this. He deliberately relaxed and flexed his fingers. "I'm not a fool," he told her. "Only a fool would pass up what you're offering." He'd like to puke.

"Lick me first."

His gorge rose.

She pointed to the floor. "Get down and lick me, Ron. You'll like it."

He sank to his knees and shut his eyes. If he concentrated hard, maybe he could make himself believe it was other skin he was tasting, other sex he was smelling.

In seconds her hips pumped. She climaxed in absolute silence and Ron dropped his head forward. At least she'd have to be more careful around him now.

"Okay," she said. "Let's finish this."

He stared up at her, at her still perfectly arranged hair and untouched makeup, at her perfectly toned nakedness, her evenly honey-colored skin—all the way to the ends of her peaked breasts. Her legs remained splayed and she beckoned him.

Resigned, Ron got to his feet. A chance for reprieve occurred to him. "Damn! I don't have anything, lovely lady. You caught me by surprise."

She leaned backward and pulled open a drawer. "No one ever catches me by surprise."

He gave up trying to stop her from slipping the condom on him herself. Then he gave up trying to resist her pushing him inside her. Placing his hands on her breasts, she dropped her back to the desk and fastened her ankles behind his back. She enfolded him in muscles that worked like an iron milking machine, and sucked at him hard and fast. A minute at the most and she came. He was a second behind her, panting, grasping the desk for support.

"Thanks." Pushing him away, she sprang to her feet. "Now we can talk."

Ron's legs quivered. With trembling hands he began straightening his clothes.

"I know what you are."

He stopped in the act of stooping for his slacks. "What's that supposed to mean?"

"Exactly what I said. I know what you are. Maryan doesn't, does she?"

He stood up and stared at her.

"I didn't think so. You were right about one thing. I can't afford to fail here. I'll admit I've had a few bad days, but I'm feeling much better now."

Ron retrieved his pants. "Glad to have been of service."

"Even if you hated it?"

"I don't know what you're talking about."

"If you say so. But I can prove it, Ronny boy."

A spasm hit his gut. "You're crazy."

"The bathroom's over there." She indicated a closed door on the side of the room opposite the mirrors. "You'd better take care of the evidence or it'll be all over your pants."

He felt himself redden. "What are you trying to pull here?"

"We've got trouble. You, Maryan, and I. Maryan doesn't know just how much trouble yet, and when she finds out she's going to be a bitch to deal with. She'll be less of a bitch if you persuade her she needs my help. That she needs to take me into her confidence."

"Against Sebastian?" He snorted. "Forget it."

"Not against Sebastian. To protect Sebastian from himself—if that's what needs to be done."

"Maryan likes to be the boss."

"She can think she's the boss, as long as I'm the boss."

Sweat stuck his shirt to his back. "What do you want? What are you trying to prove here?"

"That I can control you—and Maryan. Find a way to make her understand she needs me."

"You're dreaming."

"And you," she said, surveying her nude body in the mirrors, "are a fool. Without me to help you, Maryan's going to squeeze you dry till she finds a way to get what she really wants. Then she'll send you back where you came from."

"No—"

"Yes. You and I can be the real team here. The key is to make sure nothing changes for Sebastian. With him in place and unscathed, I'm all right, and you'll be all right. Maryan's the one who can ruin everything for us."

He needed something. A hit. He couldn't think straight anymore. "Maryan wants the best for Sebastian, too. I don't get—"

"You will. Remember two things. If you cross me, I'll tell Maryan what happened here this morning, and she isn't going to believe I raped you, is she?"

Ron couldn't form any words.

"Secondly. Maryan doesn't just want what's best for Sebastian. Maryan *wants* Sebastian. Period."

# Eleven

"Bliss! Hello, Bliss!"

Wiping rain from her face, Bliss removed her useless glasses and strained to make out the figure that approached across grass and rocky earth turned to mud by a late afternoon downpour.

The newcomer wasn't alone. Spike ambled up to Bliss and sniffed her sodden jeans.

"Fabiola said I'd find you down here." Prue O'Leary, president of Women of Today and Bliss's old friend, plodded to stand beside Bliss on the bluff that fell to the lake. "Something about you checking a fence?"

Bliss looked at her gloved hands. "One of the benefits of running an operation on a shoestring. You do a lot of your own maintenance."

Prue pulled the hood of her dark green parka farther over her serious face. "If you're on a shoestring it's because that's the way you want it."

Perhaps, Bliss decided, it was time to become less open with those she'd chosen to trust. She found she didn't like being criticized for having decided to make Hole Point a success without appealing to her family for funds.

"What fence?" Prue peered behind Bliss. "You thinking of fencing the bluff?"

Bliss pointed to an area off to her right where a circle of barbed wire coiled. "Not the bluff. And it's not really a fence.

Just the barricade around the hole. Liberty had another of her fits yesterday. Threatened to jump down there."

"Why?" Prue tramped toward the treacherously spiked wire.

"The usual. Vic doesn't love her as a woman, and so on."

"Kick 'em out," Prue said matter-of-factly while she stood on tiptoe to try for an angle on the opening into the ground. "Revamp the place. I've told you this could be a gold mine as a convention center."

"And I've told you I'm not interested in a gold mine, or a convention center."

Prue set her heels on the ground again and turned her round features up to Bliss. "How many tenants have you got?"

"Three extra cabins are let out for the summer."

"That's not what I asked."

As always, Prue knew how to get at Bliss. "Vic and Liberty are year-rounders. That's two more cabins." She couldn't lie successfully.

"I thought they shared."

"In theory they don't. Anne Snow's still with us. She's away at the moment. Teaching a summer course in native Indian pottery in Arizona. Barbara McMann will be back from Europe in September."

"Paid up before they left, did they?"

Bliss gave Prue a hard look. "You didn't come to talk about rent." Spike wound her muddy body around her legs and grinned. Bliss pushed her away and ran her eyes over the widely spaced log cabins with their surrounding hedges of unruly yews. At the northernmost reaches of the property stood the small bungalow Polly and Bobby shared with Fabiola.

"Shit's hit the fan," Prue announced succinctly.

Asking the nature of the shit and the identity of the fan wouldn't be productive. Bliss bent her head into the driving rain and started back uphill.

Prue fell in, panting a little, running to keep up with Bliss's much longer legs. "Got a response from your father."

Bliss stopped and waited for Prue to face her again.

"Don't look so shocked," Prue said. "I know you don't like the senator, but he is on our side in this one."

"My father and I don't get along. That has nothing to do with anything as far and you and I are concerned, Prue."

"Is it true you've seen Plato?"

Rainwater finally found its way through the seams of Bliss's army surplus jacket, and ran between her shoulder blades. "Did my father say I had?"

"He hinted as much. Something about how I'd better make sure our chairperson was really on board before we tried to move forward against Sebastian Plato."

Vic's motorcycle roared over the rise and shot toward his cabin. He sighted Bliss and Prue and waved. Bliss waved back.

"I don't know how you stand that man," Prue said.

Prue wouldn't have understood a positive feeling about any man. "He's okay," Bliss said. "He's always there if I need him. I regard him as a friend."

"You always had some strange notions. Bliss, you were seen at Lennox Rood's showing."

"Really. By whom?"

"Oh, I can't remember who said it."

"I don't believe you, Prue." Bliss dried her glasses on a dripping handkerchief and put them on. At least she got a smeary view of Prue's expression. Guarded. "We've been friends a long time. I thought we'd agreed to remain friends even though our interests have gone in different directions."

"We did agree to that."

"Then why are you keeping tabs on me?"

"I'm not. It's just that this is a big issue and—"

"And you want to use me to get what you want."

"Bliss—"

"You contacted my father on the Raptor Vision issue. That wasn't something we discussed."

Prue shrugged. "He's a powerful man and he shares our views on this one."

"But I didn't agree to getting involved with my father on anything political—from his point of view, or yours."

"Sorry. I assumed you'd understand."

"You also told a reporter I'd agreed to chair a committee I didn't even know existed."

"I knew you'd do it. You're the obvious candidate."

Bliss's temper wore thin. "I'm not interested. And please don't discuss me with my father or gather information on my activities."

"I thought Lennox Rood was out of your good graces."

"He's another old friend. He lived here."

"Exactly." Prue's nostrils flared. "And he got the idea that you were in love with him and tried to use that."

"All over," Bliss reminded her. "He asked me to come to his showing and I went because I wanted to. End of subject."

"Plato—"

"Sebastian Plato didn't have anything to do with what happened to that girl in New York."

"She went there to try to be taken on by his agency," Prue argued hotly.

"But he didn't kill her. Neither did anyone employed by him kill her."

"That kind of outfit is demeaning to women."

Bliss felt weary. "They aren't running a talent pageant. Both women and men model. They always will."

"We don't need Raptor Vision here. Bellevue's been very successful in driving out unsuitable influences and we're not standing still for this one."

This was what Bliss had eventually left behind when she'd parted company with her former career. "Your opinion isn't the only opinion worth considering," she said. "And in this case, it's wrong. You know how I feel about exploitation—I would never stand by and watch it if I could do something to help. But this time you're way off base."

"You and Sebastian were together at Bellevue Square."

"Damn it, Prue. Who told you this?"

"I'm not going to make you mad at someone who was just aking a passing remark."

"A passing remark. Oh, come on." She shoved her hands in er pockets and continued uphill. "Let it go. I don't have time or any of this."

"Morris said Kitten was over yesterday morning."

"Oh, this is the end." Bliss spun around. "I'm so pleased ou're on chatting terms with *Morris.* I can hardly say two vords to him without him losing his temper, but you compare otes on my activities."

"Stop it," Prue said, pressing her lips together. "I'm worried bout you. You're too kind for your own good. That man used ou years ago and—"

"You stop. Right now. I thought I could trust you with things 've never confided to anyone. I made a terrible mistake. You lready made suggestions the press could use. And you told Fab nd Polly about Sebastian when we were in school. How could ou, Prue?"

Her friend had the grace to redden. "I got carried away. I houldn't have. But neither should you have let him come walk-ng back in here the way you have."

They neared the lodge and Spike loped ahead and around to he back of the building. Bliss's lungs burned. She felt trapped—nd angry.

"You slept with him didn't you."

*"Prue!"* So furious, she couldn't think, Bliss tore off her seless glasses and stuffed them in a pocket of the olive green amouflage jacket.

"I see I've struck a nerve." Smugness didn't make Prue more ikeable this afternoon.

"I think you should leave," Bliss told her.

"You did sleep with him. My God. You haven't seen him since ou were just out of high school. He'd raped a girl and run away—ust about leaving you at the altar. And the minute he shows up, ou hop into bed with him. He must be quite something."

"He is," Bliss said through gritted teeth. "Yes, Sebastian is really something."

"Bliss, you know better—"

"Better than to fall for a fabulous face and a body that any woman would kill for? Prue, you need an hour or two with Sebastian. I'm going to arrange it. You're sex-starved, that's the problem."

"Bliss—"

"No. No, you don't have to thank me. I believe in sharing perfection with my friends. What do you like best?"

"Like?"

"You know?" Bliss gave Prue a sly grin and dug her in the ribs with an elbow. "In bed. Or on the floor. Or in the shower—or on the kitchen table. Take it from me, Sebastian does it better than anyone and he does it anywhere and everywhere. You tell me what you want and I'll set it up."

Prue's mouth hung open. Her brown eyes bulged.

"Positions are no problem. He's very athletic and he's imaginative. Let me tell you, there can't be another man on this earth who uses his mouth in as many ways as Sebastian Plato. He's got this long, slow building technique that'll drive you insane."

"That's disgusting." Prue drew her short body up very straight. "I don't know what's happened to you."

Bliss started to chuckle. Her chuckles became laughter and she bent forward at the waist.

"Was that supposed to be a joke?"

Bliss nodded, helpless to speak now.

"Well, it wasn't funny. Kitten was here early in the morning yesterday and Sebastian came downstairs without any clothes on."

"He d-didn't," Bliss said. "He had jeans on."

"That's not what I heard."

"Well it's the truth."

"Your mother was horrified. And Vic and that butterfly-brained model of his were there. How embarrassing. You would never have allowed your reputation to get mixed up with people like that until you came here."

"I should have come here years earlier," Bliss said, sober again. "Prue, we're either going to agree not to discuss any of this again, or we're going to tread very separate paths until you're through with whatever you're trying to accomplish."

"Bliss, don't do this."

"I'm not doing anything. You are. Do you want a cup of hot tea? We could forget we ever had this conversation."

A mutinous crease formed between Prue's eyes. "I've got to get back to the rest of the group. We're having a meeting. I want you to come with me."

"Not in this lifetime."

"Please, Bliss."

"Absolutely not."

"If I can prove to you that Plato's bad news will you reconsider?"

"You won't be able to prove it." Rash words, but she wasn't going to judge Sebastian again—not without gathering her own evidence against him.

"Your parents are furious with you."

"What else is new."

"Morris said Sebastian insulted Kitten."

How typical of her mother to twist the truth. "Sebastian insulted my mother by politely telling her he didn't care about her opinions of him. He also told her he wasn't ashamed of being a bastard and didn't intend to become ashamed of being a bastard. Which means my mother made a point of telling him he was a bastard from the wrong side of the tracks and that she thought he should go back where he belonged. That was because he refused to turn tail and leave *my* home when she told him to."

A dark green limousine slipped into the lane and parked beside Prue's tiny brown Honda.

"That's him, isn't it?" Prue asked, planting her feet. "Oh, Bliss, don't do this to your friends."

A chauffeur got out of the limousine and raised an umbrella. He stepped back to open a door and sheltered the tall woman who got out.

"Who is it?" Prue asked.

"Just a new tenant," Bliss said, as curious as Prue. "If you don't have any more questions, I'd better get ready to help her fill out her application forms."

"Don't be ridiculous."

"Bye, Prue. Thanks for stopping by. I'll call you."

"Have it your way. I'm going. One more question, though. Did you find out what it was you saw the other night? The ghost or whatever?"

"What—" She would have to warn Fabiola and Polly not to talk to Prue. "I was jumpy the other night. I'd had a difficult day and something put my imagination into overdrive. That's it. I didn't really see anything." Or not anything she'd been able to explain afterward, not that she'd entirely stopped worrying about it.

The chauffeur held the gate to the lane open and then had to hurry to keep up with the woman he shielded with the umbrella.

"Who is she?" Prue said. "Someone you know?"

Bliss shook her head in exasperation.

"Okay. But I'm not waiting for you to call me. You'll pass through this stage and come to your senses. Good-bye. Take care, please, you're very important to me."

Bliss felt a niggling guilt. "You're important to me, too, Prue. We're just going to have to agree to disagree on this one. Don't worry. I won't do anything stupid."

"I wish I could be sure of that." Prue walked purposefully away, her head bowed. When she passed the newcomers, she stared at the woman for longer than was polite before continuing on to the Honda.

Bliss waited for her visitors to come to her.

She'd agreed to get together with Sebastian again tonight. The scene with Kitten had been horrible, and later Bliss's father had visited the Point for only the second time in her memory. The first had been immediately after Auntie Blanche died when he'd come for the reading of the will and been furious to learn that Bliss was her aunt's sole heir.

Despite exceedingly high-heeled beige pumps, the woman

who approached picked her way rapidly over the slippery ground. The chauffeur's umbrella obscured her face. A rust-colored raincoat of some silky fabric swirled from narrow shoulders to wide hem and alternately billowed and wrapped itself around the woman's slim form.

"This must be it," Bliss heard the woman say. "The ugly log place."

Bliss smiled to herself. "Good afternoon. Can I help you?"

The woman didn't stop walking. She did jerk the handle of the oversized umbrella until she could see Bliss. "I doubt it," she said. "I want to see Bliss Winters."

Short brown hair gelled straight back. When Bliss had last seen this woman, her hair had been short, too, but combed forward around her face, and minus the gray streak that now swept from one temple.

"Good God," Maryan Plato said, taking Bliss in from her wet, disheveled hair, to the green rubber boots with yellow soles that had come from the same surplus store as the camouflage jacket. She flapped a gloved hand at the chauffeur. "Go away. Wait in the car. I'll send for you. Is this your place?" She asked Bliss, indicating the lodge.

Bliss walked silently past her to the porch. Using a toe, she worked off the heel of the opposite boot, then stood on her bare foot to remove the other boot. Maryan Plato shouldn't have the power to make her feel weak, or to make her head ache, or her arms and legs tremble.

Before opening the door, she took off the jacket and hung it on a nail beside several others.

The atmosphere in the great room was steamy. Fabiola grabbed any excuse to start a fire. Flames curled up the big chimney and two of the women who were summer renters—both poets—sat on the worn rug before the hearth, looking damp. Engrossed in reciting aloud to each other, they barely acknowledged Bliss's arrival.

Leaving the door open behind her, she walked through the

room and into the kitchens where Polly toiled over several pots on the stove.

" 'Lo, Bliss," she said. "Fab and Bobby are at the bungalow with Mom. She's dropped by to sprinkle us with her latest insights. Fab'll be right back. Sebastian called. He said—"

Bliss felt the instant when Maryan's arrival silenced Polly.

"What did he say?" Maryan asked.

Polly frowned at Bliss, who shook her head slightly. "How's dinner coming?"

"Great. Stew. You know how Fab is about storms. Any storms. Build a fire and eat stew. Beef, chicken or vegetarian. Take your pick."

"Gourmet stew." Bliss laughed. "Polly, this is Maryan— Is it still Plato?"

"Of course."

Bliss studied Maryan thoughtfully. Did that mean she believed in women keeping their maiden names after they were married, that she'd never married, or that no sane person would give up a name like Plato?

"We need to talk," Maryan said. "Where can we go?"

"Here will do," Bliss said. Under no circumstances did she intend to be alone with Maryan Plato again. The last time was already unforgettable.

Maryan eyed Polly.

Polly smiled pleasantly and, predictably, began to hum. "The Ride of the Valkyries" took on new dimensions when hummed by Polly Crow.

"I really don't think you'd want me to say what I came to tell you in front of a stranger."

"Polly isn't a stranger." And Maryan Plato didn't call any shots here. "This is Sebastian's sister," she said to Polly.

"Hi," Polly said. "Do you work at Raptor?"

Bliss gaped at Polly.

"I'm Sebastian's partner," Maryan said curtly.

"You have a talent agency, don't you?" Polly asked. "As well as the modeling agency?"

"Yes." Maryan peeled off her gloves and undid the single tortoise-shell button at the neck of her raincoat.

Polly brandished a wooden spoon. "I've been thinking of dropping by. Of course, I'm not short of work, but there might be something I could do for you."

Maryan took off her coat and draped it over the back of a chair. A soft beige sheath, cut low to showcase the only part of her that wasn't thin—her breasts—ended at mid-thigh. She regarded Polly, the spoon, and the stove. "We don't have much call for gourmet stew at Raptor."

Polly's already pink face turned a darker shade. "I'm a singer."

"A very fine singer," Bliss said, furious with Maryan.

"In that case"—Maryan's smile showed small teeth but was definitely shark style—"call Zoya. Just Zoya. Tell her I said you should have an appointment. She'll set something up for you."

Polly's delightedly flustered thanks made Bliss's heart plummet. Later she'd have to warn her to guard against disappointment.

"Now," Maryan said. "A private place?"

The door from the terrace opened and Fabiola came in.

"This is Maryan Plato," Polly said, exuding excitement. "She's going to help me get an audition with Raptor."

Fabiola looked at her sister with undisguised envy. "You're kidding."

"I'm not, am I, Ms. Plato?"

Maryan ignored her. "I'm a very busy woman, Bliss. I made time to come by because this is important."

"Do you run the modeling agency?" Fab asked, raking her fingers through her hair. "I've been meaning to come by your new offices and see if there's anything I might be interested in."

"Call Zoya," Maryan said, not even bothering to look at Fab. "Tell her I told you to call her and arrange an appointment. She'll set something up."

Bliss couldn't bear to look at either of the twins. "We can go up to my rooms," she said, leaving the kitchens almost at a run, and jogging upstairs. She didn't slow down until she was inside her room.

Within seconds Maryan came in and shut the door. She'd taken the time to gather up her raincoat. This time she tossed the wet garment on Bliss's map table and looked around the room with open curiosity.

"I don't have long," Bliss told her, suffocating on her innate dislike for this posturing woman.

"Why? Are you meeting Sebastian?"

"You said you had something you wanted to talk to me about."

Maryan grew still. She met Bliss's gaze and shook her head slightly. "This is very difficult. I need your help."

Bliss didn't trust Maryan Plato. The sharp-featured girl she'd met in the dark, in a car, on a night she'd like to forget, had matured into an arrogant, if elegant woman.

She reached into her raincoat pocket for an antique silver cigarette case and a red enameled lighter. "Mind if I smoke?"

Before Bliss could answer, a flame shot from the lighter. Maryan drew on a long, thin cigarillo, dropped her head back and closed her eyes. Smoke curled slowly from her nose and drifted. The pungent scent was faintly sweet.

"How did you find out where I live?"

Maryan looked at her. She strolled to the cedar chest, sat down and spread her arms along the brass footrail of the bed. When she crossed her legs, Bliss saw coffee-colored lace panties.

"Sebastian hired a detective. Did you know that?"

Bliss frowned. She didn't like feeling defensive on her own turf but she couldn't bring herself to sit down.

"He did," Maryan continued. "Shitty little man called Nose, if you can believe it. He had Nose find out all about you, including where you live and how long you've lived here. Same pattern as always, I'm afraid. Gets a woman on his mind and hires someone to bring him all the smutty details—or just plain details if that's all there are."

Hair rose at Bliss's nape. "Thank you for telling me." Maryan wouldn't have the pleasure of seeing Bliss get angry. "If that's all—"

"It's not all. I didn't have to come here. I do need some help from you, but I also want to help you. You're still in love with him, aren't you?"

Bliss opened her mouth.

"They all are," Maryan said, leaning to flip ash into a Spode basket. "That's his problem. Women love him. And he loves women."

"I don't know why you've come to tell me these things." Subtlety had no place here. "I'd like you to leave. Now."

"Oh, damn it." Maryan massaged her brow with two fingers. "Tact was never my strong suit, Bliss. I've got absolutely nothing against you. Can you believe that?"

"I don't think you care what I believe."

"Oh, but I do. I have to because I've got a problem and I don't think I can continue to deal with it alone. I tried everything I could think of to stop him from coming here, you know. Back to the area."

"Really?" Bliss wished she didn't feel miserable at the very idea that Sebastian might not have appeared on her doorstep a few days earlier.

"He wouldn't listen. So much talent, but he's very vulnerable. I know you'll find that hard to believe, but he is. He wants respect. To a huge degree, he's been able to buy what he wants—*who* he wants. But you can only buy certain kinds of respect, and you can't get a pedigree with any amount of money—not the real thing."

Bliss went to the nearest French door and stared out at rain that blew almost horizontally. "He seems perfectly confident to me."

"He's learned to put on a great front. When you think of what he's accomplished, it's incredible." She sighed. "Hell, he started out with an idea no one else would have touched at the time. Running an airline like a bus service. Cheap fares. Show up to get your seat. No frills. And he talked himself into the capital he needed to get started. A hell of a lot of capital. Balls, that's what it took. Balls, charm, and a brain that lets him dance over obstacles that would stop most of us."

Bliss knew the story, but she still felt proud of Sebastian.

Proud and sad at the same time. He'd made his own chances, but so much of that drive must have been spawned by an early life that came close to crushing him.

"I want to confide in you, Bliss. Trust you. Can I do that?"

Trees whipped, willow branches brushed the ground. "As long as I don't have to compromise myself, you can trust me."

"I'd never ask you to do that. I didn't want to be the one who brought you bad news all those years ago. I did it for Sebastian—and because I felt sorry for you."

Bliss bit back a retort that she didn't want Maryan Plato's pity.

"Sebastian's ill."

Tightness gripped Bliss's scalp. She turned to look at Maryan. The other woman let the heel of her shoe slip off and jiggled it by the toe. She took a long, long, pull on the cigarillo. "I'm the only one who knows—apart from the doctor."

Sebastian? Ill? Bliss visualized him in her chair, on her bed. Big, muscular, strong. Laughing, wrestling—loving. "What do you mean, ill? What's wrong with him?"

"Crystal got over him in the end, you know."

Bliss pressed her fingertips together. "They're divorced."

"Yes. Finally she couldn't take it anymore. He's never forgiven her. He still craves her."

"What's the point in this?"

"To illustrate what I'm telling you. Crystal still isn't safe from Sebastian. Bliss, I've spent a lot of years looking after my brother, but this time I'm really frightened I might not be able to save him."

"He's dying?" Each breath Bliss took was an effort.

"He's under psychiatric care."

Bliss made it to her chair and sat down hard.

"Sebastian compensates for feelings of inadequacy by proving his sexual prowess over and over—as often as he can. He's sexually obsessed. That's what drove Crystal away."

The phone on the bedside table rang. Bliss got up and answered it. Sebastian asked if she would be ready at seven-thirty. "I'll call you back," she told him shortly, and hung up.

"Sebastian?" Maryan asked.

Why lie. "Yes."

"You're going out with him tonight?"

"I'm supposed to."

"Where's he taking you? To the party in Seattle, I suppose. Or are you staying here?"

Honesty need not go too far. "We haven't decided yet."

"Will you help me, Bliss?"

"I've already told you I will if I can."

Maryan rose and stubbed out her cigarillo. "I know I can trust you. I felt that when we first met. If you care at all about Sebastian, try to keep his mood level, but don't let him get too close to you." She looked sharply at Bliss. "You know what I mean. He has—unusual tastes. I don't want you hurt."

Bliss's throat was too dry to allow her to swallow.

"I don't want anyone hurt," Maryan continued. "It's been close on several occasions, but so far I've managed to intervene in time. And for selfish reasons, I don't want any of this to get into official hands."

"You aren't making any sense," Bliss finally managed to say. "I've been with Sebastian. He isn't violent."

"That's his pattern. First he lulls them into believing in him, into wanting him so badly they can't refuse him anything. Then things change. I don't want to go into it too deeply."

"I think you'd better."

Maryan picked up her raincoat. "It isn't necessary. We both want the same thing—Sebastian's happiness and safety."

"If he just wanted a woman, he wouldn't have to come looking for me."

"It doesn't work like that for him. He wants the challenge of conquering some obstacle. He must be living out some fantasy of subduing you all over again. Also you have money. Sebastian needs money."

Bliss started to argue but thought better of it. "I'd like you to go, Maryan. I need to think."

"Of course. As long as you let him think you're besotted with him, it'll be okay. Can you do that—be nice to him—for me?"

For her? Bliss wanted to be nice to Sebastian for herself.

Maryan picked up her coat. "This isn't a game. When you're doing it for me, you'll be doing it for yourself. If you thwart him, the pattern's predictable."

"Predictable?" The solid thud of Bliss's heart was stifling.

"Nothing's been proved, but I think it's predictable. Things will happen to you. Don't misunderstand me. I don't mean you should put out for him. As soon as you do that, he'll lose interest in anything but playing his games. Painful games. Games guaranteed to scare you—to death."

Bliss didn't want to know about painful games. "How do I know any of this is true?"

"I didn't want him to come here, but leaving New York for a while was a good idea. There was too much there that might catch up with him. If you don't believe me, I can get Crystal to talk to you."

"No! No, I don't want to talk to Crystal." She wanted to be alone. "I've got to go."

"Of course, you've got to go and meet Sebastian. Just remember to be nice, but not too nice. You're too exposed here—particularly at night. Sebastian likes the night."

Bliss picked up the dirty Spode basket. "Thanks for the warning."

"There's a name for a man like Sebastian, Bliss. When he becomes obsessed with a woman—for whatever reason."

Even if that reason was only because he wanted her money? He knew she had financial difficulties here, but he also knew she would inherit a large trust fund and that this property was worth a great deal. She refrained from suggesting that the name for the type of man Maryan described might be, opportunist.

"Crystal could tell you about it. It broke her—almost ruined her life. Sebastian becomes a stalker."

# Twelve

Fab had argued against the glasses.

Polly, ever the practical one, had pointed out that whatever Bliss might gain in elegance without them, she'd lose fast when she started falling over things.

Bliss had opted for safety.

"You look terrific," Sebastian said.

She couldn't help smiling. "Thanks—again." He drove a dark gray Thunderbird tonight—borrowed from William, whoever William might be.

Driving across the I-90 bridge toward Seattle, Sebastian glanced at her, then over the choppy, gray surface of Lake Washington. They'd left after nine and the light was failing. "People tend to come back here, don't they?" he said.

Not if Maryan had her way. "I guess. I couldn't wait to get back."

"After school?"

"Mm. It's home. Always will be." She couldn't relax. Her back ached with tension.

"I don't think I've ever seen you in white before."

Few people had seen her in white. "We don't exactly have a history of attending formal gatherings—together."

He thought about that for a few moments, then said, "No," speculatively. "Does this seem unreal to you?"

She gave a sharp laugh. "Unreal's a bit weak, wouldn't you

say?" From the bridge, they'd entered the tunnel leading into industrial Rainier Valley. The rain had eased to drizzle.

"Sorry you agreed to come?" His green eyes were utterly serious.

"Wondering why I did," she told him honestly. *And unable to shut out Maryan's accusations against him.*

"This had to happen."

Bliss looked at his thigh in the slacks of his beautiful dark suit. He changed gears. Muscle flexed. His hand on the stick was broad and long-fingered—strong, very strong. He'd taken off his jacket and she smelled the scent of his freshly laundered white shirt. Against the collar his hair was black. Against his cuffs, his hands were tanned and lightly sprinkled with dark hair. Scratches on his knuckles and a bruise at the bridge of his nose reminded her of their night together.

The corner of his mouth jerked down. "You agree with me?"

She parted her lips and breathed in slowly. "That we had to go to a party together?"

His laugh was cynical. "You're smarter than that. You know what I meant. We've been moving toward this all our lives. Coming together."

"We were together once. We aren't together anymore."

"Aren't we?" His glance was no more than a flicker, but she shifted in her seat at its intensity. "We're together, Bliss. And this time we're staying together."

*He must be living out some fantasy of subduing you all over again.* Maryan had said.

"Bliss?"

"I can't make a leap like that. You can't expect me to." *As long as you let him think you're besotted with him it'll be okay.* "We're strangers." She couldn't pretend.

"Like hell we are." This time his laugh held disbelief. "We're old friends who should never have been parted. And we've already been where we'd never been before . . . before."

She ignored his last comment. "But we were parted. Your decision, not mine."

The drizzle had stopped. Sebastian turned off the wipers. "Is this because of the scene with your mother? This coolness? You were warm enough before she arrived yesterday."

"My mother has nothing to do with anything. I can't just forget. I can't forget that you . . . I can't forget, that's all. It's there."

"And you don't want to start over?"

"I"—she turned in her seat—"I can't say that, either. If I could, my life wouldn't feel as if gravity just quit."

"You, too, huh? But, hey, who needs gravity? We haven't floated away yet."

He might not have floated away. She felt decidedly separated from reality.

They drove the graceful freeway ramps that brought them to the Kingdome, Seattle's massive sports arena with its giant orange-juice strainer top. A jumble of warehouses and railroad tracks surrounded acres of parking lots.

"Seems a lifetime since I was here," Sebastian said.

Bliss felt less and less secure. "It is a lifetime." Could she find a way to bring up the subject of Crystal again?

"I don't know if I want to take you to this party after all."

"Because I'm not bubbling over with enthusiasm?" She remained where she was, swiveled to face him. "I can't pretend nothing's changed."

"That wasn't what I meant. I know I can't do the impossible and change history. I was talking about not wanting to share you."

He could make her heart flip so easily.

"I'm a selfish man." He smiled at her. "I think I'm glad you usually favor fashions by Goodwill."

Bliss chuckled. "Am I being insulted or complimented? Or both."

"Complimented only. You're the one woman I've ever known who could make anything look good." His next glance held only unnerving appraisal. "But I think I could spend a lot of time just looking at you in white silk."

She'd bought the dress to wear to a fundraising event, then been unable to go because the Crow sisters got the flu and Bliss had to look after them, and Bobby.

"I'm glad you still wear glasses."

Bliss used a forefinger to poke the bridge. "Eyesight doesn't tend to undergo major improvement."

"I mean, rather than contacts. The specs suit you. You look like an exotic, incredibly intelligent bird of some kind in all that floating white silk."

"An exotic bird?" Bliss grimaced. "Thanks, I guess."

"Did I ever tell you what a sexy body you've got?"

She felt herself grow warmer. "Yes. Quite recently if memory serves."

"Yeah. Well, you do. The dress doesn't cover enough of it for my taste. For my taste in public. Can't you pull the top up?"

She stared at him, then down at her bodice on its thin straps. The long, silk mesh scarf she wore loosely tossed around her neck didn't disguise the fact that the dress was low-cut. "I hope you're kidding."

"I am. I enjoy making other men jealous. No bra, right?"

"Sebastian!"

"Sorry." He grinned. "What can I say. I'm observant. It's one of my strengths. I like the lilies on the scarf. And the silver speckly things in the stockings, too—all the way up."

She shook her head. "Okay, you're observant."

"Hope you didn't pay too much for the dress."

He said the weirdest things. "What does that mean?"

"No top. No bottom. You're all arms and legs and . . . Well, you're all a lot of things I'd better not say if I don't want you to slap me."

They'd entered the outskirts of downtown Seattle and the concrete and glass-lined gulches swallowed the Thunderbird. Sebastian stopped for a light, then drove past the old Union Station and made a left turn from Fourth Avenue onto Jackson.

"I want you back, Bliss."

She held her breath and listened to the thrum of her pulse in her ears.

"Whatever it takes, I'm going to do it."

Her hands were cold, yet her palms sweated.

"Say something."

"I don't know what to say."

"Say you want the same thing. Say we'll never let anything separate us again."

Couples and groups swarming toward the Pioneer Square district became a passing blur to Bliss. Colors swam together, and faces.

"Why fight it? Don't tell me you haven't felt what I've felt in the past few days."

"I don't know what you've felt."

He found her hand and placed a swift kiss on her palm. He closed her fingers and let go to shift gears. A right-hand turn took them onto First Avenue, in the midst of clubs spilling patrons onto the sidewalks.

Bliss looked at her clenched fist.

"That's how I feel," he told her. "As if I'm around you and inside you, mixed with you. I don't need to know where my blood ends and yours begins, or my skin."

She dropped her head against the rest and pressed her closed hand to her throat.

"Tell me what you felt that first day when I walked into the kitchen at your place."

"Like I'd been punched," she said, settling her other hand on her stomach. "Here. Not enough air."

"Me, too. You were different, but the same. Does that make sense?"

"Yes."

"The same as the picture I remembered but with finer brush strokes added."

"I know. I couldn't believe it."

They crossed over Main. Even through closed car windows the sound of a trombone wailed blues from the Central Tavern—Seattle's self-acclaimed only second-class tavern. By the time they drew level with the jostling crowd in front of the J&M Cafe, Bliss's anxiety sickened her.

"We've got to deal with what we feel," Sebastian said. He slipped the Thunderbird into a curbside spot. "Let's put in an appearance and cut out again. I wouldn't go at all, but I'm expected."

"Too fast, Sebastian. You're moving too fast."

He turned off the ignition and pocketed his keys. "Okay." With one fingertip, he made a soft line from the tip of her shoulder to her wrist. "Okay. Sorry. I want this so badly I'm scared, I guess—scared it'll slip out of my hands if I don't tack it down fast."

Bliss regarded him steadily. "I'm not available to be tacked down. What exactly is this party, anyway?"

"I didn't mean . . ." Sebastian caught the tip of his tongue between his teeth. "These are people I'm going to have to learn to love in this area. Mostly media. TV. Radio. Print. Some types affiliated with the movies—and a lot of advertising honchos. They're the most interesting from my point of view—with the modeling agency in mind."

"Sounds awful."

He smiled and played with the long fringe on her scarf. "To be honest, I probably wouldn't have suggested this for tonight if I hadn't thought you might find it interesting. And maybe useful. There are bound to be some artsy types. Who knows, you might pick up a tenant or two. Anyway, you're bound to have something in common, aren't you?"

"Am I?" Once she'd had a clear vision of the people she wanted to fill her life with. That vision had clouded. Who a person was—inside—had gradually become more important than what they did.

Sebastian stopped smiling. His finger made the return journey to her shoulder. "Let's do it. Get this over with. Something else has definitely come up and it's going to make me want to get the hell out of this gig—as soon as possible." He pulled his jacket from the back seat and draped it over his lap. "I'm going to have to keep my eyes off you and cool down or someone's going to notice I'm a man with a mission."

Bliss got out of the car. Her skin blazed. The clammy evening didn't help her discomfort—neither did the sound of Sebastian's door slamming. She turned and stared unseeingly into the windows of the Elliott Bay Book Company. One moment she felt they'd never been separated, the next she was aware of the fantastic gulf the years had made between them. In the sophistication department, Sebastian was the lion to her lamb. And he certainly wanted to lie down with her. She had to smile.

His arm descended around her shoulders and he guided her to the corner. "Believe in me, Bliss. We'll get it right this time. I'll get it right. It's taken too long, but I'm going to convince myself that's how long it had to take."

It would be so easy, so natural to slip her hand around his waist. She was tall, but even in heels the top of her head only reached his ear. He was that presence over and around and inside her that he'd talked about.

Darn, was she going to be burning up every few minutes for as long as she spent time with him?

A man with a golden retriever sat propped against the wall. He glanced up from the impossibly long muffler he was knitting to grin at Bliss. She fumbled her small purse open and dropped a coin in a cardboard box pleading for dog food funds—and stroked the dog.

"Trust you," Sebastian said, steering her onward. "Good to the core. I never was sure what you saw in me."

"Neither was I," she said, lifting her chin and tossing back her hair. "We all have lapses in taste."

He laughed and spun her into an embrace. "You had a caustic tongue at seventeen. You've still got a caustic tongue. Oh, shit!" His grip tightened.

Sebastian grew still and so did Bliss, then she pushed away from him. "What?"

The chant of raised voices warned her of impending trouble. She turned around.

"Filth!" a woman shouted. "Filth mongers."

Bliss drew close to Sebastian's side. Ahead on the sidewalk, clustered around a doorway, and spreading out in a straining, sign-flapping clot, men and women jostled together.

"Perverts. Get out of our children's minds." A couple dressed in woven beanies, serapes and sagging jeans, swayed, a sign that echoed their words held between them.

A limousine swept to the curb and the driver hopped out. He opened the door and a blond glitter girl encased in red sequins climbed out, followed by a paunchy man in evening dress.

"Perverts! Perverts!" The cries rose higher and higher.

From behind Bliss came the complaining bay of the golden retriever.

"I want to leave," Bliss said. "This isn't a good idea."

"That won't be possible." Sebastian's voice was cold. "I don't walk away from a fight."

"It's *him!* It's Sebastian Plato!"

Horrified, Bliss realized the small crowd's attention was now firmly aimed in her direction, hers and Sebastian's.

"Silly bastards," he muttered. "Come on."

"Save our children," the serape-clad couple demanded. "Send them home."

Sebastian held Bliss firmly and strode directly at the group.

"Send our children home, *murderer!"*

Bliss stared, appalled, as the distance between her and the angry mob narrowed. She could do nothing but allow Sebastian to sweep her along.

"Save our—"

*"Bliss!"* A figure forced an exit from the group. "Bliss? For God's sake, what are you doing with him? Here?"

Confronted by Prue O'Leary, Bliss felt first disoriented, then furious. "Let me go," she whispered to Sebastian. "Take your arm off me."

If he heard, he gave no sign. His arm stayed where it was.

With his other arm he pushed a path through straining bodies to a polished oak door that opened before he rang the bell.

"Welcome, sir," the doorman, who must have been watching through a peephole, said. "Sorry about the inconvenience."

Looking over her shoulder, the last thing Bliss saw before the door closed was Prue's disgusted face.

The doorman indicated for them to go in the direction from which voices, laughter and music sounded. "Mr. Wilman's in the conservatory. They're dancing on the terrace. The buffet's in the dining room—and the bar's—"

"We'll find our way, thanks," Sebastian said. His nostrils flared and he walked fast enough to make Bliss run to keep up.

"Sebastian—"

"Goddamn fools. They don't know what they're shouting about."

Bliss shrugged free and faced him. "Maybe they don't. But they think they do."

"Hello," a smoky female voice said. "I'm Fern Wilman. You must be? . . ."

"Sebastian Plato. This is Bliss Winters."

A sinuous, too-tanned woman joined them. Carefully careless upswept black hair showed off heavy diamond earrings. Her draping pants suit glimmered as if fashioned from blue fish scales. More diamonds glittered at her throat and on her fingers and wrists. She gave Bliss a brief, but curious glance. "Morris and Kitten's daughter. How interesting." Then she concentrated on Sebastian. "*The* Sebastian." She stepped away to survey all of him. "Oh, yes, you're everything they all say you are. A dish, my dear. I'm so sorry I didn't meet you in Chicago. Larry said you throw a helluva party, darling." She smiled hugely, showing large, strong teeth with a gap in the middle.

"Good evening, Mrs. Wilman," Sebastian said, offering her his hand. "Thank you for inviting us."

"Oh, phoo." Their hostess flapped his hand away and kissed his mouth. "We don't stand on formality here, darling. Come along and meet some people. Clever of you to get Bliss to come with you."

She led the way through a foyer paneled in square blocks of dark wood. Sexless stainless steel figures stood sentry duty at the foot of a wide staircase. Green marble tiles echoed underfoot.

All Bliss could think about was the unspoken accusation on Prue's face as the front door had closed. Prue thought Bliss had sold out to the enemy.

By tomorrow, a great many people would think the same thing.

Morris and Kitten Winters would probably have heard the news.

"There are several lovely rooms to relax in upstairs, Bliss," Fern said. "Why don't you pop up there and freshen up. I'm sure you won't have any difficulty finding us again."

"Well—"

"Bliss doesn't need to freshen up," Sebastian said, gripping her elbow. "Do you, love?"

She needed to get out of here and think.

"Sure?" Fern said, rubbing the fingers and thumb of one hand together while shafts of brilliance shot from facets in a huge diamond ring.

Bliss nodded and let Fern get a little ahead before she murmured, "Did you have any idea those people would be out there?"

"How would I know about them?"

"I'm asking you if you knew. Simple question."

"No. No, I didn't. What does it matter anyway?"

She straightened her back. "I think you know the answer to that. The woman who spoke to me was a very old friend. Prue O'Leary."

"WOT," he said thoughtfully. "That Prue O'Leary?"

"I see you know her name."

"I've read it several times now. She's the one who talked to the press about your connection to me."

"Yes. And now the press will have more to say about my connection to you."

He contrived to fasten his arm around her waist. His firm grip at her side made it impossible to break away without making a fuss. "Later, okay, Bliss? We'll say the right things to the right people here. Then we'll get away on our own."

"Prue's group won't be asking me to chair their committee after this."

"Did you really want to?"

"I think you know what I'm telling you."

"Suggesting to me, do you mean? Suggesting that I wanted those freaks to see you with me so you'd lose any credibility they might have been able to use against me?"

Bliss felt his solid body from her shoulder to her thigh. His fingers kneaded her side. "You can draw your own conclusions about what I mean," she told him. "I'd like to leave, please."

"If we do that, people are going to talk."

Fern looked back and smiled, she reached to take Sebastian's hand. She drew him, still firmly holding Bliss, into a circle of guests by an opulently laden buffet table. Hanging shoji screens rested against the walls of the dining room. A chandelier fashioned into clusters of red, glass peonies cast a rosy glow over the black lacquer table and a silk rug boldly patterned in black and gold.

"Everybody," Fern said, clapping her hands. "Say hello to Sebastian Plato and Bliss Winters."

A chorus of hellos followed. Hands were shaken. Measure was taken. The conversation slid immediately to Raptor's new venture in the Northwest. Confident men and women introduced themselves, and the ritual of business mating began.

"And you're Morris's girl," a big, sandy-haired man said. He didn't smile. His rheumy eyes lingered where the tops of her breasts showed above the dress. "Small world. I was talking to Morris a few nights ago. I'm Walter DeFunk."

Muscles in her belly knotted. "Nice to meet you," she managed to say. Now he'd really have something to report to Daddy.

"My mother mentioned you just yesterday. Did you enjoy yourself at the Hunt Club?" She made sure she returned his cold appraisal. He'd get the message that she was aware of what he'd said to her father.

DeFunk grunted and filled a beefy hand with macadamia nuts. When he began funneling the nuts into his small mouth, his gaze was directed away from Bliss.

"Champagne?" a white-coated waiter asked, offering a silver tray bearing thin crystal champagne glasses.

Sebastian took one glass and handed it to Bliss. He passed for himself. "Excuse us," he said to whoever might be paying attention—everyone in the vicinity—and guided Bliss from the room. "The conservatory sounds nice. I wouldn't have expected to find one down here."

"These people can obviously have anything they want, and have it anywhere they want."

"True," he agreed. "Stylish place."

"I want to go home."

"So you keep telling me. Be a little patient, huh? We'll circulate, then excuse ourselves."

"Make sure everyone sees us together, I suppose."

He stood still. "What do you mean by that?"

The look in his eyes left her in no doubt that he knew exactly what she meant. After tonight, who would believe Bliss Winters didn't approve of Sebastian Plato. Even if she'd wanted to help Prue, which she didn't, this evening's events had made certain she'd be useless.

Sebastian seemed about to speak, but changed his mind and carried on toward a door that opened into a courtyard with a glassed-over dome. A soft, dark sky mantled the glass. Palms rustled in lush plantings. The atmosphere was fragrantly humid. Dozens of varieties of potted orchids, each one in full bloom, had been placed in groups between the trees and shrubs.

"Huh," Sebastian remarked, almost offhand. "Pretty fantastic. Typically theatrical. These people always go in for the staged event."

"Do you know many of them?"

"Yeah. A lot of them."

"I don't see any starving artists in need of cheap digs."

He raised her glass to her lips and tipped just enough to force her to take a sip. "You haven't said more than two words to anyone. How would you know who's who, or who might need what?"

"If there's a dress in this house that didn't cost thousands I'd be surprised."

With his fingers still over hers, he swallowed some of the champagne. He took his time inventorying Bliss's body-skimming dress. Bands of silk fluttered free at the bottom of each layer. The lilies on her loosely woven scarf were of silver thread.

"I'd leave on my own but it's dark," she told him. "I'm brave, but I'm not a fool."

"I won't let you leave on your own. You're wearing the best dress in the place. Too bad all I can think of is taking it off."

She inclined her head and met his gaze. "You are so sure of yourself. Whatever Sebastian wants, Sebastian gets. Isn't that what you believe?"

His jaw flexed. "Might be nice. I know what I want right now. Could we just make nice with a few more people?"

"And then? Then, what, Sebastian?"

"Then I'm going to take you away from here and finish what we started the other night."

She lowered her eyes and remembered how foolish she'd felt over the ring in his wallet, foolish and incredibly emotional. And she was a fool. He hadn't carried that ring around for fifteen years.

"Larry Wilman," Sebastian said, in a hearty, I'm-in-plastics tone. "How the hell are you?"

"Fine, fine." Balding, smoothly pampered-looking Wilman slapped Sebastian's back. "Hell of a party you had in Chicago last month."

"Glad you enjoyed yourself. This isn't shabby, Larry."

*Larry* raised his triple chins and cast a satisfied eye over the proceedings. "Did you get the stuff I sent over on my Nordstrom proposal?"

"Sure," Sebastian told him. "Yours and every other agency in the country. What makes you think they aren't satisfied with what they've already got?"

"Nothing. Never hurts to show an alternative that's better, though."

"Agreed. I'll take a look at it for you some time this week."

"Do that," Wilman said, sounding distracted. He followed the progress of a red-haired woman. Her long, green chiffon halter gown stretched tight over large breasts. The divided bodice was open all the way to a gold belt at her small waist. She wore heavily tinted glasses, and enough very red lipstick to make her white skin appear luminous.

"Stand there a minute," Sebastian said. "I've got to speak to someone."

Sipping champagne, Bliss watched him stride rapidly toward the woman in green. He slipped a hand through her arm and ushered her from the conservatory back into the house. How many women had he made love to? How many women was he involved with now?

More and more guests drifted out among the exotic plants. A deep blue parrot screeched on its perch.

Bliss felt the level of conversation drop, and the uncomfortable certainty that she was under inspection. The first pair of eyes she met were Larry Wilman's. He smiled and raised his glass. She nodded.

Every man and woman in the room had probably read about Prue's darn committee—and seen Bliss's name linked to Sebastian's. They must be exchanging theories on the nature of their relationship.

She wandered to the outer glass wall of the conservatory and walked between the palms and banks of potted orchids. The instant Sebastian returned she'd insist upon leaving.

The appearance of the woman in green had—angered him? Bliss crouched to examine a frilly yellow bloom. Sebastian hadn't been neutral, or surprised, or thrilled to see the woman; he'd been furious.

The lights went out.

An initial moment of silence died beneath a blast of excited exclamations.

"Stand still everybody!" Larry Wilman's voice boomed above the rest. "Circuit must have blown. This won't take a moment."

Bliss steadied herself with a hand on the orchid pot and pushed herself upright.

Her scarf tightened around her neck.

She cried out and tried to turn around. Her glass slipped from her fingers, but made no sound wherever it landed.

"Nothing to worry about," Larry Wilman shouted. "Relax, people."

The scarf drew tighter.

Bliss tottered backward in her high heels. A body stopped her from falling.

Blood pounded in her ears. Her lungs burned, and her throat with each breath. "Let me go," she gasped—into the hand that closed over her mouth. The hand smelled of rubber. Rubber gloves. A smooth sleeve scraped her cheek.

"Shut up," a male voice whispered against her ear. "Just listen. Scream and I'll finish this now. Believe me. No one will ever know how it happened. Can you be quiet?"

She nodded.

"That's a good girl." The odor of aniseed coated his breath, and she smelled laundry starch. "You shouldn't have come here tonight. Now it's damage control time."

"I—"

A tug on the scarf silenced Bliss. Her legs trembled. Why didn't the lights come on? Why didn't Sebastian come back?

The man took his hand from her mouth and slid his arm around her waist, pulling her against him.

She panted with horror. He was hard and he jutted his hips rhythmically against her bottom.

"Not a word," he said. His tongue entered her ear, then he bit her earlobe and his breathing grew heavy. "Stay away from Plato."

She moaned.

He chuckled softly. "You like this, huh? I like it, too." The hand at her waist slid up to cup a breast. He squeezed. "Oh, yeah, I do like it. We're going to do a lot more of this."

Bliss's control broke. She struggled and drove her elbows backward.

His hand returned to her mouth. He shook her. "Okay. End of first lesson. More to come—much more. Get rid of Plato. Tell him to stay away. I'll be watching. Got it?"

She wriggled.

"Nice," he said, and rolled his erection against her again. "You excite me, baby. Violence excites me. Too bad we can't finish this tonight, but I'm patient."

People talked loudly all around them. Why didn't the lights come on?

Bliss felt her scarf slide from her neck.

"Yeah, baby," the man whispered. "Get ready for me. I'm going to fuck your brains out."

She retched.

"Do as I tell you with Plato and I'll make sure nothing bad happens to you. Cross me, and I'll fuck you to *death,* baby—slowly. I'll eat you alive."

He released her so suddenly she staggered and almost fell.

She rubbed her neck. Her heart throbbed and her muscles felt formless.

Darkness within darkness. A sound as of roaring wind hammered at her brain. Panic. Bliss pulled off her glasses and pressed her eyes. She must not pass out.

"Let there be light!" Larry Wilman yelled, his laughter booming. "Will you look at this? Nothing wrong with the lights. Some goddamn fool leaned on the dimmer panel is all. Sorry, people. Carry on."

Bliss searched around. Mouths stretched in grins. Voices babbled. Backs were slapped, and bejeweled fingers waved. Fresh drinks circulated. It was as if a clockwork scene had been rewound and the movement picked up where it had stopped. No sign of a man anywhere near her.

Her life had been threatened. She ought to tell someone.

First there'd been the "ghost" at the lodge who told her to stay away from Sebastian. Now a maniac had pawed and menaced her disgustingly, and given the same warning—only this time there'd been the threat that she'd suffer regardless, hadn't there?

What would she say? *A man grabbed me and threatened to rape and kill me but now he's disappeared and I can't even tell you what he looked like.* She could visualize the skeptical—and pitying—response that would get. They'd think she'd panicked in the dark and imagined the whole thing.

Fern Wilman swooped down upon Bliss and said, "What on earth's the matter, love?" She frowned and snapped her fingers for a waiter. "Brandy. Get a brandy and be quick about it."

"I don't like brandy," Bliss murmured.

"I think you need it," Fern said. "Darling, you look positively deathly. All we've had here is a little light failure, for goodness' sake. It isn't going to kill you."

# Thirteen

*It isn't going to kill you?*

*He* isn't going to kill you? Bliss couldn't be certain of that. "Excuse me," she said to Fern Wilman and stepped resolutely past the woman.

"But they're bringing you some brandy."

"Thank you, but no," Bliss said without looking back. "Thanks for a lovely party. I've got another appointment." An appointment to get out of here and back to peace and safety—if there was anywhere left where she could be anything but scared.

People crowded the wide vestibule. Many more party-goers had arrived and the noise level blasted Bliss.

Sebastian materialized out of the crush and took her arm. "Sorry, Chilly, had to take care of some business."

"Don't give it another thought. I'm out of here."

"Okay." He held her still. "What's the problem?"

"You already know the problem." He didn't know half of it anymore. She needed to think things through. Alone. "I'm going to ask the doorman to call me a cab."

"No, you're not."

The trembling hadn't entirely subsided. Now it increased again. "Please let me go."

"No way."

"I don't want to make a scene. That would embarrass both of us."

"You're irrational."

Bliss turned on him. "I think that's enough, Sebastian. I don't have to take insults from you."

His black brows drew sharply together. The speculative narrowing of his eyes turned them a hard, glittering green. "What happened after I left you in there?"

"Nothing." He knew her too well.

He shook his head. "I don't think you're telling me the truth."

What shreds of control left to her began to crumble. "I don't belong here. I don't want to. You have business to attend to. Do it."

"Yeah," Sebastian said through his teeth. "I have business to attend to. The most important piece of business in my entire life." He pulled away from the throng, looking around as he did so.

With her left arm in the grip of his left hand and his right hand settled firmly on the back of her neck, he steered her behind the foot of the staircase where a huge floral arrangement filled the space.

"I want out," she told him, desperate now.

He opened a door, peered inside and propelled her into the confined area beyond. Sebastian closed them into a musty space and turned a key in the lock.

"I want—"

"Stop telling me what you want. Just for a moment, will you?" He held her in one arm and fumbled until he found what he was looking for. A single, naked bulb produced low-wattage, yellow light. Hanging from the high ceiling, the pathetic glow slithered over the contents of a storage closet.

"This is too much," Bliss said, reaching for the key in the lock. "I've had a hell of a night already and now you lock me in a cupboard."

"In a cupboard with me," he said. "Actually I thought it might be a bathroom, but this is better."

"Really?"

"Yeah. Less likely to be interrupted."

Bliss's heart turned. "Interrupted?"

"I've got a feeling that if I let you get out of this house without some serious talking, I may be chasing you all over town before I can get you on your own again. You looked spooked out there."

*Spooked?* "How did your business meeting with the redhead go?"

His jaw flexed. "Fine."

"She's quite something."

"Is she? I didn't notice."

Bliss snorted. "Do I look that stupid?"

"I want to talk about you. You and me."

"Is there anything to talk about?"

He stepped toward her.

Bliss backed up, until her back met cardboard boxes stacked almost to the ceiling. If she spread her arms, she'd touch china-laden shelves. On the floor, an open laundry bag spilled wadded linens.

"We've got something to talk about," Sebastian said softly. "Us. The future. I want you, and I think you want me."

"You don't know what I want anymore. You did once, but those days are gone."

Sebastian braced himself with a hand on either side of her head. The boxes were cool at her back. He looked into her upturned face. With the yellow light behind him, his features slanted dramatically.

Bliss drew herself up. "You're not being fair."

"Aren't I?"

"No. This is bizarre. You don't trap people in closets in strange houses."

"You aren't trapped."

"You locked us in."

"I locked other people out. Say the word and you can go."

Bliss opened her mouth.

He watched her lips and his own parted. "Don't go, Bliss."

Questions, so many questions, yet she couldn't make herself look for the first one.

"Say something."

She closed her eyes and rested her forehead on his chest. If loving him was dangerous, she was in mortal peril. She drove her teeth into her bottom lip. She did love him. Crazy as it must be, she did love Sebastian Plato.

"Kiss me," he said.

She sighed and shook her head. "This is nuts."

"So, it's nuts. Let's be nuts. I want you." He rubbed the back of her neck with his knuckles. "I'm not giving up this time, Bliss. This time it's going to work for us."

"The lights went out."

He grew still. "Yeah."

She felt the heat of his body. "It scared me."

"I didn't think you were afraid of the dark."

"I never used to be." *Tell him, tell him exactly what happened in the conservatory.*

Sebastian raised her chin. "You're safe with me."

Was she? Or was she in more danger than she'd ever been in her life?

"I won't let anything happen to you, Bliss. I want to spend the rest of my life making sure you're happy."

But he'd been able to take a fifteen-year hiatus from feeling that way.

Very gently, he took her glasses off, folded the armatures and slipped them into a jacket pocket. "You don't need them to see me, do you?"

"No."

"All you need to see is me, sweetheart." He brought his mouth to hers, caressed, skin to skin, softly back and forth. "Open up for me."

Bliss let him part her lips. His tongue slid inside and her eyes drifted shut. She felt him shift, spread his legs apart to bracket hers. His weight clamped her against the boxes. He filled the small space.

She kissed him back.

The small, hidden places inside her ached, throbbed. Sensation slipped away, all sensation but that which drew her to him, surrounded her with him. Sebastian reached into the cold, silent spaces within her body and painted them whispering hot.

Holding her face in both hands, he kissed her again and again, and she pressed closer, helpless to stop her hips from straining to meet his.

From her face to her neck, to her shoulders, his long fingers caressed, rubbed, felt their way, inch by fevered inch.

Bliss fought for breath.

She heard voices in the hall outside and vaguely registered the marvelous madness of making love in a closet while people made small talk on the other side of the door.

Sebastian kept on kissing her, but struggled out of his jacket while he did so. Bliss caught at his tie and he helped her loosen and drag it off. She undid his shirt buttons and pulled the tails free of his pants. Beneath her hands, the hair on his chest was rough, the skin heated.

His breathing was almost as fast as her own. "We were going to talk," he murmured, kissing her again, nuzzling her jaw up, breathing into her neck, following his breath with his lips.

Bliss felt dazed. She said, "Talk?"

"Wedding rings and condoms."

She blushed. "I made a mistake"—the scent of him filled her nostrils—"I was overexcited."

He chuckled, pressing his attention to the hollow above a collarbone, below the bone. "Guess who's overexcited now?"

"We both are." She felt the evidence of his words, and the evidence of her own. He was hard. She was wet, and aching. "What—"

He covered her open mouth with his own, her breasts with his hands. Bliss moaned and wrapped her arms around his neck.

"This little dress is something," he told her. "Instant turn on. Not that your purple pedal pushers don't turn me on just as much." He laughed.

Bliss didn't laugh.

She couldn't reach enough of him, touch enough of him. His

body was hot—her body burned. He pulled her arms from his neck and tugged the flimsy straps of her dress over her shoulders.

"We can't do this here, Sebastian." But she panted, and helped him free her from the bodice. It slipped easily to her waist. *"Sebastian."*

"We should have had that talk," he muttered, fondling her naked breasts, groaning faintly, maddeningly.

Bliss unbuckled his belt, unzipped his pants. "About what?"

"Wedding rings—"

"And condoms," she finished for him. "Why? I made a mistake—"

"I want you now, Bliss. I've got to have you."

"We can't. Not here." His waist was smooth, his buttocks unyielding. Bliss savored the texture of him, the power. His thighs were rock where they met her hips. She tested a flat nipple with the tip of her tongue, and smiled when he sucked in a breath.

"Bliss, I don't have anything."

She pushed his pants down. "We should stop."

"But you don't want to, either." He caught up the hem of her dress and gripped her thighs beneath. He smoothed the sensitive skin all the way to her bottom and drew her to her toes. "Do you? Do you want me to stop?"

She shook her head. His disheveled hair fell forward. His body pulsed against her. Sebastian stripped away one stocking. Bliss steadied herself on his taut biceps while she tore off the other silver-shot wisp of nothing. He cupped her mound and pressed his fingers into the dampness she was helpless to disguise.

"Oh, Bliss, I think we're just going to have to be human."

She held his penis in both hands and rubbed the tip against her, pressed it between her legs and gritted her teeth—at the searing of her own flesh, and at his tortured gasp.

Her panties joined her hose and Sebastian dipped just enough to push his fingers inside her. She played him over the hair at the apex of her legs.

"My God," he hissed. "You're killing me."

"You're killing me," she told him, her voice barely audible.

"Nice death," Sebastian said. He sucked a nipple into his mouth and she heard the laugh, deep in his throat, when she sobbed. "Better not make too much noise or we'll both be embarrassed," he warned. "If they break down the door we'll be caught bare-assed—among other things."

"Sebastian," Bliss cried into his shoulder.

He moved his mouth to her other breast.

She filled her fingers with his hair and held on.

"You want me, Bliss?" he asked between kisses. "Say you want me."

"I want you." And she couldn't think anymore.

Gripping her thighs, Sebastian lifted her. "Wrap your legs around my waist."

She did as he asked. She would have done anything he asked.

His big hands spanned the fronts of her legs and his thumbs met where the fierce excitement pooled. His thumbs massaged, and he rocked his penis upward, inside her.

He was big, huge—her delicate skin protested and tiny muscles contracted. Then, rather than push him out, those muscles clenched, drew him in.

"You are so tight," he said into her hair. He held her against the boxes, held her there and grasped her thighs, repeatedly passed the pads of his thumbs over the slick, swollen focus of all feeling.

Bliss began to move. She rose away from Sebastian, smiled when he forced her down again. Sweat shone on his fabulously demonic features, and on the bulging muscles in his shoulders and chest.

The spear of a climax pierced Bliss almost without warning and she captured her cry against Sebastian's shoulder. She sank her teeth into his skin and he yelped, but only held her tighter and moved with her harder, faster.

Their bodies jarred together.

"Baby, baby," he moaned. "This is hurting you."

"No," she lied. "No."

"Yes, it is. You're small." She heard his teeth snap together, then all she heard was the rasping, rhythmic groan he made with each thrust.

Once more the force of a climax scorched Bliss. She contracted around Sebastian, and felt the rush of his warm fluids inside her. He pushed into her once more, and leaned, holding her in a crushing embrace, against the boxes.

Tears coursed her cheeks. She sniffed.

"What?" he asked, lifting his head. "What is it? I hurt you, didn't I?"

She shook her head and giggled shakily. "Look at us."

He studied her face, then her breasts. He stroked her bare thighs and bottom. "I love looking at you. When's the last time you did that?"

"It's been a long time." She shook her head. "And I never did it like this."

His eyes narrowed again. "How many were there?"

For an instant she wasn't sure she understood.

"How many others, Bliss?"

"Is it your business?" she asked, too exhausted to be angry.

Deep sadness etched Sebastian's face. "No. No, of course it's not my business. Just the old male possessiveness rearing its head."

She touched her breasts to his chest hair, sucked in a breath at the sensation. "I understand. But you don't have any right. So don't ask again."

He smiled ruefully. "I won't. It doesn't matter, does it?"

"It shouldn't. There was one."

Sebastian drew his brows down.

"One man, Sebastian. He wasn't you. I'd waited for you and then you went away, so eventually I slept with someone else, but it wasn't right."

"My fault," he said quietly.

She said, "History," and kissed the dimple in his cheek.

"I want to take you home and tuck you into my bed," he told

her. "Then I want to do this again. And again." Slowly, he let her feet slide to the floor.

"We'd better think about putting ourselves together and doing our best to sneak out of here without everyone guessing what just happened."

Sebastian grinned. "Let 'em guess. I might just tell them anyway."

Bliss pushed him away and fished her panties and stockings off the floor. "You dare. I'd never forgive you."

"I won't then," Sebastian said, ducking to catch one of her nipples between his teeth.

"Stop it, now," she told him, but she sighed and let her eyes close again while he pulled on tender flesh.

At last he drew back. "I'm never, ever going to let you go again, you know. I want the world to know that."

Bliss struggled into her clothes.

"We're getting married."

She stopped and looked into his face. "Not just like that," she told him. "Not after everything that's happened."

"That's all behind us."

"No." She righted the bag of laundry they'd managed to up-end and pushed several waiter's jackets back inside. "It isn't all behind us. I still don't know what happened."

"You're going to have to settle for not knowing everything," Sebastian said. "What does it matter now?"

She paused. "It matters. May I have my glasses?"

Sebastian found them. "I'll tell you what I can. For the rest you'll have to trust me."

Bliss puffed up her cheeks and let the air out slowly. "I don't think so. I've been threatened, Sebastian. Because of you. I need to understand why."

He stopped in the act of pushing up the knot in his tie. "Threatened how?"

She shrugged.

"I asked you how." His grasp on her shoulders hurt. "Answer me."

Wincing, Bliss said, "At my place, the night I almost brained you with the hairbrush? A woman's voice said I must get rid of 'him.' She meant you."

"You can't be sure." He grimaced. "What am I saying? You probably imagined the whole thing."

"Thanks." She shrugged hard enough to catch his attention. He dropped his hands. "Tonight," she continued, "when the lights when out. A man grabbed me from behind and threatened me."

Sebastian's jaw worked.

She crossed her arms over her breasts. "He pawed me. He said he'd do horrible things to me if I saw you again. And he said he'd be watching me."

The door handle rattled.

Bliss flattened a hand over her mouth.

Sebastian pressed a finger against his lips and turned out the light.

The door rattled again.

"Stand still and don't say anything," he whispered. "I'm going to unlock the door."

*"No!"*

He pulled her against the shelves to one side of the doorjamb. "If they put the light on, we're sunk. We just laugh and make a run for it. With luck they won't put the light on."

Sebastian managed to unlock the door silently—a moment before the handle turned once more and light from the hall cut a wedge over the opposite shelving. A handful of wet dishtowels and another white jacket landed on top of the laundry bag, and the door slammed shut.

Bliss put the light on again. "This is freaky. I've got to get out of here."

"You're not going anywhere without me."

"Of course I am. Don't be ridiculous."

"You just told me someone threatened you tonight."

"And a few minutes ago you were saying I had an overactive imagination."

Sebastian smoothed her hair back and rested his forearms on her shoulders. "That was about the ghost thing. Not this. I'm not letting you out of my sight again."

Bliss turned her face away. "Maybe I should go to the police."

"Did you see this man?"

She propped her cheek on his forearm and shook her head.

"What will you tell the police?"

Bliss held his shoulders. "That someone grabbed me from behind and threatened me."

He watched her silently.

"It's happened again, hasn't it? I don't have anything to tell them."

"No," Sebastian said. "But you have me, sweetheart, and I'm not going to let anything happen to you."

She lowered her gaze. This was one independent woman who was beginning to like the idea of having a strong man around—a strong man whom she also happened to love.

Bliss closed her eyes and breathed deeply.

Sebastian's shirtsleeve smelled fresh, of being freshly laundered . . . and starched.

# Fourteen

"Sebastian!" Maryan's voice reached him the instant he pushed open his front door. "Is that you?"

He slung his jacket over his shoulder and considered turning around and leaving. Beater, a surefire antenna for best-avoided situations, had met him outside and refused to follow him inside. Sebastian decided he should have taken the dog's silent advice.

Barefoot, wearing a loosely belted robe, Maryan emerged from the sitting room that doubled as Sebastian's gym. She pointed a wavering finger at him. "S'you. Why didn't you answer me? There's a guy on the phone for you." Her words slurred together.

"I'm going to bed." Bliss had taken a cab back to Hole Point. He couldn't believe it. After what had happened between them, she'd walked—no, she'd run away from him and taken a cab home. He couldn't figure her out. He could figure himself out. Through all the years since he left her, he'd been working his way back. Now he was never going to give her up again.

Maryan tottered toward him. "What's the matter with you? I told you there's a phone call for you. It's not going to go away."

"Forget it." He started for the stairs.

Maryan cut him off. "You've been with her, haven't you?"

He made to walk around her.

She grasped his arm. "I know you have. Did you sleep with

her?" Her gray eyes took in the rumpled condition of his clothes. "You did, didn't you? You slept with the bitch."

*"Don't* ever insult Bliss." He shook Maryan's hand from his arm. "Do you understand me?"

She whimpered. "I'm only worried about you. You've gotta speak to that guy, Sebastian. He's mean."

"What guy?" Sebastian said. "You're drunk, Maryan."

"What I drink and how much I drink is none of your goddamn business! And I'm not drunk. Cheerful, but not drunk. You never could stand to see me cheerful. You never understood me. If you did you'd know—"

"Whoa, luvvy," Ron York said, hurrying to slip an arm around Maryan's waist. "Let's get Sebastian to his phone call. Then we all need a long chat, don't we?"

She peered at him. "Yeah. A long chat. It's Jim Moore."

Sebastian dropped his arm and let his jacket trail on the floor. "Jim Moore."

"Uh, huh," Maryan said, smiling a little. "Your dear ol' papa-in-law."

"My ex-father-in-law," Sebastian said automatically. He should have expected the old bastard to make contact. "Hang up on him."

"We did," Ron said. "Several times. He says either you talk to him on the phone or he'll come and camp on your doorstep. Why not talk to him and get it over with?"

Sebastian didn't like Ron suggesting what he ought to do—he didn't like Ron, period. But what he said made sense. He walked past the couple and into the sitting room where the telephone receiver trailed to rest on a dark gray couch.

He picked up the instrument. "Plato here." The room looked slept-in—probably appropriate.

Jim Moore's pseudo-Southern drawl announced, "You owe me."

"Plato here," Sebastian repeated, taking grim pleasure in figuring the rise of Moore's blood pressure.

"Sonuvabitch," Moore said. "You ruined my girl and you owe me for that."

"No," Sebastian said, dropping to sit on the couch and finding a space for his feet on the booze and food-littered coffee table. "Nope, sir, I don't owe you one little red cent."

"Wanna rethink that?"

"I don't believe I do."

"You're in a mess of trouble in this state, boy. People here are God-fearing. They don't take to the kind of temptation you parade before their little girls."

Sebastian's stomach turned. The man was sick, had always been sick. Jim Moore had a lot to answer for, but he probably never would.

"You hear me, boy?"

"I'm going to hang up now, Mr. Moore."

"I'm your father-in-law," Moore thundered. "You ain't got no father of your own anymore, so I'm the closest thing. You call me Pop and gimme the respect I deserve."

"You deserve to be six feet under," Sebastian muttered under his breath."

"Whad'you say?"

"I said we deserve what we get most of the time. I don't have a father, Mr. Moore. Don't want one."

"You owe me."

"I married your daughter." The argument was so old, so tired, and Sebastian had much more important pressures on his mind right now. "We gave it a good shot. It failed." And, because Crystal had suffered enough, Sebastian wasn't about to give her old man more ammunition to use against her.

"You killed my grandchild."

Sebastian closed his eyes.

"Speak up. You gonna argue that point again."

"No."

"There!" Moore's voice rose triumphantly. "Now, you gotta start paying me for that—payin' me some more. I can't find Crystal and I need money."

"Not my problem."

"But you said—"

"I said I wasn't arguing your points anymore—none of your points. And I'm not paying you off anymore. Understand?"

Maryan had sidled back into the room. She sat in a chair opposite him with her fist to her mouth. Her eyes were huge and worried. Wearing blue Spandex workout shorts and a tank top, good old Ron hovered behind her. MTV images flared on the big-screen TV. The sound had been turned off but Sebastian heard the whir of the treadmill York hadn't bothered to stop.

"Listen up." Jim Moore all but whispered this time. "A little birdie tells me you've taken up with the Winters girl again."

Sebastian's gut clenched.

"Speak so's I can hear you, boy! You're messin' with the Winters girl again. Am I right?"

Jim Moore was an animal. He'd almost killed before. Why wouldn't he be capable of physical violence of that magnitude again? "Stay out of my life," Sebastian said softly. "You've had all you're getting from me."

"You're in trouble here," Moore said, coughing. "They know all about the kind of scum you are. They know about you defiling innocent little girls that were pure before you put your filthy hands on them."

The rhetoric hadn't changed.

"You meet me and bring money, or I'm gonna give those righteous ladies exactly the kind of ammunition they need against you, boy."

"I don't think you will," Sebastian said wearily. He glanced up, surprised to see Zoya enter the room in a black swimsuit. This business wasn't for airing outside the family. "I have to go now." Had Maryan and Ron been indiscreet enough to talk about the Moores to Zoya this evening?

"You forget messing around with other women," Moore said. "You got that?"

Sebastian watched Zoya glide to sit on the arm of Maryan's chair. She held a large manila envelope.

"You hear me, boy?"

"Good night, Mr. Moore."

"Don't you hang up on me! God only recognizes one marriage. You hear me? In His eyes you're my daughter's husband and you always will be. I'm a man of God and I'm gonna see His will done. You got that?"

Sebastian felt the skin on his scalp tighten.

"I ain't never gonna stand by and watch some home-breaking trollop interfere with God's will." Moore was raving now. "Do you know what I'm saying."

"I'm not sure," Sebastian said. The old man had his full attention. "Maybe you're threatening me. No, you couldn't be threatening me. You know better than that."

"The hell I do! I know what you've been up to. I know every move you've made. Know what I mean?"

"Full of questions, aren't we?"

"Don't mess with me. Listen up. Listen good. I *know* every move you've made. I'm taking steps to protect my girl's interests. Got that? I'll do whatever I have to do to protect my girl's marriage."

Sebastian put his feet on the floor and rested his elbows on his knees. "Maybe you should explain what you mean by that."

"You figure it out."

Bliss had said she'd been threatened at the Wilmans' when the lights went out. She said some man had pawed her. Old man Moore was sick, had always been sick—was he sick enough to be menacing Bliss?

"I want—"

"That's it for tonight," Sebastian snapped. He couldn't take anymore.

"You listen to—"

"I'm not listening. And don't call back. Mess with me again and I'll take it up with my lawyers. Don't mess with me, Moore. And stay away from my family—and my friends. Got it?" He smacked the phone down and scrubbed at his face.

"He can make trouble," Zoya said.

Maryan had told her things Sebastian never told anyone. He looked up. "What are you doing here, Zoya?"

She threaded an arm behind Maryan's shoulders. "Maryan and Ron invited me over."

Maryan's eyes were glazed but she nodded. "Zoya came to swim with us. We're all worried about you, Sebby. We're all worried about what's going on here."

"This was dropped off," Zoya said, proffering the envelope.

Sebastian pushed to his feet and took it. "What is it?"

"How should I know?"

He turned the envelope over and studied the metal butterfly closure.

"The guy wanted to talk to you," Zoya said. "I told him you weren't available."

"Damn it!"

"Hey"—Zoya held up a hand—"don't yell at me. You weren't available. He came just before you got back. We're all trying to run a business here while you're all over town making a spectacle of yourself with one of those tight asses you were telling me about."

Fury turned Sebastian's hands to fists. "Stay out of my private life."

"If your private life was private, we wouldn't even know about it, would we? As it is, there are probably more photos like those in the hands of the press right now."

Sebastian stared into Zoya's eyes and said softly, "You already opened this? Thoughtful of you."

She showed no embarrassment. "You'd better take a look."

From the envelope, Sebastian slid a wad of photos. On top was a cryptic note: "Busy woman. I'm not the only one watching her. Used a Polaroid for tonight—figured you might want to see what I got at once. Nose."

Sebastian read and reread the words.

"Come for a swim, Seb," Maryan said, blinking slowly. "We'll swim and talk."

Someone other than Nose was watching Bliss. Sebastian

hadn't thought about Nose in days. The first photo showed Bliss outside the lodge with the little boy. They were talking to the painter, Vic. Sebastian flipped through several more innocuous shots and came to one that stopped him: a Polaroid of Bliss at Sebastian's side outside the Wilmans'. The expression on her face turned his stomach. Fear and anger mixed there, and confusion. The serape-clad banner wavers were prominently featured. More prominent was Prue O'Leary, shouting at Bliss.

"Did you know that was being taken?" Zoya asked.

He shook his head.

"We can pray the press don't have a matching one," Ron said.

Sebastian ignored him. There was even a Polaroid of the scene in the dining room at the Wilmans'. He flipped through rapidly, frantically, and felt his own sweat before the rush of relief at finding there were certain photo opportunities that Nose had missed.

He started again and went more slowly. A picture of Bliss with Prue O'Leary stopped him. They faced each other beside what appeared to be a tangle of barbed wire. Water showed behind them. Lake Washington? Both women were drenched and the O'Leary woman was gesturing, making a point. The photos were dated on the back. This one had been taken the previous day—probably in the afternoon before the Wilmans' party. Bliss was enmeshed with the woman.

He looked at the final shot. Bliss at the open doors to her room. Her eyes held fear. Sebastian frowned and looked more closely, and checked the date. It had been taken the night she dashed away from him—the first night they spent together. He touched her face on the print. What he felt for her wasn't going away.

"For God's sake, Sebby," Maryan said. "Stop mooning over that colorless little nothing. She's nothing, absolutely nothing. We've got important things to do."

"Shut up," he said wearily and stood up. "I'm going to bed."

"We need to talk," Zoya said. "You can't put it off any longer. We've got a company to run."

"I've got a company to run," Sebastian told her, meeting her gaze. "And I'm running it."

He began to push the photos back into the envelope but stopped. He took a closer look at the photo of Bliss on the threshold to the deck outside her bedroom. On the wall behind her—it would be the wall on the opposite side of her bed—was a large mirror with an old-fashioned gilt frame. He brought the shot closer and studied the mirror.

Faint but unmistakable was a dark silhouette. Not the substance, but the shadow of someone looking toward Bliss, someone inside her room, probably just inside the bathroom door, watching her.

# Fifteen

Zoya sat in the chair Maryan had vacated in favor of the couch. "You know where he's going, don't you?" she said of Sebastian. Damn him. She'd get more of his attention if she was his dog.

Maryan dumped gin to the top of a highball glass, slopping booze on the table in the process. She made several stabs before zeroing in on the top of the ice bucket and lifting it off. It fell through her fingers.

"Ron," Zoya said, leaning forward. "Do something with her, will you? We've got to move our plans along or Sebastian baby's going to scuttle us."

"I thought we'd agreed that things were coming along quite nicely," Ron said. "Bliss Winters isn't going to be a problem for long."

"We need to move faster," Zoya said. "Much faster. And Sebastian's tacky private eye could turn into a handicap."

Maryan held Ron's attention. He said, "Maybe he's served his purpose for us. He's already done us a favor we didn't expect."

"We'll have to be very careful." Coming out of this clean, and smiling all the way to the bank, was the only scenario Zoya was prepared to consider.

Swaying, blinking in slow motion, Maryan chased ice cubes floating in water until she trapped one against the side of the bucket. She scooped it out and managed to hit her target. More gin splattered.

Ron sat beside her and massaged her neck.

If Maryan noticed, she gave no sign. Bending almost double, she captured her glass in both hands and raised it high enough to suck almost half the contents in one swallow.

"She's going to pass out," Zoya said, resigned, but angry. Without these two she'd manage Sebastian just fine. "Maryan, Sebastian's got to be diverted. Do you understand me? We've got to get him out of the way until we've finished what we've got to do."

"Diverted," Maryan said, pointing at Zoya with a long fingernail. "Sebastian's mine. I'll divert him."

Zoya frowned at Ron who shrugged. "Luvvy, Sebastian's gone to the Winters woman again."

"Y'don't know that," Maryan said. "He likes to drive when he's uptight. Moore upset him. Without that old bastard, Crystal wouldn't have cost us so much."

"We aren't here to discuss Crystal," Ron said, avoiding Zoya's eyes.

"Crystal was his wife, wasn't she?" Zoya asked

"We don't talk about that," Ron said "Maryan, love, concentrate. Remember I told you Zoya's as worried as we are about what could happen here in Seattle."

Maryan looked sideways at him. She raised a hand and slapped his cheek repeatedly, each time with more force, and she laughed.

Ronnie flinched, but he let her hit him.

"I'm the only one who deals with Sebastian's business," she said, punctuating her words with flat-handed blows. "Do you understand that, lover boy? You keep that bitch, Zoya, away from me. And keep her away from Sebastian. She wants inside his pants. She's washed up. If the Bellevue project goes down, she goes down with it."

Zoya pushed to her feet and paced. Maryan's attitude toward her fluctuated. "Shut her up." But she was right—only the Bellevue project wasn't going to fail. "We've got to move and we've got to be sure Bliss Winters can't do any damage we can't fix."

"When exactly did it become 'we'?" Ron asked, neatly shifting his allegiance back to his mistress. He had a great body and, given what Zoya had already surmised about his predilections, Maryan's slaps had produced exactly the expected result. Ron was sexually excited.

"Do you want me to remind you about that now?" she asked Ron, tilting her head to study his crotch. "About how we became a partnership."

Ron glanced at Maryan.

"Doesn't look as if it would matter if we fucked on the coffee table, does it?" Zoya asked.

"For God's sake." Ron shot to his feet. "Watch your mouth."

"You watch my mouth," she said, and laughed, and ran her tongue over her lips. "Why don't I help you get poor Maryan into bed?"

"I don't need any help." He bent over Maryan who let the now empty glass fall through her fingers and clatter across the table. "Come on, sweets. Bedtime for us." He pulled her to her feet.

Zoya came to the woman's other side and put an arm around her, using the opportunity to squeeze Ron's very nice ass.

"Knock it off," he said, glaring at her over Maryan's head. "Go home. The show's over here."

"Uh-uh"—she pulled one of Maryan's arms around her neck—"show's only beginning, and it's going to be a doozie."

Maryan contrived to grab the gin bottle and bear it with her as they half-guided, half-dragged her toward the stairs.

"I can do this, I tell you," Ron hissed, reaching to try to push Zoya. "Our suite's in the basement. Go home."

She caught his hand and delivered a sharp bite to his palm.

He yowled, and jerked away. For seconds they stared at each other, then he looked ahead and started maneuvering Maryan down the two flights of steps that led to an airy basement.

"She's passing out," Zoya commented. "Take the bottle."

Ron took it as it began to slip from Maryan's hand. He swept her up and carried her the rest of the way to a large, starkly minimalist suite. Centrally placed, a huge brass, four-poster seemed cast adrift on a sea of blond oak flooring. Diaphanous lengths of creamy muslin wound about the bedframe and floated gently in a breeze through white jalousies.

With Maryan deposited atop the impossibly high, eyelet-covered mattress and pillows, Ron swung to give Zoya his entire attention. "Get out," he said, baring his teeth. "Get out and don't think you can blackmail me with your little stories."

She walked slowly past him to the side of the bed and undid the belt on Maryan's robe.

"I told you to get out."

"Help me. And while you help me, listen. We sink or swim together. Do you understand me?"

"No, I don't understand you. Leave her alone."

Very deliberately, Zoya pulled the belt free of the robe and rolled it up.

"Bellevue's just one operation for us," Ron said. "It'll hurt if it loses money, but it won't be fatal—except to you."

She studied him sharply. "What exactly do you mean when you say that?"

He grinned, a grin that made him boyishly handsome—as long as you didn't look into his vapid eyes. "You talked Sebastian into letting you buy a big piece of the action for yourself."

"How do you know that?"

"Maryan found out. You gambled big, baby. Desperate move, we figured. All or nothing, right?"

"I decided it was time to own something I worked to make. If we encounter a fatal hitch, it'll sting—it won't finish me."

"Not what we heard." Ron shook a knowing finger. "Not what we heard at all. We heard you were in deep in a lot of pies and trying to dig your way out."

This was not the time to lose her nerve. "Then you heard wrong. And Maryan's been keeping you in the dark. She's the one who's scared to death." Zoya drew herself up. This boy wouldn't recognize the kind of gamble she was prepared to take if it smacked him flat. "She can't afford to have Sebastian bring another woman into his life—anymore than we can."

Ron wasn't saying anything.

"Okay. Play dumb. But help me get her undressed."

"Shit, no!"

Zoya flipped open the robe. Maryan wore a beige lace teddy and cream hose. "Help me," Zoya repeated, reaching to pull the covers down beneath the other woman. "If you want to come out of this with something, do as I tell you. We need her on our side and she'll never agree unless she's got no out."

"You're mad."

"Maybe. You'd better hope not because we're in this together."

"I haven't agreed to anything."

"You don't have to. Either you do this my way and trust me to pull off a big win for you and me, or you lose. Simple as that."

He came toward her. "What if I throw you out on that sexy rear of yours?"

"Then I scream assault, call the cops, and turn you in."

"They'd never believe you."

"Wouldn't they?" She stripped off one of Maryan's stockings. "Sebastian hates your guts. He likes mine. All I've got to do is tell him you attacked me, and you're dead meat." Undressing a deadweight wasn't easy.

"You'd do it, wouldn't you?" Ron said.

She pulled the straps of the teddy from Maryan's shoulders. "You bet your life I would."

"What's in this for me?"

Zoya stopped and gave him her full attention. "We split everything."

"Split everything?"

"Everything Maryan will have to get her hands on to stop us from telling her brother exactly how sick she is. We know what she really wants. And we know Sebastian wouldn't keep her around if he knew what she wanted—or what's going to happen here tonight."

He came to her side slowly. "You really mean it."

Her answer was to pull Maryan's teddy to her waist and free her arms. "Sit her up."

"I don't like this."

"*Sit* her up."

A second later Maryan's head draped backward over Ron's arms. Her breasts were Playboy material, Zoya decided, big, with saucer-sized nipples. Watching Ron's face, she fingered them and laughed. He looked away.

"Some apples," she commented. "Mixing business and pleasure is going to be a real turn on."

"Zoya—"

"Lift her," she snapped, and pulled the teddy all the way off when he did so. "Now it's your turn. Show time."

"Forget it." He raised his palms and backed away. "I've had it with this scene."

"Don't tell me you've never done a threesome before."

"Not this way." He realized what he'd said and whispered, "Shit!"

"Always a first time. Come on," she wheedled. "Or are you shy?" Hoisting herself to sit beside Maryan's flaccid form, she rested one elbow on the mattress and teased tight swirls of dark pubic hair.

"You're sick." York walked away and rested his fists on a wall. He dropped his head forward. "Messing with a woman who can't defend herself."

Keeping him in sight, Zoya felt for the trigger point between Maryan's legs. "Let's see if we can get her attention."

"Stop it!" Ron demanded, pushing away from the wall and approaching. "If she comes to she'll blame me for this."

"Get naked."

"The hell I will."

She fondled one of Maryan's heavy breasts. "Do it, Ronnie. Or I'll strip and tell Maryan you forced me." In one swift move she sat astride Maryan's hips.

Ron rammed a hand into his hair. "Oh, my God." He pulled his tank over his head and threw it aside.

Zoya began stimulating Maryan.

The blue shorts met their mate and Ron stood, naked, muscular, and bronzed all over—and erect.

She laughed. "None of this is a turn on, huh?" She pointed at him. "And that's a mirage."

"You've had your fun, now go."

"I've hardly begun having fun. Get over here."

With obvious reluctance, he let her take his hand and pull him close. "Relax," she told him. "All I want you to do is lie down with your keeper."

Anger twisted his features, but he did as she instructed and climbed past her to lie beside Maryan.

It was all going to work. Zoya grinned her triumph. After weeks of terror, of watching everything she'd worked for dwindle away, she was seeing sunshine on her future.

Abandoning Maryan, she hopped to the floor and wriggled quickly out of her swimsuit.

"What the hell?—"

"Hush"—with a finger to her lips, she skirted the bed until she could kneel on the mattress beside him—"this is our lucky night, Ron. After tonight we're on our way to the big leagues."

"Maryan's going to chew you up, baby."

He didn't as much as look at her body—but what else could she expect? She'd enjoy using him anyway. "Don't worry about Maryan." Bending, she filled her mouth with him and bit hard enough to bring him jackknifing over her back.

Laughing, she wrestled with him, grabbing, as she knew so well how to grab, and screaming when he fought her off with slaps. He took her breasts in his big hands and squeezed them as if they were oranges and he was a man thirsty for juice.

She waited for the right moment and threw a leg over him. He was deep inside her before she fully caught his attention.

"Bitch!" he said through his teeth. He arched his chest off the bed. *"Bitch!"*

Two thrusts and he ejaculated, and Zoya bounced off him, glancing at Maryan to gauge the depth of her stupor.

"Hurry up," she told Ron. "Get up and do as I tell you."

"Let me be," he mumbled.

"You got more out of that than I did." She leaned to retrieve the robe belt and shoved it into Ron's hand. "I always get my full share. Tie my wrists to the bed."

"Fuck off."

Pressure, applied behind a trapezius muscle, got his full, yelping attention. Zoya kept her sharp fingers digging into his shoulder until he slid to the floor, moaning.

"Up," she told him. "I'm it, Ronnie, your salvation, or your destruction. Take your pick."

He staggered to his feet.

Gripping a vertical bar in the brass bed head, Zoya stretched out on her back. "Do it."

"No."

"Okay. Let's make this clearer. It's you or her. Tie me up and I'll swear you did it because she insisted. Refuse and I'll tell her you raped me while she was unconscious. Take your pick."

His chest rose and fell. "My God, you're evil."

"And you're a choirboy?"

He tied her wrists to the bed, yanking the belt hard enough to bring tears to her eyes. "What now?" he asked.

"Now we make a lovely threesome in this bed until Maryan comes to and starts screaming. Then I cry, and you protest, and I back you up. We did what she insisted we do. And I tell her I know all her little secrets. End result? We make very sure Bliss Winters isn't a problem, and Maryan becomes our golden goose. Sound good."

He chewed his bottom lip. "I don't like it."

"You don't have any choices, so let's enjoy it. Come to me, baby. Once more for the hell of it." She parted her legs and raised her hips. "What d'you say, Ronnie?"

Without taking his eyes from hers, he climbed onto the bed. "I say, fuck yourself, baby." He lay on his side and pinched her nipples, and spread a heavy leg over her thighs.

Zoya writhed. "Oh, yes. Oooh, yes. Now. I want it *now!*"

"Sometimes we don't get what we want," Ron said, rolling until she looked at his back. "See you in the morning."

# Sixteen

Sleep wasn't an option.

Bliss stared at the Delft clock. Late and getting later.

Fabiola and Polly's mother had brought the kitchen clock back from a trip she'd made to Holland with her belly dancing class.

Lots of freshly laundered shirts smelled of starch. *All* freshly laundered shirts probably smelled of starch.

Sebastian wouldn't deliberately frighten her.

Would he?

Why would he?

Why would he frighten her, tell her to stay away from him, then make love to her?

She'd never felt before what she'd felt with Sebastian tonight.

But trust had to be built, to be earned. He'd given her more reasons to distrust than to trust him.

But they'd made such love.

Seated in a chair at the kitchen table, she folded her hands behind her head and gazed at the ceiling. She felt his hands on her, felt his body pressed to hers, inside hers, his mouth . . .

From outside, Spike's bark sounded an instant before someone hammered at the door.

Bliss got up and went to shoot the bolt open.

"You didn't even ask who was out here," Fab said, charging in, her face flushed. "You're too trusting, Bliss. It isn't safe."

Barely getting out of Spike's gambolling way, Bliss leaned

against the nearest counter. "What is it? Did you forget your key to the bungalow?"

Bursts of whispers came from the terrace.

Fabiola put a finger to her lips. "This is probably dumb, but how long have you been back?"

"Maybe an hour?" Bliss shrugged. "I'm not sure to the minute."

With Liberty clutching his bare arm, Vic entered the kitchen. His gray hair streamed down his oiled back. Bobby—in his pajamas—ran ahead of Polly, and Venus Crow put in one of her rare appearances.

"Mom's spending a few days with us," Polly said, sounding uncomfortable. "Hope you don't mind."

"You know I don't mind," Bliss said truthfully. Venus never failed to amuse and entertain her. The twins' mother had permanently adopted the traditional belly dancing garb she wore tonight—including a veiled headdress that all but masked her round face.

Naked to the waist of his black leather jeans, Vic closed the door and peered through a window into the darkness. "Quiet everyone." He turned out the lights and shone a small flashlight beam at the floor. "No one talks but me. Listen closely because I'm going to whisper."

"Vic—"

"Hush," he said, interrupting Bliss. "Did you hear the bell?"

Her scalp tingled instantly. "What bell?"

"A bell," Bobby said in a hoarse whisper that ended in a squeak. "There's a bell ringing out there."

"Shh, Bobby," Polly said. "Let Vic explain."

Polly disliked Vic. Just hearing her defer to him made Bliss nervous.

"I was working," Vic said.

"We were working," Liberty corrected him.

Fabiola said, "We can imagine."

"She's jealous."

Vic shushed Liberty. "That's enough, girls."

*"Girls,"* Fabiola hissed. "The asshole called us—"

*"Fab!"* Bliss was horrified. "Bobby's here."

"Sorry."

Bobby said, "I'm not listening."

"I'll try again." Vic expelled a loud breath. "We were working and it was pretty quiet. But I think we'd have missed it if we hadn't had the windows open. A bell—like a china bell, or something—tinkling. You know the sound. It would ring, then stop. Ring, then stop. Finally Lib and I went outside to listen. It was pretty close, we thought, but we couldn't see anything."

"Maybe you imagined it," Bliss said, not without hope.

Vic flipped back his hair. "It's really important for you feminist gurus to turn the tables on a man, isn't it?"

"By suggesting you've got an imagination?" It was understood that Bliss didn't appreciate having her academic field used against her. "I'll repeat, maybe you only thought you heard a bell."

Spike pushed a cold, wet nose into her hand and she jumped violently.

"That's what we said," Fabiola told her. "Mom thinks so, too, don't you, Mom?"

"That Vic merely imagined what he heard—no," Venus Crow announced in her full voice. "That what he heard was the result of a deep, subliminal connection to an extraterrestrial aura—absolutely. This type of linking is not unusual among people of exceptional intuitive powers."

"Oh, for God's sake," Liberty muttered.

"In your case," Venus said, "You probably thought you heard what Victor heard, simply because you are accustomed to living through his intensely sensual nature. An intensely sensual man would be very likely to intercept signals from other-worldly beings—such as the sound of a celestial bell."

"Celestial bell, my ass," Liberty said curtly. "This bell was outside Vic's cabin. I don't know anything about the shit you're spouting."

*"Liberty!"* Bliss said. "Please!"

"Yeah, right, the kid. Sorry."

A bell ringing in the night? Had she mentioned the previous incident to anyone, to Vic? She didn't think so.

"We stood and listened," Vic went on. "There would be silence for a few seconds. Then it would ring again. It got more distant, then closer, then more distant."

"Like it was beckoning to us," Liberty said.

"Garbage," Polly announced.

"They don't know what happened," Liberty said to Bliss. "They weren't there. We went for them on the way back. The other two, those two poets, are away for the weekend. We thought we should all be together to decide what to do."

"Call the police," Polly said promptly.

Bobby squealed and shouted, "Yeah, call the police!"

"Silence," Venus demanded. "There may be a spirit in need of help."

"Oh, Mom," Polly said, "you'll frighten Bobby."

"We followed in the direction we thought the ringing came from," Vic said. "It went toward the cliff—or seemed to."

Bliss waited, and when Vic didn't continue, she said, "Then what?"

Vic cleared his throat. "This feels really stupid."

"It is really stupid."

"Fab," Bliss pleaded. "Let's get through this."

"Someone laughed," Liberty said. Her throat made a noise as she swallowed. "It was weird. A really horrible laugh, like something out of a bad movie or something. A kind of gurgling laugh that gradually faded."

"Look," Vic said. "It seemed to us that the laugh fell. Does that make any sense to anyone?"

"Why are we all standing in the dark?" Polly asked. "Why—"

"Because if we turn on the light we can be seen from outside, while we can't see out," Vic said shortly. "That's an advantage I'd rather not give right now."

"Because you heard a falling laugh?" Fabiola sounded disgusted. "That's ridiculous."

"What if it wasn't a laugh?" Liberty said. "What if it was some sort of gurgling noise as someone fell? Down the hole, maybe? What if they were pushed? What if the person who pushed them is out there?"

"Call the police," Polly repeated.

Bliss moved. "Wait here." She sped from the kitchen and upstairs to her room. Making her way between shapes illuminated by a cloud-dulled moon, she went to her bedside table and felt over the surface. Her fingers closed on the Steuben bell and she let out the breath she'd been holding.

What would it have proved if the bell hadn't been there? She didn't know, but finding it was a relief anyway.

When she went back into the kitchen, Vic's flashlight picked out a row of feet lined up, one pair behind the other. Bliss frowned. "Now what?"

"We've got to go out there and check around," Liberty said. "Someone might be lying injured in the dark."

"I still say we ought to call the police."

"Not without looking around first," Vic said to Polly. "They'd just tell us we were hysterical—if they agreed to come at all."

"Why are you standing one behind the other?" Bliss asked.

Bobby said, "I want to go, too."

"You'll stay with Nanny," Polly told him. "Pull out the sofabed in the great room, Mom."

"I am Venus to all," the older woman said. "Love embodied in woman. Come with Venus, Bobby. I shall watch over you."

While Polly and Fabiola groaned, Bliss stood aside to let grandmother and grandson pass. Coins clinked on Venus's swishing costume.

"Are we ready?" Vic asked. "I'll go first. I'm not using the flashlight unless I decide it's safe, or I absolutely have to, so we'll have to be very careful where we step. Holding on to each other will help."

"Not if you fall," Fabiola pointed out.

Vic snorted. "I won't fall. Keep absolutely silent. If I say, run, do it. Just turn around and run for your lives—and call the police. But if I give you the word, I want you to attack."

"Attack?"

"Attack," Vic repeated in response to the collective question. "Leap forward and yell like hell. The only reason I'd ask you to do that would be if I saw something I thought we could scare off. Like an animal."

"Oh, spare me," Fabiola grumbled.

"I agree with Vic," Liberty said.

Polly's distinctive laugh made Bliss smile. "You agree with anything Vic says," she declared. "If he said the sky was green, you'd say you'd always thought so, too."

"Come on, Vic," Liberty said. "Let's go."

"Okay, okay," Polly muttered. "Just to keep you happy, we'll all go."

Bliss knew Polly wasn't going to keep anyone happy. Much as she didn't like Vic and Liberty, she was afraid to let them go on their crazy mission alone.

"Liberty holds me. Polly holds Liberty. Fabiola holds Polly. Bliss holds Fabiola."

Fabiola sniggered. "Thank you, Victor. And thank God it's dark out there. If anyone asks if I did this, I'll deny it."

As Vic opened the door, a cool breeze swept in. Dutifully, Bliss fell in at the back of the line and gripped Fab's waist. They stumbled outside, tripping over each other's heels.

"Close the door," Vic hissed. "Now, listen up. I'm going to count to three and on the count of three put your right feet forward. We'll keep a one and two, one and two, pace. Got it?"

"He's lost it," Polly suggested.

*"Got* it?"

"Got it," they chorused and on Vic's third count, set off.

Polly hummed a conga rhythm and offered, "Dum de dum, de dum—dah!" and almost caused an instant pile-up when she apparently added high-kicks to Vic's routine.

"Shape up," he ordered. "We don't know what we're going to face out here."

"Rockettes watch out," Fabiola said. "Your days are numbered. The Vickettes are on their way."

"Silence!" Vic shouted, then whispered, "Either be quiet or go back. This isn't a joke. We could break our necks out here."

They fell silent and concentrated. Bliss repeatedly scuffled to get back in step. The ground was rough and she prayed none of them would turn an ankle. The moon had taken a vacation, and total darkness fell upon the land.

She heard a whisper too low to make out, then another and another. Finally Fabiola turned and said, very softly, "Remember, if Vic says run, run back. If he gives the word, charge and shout. Pass it back."

"I am the back," Bliss pointed out. "What's the word?"

Fab had already faced forward again.

Bliss could smell the tang of the water. They emerged from the rough circle of cabins onto the open, downhill slope of ground in the middle of the estate. The going only became rougher.

A whisper started again and quickly arrived at Bliss. "Liberty's scared."

"Why?" she asked. "Does Vic see something?"

The question made its way downstream.

Back came the answer, "He said shut up and stay behind him."

"Chauvinist," Bliss mumbled. "I'd like to throw him to Prue for about five minutes."

Fab stopped abruptly and Bliss bumped into her. For an instant there was silence, except for the sound of heavy breathing, then Vic yelled, "Shit!"

The line broke. Bliss felt movement all about her. The others shouted and she saw their shapes moving, their arms flailing. She couldn't make out what they were attacking.

"Stop it!" Vic's howl rose above the ruckus. The flashlight clicked on and he shone the beam over the group. "Stand still, will you?"

Rather than run forward, each one had chosen a spot where they could jump up and down in place.

*"Women!"* Derision loaded Vic's voice. "You think this is funny, don't you? A farce? You should see yourselves."

"You said the word," Polly protested.

"I stubbed my friggin' toe, you idiot," Vic told her. "But look at that. Maybe you won't laugh so hard."

The flashlight beam picked up what looked like a long, thin white streamer trailing in the breeze.

Bliss wiped at her misted glasses and moved cautiously closer. They were within feet of the barbed wire surrounding the hole. "Good grief, Vic. One of us could have been badly hurt if we'd run into that."

He didn't apologize. "Maybe someone's already been badly hurt."

"Ooh," Liberty moaned. "Some poor soul is down the hole."

"Not unless they managed to get over or under the wire, work the cover off, then jump and still manage to pull the concrete back over them."

"Someone else could have done it to them," Vic said, somber.

"And hung around long enough to secure the wire again," Bliss pointed out, indicating the stakes that were still in place. "Not very likely."

Vic prided himself on his single-mindedness. "Regardless, I don't like the look of this."

"What is that?" Bliss asked, pushing past him and catching the trailing white stuff. She pulled it from the wire. "Shine the flashlight on this."

Barking distracted her. "Is that Spike?"

"Sounds like a pack of wolves on the loose," Vic responded. "Coming this way."

They all drew close together. Bliss was chilly in her silk dress and already shivered. The uproar from the animals raised goosebumps all over her body.

Not a pack, but two dogs burst into the beam of Vic's flashlight, one big dog—Spike—and one huge dog resembling an English sheepdog with a long, dark snout.

Liberty shrieked and threw herself at Vic.

Polly grabbed for Spike.

"It's a St. Bernard," Fab said. "Probably got a tinkly little bell around its neck instead of booze."

"It's Beater," a cool, very familiar voice said, and Sebastian emerged from the darkness. "And he's in love. What's going on here?"

She wanted to see him, yet she couldn't stand to see him. This was the kind of emotional mess she'd avoided for a long time. She would never be ready to cope with it again—certainly not with the intensity of her every reaction to Sebastian.

"Bliss," he said sharply, looming over her. "I asked what's going on here."

He was accustomed to taking command and it showed. "You don't want to know," she told him.

"If that was the case, I wouldn't have asked."

The dogs chased each other in circles, their yips and barks joyful.

"Spike hates other dogs," Fab said.

Sebastian looked over his shoulder at the animals. "You could have fooled me."

"I take it the other dog's yours," Bliss said.

"Yeah," he told her. "Beater. Man's best friend."

"You said it."

He didn't retaliate. "There's been a problem here?"

"Vic and Liberty heard someone cry out. We were checking around. This is the hole—the one the Point's named for. We thought—some of us were afraid someone might have fallen down there."

"Did they?"

"You never did have a subtle way with words," she said quietly. "Take a look and tell me what you think."

He held out his hand to Vic and said, "May I?" The other man silently gave up his flashlight.

Sebastian inspected the deep metal spikes that secured the wire, then he shone the beam on the concrete hatch, and on the surrounding ground. "This hasn't been moved," he said. "Whatever you think you heard, it wasn't anything to do with someone falling down there."

"Gee, thanks," Vic said, his voice laden with sarcasm and dislike. "Always nice to run up against a man who knows how to take charge."

"Think nothing of it," Sebastian said. "Call anytime. It's about time you were all in your beds."

They trudged uphill with Vic muttering every inch of the way. He and Liberty peeled off at Vic's cabin. Polly and Fabiola continued on to the lodge where Venus awaited them in the front doorway.

"Okay, Mom," Polly said. "Let's get you and Bobby back to the bungalow."

"I told this charming man where you were," Venus said, looking at Sebastian with obvious approval. "He's deep, very deep. A man gifted with advanced intuitive powers possessed by few."

"You told him where we were?" Fab said. "Without even knowing who he was, you told a perfect stranger where we were when you knew we were on the hunt for a marauder."

"You didn't find a marauder, did you?" Venus said, sounding triumphant. "How could you when the sounds came from the other side."

Polly gripped Fab's arm and shook her head to silence her sister. "Drop it," she said. "Come on, Mom. Let's take Bobby."

"Poor angel's asleep on the sofabed in there," Venus said, sighing. "Really, it isn't right to disturb a young spirit so often. He'll become disoriented."

"We're all disoriented," Bliss said, grimly, walked past Venus and into the lodge. "Shh. Bobby's asleep." A small lamp showed him curled in a bump in one corner of a queen-sized sofabed.

"I told you he was asleep," Venus said, sounding aggrieved. "And I knew this lovely man was a noble soul. I felt it. Deeply noble, deeply honorable—and available?" She smiled at Sebastian through her apple green veil.

*"Mom!"* Fab and Polly moaned in unison.

Sebastian said, "Thank you, ma'am," with laughter in his voice. "Is that Bobby? The little boy who watched Beater for me?"

"Yes—"

"Nice kid," Sebastian said, interrupting Bliss. "Let him sleep. I'll stay down here with him. He'll be okay until the morning."

"Well—"

"You've got my word he'll be safe," Sebastian assured Polly. "You two ladies run along with your Mom."

"Venus," Venus said. "Call me Venus. I am love manifested to all people."

"Right," Sebastian said, his face devoid of expression. "Bliss and I will return Bobby in the morning."

Bliss didn't trust herself to look at Polly and Fabiola.

"I'm sure that'll be very domestic," Fabiola said, her tone serene.

Polly added, "Just make sure you don't forget Bobby's here."

"It won't be the first time he's slept over—with me," Bliss said pointedly, staring at Sebastian. Why couldn't she suddenly find him repulsive? "You'd better make sure you take your dog with you when you leave."

"Oh, I will," he said, his smile warm enough to melt buttons, if Bliss had been wearing any. "All I have to do is whistle and he'll come running."

"I imagine all you have to do is whistle for anyone to come running," Fabiola said.

" 'Night, Fab," Bliss said. "See you bright and early."

"Bright and early," Polly said. She smiled crookedly and shepherded her mother and sister from the lodge.

When the door closed, silence folded about the room, silence filled with sensation, with connections Bliss felt to Sebastian. She felt him as surely as if he touched her.

"Tired?" he asked.

She indicated Bobby and put a finger to her mouth.

"If that wild troupe didn't wake him, nothing will."

"They're a great troupe," she said defensively. "A little unusual, but great."

"If you say so, Chilly."

"I hated that name."

"Do you hate it when I call you Chilly?"

Small talk to fill in the empty spots. "I don't hate anything you call me." Bliss swung away. Her mouth had always had a way of betraying her with Sebastian.

"You ran away from me again tonight."

She pulled off her glasses.

"A man could get a complex about a thing like that. Especially on this night, of all nights. I'm never going to forget the first time we made love."

Her heart turned, and her stomach followed. "Neither am I. We shouldn't talk in front of Bobby."

"He's asleep."

"Just in case."

"Okay—we'll go upstairs."

She shook her head. "You should go home. I'll be here when he wakes up so he's not scared."

"I'm not going home."

"Sebastian—"

"No. I belong with you. You got a bad scare at the Wilmans' and we're going to discuss that. I think there may be things we need to keep a watch out for."

"Like what?"

"Like the possibility that someone may be trying to make sure we never get together."

This time her heart seemed to stop altogether. "I know. But I'm confused."

"Tell me about confused."

Tell him she'd wondered, at least for a moment, if Sebastian himself had tried to frighten her in the conservatory?

"Why did you refuse to let me bring you home?"

"I needed to think. On my own."

"And what did you decide."

"I didn't. Why did you come here when I told you not to follow me."

He settled a hand on her back. "I went home first."

"You should have stayed there."

"I planned to."

"What changed your mind?"

"You don't want to know." He cleared his throat. "It's only fair for me to warn you that I'm potentially dangerous to your health."

Laughing when she felt like crying, Bliss turned toward him. "Do you think you have to tell me that?"

"Yes." His face was absolutely serious. "I think I'd convinced myself certain problems had gone away. They haven't. Bliss, I need to keep you where I can watch you."

The next flip in her stomach wasn't pleasant. "What do you mean by that?"

"I'm not sure. You told me earlier that you've been warned to stay away from me twice."

She nodded.

"Once here, and tonight. But tonight the guy got physical."

"Yes." The kind of physical she didn't want to think about.

"What exactly did I walk into when I arrived here?"

Bobby rolled over. "This will have to wait," Bliss said. "I don't want him to wake up."

He looked down at her mouth.

Bliss moistened her lips.

Sebastian bent toward her.

"Bobby!"—she backed away—"You'd better go before Bobby wakes up."

"I'm not leaving you alone here."

"I'm not alone."

"You know what I mean." He glanced at the boy. "He likes men."

The change of subject threw her.

"I felt that in him that first day."

"He's never really known his father," Bliss said. "He's the nicest boy. I love him."

Sebastian turned back to her. "You've got a lot of love to give, sweetheart."

"Go home, Sebastian."

Rather than make any move to do as she asked, he took off the dark green windbreaker he'd put on over the same shirt and suit pants he'd worn earlier. "Go on up to bed. I'll be comfortable here."

"No," Bliss told him. "Absolutely not. Bobby would be scared if he woke up with a stranger."

"He won't be scared. Take it from me, he'll like waking up and finding me here."

"You can't know that."

"Go on up to bed, Bliss. See you in the morning."

"Where will you sleep?"

"I'm great at recliners, remember?"

"Okay." Arguing had become too strenuous. "Have it your way. You'll call me if Bobby wakes up and he's scared?"

"Sure. But he won't be." He kicked off his shoes and rolled up his shirtsleeves. "Off you go."

Still she hovered. Bobby had only met Sebastian once.

"Go."

Bliss climbed the first few stairs and stopped again.

Sebastian looked up at her, his face all but obscured by Shadow. "Go, Bliss, or I'll have to take you upstairs myself. If I do that, I may not have the willpower to come back down again. Not without doing what I want to do right now."

"Don't say that," she whispered. "Please."

"You're beautiful."

"You're beautiful," Bliss told him, and meant it. "Why couldn't things have been different?"

"They're going to be. I'll make sure they are."

When he spoke like that, with utter conviction, she could

almost believe him. "You should go home. I should stay with Bobby."

"Go to bed. I'll stay with him. Go on."

When she still hesitated, he pointed toward her room, "Go, my love. I'll be here thinking about you up there. And I'll think about all of you, all of you and all of me—"

"Good night," she told him and ran the rest of the way up the staircase.

When she leaned over the railing along the landing, he was standing with his back to her, his hands on his hips. His hair shone black, his shirt very white. Then he turned to the sofa bed and pulled the sheet higher over Bobby.

Bliss ached with longing.

She went into her room and left her door slightly open. Surely Bobby would yell when he woke up and found himself with a stranger, a stranger she couldn't seem to stop wanting.

She stepped out of her shoes and went into the bathroom. A peek in the mirror was enough to remind her that this had been a tough night.

"Hag," she muttered, and threw the crumpled streamer she still held onto the counter.

It sparkled faintly.

Bliss picked it up and smoothed it out. Several long strands of white silk—and one strand of silver thread.

Her hand went to her throat.

In the conservatory, when the man had grabbed her, he'd tightened her scarf, then pulled it away. Bliss looked into the mirror again, looked at her bare throat above the low-cut bodice. She'd completely forgotten the scarf. A small red graze showed on one side of her neck.

With fingers that trembled, she smoothed the strands of silk. Pulled from her scarf—she was sure they were from her scarf. And she was sure that they were a message—for her. He would do anything he needed to do. And he could get at her whenever he chose.

Who could get at her? And why?

# Seventeen

"I'm not asleep."

Sebastian opened his eyes and looked into Bobby Crow's slender face. "You're not?"

The boy sat up and crawled closer. "Nope. I waited till Bliss stopped moving around to tell you. She's stopped moving around." He cocked his head. "Listen. She's stopped."

Sebastian already knew Bliss was in bed. He'd been thinking about that. "You ought to be asleep."

"You said I wouldn't be afraid to wake up and find you here."

"I said that, yes. Kids know when people like them. People who like them don't scare them."

"I don't get scared."

"You're past that phase, huh?"

"I look after my mom. I'm the man of the house."

"Your mom told you that?"

Bobby sat straighter. He wore Batman pajamas that probably hadn't been new when he got them. They were well-washed, and threadbare over the knees. His thin wrists and ankles protruded from too-short sleeves and legs. "Mom says we gotta stick together 'cause there's just us, and Auntie Fab. And Nanny."

"People should always stick together."

"Uh-huh." Bobby sucked in the corners of his mouth. His blue eyes were solemn. "You called Auntie Bliss beautiful."

"She is."

"Uh-huh. She said you were beautiful, too."

Sebastian felt himself color. "She was joking."

"She just meant she likes you a lot."

"You think that's it?"

"Uh-huh."

The boy's body had a bundle-of-sticks quality—bony, vulnerable. Sebastian glanced at the hands that seemed constantly in motion. They had the scrubbed, but never-quite-free-of-dirt appearance peculiar to small boys. Bobby's tow-colored hair was mussed and stood up at the crown.

A kid's face shouldn't show strain. Bobby's features formed a gut-wrenching picture of anxiety. "Something bothering you?" Sebastian asked.

The boy shook his head.

Sebastian shrugged and tried to stretch out more comfortably in a recliner close to the empty fireplace. Sagging recliners seemed to be Bliss's specialty.

"I guess you don't like kids."

The frightened note in Bobby's voice grabbed Sebastian's full attention. "What makes you say something like that?"

This time Bobby shrugged, brought his pointed shoulders all the way up to his ears. "Vic doesn't."

"I'm not Vic."

"My dad doesn't."

Sebastian swallowed. This was strange territory. "I'm sure your dad likes you."

Bobby frowned and shook his head.

If there were magic words, Sebastian didn't know them.

"My dad came here once. I was just a little kid then."

This was more than Sebastian had bargained for tonight. Or any night. "Sometimes it's hard for adults to say the right things to kids."

"Does your dad like you?"

"I don't have a dad."

"Oh."

They fell into a silence no more comfortable than the conversation had been.

"My dad doesn't like me," Bobby said with finality.

"You don't know that."

"He said so. He told me he didn't like boys with blue eyes and blond hair."

For the first time in his memory, Sebastian felt the sting of tears. "Sometimes grown-ups make jokes children don't understand."

"My mom picked me up for him to hold, but he wouldn't. He put his hands behind his back like this." Bobby gave a demonstration.

If the ground had slipped beneath him, Sebastian couldn't have felt more unsure of himself. "Maybe your dad's got a bad back." Stupid, stupid comment.

"Maybe," Bobby said. "He never came again."

Sebastian sat upright. "That's tough."

"He gave me five dollars."

"Wow."

"And some candy."

"Hmm."

Bobby strained his eyes upward and said, "My hair's brown now, isn't it?"

"Uh-huh."

"My dad said he'd be back through someday, but he hasn't come yet."

Sebastian felt a rare urge to kill. "Your dad's the unlucky one."

Bobby crossed his legs and watched Sebastian intently.

"He's missed out on being around a great kid. But your mom loves you, and your aunt and grandma. So does Bliss."

"Yeah."

Yeah, but a boy needed a man around. Sebastian looked at his fingernails. As long as the man wasn't like the one who'd made him spend his own childhood planning escape. "I was adopted," he said, and wondered why.

"Your dad went away, too?"

"I don't know what happened to my real father and mother. When I was adopted they had what was called closed adoptions. You didn't know all the details. I could go and try to find out now."

"You gonna do that?"

"No."

"Why?"

"Some people need to. That's great. They should do it. Other people don't. Maybe it's because they've decided . . . Oh, hell—I mean, I don't know why, but it doesn't figure in my life anymore." He was talking the philosophy of his life to a five-year-old in the middle of the night. "Go to sleep, Bobby."

The phone rang. He saw a cordless on the mantelpiece and jumped to grab it, hoping to stop Bliss from waking up. It rang a second time before he could press the talk button.

Bliss's sleepy voice said, "Hello."

He should hang up.

"I know it's late," a man said. "I had to call. I can't stop thinking about you."

Sebastian drew his lips back from his teeth and held his breath.

"Lennox?" Bliss said. "Is that you?"

"Who else? It was great of you to come to my show. Meant a lot to me."

"It wasn't anything. It is late."

"I can't sleep."

Bliss didn't answer.

"What happened was a mistake," Lennox said. " 'I shouldn't have pushed the way I did."

"It's history," Bliss said. "Forget it, Lennox. Move on."

"When you came to the show I thought—"

"I shouldn't have come. I just wanted to support you."

Bobby's upturned face was as still as a carving. The kid was too old for his years, too clued in to doing what would please adults.

"You shouldn't get involved with that Plato guy, Bliss."

Sebastian stood straighter, listened more intently.

"He's bad news. I've been doing some research on him, he—"

"Good night, Lennox."

"Bliss! Don't hang up. I want to see you."

"No."

"Please. I'd like to talk about moving back to the Point. I did some of my best work there. And we were great together."

"Memory has a way of turning into imagination."

"Stay away from Plato."

Bliss fell silent. While Sebastian held his own breath, he heard hers. Then he heard her hang up the phone, and, after several seconds, the click of Rood cutting his end of the connection.

Sebastian set down the phone.

"Are you mad about somethin'?"

He glanced at Bobby. If possible, the child's face had grown even more tight, his eyes more huge.

Sebastian smiled. "Of course I'm not mad." Puzzled. Suspicious. But not mad. He'd have to send Nose on a new fact-finding mission. "You'd better get some shut-eye." Before setting out to find Bliss tonight, he'd spent more time studying the photo with what appeared to be a human form looking toward Bliss in her bedroom. It could have been Rood. Or Jim Moore. Or a trick of the light and shadows . . .

"You got any kids?" Bobby asked, resuming his spot in one upper corner of the sofabed.

"No." Sebastian stood over the boy and pulled the covers up again.

"You gonna have some?"

Only a kid would ask a question like that so baldly. Sebastian smiled. "Maybe."

"This is a big bed," Bobby said, squinting up at him. "You can have the bit over there if you like."

Sebastian blew out a long breath. "Nice offer." Forming any

kind of a bond with a needy child when that bond would be short-lived, was wrong.

Bobby pulled one of the two pillows from beneath his head and pushed it to the far side of the bed. Without another word, he curled up again and squeezed his eyes shut.

With a glance toward Bliss's room, Sebastian lowered himself to the sofa and stretched out. He stacked his hands under his head and listened to the faint sound of the child breathing, breathing as if he was trying not to make any noise at all.

Lennox Rood hadn't entered his mind since the night of the incident in Bellevue Square. But the guy had warned Bliss to stay away from Sebastian.

And Jim Moore was moving in again—just when there'd been some vague hope the man might finally have let go.

Jim Moore knew about Bliss.

"You asleep?"

Sebastian turned his head toward Bobby. "No. But you should be."

"You got a dad when you were adopted."

After trying to see beyond the comment, and failing, Sebastian said, "Yes, I did."

"You were lucky."

No point in burdening a five-year-old with trouble he didn't already have. "I guess I was. The people who adopted me are both dead. They weren't young when they took me."

"Hmm."

Bobby fell silent. After several minutes he said, "You any good at telling stories?"

Sebastian's mind went blank.

The boy rolled over. "I didn't mean I wanted you to tell a story," he said, pressing his eyes tightly shut. "I just wondered is all."

Sebastian studied the young face with its promise of strong features to come. He stretched out his arm and ruffled hair turned the texture of straw by the sun. Bobby wriggled closer.

"Long ago and far away, at the very top of the world, there

was a family . . ." Sebastian paused. "It's the middle of summer and I'm telling a Christmas story."

"I like Christmas stories best of all."

"Good. It's the only one I can remember right now. At the North Pole there was a family of master chocolate makers who worked for Santa Claus . . ."

Sebastian awoke with a cramp in his shoulder.

He blinked at faint bands of early-morning light through warped venetian blinds. A scent of dust, overlaid with soap, emanated from the child bundled against his side, with his head resting beneath Sebastian's chin.

Very carefully, a little awkwardly, he patted the boy's arm. Making a child happy didn't have to be so hard. Why did some people make it impossible—and so painful for the kid? Not that Bobby's mom wasn't doing her best. Sebastian could tell how hard she tried and how much she loved her boy—and how much he loved her.

He heard another sound and turned his head. Bliss sat halfway down the stairs, looking at him through the balusters. Her hands were crossed on her knees, with her chin on top.

He mouthed, "hi," and she mouthed, "hi," back and wiggled her fingers at him. The sadness in her eyes turned his heart.

Bliss got up and came slowly to stand at the side of the bed. She offered him her hand and he took it, and squeezed. She bent and kissed his palm, released him, and went in the direction of the kitchen.

Sebastian eased away from Bobby, who scarcely stirred before nestling deeper into the covers.

Swathed in a worn, blue poplin wrapper, Bliss stood in the open doorway from the kitchen to the patio and vegetable garden. The earliest rays of the sun touched her hair, lighting a fiery nimbus around the auburn. Carefully shutting himself in with her, Sebastian approached on silent feet to stand only inches behind Bliss.

When he rested a hand on her shoulder, she didn't move.

Birds sang outside.

A light wind brought scents of lavender, and rose, and mint and sweet basil into the kitchen.

He touched Bliss's hair, and smiled when it clung to his skin, and sprayed upward as he lifted his fingers again. Sun shone through the drifting strands, picked out sparkling lights.

There had never been tenderness for him. Except with Bliss. Not before her, nor after her—until now. Now there was the chance to recapture tenderness, and he wouldn't let that chance go away.

"The wanderers return," Bliss said.

He held her waist and looked past her. Sighing in the sun, Beater and Spike lay in an untidy heap. "I told you Beater was in love."

"Good job we're responsible pet owners," Bliss commented. "Looks as if those two made quite a night of it. They're worn out."

"You remind me of everything I've never had," Sebastian said. He pulled her hair aside and kissed her neck. "I didn't even know how much I wanted them until I met you."

"Which time?"

He rotated her toward him. "The first time. Now I'm remembering all over again. You know what's so amazing?"

She shook her head. Freshly washed, her skin had a transparent quality.

"It's amazing I can love."

Her eyes closed. The frown that drew her brow down was filled with pain.

"Forget I said that," he told her hurriedly. "It doesn't matter."

"It matters to me. So you mean it's amazing you can love because you never had any examples—of love—to follow? To imitate?"

"Maybe. Yeah, I do. Until you. When you let me hold your hand for the first time I was a goner, lost—lost to love. I never had a chance after that. Corny, huh? I couldn't believe the feeling. You made me crazy. I wanted to shout. My throat quit working properly."

"I know."

He rubbed the sides of her face with his fingertips. "How could you know?"

"How do you think? You always said we were the same."

"We're not, though, are we? We're just different enough to make one hell of a couple."

"But can we get through all the stuff, Sebastian? So much *stuff*."

Hope burst in his breast. "We can do it, love. Trust me, we can do it."

She lowered her eyes.

"What?" He shook her gently and kissed her forehead. "What is it?"

"You want to make everything go your way. You think you can just say, this is the way it is, and make it so. Life isn't like that."

"It can be."

"No, Sebastian." She took his hand from her waist and stepped around him. "No. We've got too much to work through. I've got to know all about you, all about the years when you weren't around. Starting with the day you didn't show up to marry me."

"Bliss—"

She held up a hand. Her long legs were a clear silhouette through thin cotton, a lovely silhouette. He looked away.

"Last night I got another warning. Of sorts. I'm not even sure what it meant. But that was number three."

"Two." Or was she counting Lennox Rood?

"Three. Look at this." She pulled the collar of the robe aside to reveal a red mark on her neck. "See that?"

"From when the guy grabbed you by your scarf?"

"Yes."

"That was the second—"

"The third was all that nonsense you ran into outside. With

the ringing bell routine, and threads from my scarf on the wire around the hole."

"You didn't say anything about that."

"I forgot. There was a lot going on."

"Threads from your scarf? How can you be sure?"

She opened the dishwasher and took out two clean glasses. "My scarf's gone."

"You didn't say—"

"I didn't say it was gone at the time? Maybe that was because I had my hands full with other . . ." She tossed back her hair and blushed. "I was busy with other things."

Sebastian smiled and went to rub her back. She held the edge of the sink and leaned against the pressure.

"We were very busy, weren't we?" He slipped a hand around her and inside the robe to cover her breast through a silky gown. "We've got lost time to make up. Don't you think it's time we got started in earnest."

"Bobby's out there."

"He's sleeping. And I'd hear the door. I wasn't suggesting we get naked right here and now.

"I can't think with you doing that to me."

He smiled into her hair. "That's the idea. Can I tell you what else I'd like to do to you?"

"No."

Her nipple was already erect and he made circles over it with his palm. "I'll tell you very quietly."

"Oh, stop."

"You don't want me to."

"No, but you've got to stop. Now. Sebastian, someone took my scarf at the party. Then they hooked some strands from it on the wire by the hole. Do you know all about the hole?"

He grew still. "I know it's there. That's all."

"It's covered because it's dangerous. Big enough for a good-sized person and apparently vertical for a long way before it takes a slight turn. If you fell down there you'd get lodged before you reached the bottom—not that you'd still be alive—or at least conscious. It was filled once but the way the water enters some sort of shallow cave underneath gradually sucks the fill out. It washes away."

"Plug it with concrete."

"I intend to. When I can afford it."

"I can afford it." He knew his mistake as soon as he'd made it. "I mean I could float you a loan—lend—*hell,* I could fill the damn hole for you, period!"

"Don't swear at me."

"I—yi—yi," he dropped his hands. "I'm so frustrated."

"You want to control everything in sight. I'm not someone you can control. Get used to the idea."

He'd let that go—for now. "You can access money of your own."

"Not without my father's agreement. He and my mother don't believe in this venture. My dad hates it that my aunt left Hole Point to me. I'm not asking him to help me keep it going."

"With your own money?"

"I'm not asking."

"Okay." He pulled a chair across the floor and sat down in the slice of sun through the open back door. He stripped off his shirt and draped it over his knees. The warmth felt good on his skin. "What are we going to do?"

"Drink our orange juice."

He took the glass she offered and drained it. "Now what?"

Bliss drank her juice. Her upturned throat was pale and smooth, smooth all the way to the shaded cleft between her breasts. She took both of their empty glasses to the sink and set them inside.

"You've been warned to stay away from me."

"I don't know why," Bliss said, crossing her arms. "Who would want to stop us from being together?"

At least she spoke as if their being together was something that had to be worked out.

"You don't have any ideas?" He couldn't talk about Crystal and Jim Moore—not yet, maybe not ever.

Looking at her bare feet, she walked slowly to stand between Sebastian and the open door. "I've never been good at lying—even when it might be good for me."

"What does that mean?"

"I did another of my stupid running away acts last night."

Her downcast lashes were dark red, but tipped blond. He just wanted to hold her and never let go. "You want to talk about that."

"No. But I'm going to. The guy's sleeve smelled of starch."

He inclined his head.

Her blue eyes flashed at him and down again. "The guy at the Wilmans'. Then—when you put your arms on my shoulders after, after we made love." Her lips made a small O as a breath whistled out. "Your sleeve smelled of starch, too."

Sebastian narrowed his eyes and considered. "Maybe I'm not getting this straight."

"Yes you are. I'm stupid sometimes. Or, as my daddy loves to say, I'm book-smart, but street-stupid."

"You think—"

"Thought. For just long enough to make a fool of myself—again. I decided you might have done it to make me run to you because I was afraid."

He considered himself an intelligent man, but he was having trouble with her logic. "You thought I told you to stay away from me so you'd come to me because you were scared? Is that what you're telling me?"

Her laughter surprised him. She pressed her hands to her cheeks and laughed the way she used to when they were teenagers. "Idiot. I'm an idiot. What can I say? I never said I'd become any wiser about worldly things."

"You aren't worldly." He struggled with his own desire to laugh with her. "You never were. I remember how you never got jokes."

"I—still—don't." Bursts of giggles replaced her laughter. "I'm sorry, Sebastian. Honestly, I was so rattled it just washed over me and I couldn't think straight. When the waiter opened the door, I thought I'd die. I'm still rattled, only . . ."

When she didn't continue, he reached to clasp her hips and guide her closer. "Only?"

"Only now I'm with you and nothing else seems important. I watched you in there with Bobby. Sebastian, you are a nice man. A special man. You wouldn't do anything to hurt anyone—not deliberately."

He shook his head. "No, I wouldn't. And, if you're very good, I'll forgive you for thinking evil—stupid, evil things about me."

"Oh, *you.*"

Sebastian rubbed the dips in front of her hip bones with his thumbs. That tenderness, that great, dangerous, irresistible tenderness charged again. He wanted to lose himself to her.

Sun through the door outlined her legs with a golden line. When he looked up at her, the same light shimmered about her hair and threw shadows into the hollows of her pointed face.

The tenderness overwhelmed him and he wrapped his arms around her hips, buried his face in her belly. If there were names for the feelings he had, he didn't know them.

Bliss stroked his hair, bent over his head and rested her chin on his bare back. She rocked him. Rocked him gently as no one had ever rocked him.

"I'm tough, y'know," he murmured. "Ask anyone how tough I am."

"You're tough," she agreed. "Me, too. Tough, independent champion of independent women, that's me."

"Uh-huh. Bliss, don't leave me again."

Still she rocked him.

"There's no point in my covering up with you," he told her. "You know where I came from, and what I was."

"You were a great kid in a lousy situation."

"I loved you then, Bliss. I love you more now, if that's possible."

"It's possible. I . . ."

"Finish," he said, when she didn't.

"I want to try to work it through, Sebastian. You and me. Really work it through. But we're going to have to deal with whatever craziness is going on first. There is something going on."

"Yeah. I know." The sun made her warm to the touch. "Leave it to me, please." Jim Moore had done his worst. From now on, Sebastian would call the shots with him.

He heard loud knocking on the front door, followed moments later by Bobby calling out for his mother.

Bliss shot away and dashed into the great room with Sebastian at her heels. "Wait," he told her, dragging on his shirt. "Don't open the door until we're sure who it is."

"Auntie Bliss!" Bobby had jumped to sit on the back of the sofabed. The knocking resumed and the boy pulled his feet beneath him. "Auntie Bliss!"

"It's okay, Bobby," Sebastian told him. "Stay real quiet while I see who it is."

He caught Bliss as she started to open the door and swung her behind him. "Who is it?" he called.

"You don't know me. Name's Cozens. Someone's in trouble out here. I need to get help."

Sebastian considered.

"On the bluff!" the man shouted. "I saw him from the water. He's on a ledge."

"Oh, my God," Bliss said. "Open the door."

"I'll be right out." Sebastian turned to Bliss and held her arms."You stay here with Bobby until I make sure this guy's for real. Understand?"

She stared at him.

"Coming," he shouted. He opened the door to a middle-aged man in a sweat-stained orange T-shirt and green oilskin pants.

"I'm Gil Cozens." Pointing south, he inclined his head. "We live a few miles from you. I was fishing. There's an easement. I hauled the boat out of the water and ran here."

Sebastian felt the man's anxiety and it was real. "Okay, let's go."

Cozens peered into the lodge at Bliss. "You better come, too, ma'am. Someone will probably have to stay with him and someone'll probably have to go for help. Or we could be lucky and get him. It's not too far down there. I think he may be hurt pretty bad, though."

"Take Bobby and go for Vic," Sebastian said. He followed Cozens, started to run when the other man did so.

They almost collided with Vic as he came from behind the yew hedge that surrounded his cabin. Shirtless, Vic stretched and frowned. "Whassamatter?"

Every time Sebastian saw Vic, he liked him less. "Come on," he told him shortly, not breaking stride.

Cozens bypassed the wire-enclosed hole and didn't stop until he arrived at the edge of the bluff. He dropped to his knees and cautiously extended his head.

Sebastian reached Cozens's side and looked down.

"Shit," Cozens muttered. "Oh, shit."

Sebastian leaned farther out—and immediately knelt beside the fisherman. No more than twenty feet below, on a craggy ledge, lay a man. One arm and leg lolled over the edge. The other leg bent double between the man and the bluff.

Vic joined them. He stretched out on his belly and stared downward. He said, "Holy . . . The falling laugh. That's what it must have been."

Rumpled khaki pants and shirt littered with many sagging pockets. Thin, bruised, blood-streaked face—the eyes staring at the sky.

"My fault," Sebastian said. "My fault, dammit."

Nose wouldn't be taking any more candid camera shots.

# Eighteen

"His poor wife," Bliss said. She stood beside Sebastian and Vic while a gurney bearing the dead man's body was lifted into an ambulance. After hours of questioning, Gil Cozens had been told he could go home.

"Yeah," Sebastian said. "I'll have to go and see her. I feel responsible."

Vic hitched at his pants and slouched. "Jealousy's a dangerous animal, friend."

"Are you talking to me?" Sebastian gave Vic his full attention.

"If the cap fits." The sky interested Vic. "Bliss is important to all of us here at the Point. She's not like most women. Not like most people."

"You're telling me this?"

The ambulance pulled away, followed by a second aid unit. Four police cars had responded to Bliss's emergency call. Three had left ahead of the ambulance, the fourth remained while final photographs were taken at the accident scene.

"Most guys don't hire private eyes to make sure a woman doesn't step out of line."

"Not now, Vic," Bliss said. Sebastian knew—had known the man. A Mr. Nose who was a private investigator in Sebastian's employ. Later Bliss's anger over that would explode. For now sadness blunted any other feelings. When Maryan Plato had spoken of a private detective, Bliss hadn't taken her seriously. That Sebastian would have her watched was unbelievable.

Vic wasn't deterred. "Hey, some poor bastard's dead because of this creep. I never did get it quite straight about you two, anyway. Old friends, is that right?"

"Yes," Sebastian said with an icy edge that scared Bliss. "Very old friends. And you rent one of Bliss's cabins, is *that* right?"

Vic gathered his hair in one hand and gave it a shake. "We aren't just landlady and tenants here. This is a community. Bliss has made a commitment to further the arts by providing peaceful, affordable refuge to deserving artists."

"You sound like a commercial," Sebastian commented. He was absolutely still. "I am not a jealous man."

"No? You just hire a snoop to watch Bliss for kicks? Take it from me, buddy, this is a lady who lives a squeaky clean life. She doesn't have a thing to hide. Not a thing for you to be worried about. As in, I never saw her with a man before you—except Rood, and that was a mistake she soon wised up to. And I never saw Rood coming out of her bedroom."

*"Vic!"* The morning's events had left Bliss shaken. She couldn't bear this bickering. "A tragedy happened here last night. Sebastian didn't want it anymore than you or I did. Could you please go back to Liberty? She's upset, too."

"And leave you with him? Bliss, you're a babe-in-the-woods. Jealous men are often violent men."

"How true," Sebastian said, his voice deceptively even.

Bliss shot to stand between the two men. "I've known Sebastian since we were kids, Vic. He is not violent. If you do care about me the way you say you do, please go home."

"Yeah, Vic. Go home."

"Sebastian!" She swung to face him. "Stop baiting him."

"I don't have to give an explanation to Vic, here, but for the record, I hired Nose to help me when I was trying to locate Bliss. We'd lost touch a long time ago. I intended to tell him I didn't need his services now, but things have been a bit hectic."

"Nice little story," Vic said.

Bliss thought, *pat little story.*

"The only story you're going to get," Sebastian said. "Now cut out."

A sand-colored Mercedes bumped down the potholed drive, paused in front of the police car, and veered sharply toward the lodge. It drew to a halt beside Sebastian's black pickup.

"Oh, no," Bliss moaned. "This is too much."

Morris Winters got out of the Mercedes, regarded the police car for too long, and slammed the heavy door of his car. Jutting his formidably square jaw, he strode toward his daughter with the purposefully sharp-eyed stare that had become his trademark. Hawk Winters, Eyes of the People, Eyes for the People.

Bliss had learned that her father's eyes looked only inward—toward himself, and whatever would serve his ambitions.

"Bliss," he said, bearing down on her. "Get rid of these two clowns. We've got to talk, my girl."

"Dad—"

Her father waved her to silence. "Still a complete mess," he said, sweeping his eyes over the cropped pink T-shirt and worn denim skirt she'd grabbed that morning. He curled his lip and pointed at Sebastian. "Plato?"

Vic said, "You know where to find me, Bliss."

She nodded, and managed to smile at him before he set off toward his cabin.

Sebastian and her father faced each other. "Damn you," Morris Winters said. "I recognize you from the paper. What's that doing here?" He indicated the police car.

"A man died here last night," Sebastian said succinctly. "The police think he tripped and fell at the edge of the bluff. Hit his head and died."

"Oh, my God." Morris pushed back his corduroy jacket and gripped his slim hips. Not a sandy hair was out of place. "The press will make something out of that, too."

"Daddy," Bliss said. "A man died. It's tragic. And that's what you should be thinking, instead of worrying about how it'll affect you. Why are you here anyway?"

"Don't tell me how to react," he snapped. "You never did understand the score, did you? You've always had to make yourself a liability to me. Well, it's going to stop. Now."

"Make sure you don't hit my truck on your way out, Winters."

Bliss gaped at Sebastian.

Her father swept past them both and went into the lodge—and a familiar dark green limousine crawled onto the property. Masked in dark glasses and a red head-scarf, Maryan Plato got out before the chauffeur could come to her aid. The same shiny raincoat she'd worn on her last visit was in place, but this time her high-heeled shoes were red.

Sebastian crossed his arms and waited until she reached him. "What the hell are you doing here, Sis?"

"Trying to save you from yourself," she said, ignoring Bliss. She flapped a newspaper. "Have you seen this?"

"Bliss and I have already had a very long, very difficult day."

"There's a photo of you with all those bleeding-heart, save-our-children types screaming at you. She's in it." Maryan pointed the paper at Bliss. "That bitch O'Leary scored a great point. She said Bliss Winters is a rebel who'd do anything to hurt her father. She said she's deliberately hanging out with you to try to hurt his political career."

"Maryan. I want you to get back in that car and go home."

"Don't you tell me what to do," Maryan shouted. "Don't you understand the inference. She can hurt her daddy's career by being photographed with a man who lures nubile girls to their deaths, a man who feeds them like tadpoles to his shark buddies in the porno biz. She's *using* you."

A queasiness attacked Bliss's stomach. Her head buzzed.

"Notice she's not saying anything," Maryan pointed out. "What the paper doesn't say—because they don't know—is that she's paying you back for having the sense to duck out on her years ago. So don't fuck everything up now, Bro. We've been through too much to get where we are. What do you think you're doing? Chasing your lost youth? You need some entertainment—real entertainment. I'll make sure you get some. Now, let's get out of this dump."

"Bliss!"

She heard Sebastian say her name and realized she'd clutched his sleeve. "Sorry." She started to let go, but he covered her hand on his arm.

Without replying to Maryan, Sebastian led Bliss inside the lodge. "You don't look good," he said, as if Morris Winters weren't pacing the shabby great room, and as if Maryan hadn't followed them into the building. "I want you to go upstairs to your room. I'll help your father calm down."

"Help me calm down!" Morris all but charged Sebastian. He halted inches in front of him, his hands opening and closing at his sides. "You upstart. You piece of trash. You are nothing. I know it and you know it. And if you don't gather up your marbles and get out of town I'm going to make sure you get kicked out of every game in the country. Do we understand each other?"

Bliss watched, paralyzed, as Sebastian narrowed the distance between himself and her father to a short breathing space. "I know who I am—and what I am. Do you know who and what you are, or would you like me to explain those details to you?"

"Get out of Washington State." Morris's voice had lost a trace of its certainty. He was a tall man, but not as tall as Sebastian. Suddenly Bliss's father seemed smaller than he ever had—and older.

"Darn it, Dad. You're making a fool of yourself—and me."

Her father turned an even darker shade of red. "Don't you *ever* speak to me like that, my girl."

"Bliss isn't a kid you can push around anymore," Sebastian said. "I'm here and I'm staying. I'm staying until I decide I don't want to stay anymore. And as long as Bliss is here that won't happen, so I guess you're going to have to get used to knowing we inhabit the same territory."

"I'll put you out of business." Morris saw Maryan. He stared at her. "Big sister to the rescue as usual?"

Sebastian eyed Maryan. "Have you two met before?"

"Not in the flesh"—Maryan showed her sharp little teeth—"fortunately. I called his office earlier and asked for a few words with the great man. I was told he wasn't in, but evidently he just wasn't in to me."

"You've got it, girlie."

Bliss sat down hard on the couch. "Girlie, Dad? For God's sake."

"Peddle your politically correct crap somewhere else, Bliss. And remember whose side you're on."

"Mine," Sebastian said calmly. "I'd have thought political correctness came pretty high up on your list."

Morris rolled from his heels to his toes and back. He sniffed. The color in his face notched down from puce to pink. "Okay. Okay, let's back off and calm down. Tempers got a bit out of hand for a moment there. We're reasonable men. Let's talk." A gesture of his left hand took in Bliss and Maryan. "Why don't you two gir— You ladies must have other things to occupy you. Run along. I'll say good-bye before I leave, Bliss."

She laughed. She couldn't help it.

No one laughed at Morris Winters. "Get a hold of yourself. Damn it, you were a difficult child and you're still difficult. You've got a lot of growing up to do. Good thing your aunt made sure you couldn't get your hands . . ." He twisted his neck inside his collar. "We'll talk about that later."

"Maybe you should talk about it now," Sebastian said, all silk.

Maryan met Bliss's eyes and the message was clear, *I told you he wanted your money.*

"Dad," Bliss said. "Maryan can go where she pleases. This is my home and I'm not going anywhere."

Maryan started a slow hand-clap.

"Shut up," Sebastian said. "And either go to the office, or wherever you're supposed to be, or sit down and be quiet."

Morris's withering glance in Maryan's direction was a wasted effort. She took off her coat, left on the glasses and scarf, and arranged herself at the opposite end of the couch. A red tank top clung to her breasts and pouted over her nipples. A matching, rib-knit skirt barely covered her panties—also red from where Bliss sat.

A police officer tapped the door and entered, taking his cap off as he did so. He nodded at Bliss, cast a speculative eye over Morris and Maryan, and beckoned to Sebastian. "Could I ask you to step outside, sir. Just one or two more questions have come up."

Maryan made to get up. A glance from Sebastian subdued her.

"Can we talk some sense now?" Morris asked when Sebastian had left the lodge. He spoke as if Maryan were absent or deaf. "Your mother took time out of a busy schedule to come and see you."

"Made her late for a hair appointment did I?"

"Don't put your mother down to me."

"Sorry." She wasn't.

"She told me what she found here. What happened."

When Bliss didn't respond, Maryan said, "What did happen?"

"Be quiet, or get out," Morris told her.

Bliss smiled sweetly and said, "Mother was a bit surprised when Sebastian came down from my bedroom—it was early in the morning and she has such a suspicious mind."

Maryan's already thin mouth all but disappeared.

"Disgusting," Bliss's father said. "A woman of your background fornicating with a—"

"That's enough," Bliss told him. "Don't talk about Sebastian like that. You don't know him."

"I don't want to." His eyes returned repeatedly to Maryan. "I didn't get your message until I'd already left to come here. If I'd known you'd called, I'd have made a point of speaking to you. Maybe you can help me sort out this mess."

Maryan crossed her legs.

The glimpse of red satin between her thighs wasn't wasted on Morris. "You left a number. Can I be forgiven for being an overbearing male? Will you allow me to call you later and discuss our common interests?"

Once Bliss would have wilted in the presence of her father's blatant sexual overtures to women other than her mother. At this point, his apparently flourishing appetite simply interested her—and disgusted her.

"We can talk," Maryan said, crossing her arms beneath her breasts with predictable results. "My brother is a hothead. He doesn't always think, but he's a helluva businessman—a natural—I'm sure he'll come around."

And she, Bliss thought, might as well be an annoying piece of wallpaper that needed to be hidden by a coat of fresh paint.

Sebastian returned with a deep frown line between his brows. "Are we finished, Mr. Winters? Yes, we're finished. Good. Have a great day."

Maryan rose from the couch and went through the pointless exercise of smoothing her almost nonexistent skirt. "I'll be at the office later this afternoon, Seb. We both need some time to cool down. Be there, will you? Around, ooh, four?"

"Bye, Sis."

"Four?"

"*Bye,* Sis."

Turning her mouth down, Maryan swept up her coat and flung it around her shoulders.

Pounding footsteps of the small, bare variety, made their way through the kitchen and exploded, with their out-of-breath owner, into the great room. "Sebastian!" Bobby yelled, and threw himself at his new favorite person. "Mom's coming. She wouldn't let me out till those police cars left. I wanted to come and see."

"Your mom knows best," Sebastian said, swinging the boy off his feet. He hiked a delighted Bobby onto his shoulders and wrapped his arms around the child's legs. "This is my buddy, Bobby," he told Maryan, whose mouth appeared likely to remain permanently open.

Polly came into the room. At the sight of Maryan she stopped as if stunned.

"Hi, Polly," Bliss said, freshly angry at the memory of Maryan's previous callous behavior toward Polly. "Oh, I forgot to ask how you made out when you called Raptor. Polly's a singer, Sebastian. She's very good. Needs the right break, like most people. Maryan told her to call someone called Zoya? She runs the talent agency for you? Maryan said Zoya would arrange for Polly to come in to see if there might be something Raptor could do for her."

Sebastian was staring at Maryan. "When would that have been? You were here before?"

"Just stopping by to say hi to an old friend," Maryan said smoothly. "After all, it isn't as if Bliss and I are strangers."

"No," Bliss agreed. "We met once before—for five minutes."

"Why did you come here?" Sebastian asked Maryan.

"I told you. To say hi."

"Garbage," Sebastian told her. To Polly he said, "Can you be reached here?"

"Y-yes." Polly's mouth trembled.

He smiled reassuringly. "Zoya will call you and set up an appointment. This is a fine young man you're bringing up. You must be very proud of him."

Bliss could have kissed him. She'd known for too long that Bobby's confidence was almost zilch. This afternoon, using Sebastian's ears as handles, he glowed.

A swish of silky raincoat drew Bliss's attention back to Maryan. Fury drew her features tight. She spared Bliss a withering look that traveled her length, then made for the door, not, Bliss noted, without a parting glance in Morris's direction.

"Thanks for coming," Bliss said, and instantly regretted her mean effort. "It'll be okay, Maryan. Trust Sebastian to do the right things for everyone."

The sunglasses came off, revealing puffy eyes underscored with dark lines. "You trite bitch," Maryan said. "The first time I met you, I detested you for what you are."

Such bald hatred stunned Bliss.

Her father busied himself checking his pockets for some mystery possession.

It was Sebastian who gave Maryan his full, furious attention.

"That's really too bad," he said. "A real shame. It's going to make things pretty complicated."

"Not from where I'm looking," Maryan said, replacing her glasses. "You're no fool, Seb. You know who your best friend is. You know who'll always be there for you—who'll make sure you get whatever you need."

"I think I do," he told her. He lifted Bobby from his shoulders and put the child's hand in his mother's. "D'you suppose you two could track Beater down for me?"

"He's—"

Polly interrupted Bobby, "Of course we will. Come on. Bobby. We'll make sure he gets some water and food, too."

Without waiting for the door to entirely close behind Polly and Bobby, Maryan swaggered to hang on Sebastian's arm. "I'll send the car back and come with you."

Firmly, but gently, he disengaged her grip. "Go in the car. We'll talk later."

Maryan's gray eyes sparked. "I need to discuss some things with you and they can't wait."

"And I need to discuss some things that can't wait," Sebastian said. "But not with you."

Bliss felt uncomfortable.

"Morris?" Sebastian said.

"I think Mr. Winters would be more appropriate."

"You asshole."

"Sebastian!" Bliss said.

"Yeah. Sorry, *Mr. Winters*. Your daughter doesn't like me to swear—so I try not to."

"Shit," Maryan muttered.

"Do you have anything to say to me before you leave, Plato?"

"Sure do, Mr. Winters." Sebastian smiled—the picture of charm and respect. "I'm going to marry your daughter."

# Nineteen

Some might say he'd made a tactical error. Sebastian preferred to consider himself a brilliant wartime strategist. Bliss was definitely not dripping honey all over him in the wake of his announcement, but desperate conditions called for desperate measures and he'd been damned desperate. He'd risen to the occasion.

She wouldn't look at him.

Morris had been the first to thunder from the lodge, spewing threats—and assurances that Bliss would never be Sebastian's wife. Maryan had hung around a few minutes longer to question Sebastian's basic intelligence quotient, then, finally and blessedly, left in a shoe-slapping flurry.

Bliss still hadn't said a word.

But she hadn't told him to fuck off and die, either.

No, he'd better try to stop even *thinking* those words. She hadn't told him she wouldn't marry him, or that he was all kinds of a fool, a presumptuous fool, for saying she would.

"I think you've lost your mind, Sebastian. I'm not going to marry you."

And that exploded whatever small reassurances he'd allowed himself until now. "Yes, you are."

"No, I'm not." She delivered the statement with her pointed chin raised and mutiny in her blue, blue eyes.

And he never backed away from what he wanted, and what he was going to get. "You will marry me. You may fight what you really want, but in the end you'll give up and give in. We're going to be married."

"You're arrogant."

He bent forward from the waist and went to her, brought his face close to hers. "Why don't you let it all hang out? Say something really terrible, like, mmm"—for an instant he couldn't find the words, then they came to him—"Like, you nasty man, you. Try it, babe. I promise you I'll still respect you, even if you do sully your pristine lips with such epithets."

"I hope you never call me *babe,* again"—she tried to make more space between them—"Darn, you, Sebastian, you're so abysmally sarcastic."

He frowned. "A-bys-mal? Great going, Bliss. That sounds really obscene. I'm proud of you."

"I didn't believe Maryan when she told me you were having me followed."

"Maryan"—he processed the comment—"Maryan told you that?"

"Maryan's a miserably unhappy woman. Maybe you should give her a break. She obviously loves you too much. And yes, she told me you'd hired a private detective to follow me around."

In other words, Maryan had come to Bliss to mix things up, to point out what a worthless shit he was, and how wise Bliss would be to wish him *adios.* His sister would get her chat, but she wouldn't like it.

"You hired someone to spy on me," Bliss said, her voice rising.

"I did do that. Before I got here to Washington, and for a while afterward. I needed to be sure I wasn't breaking in on you if you had a husband and ten kids."

"I don't. You knew that some time ago. That poor man died last night and it was completely pointless."

"And I feel partially to blame. I should have told him to"—he recalled the shadowy shot of the inside of Bliss's bedroom—"I intended to release him. The appropriate moment didn't occur before it was too late."

"You don't like losing women, do you? It makes you angry and vengeful."

"Where did that come from?"

"I don't know." She shrugged and turned a little pink. "Just an idea I had. Forget it."

"I don't think so, Bliss. What do you mean?"

"I don't know what I mean! Just drop it."

"Was it something else Maryan said? Another of her persuasive arguments?"

"Drop it, please. I don't know most of what I'm saying. I haven't slept in almost two days."

"Neither have I."

"Of course." Sliding along the couch, away from him, she pushed to her feet. "Are you in financial trouble?"

She caught him off guard. "Huh?"

"Financial trouble. Short of money."

"Good God . . . No, I'm not short of money, Bliss."

"Good."

She made for the stairs.

Sebastian cut her off. "Not good enough. Why would you suddenly ask if I'm short of money?"

"I don't know. You did point out to me that I've got a trust fund."

"When?"

"I can't remember."

To stop himself from touching her, he stuffed his hands into his pockets. "Try."

"Okay." She appeared short of breath. "We were talking about my having a tough time making ends meet here. You said I should go into my trust fund."

"If you need money, I think you should. It's yours."

"I'm going upstairs."

The sound of his footsteps behind hers on the stairs didn't slow her down.

She hurried.

He speeded up and passed her, and reached the bedroom door in time to throw it open for her. "Allow me."

"Thanks." She went inside and made to shut the door again.

It was Sebastian who shut the door—from the inside. "What point are you trying to make about money?"

She looked trapped. "Forget it."

"My sister is . . . She's my sister. The closest thing to family I've got, but she's possessive. I don't even like thinking that. Saying it burns me. She's afraid someone else is going to hurt me."

Bliss pushed at the bridge of her glasses. "I've got enough trouble all on my own. I'd like you to go."

"I'm pissed, Chilly." He parted his lips over clenched teeth. "Now I remember when the subject of your trust fund came up. We were talking about that damned dangerous hole you've got out there. You said you'd fill it—"

"If I had the money, I know."

"And, if I remember the way it went, I said I'd fill it for you and you lost your wool over that."

"Right. All absolutely right. I'm sorry. Yes, that's the way it went. Forget it, okay?"

"I'm trying. Marry me, Bliss."

"You're pressuring me." She crossed her arms over her middle. "Crushing in on me from all sides."

"Marry me."

"No," she told him. "I've already told you, no. This has happened too fast and there's too much going on for me to trust any decisions I make now."

"True. Particularly a decision not to marry the man you love." Her long stare unnerved him. He said, "What? What are you thinking?"

"Look at you. Rumpled. Who remembers how many hours' growth of beard that is. Your hair . . . Wind and too many trips through it with the fingers would make some men a mess. Not you, Sebastian. You're a picture no woman would look away from. You're gorgeous."

When he could finally speak again he said, "I'm angry. That's what I am. Simmering with it. It's so close to the surface, I'm shivering. Just under my skin, Bliss."

Her eyes never left his face.

"Bliss." He strolled toward her with a nonchalance he didn't feel—and that couldn't fool her. She held her middle tighter. "You couldn't wait to marry me once."

She stood her ground. "True. But you found you *could* wait, Sebastian. You found you could wait a very long time. Then, for some weird reason, you had to show up here and demand another chance. Why?"

"Because nothing's changed about the way I felt about you back then. Except it's even more intense, more desperate. Remember how we tried not to talk about the end of the school year? How it was getting close?"

"Of course."

"Remember how we didn't talk about it, but we knew the end of school could mean the end of us?"

"We'd only known each other three months and you sold your truck." Her short laugh hurt him as much as it must hurt her. "You sold it to buy me a ring. We both knew we were crazy but we—I wasn't afraid of having nothing as long as I had nothing with you."

"Bliss, you don't get to love like that more than once in a lifetime. Not exactly like that."

"I haven't," she said quietly.

She was the most beautiful woman in the world. Who she was, what she was, showed in every glance. Honest and true—and his love.

"Neither have I," he told her. "I don't want to."

"But you did something that made you leave me. And you never even sent me a note, Sebastian. Why?"

"It's a long story. You'll hear it all eventually—or as much of it as you need to hear. But I've told you I never stopped loving you—wanting you. I sure as hell want you now."

The echo of his meaning glittered in her eyes. He tasted triumph.

His body answered the desire he saw in her. Heat and a deep ache only sharpened his need. "There's something physical between us. We can't deny that. But there's so much more."

"I'm not interested in sex for the sake of sex."

"That didn't stop you at the Wilmans' last night. You were all over me then. You couldn't get enough."

Her face turned scarlet. "What a cheap shot."

"I'm only human. Tell me about Lennox Rood."

Bliss faltered. "I thought I heard a click on the line when Lennox called last night. You heard it all, didn't you? So there's nothing else to tell."

"Don't lie to me."

"What is this? Jealousy?"

"Hah! Hardly. Curiosity maybe."

"I believe honesty's the best course. You listened to his call last night."

He shrugged. "I tried to get to the phone before you. I wanted you to sleep."

"At least you're straightforward about listening in."

"I'm straightforward about everything."

"Are you?" Their eyes met and Bliss told him, "Lennox is part of my past. A very small part. You know? Like you have parts of your past, big and little. The end. There's nothing more."

"Good enough. Why don't you trust me?"

"You know why."

"Things happen. We went through hell. *We,* Bliss. Not just you. But it's over. We can start again."

"Oh, sure, start again with threats on all sides. I've been warned to stay away from you—with special effects to back up the warnings."

"I'll deal with the warnings, sweetheart."

"Sebastian, Sebastian. The term 'torn' is taking on a whole new meaning. I think there's too much for us to overcome. Maybe we should just forget anything ever happened between us."

Sebastian caught her arm and pulled her so close she had to raise her face to see him. Fury mounted again and he felt himself pale. "Forget, huh? Why? Because you don't mind making love to white trash, but you're sure as hell too wise to marry it now?"

Bliss slapped his face. He grasped her wrist and stared into her eyes. A sob choked from her throat.

"I've never hit anyone in my life," she told him.

"Until now. But you're dealing with trash. The rules change then, don't they?"

"Stop it!"

His tension didn't ebb. "You don't want to make love with me again? Isn't that what you're telling me?"

"I didn't say that." Her mouth trembled. "This is too much. Too hot, too powerful. Too *dark.* It frightens me."

"But you are saying you don't love me."

"I should never have let this begin again. I let you know I loved you once before and you turned away."

"This is different."

"Yeah. Different."

"You think I want to marry you for money."

"I don't know."

"No, you don't. That's asinine. If you knew more about me—about—hell, it doesn't matter. I don't need your money. I want to possess you."

She averted her face. "I'm not available to be possessed."

Bliss yanked her arm from his hand and spun away. She stumbled into a shaft of sunlight through thin drapes over a door.

"I can't live without you anymore, Bliss. I've done it for too long, now I have to have you."

She held the back of a chair and said, "And I want you," very low. "The girl I was would take you in her arms and convince herself that this time there won't be any heartaches. The woman I am knows better. There aren't any fairy tales."

"Bliss?" He stood behind her, so close he all but touched her. "Tell me you want me again."

She hung her head forward.

"Tell me."

"I don't know about anything anymore."

The touch of his fingertips at her bare waist made her jump. He rubbed her sides, her back under the short T-shirt, undid the fastening on her bra.

"No!" Bliss said. "Sebastian!"

"You want me to stop?"

Each breath she took was a pant. "We shouldn't do this. Not like this!"

"Why not now? How should we do it? When?" Around her ribs and beneath her bra he stroked, trailing fleeting caresses on the undersides of her breasts. He layered himself against her and kissed the back of her neck. "I can't help myself with you. I don't want to."

"The police might come back. They might want to ask more questions."

"Forget the police." He pinched her nipples gently, pulled. "Forget everything but this."

Bliss covered his hands. The need blossomed. His hips met hers. She was hot, so hot.

"Bliss," he whispered against her neck, "Just go with it. Go with me. Grab the chance. Don't let us be the losers again."

She didn't answer.

The sound of his zipper must be as clear to her as it was to him.

He pulled her skirt up to her waist.

"Sebastian!"

In one motion, he tipped her forward over the chair and shifted behind her until he nudged past her panties.

"Oh, God, Sebastian!"

He was inside her, holding her breasts, coming into her with a relentless rhythm he knew neither of them could have stopped if they'd tried.

"Oh, my . . . Here? Oh, Sebastian."

"Yes." He laughed, and gasped and his speed increased. "Yes, yes, yes, love. Now!"

Spasms broke over him, the spasms of her climax, and his own—the product of his climax, and hers. She shuddered, and whimpered. Sebastian cried out, and fell over her, still cradling her breasts, his penis still deep within her, his hard thighs parting hers.

"This isn't me," she murmured.

"But it is you," he gasped. "Oh, it is now, my love. And it's just the start of knowing who you are."

"No one should love in anger," she told him. "Like animals."

The humiliation he heard in her words turned his stomach. "You didn't like it?"

"I don't like myself for liking it."

He nuzzled her nape with his rough chin and laughed softly. "I love you. I love you. Got that. It's real simple. I love you and any way we choose to make love—as long as you love me, too—is okay."

"I love you," she said, and covered her face.

"I know you do," Sebastian told her. "We're going to sort out whatever's going on around us and then the education continues."

"Education."

"Learning just how many ways there are to say I love you, without the words."

# Twenty

Bliss sidled into the bathroom, filled a glass with cold water and climbed onto the toilet seat. Standing on tiptoe, she could see into the shower, see Sebastian's plastered black hair, his upturned face, his spiky eyelashes squeezed together.

Very carefully, she rested the glass atop the sliding doors and leaned a little closer until she had a better view—of all of him.

*Oh, my.*

Soap streamed from his face and over the bunched muscles in his shoulders and chest. His braced thighs echoed the power in his torso. And in between . . . In between, his skin was paler. Bliss leaned to her left. Bullets would bounce off those buns. She leaned to her right. Tensed belly. And there ought to be a fantastic name for a penis that even when wet and soapy, didn't manage to look vulnerable. Bliss studied . . . Mr. Happy. She'd heard that term somewhere. Yup, she'd think of it as Mr. Happy, one who was always alert and ready to go at a moment's notice.

Steam tickled her nose and she sneezed.

Enough peeking for now.

"Bliss?"

"What?" She started, looked into his green eyes, and gripped the glass.

Sebastian slicked back his hair and swiped at his face. "I'm shocked," he said, looking anything but shocked. Dangerously smug was closer. "Can't get enough of me, huh? Gotta creep up on me in the shower."

She clutched the glass. "There's nothing wrong with getting off on a good male body."

"Getting off?" He rested a shoulder against the tile. Moisture beaded on his skin. "This can't be my little Bliss, my little puritan. Not that you were a little puritan last night."

Last night would always be unforgettable. "Don't be condescending." She gave Mr. Happy a long look and held her tongue between her teeth. "Men have always enjoyed looking at women. It's a myth that women don't enjoy looking at men just as much."

He shifted a little.

"Am I embarrassing you, Sebastian?"

"Of course not."

Yes, she was. "I do believe I am. And look, Mr. Happy's coming to attention."

"Mr."—Sebastian glanced down, then back at Bliss—"You've gone to the dogs. I've created a monster." He'd reddened.

"I love it when you blush." She smiled at him and lifted the glass.

His eyes left hers slowly. "What's that? Oh, Bliss. Oh, no. Don't do it."

"It's good for you. Good for the heart. In Scandinavia they get out of saunas and roll in the snow."

"This isn't Scandinavia." He made a grab.

Bliss raised the glass out of his reach.

"I'm not telling you when," he said. "And I'm not telling you where. But if you dump that water on me, I'll get you."

She began to tip.

He wagged a finger. "It's warm water, isn't it? You're torturing me with . . . Aaah!"

Bliss hit the bathroom floor at the same moment as the shower door shot open.

"Help!" She made a dash across the bedroom, shrieking and giggling as she went. "Don't run with wet feet. It's dangerous."

"What did I do to deserve that abuse?"

"Nothing! I just feel wicked. I've become an abandoned woman. Your fault."

*"My* fault? That's it, Bliss. You're dead meat."

Choking on laughter, she wrenched open the bedroom door and rushed along the balcony to the stairs. Sebastian's feet pounded behind her—and his hand descended on her shoulder.

"I'm gonna get you."

"I just felt like playing." She tried to squirm away. "We never had a chance to play when we were kids."

"I know. And now it's my turn to catch up. I'm going to teach you all about torture."

"No," she shouted. "I'll scream!"

On the stairs she managed to slip his grasp—in time to leap down and collide with Polly and Fab.

"You're evil," Sebastian said. "Twisted."

He took the back of her neck in a large hand, and grew still.

Fab said, "Wow," in a reverent tone.

Polly said, "Oh, my."

Sebastian said, *"Shit,"* and moved behind Bliss.

Bliss scrunched up her face, held in the laughter, and didn't say a word.

"Good morning." Fab's eyes were round. "I guess you're all right then, Bliss?"

"I'm fine."

"You don't need any help?" Polly said.

"No help at all."

"Nice day," Polly said, smiling, and breaking into a snappy, hummed version of "Hello Dolly."

"We heard you scream." Fab definitely wasn't looking at Bliss. "So we thought you might be having another Lennox—another *thing."*

Bliss gave Fab a wolfish grin. "Don't let us keep you from what you were doing."

The twins hesitated several seconds longer before turning away. In a full, husky, alto Polly sang, "You're looking *swell,* Dolly," before she disappeared into the kitchens behind Fab.

"Cute," Sebastian remarked. "Great voice."

"I'm sorry," Bliss muttered, feeling penitent. "I forgot they might be in."

"I'm not telling you exactly when or where," Sebastian responded. "Probably not here because this is a crazy place. I'm taking you away from here. Yes, siree. You are coming to live with me."

"I'm staying right here and running my business."

"You'll marry me, move into my house. Run this disaster from there if it'll make you happy—and we're going to make love in peace. Think of that. And run around naked if we feel like it."

"You're having a fantasy."

"Yes, ma'am. A fantasy about to come true. I saw the way you looked at *Mr. Happy*."

Bliss made sure the kitchen door was closed. "Don't say things like that out loud."

"Tough to say them any other way." He tweaked a nipple through her white cotton blouse and grinned when she slapped him away. "You'll want to stay close to Mr. Happy, and he's with me."

He made it so hard to be either serious, or logical. "We've got a lot to deal with, Sebastian. But this discussion will have to wait."

"Bliss! Bliss, where are you?" Venus Crow's fruited voice bellowed through the lower floor of the lodge.

Sebastian sprinted upstairs and Bliss followed, calling, "Down in a minute, Venus," as she went.

She didn't close the bedroom door behind her, but watched Sebastian from a distance instead. "You're a forgiving man."

"No, I'm not. I never forgive. I bear grudges deeply and forever."

When he'd said he couldn't face putting on his rumpled suit pants and dress shirt again, Bliss had found him a pair of tan shorts from the Lost and Found Box. He pulled them on, working them over thighs that needed much more room, and barely managing to close the zipper. One of Bliss's oversized white T-shirts stretched across his shoulders until the seams strained. He stuck a finger into a hole over his navel and curled his lip.

"It's early," Bliss told him. "You'll have plenty of time to eat breakfast and get to the office."

"I'm going to make a few calls now, if that's okay. Then I think I might want to change before I show up at the office. Think that's a good idea?"

She spread her hands. "Well, I didn't mean you should go to the office like that."

Sebastian lifted the phone and dialed.

Bliss turned to leave, and turned back. She went to the bedside table where the phone rested and picked up the crystal bell.

Sebastian said, "William. Good morning. Sebastian here. If you need me, you can reach me at that number I gave you. If I'm not here, try my home. I'll be in later." He sat on the edge of the bed and rested an ankle on the opposite knee. "I have nothing to say to them. Have Zoya field those calls. And let my lawyers know I want them to stand by." He hesitated, then said, "Maryan isn't herself. Would you please talk with Zoya? Tell her to keep Maryan busy till I get there," and he hung up.

"What's wrong?"

"Your WOT friends need a reality check. And my sister's flipping out. Crises on every side."

"I'm sorry about Maryan. The WOT people aren't my friends."

"Prue O'Leary isn't your friend?"

Bliss rang the bell softly. "She used to be. She may be again if we can get past this."

"I'd better think about leaving," Sebastian said, getting up.

"The bell's gone."

He looked at her. "What d'you mean?"

"This isn't the bell. It's a different one."

For an instant his brow furrowed. "Are you sure?"

"Sure, I'm sure. I know the bell I keep beside the bed. My

aunt's favorite bell. This isn't it. The night before last when the others came to get me, they'd heard a bell ringing."

"So?"

"I heard a bell that night when I nearly killed you with my brush."

"Don't exaggerate."

"When the others talked about a bell I ran to make sure it was here and I thought it was. I think someone had already taken the Steuben to use in whatever twisted little stunt they're pulling to frighten me. I just didn't notice until now."

Sebastian rubbed the space between his brows. "If they think they're doing some ghostly number they've got it all wrong. It would have to be very solid fingers that pulled the switch. If the bells have been switched."

"I told you—"

"Okay, I believe you. But what's the point?"

"To prove they can get at me. To remind me I'm in danger whenever I'm with you."

"I wasn't here when the bell rang."

"No, but I'd been with you earlier, hadn't I? And they'd already warned me—in more ways than one."

Sebastian draped his arms around her shoulders. "You certainly had been with me. We'd better let the police know, Bliss. Just as a precaution."

"And tell them what?"

"That someone stole a Steuben bell. Then I want you to come where I can keep an eye on you at all times."

Bliss heard someone at the door downstairs. Footsteps hurried from the kitchen, followed by the murmur of voices, one female, the other low and male.

"Maybe Daddy's come to visit again," Sebastian said.

Bliss went to look over the balcony railing. A policeman stood with Venus Crow in the room below. Today Venus's diaphanous harem pants and veils were of gold-trimmed magenta.

"It's the police," Bliss said over her shoulder.

"Right on cue."

Sebastian ran down the stairs beside Bliss. The policeman was the same, middle-aged man who had called Sebastian away the day before.

Venus swayed and her coins clinked. "I've told him he'll have to have a search warrant." She pressed her palms together.

"We were just going to call the police," Sebastian said.

"Is that right, sir?" The officer appeared mildly interested. "Something you wanted to tell us, was there?"

"Theft," Sebastian said.

The policeman frowned "Theft?"

"A Steuben bell," Bliss told him. "It was my aunt's. I kept it beside the bed the way she did."

"I'm Officer Ballard," the man said, slipping out a notebook. He screwed up his weathered face and stared hard at Bliss's middle. "I'd like to have a look around, if you don't mind."

"That would be fine," Bliss said. "Great, in fact. I know this sounds ridiculous, but I've heard some really strange things around here lately."

Ballard nodded without raising his eyes. "I wouldn't be surprised. Ringing and what not, I suppose."

Bliss was amazed. "How did you guess? Did one of them tell you?"

"Maybe you should sit down, Ms. Winters. Perhaps this nice lady would get you some coffee." He indicated Venus who wound and unwound her wrists before her face while she slid her head sideways.

"I don't do coffee," Venus said. "Tell him to leave, Bliss. His aura is troubled. I can't relax around troubled auras."

Ballard pointed his pen at Bliss. "You've had a lot of stress, ma'am. People don't realize the trauma they can suffer when they've been at the scene of a sudden death."

"We've all had a shock," Sebastian said. "But I get the feeling we aren't talking about the same things here."

"The lady's holding her bell, sir," Ballard said. He cleared his throat. "I expect she just forgot. It was another missing item that I came about."

"This isn't the bell," Bliss and Sebastian said in unison.

"Too many bad auras," Venus said, raising her nose and looking from Ballard to Sebastian. "I believe I was wrong about this man, too. He's brought trouble here."

Bliss glared at her. "Isn't there something you could do to help Fab and Polly?"

"They've gone back to the bungalow."

Ballard shifted from one shiny shoe to the other. "I do need to get on here."

"So do I," Sebastian said coldly.

"This cheap bell was put where the Steuben used to be, just to throw me off," Bliss said. "So I wouldn't notice it had been taken."

"Worth a lot of money, is it?"

"Look," Sebastian said. "You're not getting it. This isn't about value. It's about bells ringing at odd times, and voices, and threats whispered in the dark."

Ballard tapped the end of his nose with his pen. "Is it? I see. We'll, I'd better make a note of that."

"You can look upstairs in my rooms," Bliss said, growing furious. "It's gone. It's smaller than this and much more ornate, and it's gone. It has a very high, clear sound, not like this." She gave the cheap glass a hard shake and produced a dull clatter.

"I need to take a look around the scene of the accident, ma'am," Ballard said, turning slightly pink. "I can get a warrant if you'd be more comfortable with that."

"I don't care—"

"Whoa," Sebastian said, cutting Bliss off. "I'm sure Bliss won't mind you looking at anything you want to look at. But I don't appreciate you treating her like a fool."

"I didn't treat her like a fool, sir."

Sebastian rolled his shoulders and Bliss could see him trying to relax. "It's okay," she told him. "Someone took my bell from beside my bed, Officer Ballard. And Vic Taylor and Liberty heard a bell outside Vic's cabin on the night before last. I think someone took it to frighten me with."

"Why do you think that, ma'am?"

"Because"—she blinked rapidly—"I don't know really."

The policeman sighed hugely. "Well, I'd better take a look at the room. Upstairs, you say?"

Bliss concurred and the officer lumbered up, his holster creaking.

"You two would not be a good match after all," Venus Crow said. "I advise you to banish him, Bliss."

"Oh, for God's sake." Sebastian held Bliss's elbow and propelled her upstairs behind Ballard. "I've got to get you away from here."

"I know about these things," Venus called. "I would never dance at a wedding unless I could be sure the coming together had been blessed in a higher place."

Sebastian's fingers dug into Bliss's arm and he turned back. "It has been blessed in a higher place," he told Venus. "Way above your head." With Bliss firmly in his grip he continued on to her room. "If she'd been up here last night she'd know just how blessed our coming together was—on several occasions."

She smiled a little, but sobered at the sight of Officer Ballard poking around her private domain. "The bell was beside the bed," she said shortly, and immediately regretted bringing attention to the tangled mess of sheets that trailed to the floor, and the pillows piled together against the headboard.

If Ballard considered the condition of the bed interesting, he hid his feelings well. "Steps up to the balcony, are there?" He went to the nearest French door and parted the drapes.

"Yes. They lead down to the kitchen gardens," Bliss told him.

"Locked," Ballard said, turning a handle. "You always keep them locked?"

"Since the first time."

Ballard cocked an enquiring brow.

Bliss said, "Since the first time I heard the bell and saw the face."

The man stared at her. "Someone was outside looking at you and ringing your bell?"

"No! Of course not. They were inside looking at me and ringing my bell. I was outside."

"Ah." Ballard made artful squiggles on his pad. "Did you think you might know the person?"

"She was wearing a mask."

"A mask? A woman?"

"I heard a woman's voice."

"I see. What did she say."

Bliss felt heat under her skin. "Oh, just some sort of silliness. I didn't really hear." She wasn't about to pull Sebastian's name into this.

"Hey!" Sebastian crossed the room in a few strides and pulled the drape back farther. He stooped and swept up a bell. "This is it, isn't it, Bliss? The Steuben?"

Feeling stupid, Bliss nodded. "Who would put it there? This is . . . I don't like it, Sebastian."

"Well, ma'am, that seems to solve that."

"It does not," she said angrily. "Someone deliberately switched bells on me."

The notebook was replaced in its pocket. Ballard waved his pen. "Wouldn't be hard to do, would it? Not with so many to choose from."

Bliss followed the direction of his pointing pen to the high shelf that held Aunt Blanche's bell collection.

Ballard went from French door to French door, checking the locks. "Still locked. Were they unlocked two nights ago?"

"No."

"There's no sign of forced entry."

Bliss wished the man would go away, and she wished she'd never mentioned the stupid bell.

"I'd recommend you put the little bell back where it belongs and get the other one up where it came from"—Ballard pointed to a space on the end of the shelf—"I expect you're feeling a bit upset, ma'am."

"Annoyed would be more accurate."

"As you say." He looked at Sebastian. "We won't dwell on this, will we, sir. Sometimes people need a bit more attention, especially when they're unsettled."

"Are you saying you think I switched these bells to draw attention to myself?" Bliss said, sputtering.

Ballard was already on his way out of the room. "I'm not saying anything. Call the station if you hear any more odd ringings. It was something Mrs. Nose said that I wanted to look into this morning."

"What would that be?" Casting Bliss an apologetic smile, Sebastian jogged downstairs behind Ballard.

"The dead man's personal belongings. I'd like to take a look around the bluff and see if we missed anything."

"Lots of people have looked," Venus said dreamily. She hadn't left her station at the foot of the stairs. "Death always brings such legions of souls who want to keep watch with the departed."

"Venus," Bliss said sharply. "Whatever this new psychic twist is, drop it."

"You never understood these things. Greater understanding of the body brings greater understanding of the mind. Mr. Nose is out there still. I feel his sadness, his confusion. He had no time to prepare. The others come because they feel it too, only they don't understand that's why they come."

"They come because they're ghouls," Sebastian muttered. "This is private property and they won't be coming anymore."

He marched out with Ballard and immediately hopped as his bare feet met the gravel path. Bliss ran after him. "Get your shoes on."

"No need." He sidestepped to the muddy grass and cast a disgusted glare at his instantly filthy feet.

"Too bad if we've had a lot of activity," Ballard said. "Someone could have picked it up."

"Picked up what?" Sebastian asked.

Ballard marched ahead to the edge of the bluff and prowled

back and forth. "Makes you think," he said. "Hardly any distance. That's where he fell. Hardly any distance. Just caught his head wrong, poor devil."

Bliss hugged her ribs. "It's awful."

"What are you looking for?" Sebastian persisted with his trademark single-mindedness.

"We already know he was working for you, Mr. Plato. And he was here doing his job." Ballard peered down the shallow slope to the water. "His wife says he never went to work without them. There were two, y'see. One was in the car."

Bliss met Sebastian's exasperated gaze.

"Maybe the other one fell in the water and got swept away by the currents. Probably never find it."

"Find what?" Bliss asked.

"His other camera."

# Twenty-one

Whatever it took, he would wrap Bliss so snugly inside his life, she'd never want to get out again. Sebastian stared ahead through the windshield at an afternoon turned to smudgy gray. His need for her only grew stronger, his need for her just as she was, without changing. He would never want her to become less of herself because she was part of him—and he was part of her.

She'd been very quiet since he'd persuaded her to leave Hole Point with him and go to Raptor for the first time. She had changed her clothes. Sitting beside him in the Ford with her hands folded in the lap of a long, loosely fitting denim dress, she looked remote.

If she wanted to talk she'd let him know. He knew he wanted her beside him for the rest of his life. He also knew he wanted to get his hands on whoever was trying to mix things up between them.

"Are you sure this is a good idea?" she asked.

"Absolutely certain."

Bliss bowed her head and her heavy, red-brown hair swept forward to hide her face. "Maryan isn't suddenly going to change her mind and love me."

He waited his turn at a fourway stop. "Maryan is a difficult woman. She's my sister, the only family I've got, but I don't wear blinders where she's concerned."

"She can make things difficult, can't she? If she doesn't approve of me?—and she doesn't."

"She can make things difficult for herself. But she's no fool and I don't think she'll do that. That's why I wanted to bring you in with me. It's time we started letting everyone get used to the idea that you and I are together."

He waited and got the silence he expected. Bliss wasn't ready to commit to him, not completely, not without a lot more explanation of what had driven him away from her in the first place.

"There haven't been many women in my life." He worked the muscles in his jaw, uncertain why he'd told her that, beyond feeling he had to.

She leaned away from him, rested her head on the window.

"Bliss—"

"Don't. Please don't say anything else right now."

How could he tell her all she needed to know, wanted to know, when there were parts of it that were still a puzzle to him?

"If the rain's going to keep up I'll have to put the canopy on for Beater."

"I like him." Still Bliss didn't look at him. "You always wanted a dog, didn't you? I remember you telling me you did."

Long ago and far away. Another planet. "Yeah. Beater Two is son of Beater One. His dad was mine, too. You'd never believe they were related. Beater One had some greyhound in the woodpile. Weirdest-looking dog you ever saw."

She laughed lightly. "Beater isn't exactly show material."

They were saying everything but what needed to be said. "Will you just say something along the lines of—I'll follow you anywhere, Sebastian? And, maybe—I trust you, Sebastian?"

"Please don't push me."

"I don't have any control over my mouth anymore." Absolutely true. "From the rotten day I left Seattle until the day I showed up on your doorstep, I was swimming through deep emotional water just to get back to you."

"And I was treading water," she told him with almost no inflection.

"How about I say I'll follow *you* anywhere?"

She laughed again. "You seem to be doing that already."

"And you hate it?" The rain grew heavier. "I'm sorry, Bliss. I knew I had no right to barge back in, but I'd held off till I couldn't hold off anymore. I could never shake you out of my mind."

"What if I had been married and had those ten children you mentioned."

"I'd have kidnapped you."

"Sure, you would."

"I don't want to think about it." He wanted to give thanks for finding her unattached and still caring about him. "You do still care about me, don't you?"

"I've told you I love you. If I had any sense, I wouldn't have told you, but I've never been good at protecting myself."

"You don't have to with me." He squeezed her hands in her lap. "Your fingers are cold. You're tense."

"You're taking me somewhere where they probably think I'm spearheading the enemy. I don't know what to expect."

"But you've agreed to come."

"You said you wouldn't go to the office unless I agreed to go with you."

He considered for a moment. "That's true. And from now on, I'm going to keep on hanging around until you give up and give me whatever I ask for."

"That's coercion."

"Uh-huh. Whatever it takes, Chilly."

Sebastian turned off Bellevue Way onto the street in front of his building and parked at the curb. He saw Beater—who made new homes with remarkable speed—leap from the back of the truck and shamble to the revolving glass doors.

By the time Sebastian had helped Bliss out, the dog had nosed the door into motion and sashayed into the lobby.

"He's incredible," Bliss said. "Smart as a fox."

"Smarter," Sebastian said, not without pride. "Would I choose a dumb dog—or a dumb anything?"

She stood quite still in the increasing downpour and looked upward. "This is yours?"

"Some of it. A lot of it."

"Yes, well, it's impressive. Why don't I wait in the truck."

Sebastian stepped behind her, held her waist and marched her firmly toward the building and into the revolving door. He nodded to the doorman and headed to where Beater stood in front of the door to the private elevator.

Once inside the elevator, Bliss retired to a corner. Beater sat on Sebastian's feet and gazed up into his face. Bliss was right, he'd wanted dogs all the years he'd been growing up. Now he couldn't imagine life without one.

A slight, cushioned bump heralded their arrival on the top floor, and the doors slid smoothly open. Sebastian offered Bliss his hand and she took it reluctantly. Rain had dampened the shoulders of her dress and wetted her hair. As they got off the elevator, Beater gave a mighty shake and peppered them both with raindrops.

William wasn't at his desk and the first words Sebastian heard came from his office: "Get the sonuvabitch then! Find him and get him here or I'll tell them papers some things they never guessed about that whore-maker."

"I think I should return to my desk." This time it was William who spoke. "You can call me if—"

"Stay put," Ron York demanded. "We'll want you to explain to Sebastian that you're the one who made the mistake of letting this clown in here."

Bliss's death-grip told Sebastian all he needed to know about her reaction. She tugged, but he didn't let go. "Hang in here with me," he told her.

"We did right by you." Maryan's voice was unmistakable. "We paid what we didn't owe."

"You paid to keep me quiet. You and that bastard brother of yours never knew a moment's remorse for what you did. You bought me off and I shouldn't have let you do that."

"But you did let them," Ron York said, sounding pompous. "You took every penny Sebastian and Maryan gave you. Now you think you can get more. Forget it, old man. Take your sorry ass back to whatever hole you crawled out of, and *die.*"

Pulling Bliss with him, Sebastian approached the door to his office. William, standing beside the desk, was the first to see Sebastian and Bliss. Sebastian motioned him to silence.

Jim Moore, Crystal's father, sat in the Z chair Nose had once occupied. Maryan and Ron flanked him. The three were too absorbed in their hate battle to notice Sebastian's arrival.

"He's somewhere around here," Jim Moore said, turning his haggard, gray face up to Ron. "Don't you tell me he isn't. I read it, see. In the papers. And I already talked to him. You were there. You're all against me."

Maryan fingered the collar of the old man's frayed brown shirt. "And I suppose your God sent you running over here to demand more payoff."

Bliss's grip on Sebastian's hand tightened. Her short fingernails dug into his skin. She'd have to know it all before they could have anything permanent together. Now was as good a time as any to let her start hearing how he'd made a mess of his private life. Better from Jim Moore's mouth than his own.

Even at a distance Sebastian saw Moore tremble. The man was a shrunken, fleshless version of what he'd been the last, the only time Sebastian had seen him.

With the pointed end of a pencil, Ron York made little jabs on top of Moore's stooped shoulder. "When a lady asks a question, a gentleman answers," he said, sending his next lead poke into the man's neck. "Who sent you here? God?"

"My Crystal," Moore muttered, straining away from the pencil point. "She was untouched when that boy took her."

"This is old," Maryan said, yawning theatrically. "And Crystal doesn't talk to you anymore. Crystal hates you, old man. If she hadn't been so scared of you she might not have gone looking for love somewhere else."

"God will strike you down!" Jim Moore's voice rose to a querulous rail. "All of you. That man defiled a pure girl. He twisted her mind and made her into a foul thing God turns his face from."

"My brother did very well by your daughter," Maryan said. "He married her and he paid you for the privilege."

"He paid me because he was afraid I'd let on how he raped my girl."

William stared directly at Sebastian.

Maryan's and Ron's eyes met over Moore's head.

"Wouldn't have done her much good if you'd done that when Sebastian was her husband, would it?" Maryan said.

Moore got unsteadily to his feet. "He says he ain't her husband no more," he shouted. "But he's still up to his tricks. Those loudmouth women came to my place. I know things they'd like to know, and maybe I'm going to tell 'em."

"What things would those be?" Sebastian said.

Moore, with Maryan and Ron, swung to look at him.

"What things would those be, Mr. Moore?" Sebastian repeated.

Jim Moore's watery eyes shifted between Sebastian and Bliss. "Who's that then?"

Sebastian ignored the question. "What do you think you could say that would hurt me?"

"The papers only hinted at what you were up to before you left all those years ago. I can tell them the truth. I can tell them you raped my girl and got her pregnant."

Sebastian released Bliss and strolled to stand in front of Moore with the chair between them. "And will you tell them you threatened to kill her if I didn't marry her? Will you say that as I began to build a name for myself, you arranged for us to pay what you called a *pension* to guarantee you wouldn't make things difficult for me?"

"I got nothing to lose anymore."

"Crystal remarried." He knew what Moore was going to say next. "Isn't she taking care of you?" He'd never felt the depth of loathing he felt for this man—except, perhaps, for his own adoptive father.

"Divorced him, too," Moore said. "Not that she could ever

be married again as long as the two of you are alive. Married to you for life, she is."

"We won't start that discussion."

Maryan went to the bar and poured vodka into a tall glass. "Tell the little fart to get lost, Seb. He can't do anything to us anymore."

She was probably right, but some shred of pity for Crystal made Sebastian ask, "What is it you want from me?"

"Money," Moore said. "Big money. Or I'll tell those women what they want to know. I'll tell 'em what they asked me about."

From the corner of his eye, Sebastian saw Bliss move for the first time since they'd come into the office. She took several rapid steps forward and Jim Moore's head snapped toward her.

"What did they ask you?" Sebastian said.

"Who's she?" Moore asked, pointing at Bliss. "You're his latest whore, aren't you?"

"Shut your mouth, Moore," Sebastian snapped.

"You're that Winters bitch. I warned you to stay away from her, Plato. You can't afford another whore."

Maryan sniggered.

Sebastian said, "That's enough," too numb to feel the full force of his anger.

"Mr. Plato," William said in an admirably even tone. "Perhaps I should summon someone to escort this man from the building."

"Perhaps you should toddle off to your desk, Billy boy," Ron said. "And forget every word you've heard here if you know what's good for you."

"I am Bliss Winters, Mr. Moore," Bliss said clearly. "I was in school with Crystal, but I haven't seen her for years. How is she?"

Sebastian swallowed acid self-hatred. Of course Bliss had always outclassed him, but she'd loved him, probably still loved him now—or had until a few minutes ago.

"Crystal needs help," Moore said to Bliss. "Aren't you the one who's in with those women who want Plato out of Washington? Didn't you have trouble with him, too?"

"No."

Sebastian met her eyes and she stared back without blinking. He wanted to thank her, but now wasn't the moment.

"Don't you have nothing to do with him, then. He raped my girl and got—"

"I already heard what you suggested," Bliss said. "And he did marry her, didn't he?"

"Doesn't take the act away."

"If there was something to be prosecuted, you should have done it at the time, shouldn't you?"

"He doesn't know I've found out other things," Moore said, the corners of his colorless mouth jerking. "I know all about the girl who died."

"Do you want to get back to your desk?" Sebastian asked William, who raised his brows and left the room, closing the door behind him. "Look, Mr. Moore, if your daughter hadn't once been my wife, I'd have you thrown out. On the long shot that there's still some way you might be able to punish her if I did, I'll ask you to leave quietly instead."

"You think because everyone believes you don't make filthy movies you're off the hook for that girl's death."

"I was never on the hook for the poor girl's death," Sebastian said. "Ron, why don't you go over to Bellevue Square and spend some more of Maryan's money."

"Sebastian!" Maryan's thin lips all but disappeared.

"All right," he said to her. "Sorry. Why don't you go and spend some of your money on him. This is private."

His sister's face turned white. A bright spot of red burned on each cheek. "How dare you speak to me like that in front of her." Her nostrils flared and she glared at Bliss. "Get rid of her *now.*"

"Not unless she wants to leave." He looked at Bliss, sent her the message that she could choose to be for him, or walk away now.

"I came with you," she told him. "If you want me to stay, I will."

Maryan insinuated herself between them and faced Sebastian. "You've never needed me more than you do now. Listen to what this old leech is going to say, will you. He can hurt us, Seb, and he knows it."

"No he can't. I don't have anything to be ashamed of—nothing that isn't very old."

"You made that girl take off her clothes," Jim Moore said. "Then, after you'd had your way with her, you got that killer who makes porno movies to come and look at her."

Maryan covered her mouth.

The only noise Sebastian heard was Bliss's small cry. He shook his head. He couldn't afford to lose control. "I don't know where this is coming from and it won't work, Moore, so forget it."

"You'd like that, wouldn't you—for me to forget it. Well I've got my duty to do so I can't."

"Unless I pay you to?" Sebastian said.

Moore hitched at his baggy gray pants. "Only so I can help the family she left behind."

"I never met the girl who was murdered," Sebastian said, skirting the chair to stand, toe-to-toe, with Moore. "I never met her. I never touched her. I regret her death, but it had absolutely nothing to do with me. Do you understand?"

"One of them women came to me and told me all about it. And if you won't pay me not to talk about what you did to my Crystal, she'll pay me to tell everything."

Bliss made another sound.

"What's that supposed to mean?" Sebastian asked Moore.

"The girl who died had a friend. She told this friend everything, see. How you said you'd help her if she did what you wanted. Then how you made her go with that killer."

Bliss crossed the room and touched Jim Moore's sleeve. "Who told you all this?"

"I ain't sayin'. But all I got to do is let on what Plato did to Crystal and everyone's going to stop believin' his story."

"That's blackmail," Bliss said. "Sebastian, he can't do this to you."

"No he can't," Ron agreed.

Maryan pushed Ron aside. "Shut up, all of you. And get out. Leave this to Sebastian and me. We'll deal with it."

"There's nothing to be dealt with," Sebastian said. "As Bliss and Ron have already pointed out, there's no threat here."

Maryan upended the vodka she'd been steadily drinking and drained the glass. "She's on their side," she said, pointing at Bliss. "You're so stupid, Seb. She hates you because you chose Crystal instead of her."

"Be quiet," Sebastian said. "Mr. Moore, I'd appreciate it if you'd leave."

"She's the one Crystal talked about," the old man said. "The one you were going to marry, only you got Crystal pregnant."

"That's right," Bliss said. When Sebastian started to speak she shook her head emphatically. "I can deal with this. I am the girl Sebastian was going to marry when he had to leave Seattle with Crystal. It's all very sad, Mr. Moore, and I think I understand it now. He did it to protect her from you, didn't he?"

"He wanted her," Maryan shouted. "Every male in miles wanted her."

Ron reached for his mistress. She tried to hit him, but missed.

"I wanted you Bliss," Sebastian said. He hadn't had any idea this would become so ugly. "But I thought . . . I had a responsibility to Crystal. She told me what her father was like. He'd told her he'd kill her if she ever *disgraced* him as he put it."

"You forced yourself on her." Moore ranted now. "I'm going to tell that O'Leary woman I'll tell anyone who wants to know. Then see if you don't get run out of this town."

"Go for it," Sebastian told him. "If Prue O'Leary's so desperate she'll try using you as a witness for the prosecution, she's already lost her case."

Jim Moore backed away toward the door. He raised a fist and shook it high. "It won't be me who'll be the star witness against you," he said. He leveled an arthritic finger at Bliss. "There's evil here. If you know what's good for you, you'll get away before you end up like my Crystal—locked up in a place for mad people."

# Twenty-two

Bliss watched early evening rain beat against the windows in Sebastian's conservatory. He'd gone to the front door to pay for the pizza he'd ordered.

She blinked back the all-too-familiar tears. He thought they could pretend nothing stood between them anymore. Coming here to his home was probably a mistake, but she couldn't have refused him, not after what she'd seen him go through in his offices.

She'd wanted to come.

"It's dinner!" Clad in black sweats, he arrived bearing the pizza box aloft. "I hope you're not very hungry because I am."

Bliss got to her feet. "I suppose that means you want the whole thing?"

He put the box on a green wicker table and took a wad of cocktail napkins from a heap on the wet bar. "Not the whole thing, just most of it. Sit down. Let me wait on you."

Bliss remained standing while he opened the box and poured two glasses of red wine without asking if she wanted any.

He gave her a glass and tapped it with his own. "Here's to us, Bliss." His smile had fled. He looked into her eyes and his own held question, and sadness—and hope? "Can we drink to us?"

Bliss put her glass on the table, took Sebastian's and set it beside her own. She wrapped her arms around him and pressed her face to his chest.

"Sweetheart?" A second passed, and another, before he held her, held her so tightly it hurt. She didn't care. He pushed a hand beneath her hair to clasp her neck. "It's all been such a goddamn waste."

He'd feel her tears. She tried to blink them away. Instead her throat closed and she gasped for breath.

His hands trembled. "I didn't do it."

Bliss kneaded his back. "I know." She didn't have to ask what he meant. "I've always known."

"There can't be any more lies between us. I did sleep with her. At one of those damn parties after the games. Before I met you."

Her heart drummed, she heard its wild flight.

"I don't want to say anymore. I slept with her. And I married her when that old man threatened to kill her. She was my wife. I didn't know she'd been in a clinic until old man Moore told me. Not that I'm surprised. I owe her some dignity, even if it was all so wrong. But do I have to give up the rest of my life for it?"

"No one's asking you to do that," she said.

He drove his fingers into her hair and forced her head back until he could see her face. "You are, if I have to lose you again."

"I can't let you go, Sebastian." She waited for his kiss and closed her eyes at the tender warmth of it. He kissed her lips softly, kissed her eyes shut.

Something wet and lumpy brushed her leg and she jumped. Her forehead bumped Sebastian's chin and she looked down to see Beater offering up an ugly, orange rubber spider.

"He really likes you," Sebastian said, his voice heavy with emotion. "I'm the only one who gets to throw his spider."

Bliss took the toy and looked for a clear path to throw it.

"You're going to marry me, aren't you?" Sebastian asked, covering the spider and her fingers with one big hand. "Beater and me, that is? You'll take us on, please?"

Her legs didn't want to hold her anymore. She clung to him.

"How could a woman turn down a dog like that?" The dog in question watched his spider with unwavering concentration.

"Or a dog like me?"

"I don't seem to have any choice anymore."

"That's a yes?"

"That's . . . Yes, Sebastian. I've got to say yes, because if I say no, I'll only have to come back and beg you to let me change my mind."

"We shouldn't be eating pizza," Sebastian said, holding her shoulders in another crushing grip. "I need to take you somewhere. We've got to get a ring." He swung her around. "I'll have rings brought here. I'll make a call now."

Bliss laughed and shook her head. "I want pizza. I don't want red wine. I do want beer. And forget the ring."

"No." He kissed her again, and again. "No. Yes. Beer coming right up."

Pressing her fingertips to her lips, she watched him turn in a circle. "What?" she asked him. "What is it?"

"Beer? I can't remember where the beer is."

"In a refrigerator somewhere?"

"The kitchen." He started from the conservatory, only to retrace his steps and grab her hand. "I'm not going anywhere without you. I know someone who'll come over with rings. I'll call him from the kitchen."

"Not now," she told him, dropping Beater's spider. "All I want now is you."

"You've got me." He made to draw her to him again, but Bliss placed a firm hand on his chest. He said, "I thought you said all you wanted was—"

"After the beer"—she smiled—"and the cold pizza."

Beater growled softly.

"Damn," Sebastian groaned. "We must have visitors," and the front door opened and slammed a moment later. He narrowed his eyes and pulled her against him. Side by side, with his arm around her shoulders, they confronted Maryan and Ron.

Maryan came into the conservatory in front of Ron. "Seb," she said quietly, "I've been an ass. I'm sorry."

"Yeah," Sebastian said. "You have been an ass."

"You're my kid brother and I want the best for you. I was wrong to interfere, but I was afraid you could get hurt again. Is that a sin?"

Bliss was grateful for the warmth of Sebastian's arm.

"Do you think it's a sin to worry about your brother?"

Maryan was talking to her. "No," Bliss said when she could make the word. "No, of course not."

"When we were growing up there were only the two of us, weren't there, Seb?"

Sebastian didn't reply.

Maryan threw down the purse that matched her chartreuse dress and jacket. "What else can I say?"

"We brought you these, Bliss," Ron York said and held out a huge bunch of multihued day lilies. "I'm the outsider in all of this, but Maryan means everything to me. If you can help her by making this easier, you'll make me a happy man."

His blue eyes were serious, his fair eyebrows drawn down.

Bliss took the lilies. "Thanks." She could try to forget that Maryan Plato had all but accused her brother of being unbalanced, and that she'd tried to make Bliss distrust him.

"Seb?" Maryan said, stretching a hand out to him. "Forgive me?"

Sebastian felt rigid at Bliss's side. She glanced up at him, then at Maryan and said, "I never had a brother. If I had, I'd probably have been pretty protective."

"Thank you," Maryan said, and her gratitude shone in her tense face.

"Okay, Sis," Sebastian said. He squeezed her outstretched hand and released it. "I don't think I can stay mad about anything tonight. Bliss has agreed to become my wife. You can be the first to congratulate us."

Maryan's mouth opened and remained open.

"God, that's wonderful," Ron said. He grinned and slapped

Sebastian's shoulder. "Congratulations, man. This is one of those stories that isn't supposed to come true. I'm glad it has for the two of you."

"Oh, Seb," Maryan said. "Oh, what a day. Ron, we've got to drink to this."

"We were going to have a beer with our pizza," Sebastian said. "Bliss's choice."

"Of course," Maryan said. "Bliss's choice."

Ron was the first to leave the conservatory for the house with Sebastian behind him. Bliss smelled her lilies and walked beside Maryan.

If Beater hadn't yelped, Bliss wouldn't have known that Maryan kicked the dog as they passed.

He was still slim, still tall and straight, and too fucking sure of himself. Morris Winters's face bore subtle signs of aging, but his arrogance and preoccupation with himself had served him well. Undoubtedly he slept the peaceful sleep of the selfish, and that sleep had kept his skin smooth.

Maryan felt him watch her while she toured his study in what, fifty years earlier, had been a summerhouse in the grounds of the Winters's luxurious Laurelhurst home. She felt him assess her—physically and mentally. Morris Winters was a man who took careful stock of any enemy before he struck.

Only this time the positions were reversed. This time she would do the striking and he would bleed. He'd bleed to death unless he gave her what she wanted.

"What would make you come here like this?" he asked in the deceptively soft voice she'd never forget. "What would make you take such a risk?"

"You should have spoken to me when I called your office the other day."

"You shouldn't have called at all. We have no business together."

Maryan slipped off the short jacket that matched her chartreuse halter dress and let it trail. "This room hasn't changed."

"Everything's changed."

"Not really. You haven't, and I haven't. We both still know what we want."

"It's two in the morning. I want to get back to sleep."

Maryan approached him. "You woke up easily enough. But then, you always did, didn't you?" He'd put on a navy-blue silk robe over matching silk pajamas. The robe pocket bore his monogram and she'd bet the pajamas did, too. "Didn't you change the signal over the years? Or have all your women rung your private line from a pay phone and hung up—the way I did? Who did you expect to find waiting for you out here?"

"You were never my woman."

"Never?"

He looked at her with a loathing that excited her. Angry men made great lovers.

"I didn't take any chances, *Morris*. Somehow I guessed you hadn't started spending your nights tucked up with your little Kitten."

"Say what you came to say and get out."

Maryan took the stopper out of the neck of a crystal decanter and poured Scotch. Not her favorite, but all he'd ever kept in his private sanctuary. She held the decanter up to him. Morris shook his head. Maryan poured him a glass anyway.

"It's not going to be so easy this time." She grimaced at the taste of the whiskey. "Here, you're going to need it." He took the glass she gave him but didn't drink.

Everything in Morris Winters's lakeside home reeked of money. Not that she'd seen inside the main house—she didn't need to. From the authentic Chagall over the study fireplace, to the collection of Renaissance and Baroque glass ranged in a floor-to-ceiling display case—to antique maps visible through the top of a leather-covered chart table, this room shouted, with elegant subtlety, that Morris Winters was a man of considerable means.

"We have to act. You know that, don't you?"

Morris looked into his whiskey.

"Neither of us can afford to risk them coming together again now."

"She won't have him. Not after what he did."

Maryan laughed without mirth. "She's already had him, Morris, love. She's probably having him again as we speak."

He winced.

"They're together at his house."

"Tramp," Morris muttered. He swallowed half the whiskey in his glass.

"My brother says he's going to marry that tramp."

"He can't!"

"Ah." Maryan draped her jacket over the chart table. "Got your attention at last."

"He's not going to get in my way," Morris said. His mouth was a taut white line. "You're going to make sure he doesn't."

"Am I?"

"I know about you, Maryan. I've always known."

He wasn't supposed to threaten her. "The way I see it, it'll only be one short step from the news that your daughter's marrying Sebastian Plato to a lot of questions about why she hates you enough to sleep with a man who stands for everything you pretend to detest."

"Fix it," he said. He set his bared teeth together. "I don't care what you do, but make sure it doesn't happen."

"Not this time," she told him softly. "You were right when you said we're not the same—not in some ways. I'm not a desperate kid anymore."

"You're a desperate woman."

"Almost as desperate as you."

He grew restless and paced. "She was always a liability."

"Things worked out before. We can make them work out again."

"It's too dangerous now. Too dangerous for me to get involved."

Maryan laughed. She poured herself more whiskey. "It's too dangerous for you not to get involved. Old man Moore came to the offices this afternoon."

"Moore?" Morris's face paled to match his lips. A sheen of sweat showed on his brow. "I warned you years ago that he could be trouble."

"And you were right." She didn't feel as casual as she sounded.

"What does he want."

"What he always wanted."

"Pay him."

"Sebastian won't give him any more money."

Morris downed the rest of his drink. "I said, *you* pay him."

"You're the one who'll pay," she told him calmly. "Until we figure out a permanent fix."

He turned his back on her.

Maryan kicked off her shoes. "Morris," she said, very quietly. "We're going to be partners again. Why not enjoy it?"

He looked over his shoulder at her. "No one's going to get in my way."

"No one," she agreed.

"You know what I like."

"How could I forget?"

"You didn't like it before."

"I was too young, too scared. I'm not scared anymore, Morris."

"Show me your tits."

"Make me."

"I don't have to. Do it."

He advanced and she reached behind her neck to undo the buttons that secured the halter. She held it in place and smiled at him.

Morris didn't smile. He went to a paneled wall and pressed a spot that clicked before an entire section swung inward and slid aside to reveal a shallow recess hung with paraphernalia that made Maryan's heart trip with excitement.

Tapping at the draped windows made them both jump.

"What the *fuck* is that?" Morris hissed. "Is this a setup?"

She shook her head. "Ignore it."

The tapping sounded again. "Maryan," a familiar voice called urgently. "I know you're in there with Winters. Tell him to let me in."

"Who is it?" Morris asked.

"Zoya. She's the woman who—"

"I know who Zoya is. What's she doing here?"

Ron must have told the bitch where Maryan was going. "Let her in."

Morris swallowed audibly. "What are you trying to do to me?"

"It'll be okay," she told him. "She's got as much riding on all of this as we do."

"There isn't any we," he said. He parted the drapes an inch and peered out. *"Fuck!"*

Maryan thought of the two nights she and Ron had spent with Zoya, of the way the woman had manipulated her, and Ron. "She's okay. Let her in." If there was one thing Zoya did really well it was scare the shit out of any man who got in her way.

After another hesitation, Morris unlocked one of the French doors and stood back to allow Zoya to pass. He promptly locked the door again and replaced the drapes carefully.

"I was worried about you, sweetheart," Zoya said to Maryan. "You've got to tell me when you plan to go out in the middle of the night. You need me to protect you."

Maryan's stomach flipped. Zoya patted Morris's face in passing and came to kiss Maryan. She kissed her open-mouthed, her tongue snaking deep into her mouth.

And Maryan's eyes closed. Her breasts throbbed and she was instantly wet. She heard Morris laugh but didn't care.

"I hate to break up this touching scene," he said. "Maryan tells me we share some interests."

Zoya drew away from Maryan and looked at him. "Maybe

we do." Her eyes flickered over the recess behind the paneling. "Maybe we do. Looks as if I've interrupted a reconciliation."

"Morris and I are old friends," Maryan said, her excitement all but choking her now. "We go way back. Way, way back."

"So Ron told me. We talked and decided you might need me to make sure Mr. Winters here fully understands our commitment to the cause—his and ours."

Maryan saw how Morris stared at Zoya. He passed his tongue over his lips. Zoya had the same effect on all men—they all wanted her.

"Don't let me stop you," Zoya said. Dressed in black, a loose silk tank top and long skirt unbuttoned from hem to thigh, she sat in a straight-backed chair and crossed her legs. The skirt fell open, revealing that she'd been too warm, or too hot to wear panties. She clasped her hands behind her neck. The only thing covering her pointed breasts was one thin piece of silk.

With obvious reluctance, Morris looked at Maryan again. "I think your lady friend wants what I want."

Slowly, she began to take her hands from her neck.

"She's got great boobs," Zoya said. "And right now she's got the biggest wide on. I can vouch for that. We know these things about each other, don't we sweetheart?"

Maryan felt suddenly awkward. It was one thing to play along with Ronnie. She could control him. Ronnie might not think she knew he was a switch hitter, but she hadn't bought his story about wanting out of the homo scene completely. Morris Winters was another matter. Maryan didn't know how Zoya's act would affect what had to be accomplished here.

"Show Morris your big brown eyes," Zoya almost crooned. "Come on, uncover 'em, Maryan. The man's waiting."

Maryan let the top of her dress fall and warmed with pleasure at Morris's rapid intake of breath. She stroked her own naked flesh and watched him watching her.

"I do believe the man's Magnum is loaded and ready to go."

Morris ignored Zoya. He pushed Maryan's hands aside and squeezed her breasts until she whimpered. He used his hold on her breasts to push her against the recessed wall. One by one he raised her hands above her head and fastened them in manacles. Swiftly, he pulled off her dress and panties, spread her legs and secured her ankles.

He stood back.

Maryan stared at him. She strained against her bonds. "Get out, Zoya." Agitation mounted until her skin crawled. "Send her away, Morris. She won't be any trouble."

He offered Zoya a hand and she took it, let him pull her to her feet. With his spare hand, he delved beneath her skirt. She undid the belt on his robe.

Maryan squirmed and moaned.

"Sebastian and Bliss can't be allowed to get together," Zoya said. Her black hair streamed over her shoulders. "Ron and I have figured out a way to make sure it doesn't happen." She released Morris for long enough to pull the tank top over her head.

"Oh, God, yes," Morris whispered. "Oh, yes, baby."

They didn't bother to dispense with more clothes. Morris went after Zoya's pointy breasts like a man on forced withdrawal from a very old habit. He worked between her legs until she screamed with pleasure.

"Morris!" Maryan tugged at the manacles until her skin burned. "Stop it! Do you hear me?"

"Whoa, look at this maypole, sister?" Zoya released Morris's prick and whooped when she sprang to loop her legs around his waist and impale herself on him.

A few wild bucks and shouts, and Zoya's feet slid slowly back to the floor. She and Morris clung together, panting.

Maryan felt the stirrings of fear.

"Poor Maryan," Zoya said, her voice husky. "And she's being so good. She needs a reward."

"She'll get one," Morris said, but his exhaustion showed in the rapid rise and fall of his chest. "And we'll work together to get what we want."

"Together," Zoya said. She left Morris to pour a drink. She pushed him into the chair she'd vacated and gave him the glass. He slumped.

"Your turn," Zoya said. She came close to Maryan and brushed their breasts together.

Maryan grew hot. She couldn't look at Morris, but she heard him chuckle.

"What would you like, sweetie?" Zoya asked, sinking to her knees. "Ask and it'll be yours."

"Nothing," Maryan said. "Let me out of these things. They hurt."

"Give her a mustache ride," Morris suggested, breaking into loud laughter. "Give big-tittie Maryan a mustache ride."

Zoya joined in his laughter and draped a length of her hair over her upper lip before she buried her face in Maryan's crotch.

Writhing in an attempt to free herself only brought the waves of Maryan's climax faster. She cried out and slammed her butt helplessly against the wall. Then it was over. Zoya took off her skirt, spread it on the floor and stretched out, stark naked and sickeningly beautiful, on top of it.

"Bravo," Morris said.

"Hmm," Zoya sighed, and stretched luxuriously. "Ah yes. Everything's going to be all right. Know why?"

Morris closed his eyes and drank, and said, "why?" as he wiped his mouth with the back of a hand.

"Best reasons in the world," Zoya told him. "We've got everything to win or lose—and we don't trust each other."

# Twenty-three

Bobby Crow rushed up the drive to meet them. His arms flailed in windmill circles until he hurled himself at Sebastian. "Nan said you'd stolen Bliss and locked her up," he said. "I knew you wouldn't do that."

Bliss made owl eyes at Sebastian. "You were right, Bobby. Sebastian wouldn't do that."

"But you've been gone since yesterday," Bobby announced, looking thoroughly satisfied when Sebastian swung him onto his shoulders. "I said you'd probably gone away to get hitched."

Sebastian and Bliss laughed and Sebastian said, "Where did you get a word like that?"

"They say it on TV all the time," Bobby said, bouncing contentedly as they went into the lodge. "And Auntie Fab says she never wants to get hitched. I wish my mom and dad were hitched."

Sebastian rubbed the boy's legs. "Your mom and dad got you. They couldn't have wished for anything better."

How could she ever have thought this man was other than a wonderful human being? Bliss smoothed his back above the waist of his jeans and followed along toward the hubbub emanating from the kitchens.

Sebastian stood aside to let Bliss go in first. She mouthed, "Thanks a lot," and prepared to face her fate.

"Bliss!" Venus Crow enveloped her in a heavily sandalwood-scented embrace, then held her away while she studied her anxiously from head to toe. "Oh, my dear, they wouldn't call the police. I told them you could be lying dead somewhere, but they still wouldn't call them."

"I should hope not," Bliss said. "You all knew I left with Sebastian. That means you all knew where I was—if I'm supposed to keep you informed."

"Well, you are." Vic's bare chest expanded. Today his black leather pants were silver-studded at the sideseams. His gray hair hung loose. "We've got a family here, Bliss. Families look out for each other."

"They do, Bliss," Liberty said. Her eyes were puffy as if she'd been crying.

"Thank you," Bliss said. Their concern touched her, but today she was in the mood to love everyone, to embrace everyone. "Any problems Polly? Fab?"

The sisters grinned. "Not a thing," Polly said. "Prue called in a snit again, but I told her you were out."

Fabiola shook her head. Her eyes never left Sebastian. "We got calls from Zoya," she told him. "Polly and I did. We've got interviews tomorrow."

"That's great." He swung Bobby to the floor but kept a grip on his hand. "I'll stop by her office and find out what she's got in mind."

Polly crossed her arms so tightly Bliss hid a smile.

"The police came again just after you left," Fab said. "They keep looking around by the bluff, but I don't think they're finding what they want."

Venus made sounds that might have been a foreign language or an incantation. She wore magenta again. A wide band of black edged blue shadow around her eyes.

"Please, Mom," Polly said. "Relax, will you?"

Venus held up both hands. "I must be open to any messages they want me to receive."

"I want you to receive a message," Sebastian told her. "All of you. Bliss and I are getting married."

In the furor that followed, Bliss struggled beneath the hugs that came from all sides—including from Sebastian, who took his opportunity to kiss her soundly. Cheers went up.

Bliss had noted that Vic wasn't brimming with enthusiasm at the announcement. She smiled at him. He looked at Sebastian and said, "Take good care of her."

Sebastian studied the other man speculatively. "I intend to."

Bliss hadn't noticed Liberty slip away. The kitchen door opened and she came back in carrying one of the large, gaudy fish she made to sell at local fairs.

"Liberty?"

She shushed Vic. "I want to be the first to give them a gift," she said, holding the pottery piece in both hands. "An engagement gift. I've always thought it would be great to get engaged and for everyone to be happy for you."

Bliss accepted the fish and examined its shiny green and yellow stripes, and popping purple eyes. "It's wonderful, Liberty. Thank you."

"Never be another like it," Vic remarked and Bliss frowned at him. He didn't seem to get it that Liberty loved him. He looked away and added, "Each of your pieces has a lot of energy and humor."

Liberty glowed. "Thank you, Vic."

An awkward lull fell.

"You forgot to tell her Lennox called, too." Liberty said. "Says he's at the Bellevue Arts and Crafts Fair if you can get by."

Bliss observed that Sebastian didn't even react to the mention of Lennox this time. He said, "We can stop by this evening if you feel like it."

Polly wiped her hands on her jeans and went to open the oven. The smell of roasting garlic escaped. "The poets are eating in," she said, shutting the door again. "How about you two?"

"I'm just picking up some things," Bliss said. "I'll be back later, but don't wait dinner for me."

Venus took up her incantation again.

Polly hummed, "So Long It's Been Good to Know You."

"Well," Fab said, too loudly. "Are you going to give up the Point, then?"

Everyone grew still.

She should have known they'd be worried about the future of Hole Point. "No, I'm not giving it up. This place is special to me. It always will be."

Even the air seemed to relax. "But you won't be around?" Polly said. "Dumb question. Of course you won't."

"I'll come and go," she told them. "I don't intend to stay home and do nothing. And I don't want to teach again. So Hole Point remains my thing."

Vic took the fish from Bliss and set it at the back of a counter. "Better take care of that. Could be worth something." He grinned. "Shit, if things get—"

"Vic!" Bliss frowned at him.

"Okay. Sorry about that. Shoot, if the shit—I mean, if the sugar gets any deeper around here I'm going to throw up." He opened the door to leave and Spike ambled in as Vic and Liberty left.

Polly and Fab busied themselves around the kitchen while their mother moved into a tinkling, tummy-rolling dance.

"How are the repairs coming on your place, Venus?" Bliss asked. "You must be looking forward to going home."

"I don't have a place anymore." The woman didn't miss a step. "They raised the rent and I couldn't afford to pay it. There aren't any allowances for extraordinary people with extraordinary talents, unless they make a lot of money. I no longer have a home."

Sebastian, Bliss noted, avoided meeting her gaze. "There's room at the bungalow," she said. "I'm sure Polly and Fab will be glad to have you as long as you need to stay."

If Venus was grateful, Bliss noted no sign of it, but the twins stopped working and flashed her their pretty smiles. "I'm going to pick up a swimsuit," she told Sebastian. "You promised me a dip in that beautiful pool of yours before the sun decides to quit again."

Bobby went with Bliss and Sebastian into the great room.

"Leave them alone, Bobby," Polly called.

Sebastian ruffled the boy's hair and said, "He's okay."

Promptly, Bobby ran ahead and up the stairs.

"He's getting very attached to you," Bliss said. "He's needy, Sebastian."

"Of course he is. Not a problem. Not to me. I've been there." He went ahead of Bliss, taking the stairs two at a time. "I want to make sure you understand some things about Maryan and Ron."

"We do need to talk some more," Bliss agreed. "Later, though, huh?"

"Yeah, later."

Bobby stood in front of Bliss's door, a brown paper sack in his tanned arms. "I put it up here until you came."

"What's this?" Sebastian settled a hand on one of Bobby's thin shoulders. "Another engagement present?"

"Uh-uh."

Bliss and Sebastian exchanged a look and Bliss said, "Okay."

In her rooms, the boy put his parcel on the recliner. "I found it. Then I was scared."

A tightness squeezed Bliss's stomach. "Can't be that bad."

He drew up his shoulders. "Nan said there's bad stuff around here and we shouldn't let it get close to us."

"Your nan means well," Sebastian said. "But she's got a big imagination. It's probably because she's so creative."

"So, what's in the bag?" Bliss reached for it.

Bobby snatched it up again. "Nan says the police are always bad news. That's what she calls them, bad news. That means they're bad."

"Not always." If Bliss had her way, Bobby Crow wouldn't look so troubled. He'd have more carefree moments, more chance to just be a child.

Bobby set down his bag again, opened it, and drew out what it had hidden.

"Oh, God," Sebastian murmured. He found Bliss's hand.

She asked, "Where did you find it, Bobby?"

He scrubbed his eyes with his fists. "I was going to throw it away."

"Why?"

"So's the police wouldn't get mad at you."

"Bobby?" Sebastian dropped to his haunches and looked into the boy's face. "Tell us where it was."

"In the back of your truck. Under Beater's blankets."

Bliss stopped breathing. "Sebastian," she whispered. "It's Nose's, isn't it?"

"I'm sure it is," he said, staring at a badly scratched miniature camera, its back gaping open. "Exotic little number. Too bad the film isn't still in it."

Another hour or so and the sun would set.

Bliss sat beside Sebastian on the side of his pool and splashed her feet. Maryan and Ron lay side by side on chaises. Using an economical crawl stroke, the beautiful super-model, Zoya, did lazy laps.

Sebastian and Bliss had decided not to talk to anyone about the camera, or the subsequent lengthy session with the police, until forced to do so. Bobby had made his find the day before and hidden it because he feared Sebastian would get into trouble for "fibbing and stealing." His fears had been quickly put to rest, and his absolute faith in Sebastian rapidly restored. Bliss and Sebastian weren't so certain the police were equally convinced.

"This is a beautiful house," she told him. "I grew up on the lake."

"Yeah, I know." He settled a hand on her thigh. "I didn't."

With the discovery of the camera, from which the police

clearly assumed the film had been deliberately removed, the joy had gone out of the day.

"You're not really worried about the police, are you?"

He stroked her leg absently. "I meant it when I said I don't want you out of my sight."

She linked her fingers with his on her leg. "No one's going to hurt me."

"No, they're not. I'll make sure of that."

Nearby, Zoya pulled herself from the pool and picked up a towel to blot her hair and skin. "Can I get anyone a drink?"

Bliss and Sebastian declined, as did Maryan and Ron. Zoya strolled into the house.

"I think Maryan's relaxing with me," Bliss said. "It was sweet of her to buy me more flowers."

"Place is beginning to look like a funeral parlor."

She bumped him with a shoulder. "Don't be a cynic. She's trying."

"Sorry. She is trying. She's also drinking less, thank God."

Bliss didn't pursue that. "I'm going to take that dip. How about you?"

"Me, too. Then we'll take a wander around the fair and find some dinner."

"Sebastian," Zoya called. "Phone for you. Sounds important."

He said, "Damn," and hopped lithely to his feet. "I'll be right back."

Bliss slid into the water and watched him move toward the conservatory. His shoulders swung with the natural grace he'd always possessed. She took in every inch of him and her tummy contracted with the desire she'd started to expect whenever she as much as thought about him. Desire? Or lust? She smiled and pushed off the wall with her feet.

Lust was allowed. Lust was okay.

She swam to the middle of the pool and heard almost twin splashes as Maryan and Ron dove in to join her. They still made her uncomfortable, but she smiled as she slicked her hair back.

With his right hand, Ron smacked the surface of the water and sent spray over her face. He laughed. Bliss returned the favor.

Maybe they'd all be able to get along after all.

"I've never seen Sebastian look so happy," Maryan said. She wore an embarrassingly low-cut pink swimsuit. "You're good for him."

"Thanks." Bliss felt a flush of warmth toward the other woman, and gratitude. "He's good for me, too. Isn't it funny how life is? Who'd have expected this after so many years."

"Not me," Maryan said, smiling.

"Race you two for the bottom," Ron said and promptly flipped up his bottom and shot downward.

Maryan looked bored but obligingly followed.

Bliss, who loved the water, dove after them.

The center of the pool was deep. She reached the bottom and touched with a hand. Ron's face turned toward hers, a distorted grin stretching his mouth. He twisted over and caught her ankle, and she swatted at him.

Her head touched the bottom.

Ron tickled the bottom of her foot and she kicked out at him. In the future she'd call him Iron Lungs. She wanted to go up.

He saluted and headed upward. Bliss saw Maryan's pink swimsuit headed in the same direction.

She made to revolve herself. Her scalp hurt.

Reaching for the top of her head, she pulled.

Something trapped a length of her hair.

Looking up, pumping her legs to stay in place, she vaguely saw the bottoms of Ron and Maryan's feet. Then they paddled until she couldn't make them out.

She pulled again, but couldn't turn to see what held her.

Panic, deep and dreadful panic swelled. And her lungs swelled.

The blue water took on a hazy quality. Working frantically, she grappled with her hair.

Caught in a drain.

Her brain clamored. Her hair had snagged on a drain. Pulling, tearing, she squirmed. Too much hair.

Her swollen lungs began to release their air. She mustn't let them.

Burning in her throat.

She wanted to scream. Inside her head she yelled for help.

Bubbles streamed upward from her nose.

The hair was under the drain, under the rim, battened down there. Desperately, she groped for some way to release the grill and found a screw.

She managed a turn.

No air.

The water pressed in, pressed her body, her insides.

No air in her lungs.

She had to take a breath.

Chlorine burned her eyes, stung her nose. Her fingers stopped working.

Drowning.

A roar filled her ears, seeped over her brain. If she breathed, she'd drown. The roaring got louder. The water crushed her, then cradled her. Warm water.

Her eyes closed. It grew more quiet. No need to fight anymore.

She opened her mouth to breathe in the warm, cradling water.

# Twenty-four

Sebastian slammed down the phone on Morris Winters. Warning him to stay away from his daughter! As if they were both still kids to be manipulated.

The phone rang again. He looked at it, turned away and walked outside. Mentioning the call to Bliss would only upset her. Damn it, they were going to be happy. No one would get in the way of that.

Scooping water into each other's faces, Maryan and Ron shrieked and shouted in the shallow end of the pool.

Sebastian smiled and looked around for Bliss. She must be swimming. He walked to the edge and scanned the surface. Not a sign of her. And she wasn't on one of the chaises. Lowering sun glittered off the nearby lake.

He glanced down, hesitated an instant, and dived. *Bliss!* She was on the bottom of the pool.

When he reached her, wrapped an arm around her, he couldn't pull her with him.

Her hair was caught in a drain. Running on instinct, he found a central screw, jammed a thumbnail into the groove and turned. She swung sluggishly against him. He raised an arm and surged to the surface.

Dragging her from the pool, he gripped her middle and let her hang forward, slapped the middle of her back while water poured from her mouth and nose.

"Call Medic 1," he yelled, stretching her on her back. "Maryan! Call Medic 1!"

He heard the babble of voices as the others approached. "Come on," he muttered, lifting Bliss's chin. "Come on, sweetheart."

He brought the heel of one hand down in the middle of her chest, tipped her chin even higher—and her eyes opened. She reached for his wrist with fingers that couldn't hold on.

"Oh, my God," Sebastian said when her breath crossed his face. Gradually her eyes focused. "Bliss, you almost drowned. Oh, thank God!"

He registered three pairs of ankles nearby but could only look at Bliss.

"Still want the medics?" Ron asked.

Bliss coughed and said, "No." She rubbed her scalp and tried to sit up. "Caught. I couldn't unscrew it."

"What happened?" Maryan asked in a voice that trembled. "We were all in the water. Playing around. She was right behind us."

"Drain," Bliss gasped. "I tried to unscrew it."

Sebastian frowned. He picked her up and carried her toward the house.

"I bet she turned the screw the wrong way," Ron said, hurrying along beside them. "Geez, I didn't even notice she wasn't with us anymore."

Grim suspicion sickened Sebastian. "You wouldn't think her hair would go underneath unless the screw was loose, would you? It should have come free as soon as she moved. Makes you wonder how the screw tightened down again."

Vague threats. An "accident" that almost killed Bliss. An accident that had killed Nose. Sebastian observed the preoccupied way Bliss pushed strawberries and cream around her dish and figured she was mulling the same thoughts.

The colorful melee of people at the fair streamed through the lengthening shadows. She'd insisted she was fine, insisted getting out and having some "fun" would be the best medicine—for both of them. Her face was still so pale.

They sat at a table in the driveway between a multistory car park and the massive block of Bellevue Square's shops. Stalls of arts and crafts ranged the rest of the drive and stretched throughout the lower level of the car park.

"You don't really want that, do you?" he asked.

Bliss pushed her paper plate away. "I thought I did."

"Sweetheart, would you just let me get a doctor to check you over?"

"No."

He suppressed a smile. "I wish you'd say what you mean. Okay, no doctor. But that was quite a shock you had."

She nodded. "You, too?"

"Oh, I guess you'd say I was shocked." Leaning toward her, he framed her face. "I nearly lost you just when I've finally found you again. How shocked do you think I was—am?"

Her eyes grew larger.

Sebastian kissed her. "I vote for a speedy marriage, then we get away from here for a long honeymoon."

"I thought you had a business to run."

"I do. And I can run it from anywhere in the world."

"I have a business to run."

"You know how to use a phone, too."

She looped her arms around his neck, studied his mouth, and brushed her own slowly back and forth over his lips.

"Mmm. I think we need to go where we can be alone."

"We're going to do that." Her voice was husky. "But I do want to see Lennox. And take a quick look to make sure there's nothing at the fair I can't live without."

"You're the only thing I can't live without."

"Ooh, you know how to make sure I can't think straight anymore."

"Good." He stood and offered her a hand. "Let's find your friend Lennox's stuff, then go home."

"You're being very nice to him."

"No I'm not. I want him to see us together. I'm human. I want to gloat a bit."

She punched him playfully. "You're rotten."

"How well you know me."

By the time they found Lennox, Sebastian had bought Bliss a tiny, pottery water garden, a coat made of bright yellow hand-woven silk, a wooden, heart-shaped box so smooth its opening was invisible, and a set of twelve prints of Seattle she'd paused to admire.

"No more." She laughed up at him. "I hate everything else at this fair. There isn't another thing I want."

"Good," he said, and spotted two rows of brass buttons on a navy-blue blazer. Lennox Rood stared hard at Sebastian and he was reminded of the old saying about looks that might kill. "Here's your buddy, Lennox," he told Bliss.

She spun around and hugged the man!

Lennox enjoyed every damned second. He hugged right back and smiled over her head until she stepped away.

Sebastian stuck out a hand and the other man shook it—limply.

"Sebastian and I are getting married," Bliss said happily. "I wanted you to know. I wanted to be the one to tell you."

The man deserved admiration. His smile barely slipped before he transformed it into a grin. Within seconds he was pressing one of his paintings on them. "An engagement gift." Sebastian had the fleeting thought that they might actually have to display the gifts they received from Bliss's oddball friends—at least if there was warning that they intended to visit.

"I'll wrap it for you," Lennox said, and Sebastian felt how the man welcomed a chance to look somewhere other than at Bliss.

She examined a profusion of brilliant windsocks trailing from wires and all but brushing the ground. "Hah! Look at this one. A big, pink pig."

Sebastian looked.

"I hate it." Bliss laughed. "I certainly don't want it!"

"Could you hold that corner," Lennox said of the brown paper he was using to wrap a painting entitled, *Sea Music,* for reasons Sebastian couldn't determine.

Several minutes, and numerous pieces of tape later, he juggled packages and took the latest one beneath an arm. "Thanks," he said, with all the warmth he'd could muster. "Will you visit sometime?"

Lennox clicked his jaw from side to side and nodded. "Sometime. Take care of her."

"I wouldn't dare not to." Men certainly lined up to look after Bliss.

He turned to leave, but didn't immediately see her.

She emerged from the forest of windsocks, clutched his elbow and hurried him away with only a brief, "bye," to poor old Lennox.

"I think we'll have to leave," Sebastian told her. "I don't think we can carry anymore."

She waited until they were out of sight of Lennox's stand before stopping and pulling Sebastian to face her. "We've got trouble. Big trouble."

"It'll be all right." He refused to believe Ron or Maryan had tried to drown Bliss. "We've just had a bunch of rocky times to go through. We'll get away and everything will be fine."

"I'm not so sure. I just got another of those *damn* warnings." Pallor made her eyes an even darker shade of blue. "He told me to stay away from you. *Again.*"

Sebastian screwed up his eyes. "Who told you? When? We were—"

"*You* were busy with the painting. It only took a few seconds."

"*What?*" People bumped them in passing. "What only took a few seconds?"

"Pulling me backward into those windsocks. Covering my mouth, and telling me you were bad for my health."

"I don't believe this."

"Believe it," Bliss said, and drew several long strands of white silk and silver thread from her neck.

Officer Ballard tucked his pen back into his pocket. "Very interesting."

*Very interesting and I think you're a nut case,* Bliss thought. Sebastian had insisted upon calling the police and having them send someone out to talk to them at the Point. Evidently Ballard had inherited the dubious honor of dealing with what he probably considered nuisance calls relating to Bliss. At least the man had told them the police thought some curious spectator had probably found Nose's camera, then become scared and disposed of it in the back of Sebastian's truck.

"I'll go back to the station and file a report," Ballard said politely.

"I want Bliss watched," Sebastian said, while she raised her eyes to the ceiling. She could almost hear Polly and Fab breathing on the other side of the kitchen door while they listened. "She's been threatened and she's been hurt. There aren't going to be any more risks taken. If she's not with me, she's to be watched by you people."

"We can have a car drive by now and again," Ballard said.

"I didn't say—"

"Sebastian! Please. You can't expect the police to spare men to watch me all the time."

"Then I'll hire someone."

"Better make sure he keeps away from that bluff," Ballard said mildly.

"I don't find you funny." Sebastian didn't sound as if he found anything funny. "From now on, until we get to the bottom of this, you'll be with me, Bliss. Understand?"

"How exactly are you hurt, miss?" Ballard asked.

She touched her neck. This time the threads from her scarf had been applied over the collar of her shirt. "He yanked on my neck. There aren't any marks."

"Right. Like you already said."

"This afternoon she almost drowned in my pool."

"Really?" Ballard's impassive expression changed a little. "You didn't mention that."

"It was an accident," Bliss said. "I caught my hair in a drain."

"I see."

"No you don't," Sebastian said. "She should have been able to pull free."

"But she couldn't?"

"If I'd been a few seconds longer going after her we might not be having this conversation."

"Ah. So you think someone tried to drown Ms. Winters?"

"They absolutely did not," Bliss said. "It was just one of those freaky things. You're too jumpy, Sebastian."

"That's not what you said at Bellevue Square."

"It's what I'm saying now. Someone put that silk around my neck, Officer. Like I told you, it's the second time it's happened and I don't know why. I'm not frightened by it because I think that's what this person wants. I just think it's a good idea for the police to be aware of these events."

"Right." Ballard brightened considerably. "Absolutely right. And we'll be keeping an ear open in case you need us. You just let us know, Ms. Winters."

"I will," she told him. "I certainly will."

*"I certainly will,* " Sebastian said venomously when Ballard had left. "The truth is that unless you're dead, they aren't going to do anything."

"Don't say that! You frighten me."

"Oh, love." He enfolded her in a big hug. "I'm sorry. This has been a helluva day, is all."

"I hate it when you—"

"Swear?" He chuckled into her hair. "Yes, I know. It's still been a helluva day."

"Woman from the Arts Commission on the phone for you, Bliss," Liberty said from the kitchen doorway. "Says it's something about grants."

"Ooh!" Bliss leaped away from Sebastian. "Sit right there on the couch. Grants are a language I speak fluently."

She left him and ran to pick up the kitchen phone. "Hi! Bliss Winters here."

"It's been a long time," a woman's voice said. "I owe you some explanations."

Bliss looked up, and through the window. "Who is this?"

"Can we meet? Just the two of us?"

The voice wasn't familiar.

"If I thought anyone else would know, I couldn't come. It'd be too dangerous."

"All right," Bliss said slowly. "We can probably meet."

"I'm doing it for Sebastian. I owe him that much. You won't tell him, will you? If you tell him I won't feel I'm finally free of the guilt."

Bliss bowed her head. "I won't tell him," she said, knowing now who she was speaking to.

"This is Crystal."

# Twenty-five

"Little Point," Polly said.

"Appropriate," Fab responded, her face folded in concentration. "But it doesn't make the point, does it?"

Bliss and Vic chuckled.

Polly wrinkled her nose and said, "She doesn't even know she made a funny."

"Mm," Fab said, but she grinned. "Pretty little funny, if you ask me. But we can't call the place Hole Point if Sebastian's getting the hole filled."

Bliss's full attention wasn't on the discussion. She'd successfully persuaded Sebastian to go to his office to take care of some European business, but timing would still be close if she was going to keep her appointment with Crystal and get back before he did.

"No Point," Vic said triumphantly. "Hole Point today. No Point tomorrow, when Sebastian's filled the hole with concrete."

"He isn't doing it himself," Liberty reminded him.

"Shit!" Vic said. He scowled at her. "Do you have to pick on every word I say?"

The twins burst into a flurry of motion, clattering clean dishes into cupboards.

Liberty's cheeks had turned bright red.

"Vic"—Bliss stared at his angry face—"Liberty didn't mean anything. You're so touchy. And you don't appreciate her." Her palms sweated. This confrontation was overdue, but that didn't make it easier.

He looked away. "I appreciate Liberty. She's the best. We're all a bit shaken up by so many changes, so fast."

"That's right," Liberty agreed. "Come on, Vic. I've got to work for a while."

"Yeah. Me, too."

The instant the twins were left alone with Bliss, they talked excitedly about the interviews they were to have at Raptor. Bliss half-listened, showed enthusiasm in most of the right places, and worked out how she'd get to her meeting with Crystal.

"Can I come in?"

The sound of her mother's voice startled Bliss. She swung around to see Kitten already walking into the kitchen.

"I know I should have called, but I don't see enough of you, darling." She didn't meet Bliss's eyes. "So I decided to take a chance on finding you at home." Her voice broke and she rushed to fall into a chair at the kitchen table and bury her face.

Bliss was aware of the twins slipping quickly from the lodge and closing the door softly behind them.

"Has something happened, Mom?" Bliss asked awkwardly.

Kitten's hair was as perfect as ever, her powder blue outfit as impeccable as ever, but her shoulders heaved, and her sobs tripped Bliss's heart into a runaway rhythm.

"Mom?"

"I've been a bad mother to you."

Bliss rubbed Kitten's shoulders and pulled a chair close beside hers. "I'm okay," she said. "I'm happy. Really happy."

Kitten raised her face and Bliss noticed what she hadn't noticed before; streaked mascara and the signs that her mother had been crying for a long time.

"Oh, Mom, what is it? Is it something with you and Daddy?"

"No! No, it's never been that. Morris and I have a wonderful marriage. We always have. But I shouldn't have ignored you the way I have." She fumbled in her bag for a pack of cigarettes and a lighter.

"I didn't know you still smoked," Bliss said, grateful for any diversion.

"Never quit," Kitten said, lighting up. "I just made sure you didn't know—or anyone else but Morris. I'm not young anymore, Bliss."

At a loss for words, Bliss resumed awkwardly patting her mother's back.

"I don't have the right to ask, but I need you. I need to feel close . . . No. I do feel close to you. It's just that I've never been good at affection."

Why tonight, of all nights? Bliss thought, and instantly disliked herself for being self-absorbed. She sighed. "I'm okay, Mom. You took care of all the important stuff."

"No, I didn't. I took care of your needs."

And put her own needs first. Her own and those of Morris Winters.

"Morris is very demanding, Bliss."

The statement shocked Bliss. "I know that, Mother."

"He's always known exactly what he wants, and what he needed from me as his wife. And from you."

"Yes."

"I'm not criticizing him."

"No."

"But I am criticizing myself. I should have made up for what he didn't have time to give you."

Once again words failed Bliss.

"Will you let me try to do that now?" Kitten stubbed her barely smoked cigarette out among thumbtacks in a shallow bowl. "Will you? Could we try to start being mother and daughter like other people are? Bliss—"

"Hush." For the first time, Bliss saw Kitten Winters's vulnerability, her insecurity. "I don't know what to say, except I'd like it if I thought you felt something for me."

"I do! I love you! And I hate myself for never knowing how to show you."

"Mother—"

Kitten got up abruptly. She found a tissue in her purse and wiped her eyes. "Of course you can't forgive me. Just forgive me after a lifetime of never being able to turn to me for anything. Anything but money and lectures on what you should or shouldn't do. Why should you forgive me?"

"Because it would make me feel very good," Bliss told her. She stood and took her mother into her arms. "Give it time, okay, Mom? Give *us* some time. You've made me glad tonight. Is that a good enough start?"

Kitten's renewed sobbing tore at Bliss. "It's okay. It will be okay. I don't think either of us has known too much happiness."

"I've always been trying to do what I thought I was supposed to do," Kitten said into Bliss's shoulder. "I was relieved when that boy left town. I thought I was supposed to be, because Morris was relieved."

Bliss stood absolutely still. "You knew about Sebastian from the beginning?"

Kitten sniffed. She raised her tear-streaked face and blew her nose. "Everyone knew, didn't they? I was on the PTA and Morris was very active with the sports program—the stadium and so forth."

"But none of those people knew about Sebastian and me. Not until afterward when the stories about Crystal Moore circulated."

"That's what I mean. We knew afterward." She dabbed her eyes. "Everyone knew afterward."

"You never said anything to me."

"I know." Kitten cried again, but quietly this time. "So wrong. I should have comforted you, but Morris was angry about what it would have done to us if you had gone away with the Plato boy."

"You'd have survived."

"Oh, darling, things were different then. You couldn't get away with the things public figures get away with now. Morris's opponents would have made a meal out of it. If Morris couldn't take care of his child, how could he be trusted with the good of his constituents. That sort of thing. We needed a united front."

"And you got it," Bliss said without bitterness. She no longer had any reason to feel bitter.

"At your expense. Whatever happened to that dreadful Crystal girl? I assume he divorced her."

"You can certainly assume so, Mother. Sebastian and I are going to be married."

Kitten's mouth fell open in slow motion. "Well . . . Well, obviously I knew you were seeing him. After all, he was here and so on. Morris said he'd spoken of marriage, but we thought that was Plato trying to make your father upset."

How quickly the mood changed. "I'm going to marry him."

"I see." Kitten selected a thumbtack from its bed of ashes and rolled it between finger and thumb. "Well, you know what's best for you."

"Mother?" Bliss ducked her head until Kitten met her eyes. "That's it? You're not going to berate me or say how bad this is going to look for Daddy? Because of his stand on child pornography—which Sebastian would have absolutely no part of, by the way?"

Kitten straightened her back. "I'm going to make sure your father and I support you in whatever you decide to do. Morris will manage very well. I'm convinced he's going to go all the way to—well, you know. We don't actually say it."

"I hope Daddy agrees with you."

"He will." Kitten actually smiled. "You'd be surprised how much influence I have over your father. He hides it very well in public. His strong image, you know. But in private he's a pussycat. With me."

That wasn't exactly the picture Bliss recalled, but if it made her mother feel good, so be it. "Then I'm happy. I'd like us to be a family." She couldn't say "again," because it would be for the first time. "Actually, I'm happier than I've been since Sebastian and I agreed to marry when I was seventeen. What happened then wasn't his fault. Not really."

"What do you mean?"

"He was young. He made a mistake. I think Crystal's going to try to tell me—"

"Crystal?" Kitten wrapped her fingers around Bliss's wrist. "You've heard from her?"

Bliss looked away.

"She contacted you?"

"Yes. We're all a lot more mature than we were in high school. She wants me to know exactly what happened."

"Oh, my dear," Kitten said, her eyes filling with tears yet again. "Wouldn't that be painful for you?"

"Probably. But she told me she owes it to Sebastian." Perhaps this was appropriate, sharing the saddest part of her growing up years with her mother. "She's staying with her father and I'm going to go and talk with her."

Kitten shook her head. "I hope she really means well. She could intend to try to make him look bad in your eyes again."

"I've thought of that."

"Of course you have. You are so brave. I suppose that's one of the few good things that came out of having to rely on yourself so much when you were growing up. It made you strong."

Bliss turned the corners of her mouth up.

"But it didn't give you a high opinion of your parents, did it?"

"Mom—"

"No. No, you don't have to answer that. I don't have any right to expect you to throw your arms around me and tell me I was wonderful after all. But you are going to give me a chance, aren't you?"

"Yes," Bliss said. "Yes, I am. I'd like to."

Kitten took several moments to gain control enough to say, "Thank you. When are you meeting that woman?"

Bliss looked at the Delft clock. "Quite soon." Her stomach turned over.

"Shall I come with you, darling? I will if it'll help."

"No. This is one of those things you do alone. But I should think about getting there."

Kitten gathered her purse and gloves, and faced Bliss again. "May I call you tomorrow? I'm going to try anyway. And I . . . I'm going to suggest to Morris that we give a party for you and Sebastian. Good night, Bliss." She rose to her toes to kiss Bliss's cheek. "I'll talk to you tomorrow."

Bliss didn't attempt to follow her mother, or to say anything else. She allowed herself a faint spark of hope for the future. Morris Winters had crushed his wife into the shape he'd needed her to be—he'd continue to crush anyone who needed to be changed for his purposes. A relationship with her father would never be in the cards, but perhaps Bliss could draw close to Kitten anyway.

On the way to her room to gather a jacket, Bliss recalled the many times she'd watched her father humiliate her mother, ever so subtly, of course, with his dismissal of her, and his attention to any attractive female in sight.

Morris Winters had a great deal to answer for. He would hate her marriage to Sebastian and he'd let them both know it, but he couldn't hurt them. And, despite Prue O'Leary's best efforts, Bliss's relationship with Sebastian wouldn't harm Morris's career. Bliss didn't regret wishing it might.

Getting a cab to come to a private address in Bellevue would be almost impossible. Wearing a sweat suit and tennis shoes, she put money in her pocket and set off to catch a bus into Bellevue. At night the route was sparsely served and almost an hour passed before she arrived at the Bellevue bus terminal. She cut through narrow side streets to the closest hotel, where she flagged a waiting taxi.

After his wife's death, Jim Moore had moved from Seattle to a trailer on a lot in the hills east of Bellevue. The silent cab driver followed Bliss's directions with only the snap of his gum in response.

They took I-90 and headed away from Bellevue. A few miles west from the town of Issaquah, the taxi left the freeway and veered south. Dense stands of fir all but obliterated the moon-filmed sky over a narrow road that climbed Cougar Mountain.

Too nervous to sit still, Bliss pushed to the edge of her seat. "D'you know, I've lived in the area most of my life and I've never been up here."

The driver snapped his gum.

"There's a sign that says Beware of the Dog. We've got to look for that. It'll be on the left. Black and white sign."

The gum snapped.

Another switchback bend in the road, followed by another, and another, brought Bliss's stomach into her throat.

The driver's sudden, "Shit! Goddamn sonafabitch, fool!" and a sharp veer to the right, all but knocked her from the seat. "D'you see that? See it, huh? Goddamn fool."

She'd felt more than seen a car overtake. Traveling fast and showing no lights, the suggestion of its pale shape immediately disappeared into the darkness ahead.

"No lights! Shit! Round the bend and all over me before I knew it. Good job I'm on top of things."

"Yes," Bliss agreed weakly, wishing the man would go back to snapping his gum. "Very foolish person."

The man subsided, muttering unintelligibly.

They took an almost horizontal left. "I think we're getting close," Bliss said. "I'll need you to wait for me."

That earned her a grunt.

"There it is!" Bliss pointed to a sign beside the road. "You pull onto the shoulder and wait here. I'll run in and"—she thought rapidly—"I'll get my friend and have you take us both back to Bellevue." She didn't trust the cabby to hang around long.

With his protests following her, she leaped from the car and dashed past the dog sign, sparing a thought for the nature of the animal, but instantly discarding that thought.

Pale gravel gave her a route to follow.

Moving more slowly, she advanced. The only sounds were of wind sighing through tall trees and the distant baying of coyotes serenading the moon. Her stomach cramped, and sweat turned cold on her back. Another hundred yards and she arrived at a clearing.

Light shone in one window of a trailer parked at the far side of the area. Dimly, Bliss could make out shapes spilling over the ground in all directions. Her eyes began to adjust and she saw barrels and boxes and lengths of wood and metal. Objects she couldn't identify lay among plastic bags that had never been closed. Whatever bulged from the bags was probably responsible for the odor of rotting garbage.

Bliss pressed a hand over her heart and approached.

Something moved by her feet.

She looked down and barely contained a scream. The sinuous body of a snake passed over one white tennis shoe.

Bliss kicked, kicked at nothing. The only remaining evidence of the reptile was a sibilant rustle.

Muscles in her thighs ached. Sweat stung her eyes.

Two steps leading to the trailer door had broken free on one side. Bliss reached up and knocked, and the door eased open a few inches. She made herself take a deep breath and said, "Crystal? It's Bliss Winters."

Inside the trailer a radio blared crackling, distorted gospel music.

Bliss knocked harder. "Crystal?"

"Come on in," a man's voice shouted. "She's primpin' as usual."

She didn't want to go in. She wanted to run, and she wanted to run right now.

"I can't get up," the man's voice announced. "The arthritis is too bad."

The cab driver was a few hundred yards away. If she didn't come back soon, surely he'd come to find her. And how much harm could one arthritic old man do? Crystal wanted to set things straight. Bliss had heard remorse in the other woman's voice.

Avoiding the broken steps, she gripped the doorjamb and pulled herself up to the threshold.

She wanted to hear Crystal's version of what had happened—before, and after she left Seattle with Sebastian.

The instant she entered the gloomy trailer, the door slammed shut behind her.

Bliss jumped.

A lone candle, waxed to a plate, burned beside a sink overflowing with dishes.

"You sit yourself down, missy. We got talkin' to do." A stooped old man shuffled forward. He pushed her toward a split bench seat from some old vehicle.

She didn't sit. Her head felt light. "Who are you?"

"Crystal's dad. Who else would I be?"

Of course. Bliss struggled to calm down. "Where is she?"

"Doin' like she's told for once. Lettin' me have my say first."

Bliss glanced toward a glow around the door into another room. "Can we put a real light on in here?" The sour stench of old food and unwashed bodies brought acid into her throat.

"Light don't work no more. Electricity's been cut off."

Bliss looked toward the other room again.

"Oil lamp," the man said, shuffling through the gloom. He hovered close to Bliss, then moved on to place himself between her and the room she couldn't see. "That Plato's got a lot to answer for. And I'm goin' to get my due. You're goin' to help me."

He couldn't make her stay. She felt a breeze behind and to her left. The door was still open.

"You gotta do what's right," Crystal's father said. "You gotta leave a married man alone. My girl ended up in an institution because of him. She's better now. But he's gotta look after us."

She took a step backward, and a ball of flame parted thin curtains covering a window over the sink.

Bliss screamed.

The curtains ignited instantly.

"Get out!" Bliss flung the door wide open. "Come on!"

Transfixed, Moore stood where he was.

"Crystal!" Bliss shouted. "Crystal, run. Now!"

The sound of shattering glass exploded in the small space. Fire burst toward the roof, shutting Bliss off from the sight of Mr. Moore's staring eyes.

Smoke filled her lungs and heat blasted her face.

There was no path to reach Moore—or the other room.

"Crystal!" All she saw was leaping flame shooting along the floor and curling up walls. "Come on! Oh, please, come on!"

She threw herself through the door, crumpled on rock-strewn ground.

Another explosion, bigger this time, shook the trailer. The roof broke open and flames shot into the sky.

Bliss shook so hard, her teeth clattered. She shook and sobbed, and drew back from the intensity of the heat.

"Help!" she cried feebly. "Help!" Help would come too late. Jim Moore would be dead. Crystal would be dead.

She turned and fled, dashed back the way she'd come with feet slipping and her throat making dry, shrieking sounds.

# Twenty-six

The surface of the lake resembled pink satin.

Sebastian stood beside Bliss and watched the sun come up. International calls had kept him at Raptor for hours. He'd left a message on Bliss's machine, warning her he'd be very late, and assumed she was busy somewhere other than in the lodge. When he'd arrived back from Bellevue shortly before five in the morning, he'd confronted the unwelcome and too familiar sight of a police car parked in front of the lodge. Inside he'd found Bliss offering coffee to two police officers—one of them Ballard, naturally.

The police had looked at Sebastian, said their business was complete—for now—and left.

And Bliss had walked out of the lodge and kept on walking until she arrived at the foot of an easement leading to the edge of the lake.

Sebastian had followed, a stride behind.

She hadn't spoken to him yet.

Sebastian could wait.

A small boat slipped through the water, its engine puttering. A single occupant lounged over the tiller in a quiet world he owned for the moment.

The peeling, red limbs of a madrona tree curved overhead. Dew dripped from leathery leaves, and glittered in trembling spider webs.

Bliss crossed her arms tightly and gave a small shudder.

He tapped his knuckles together. Her hair was gathered into a rubber band. The skin on her neck was pale, and vulnerable. If he kissed her there, very softly—just rested his mouth there, and waited—she'd come into his arms.

Sebastian touched her back.

"You can't blame me for wanting to hear her side of the story." Her shoulders rose. "I'm only human."

"Bliss—"

"Now she's dead and I know it wasn't an accident. I saw the fire start. I think someone watched me. Followed me. I think they wanted me to die, too."

"Whoa." He turned her toward him. "What are you talking about?"

Dirt streaked her sweatsuit, and her face bore faint gray smudges. She said, "It'll be all over the papers soon enough."

"I'm asking you now."

"Oh, Sebastian, you're going to be so angry with me."

"I couldn't be angry with you, my love"

"Crystal called and said she wanted to set things straight. I went to meet her at her father's trailer on Cougar Mountain. While I was there someone set fire to the trailer. If I hadn't been closest to the door, I wouldn't be here. The trailer burned. It just burned and blew up and Mr. Moore and Crystal never had a chance to get out."

The information processed in laborious detail. Sebastian gathered a fistful of her sweatshirt. Dead. Crystal, dead? He ought to be glad, but he wasn't. "You arranged this meeting and you didn't tell me?"

"You wouldn't have wanted me to go."

"Damn right, I wouldn't. I wouldn't have allowed you to go."

She tried to shrug off his hand. "You can't allow or not allow me to do anything, Sebastian."

"I could probably figure out a way to stop you."

"You said you wouldn't get angry. You said I couldn't do anything to make you angry."

"I was wrong. I'm goddamn enraged, you little idiot. And scared out of my wits. *Shit,* I could have lost you."

"Don't swear at me."

"I'll swear"—he breathed long and deep—"You could have died."

"Yes, I know. I already told you I think I'm supposed to be dead."

"You went because you still don't trust me."

She shook her head vehemently. "That's not it. I heard the remorse in Crystal's voice and I wanted to do what she asked."

"And you wanted to find out more about what happened."

*"Yes!* All right, yes. I did want to find out more. I still don't understand, and you haven't told me everything."

He felt stripped, as if his nerves were open to the wind. "I told you everything you needed to know. Most importantly, that I didn't rape Crystal. I've never raped any woman—I never could."

"I believe you."

"Gee, thanks."

Bliss pushed past him and started uphill. "Sarcasm is ugly. It doesn't suit anyone. It doesn't suit you."

He walked after her. He didn't have to hurry to keep up. The swinging of her arms and her furious breathing sapped her energy, and slowed her pace.

The easement flanked Bliss's property. Before they reached the top she veered to the right, between fuchsia bushes loaded with tiny red blossoms, and broke into a run toward the back of the lodge.

She made it inside the kitchen only seconds before Sebastian. They both stopped at the sight of Bobby Crow, barefoot and still in pajamas. With Spike at his side, he hovered in the doorway to the rest of the building. The boy and the dog made a rag-tag, anxious-eyed pair.

"Bobby," Bliss said, hurrying to gather him into a hug. "What are you doing here?" The dog growled at her.

"They're going to fill up the hole today, aren't they?"

When Bliss didn't immediately respond, Sebastian said, "Yes. This morning."

Bobby pointed across the room. "See?"

Sebastian looked, but didn't see anything unusual.

"It's gone," Bobby said. "Liberty gave it to you and Bliss for a present. He took it and threw it down the hole. He made Liberty cry."

"The fish," Bliss said, going to where the piece of pottery had been on the counter. "Why would he do something so mean?"

Sebastian dropped to his haunches in front of Bobby. "Hey, buddy, shouldn't you still be in bed?"

"There was a police car here. It brought Auntie Bliss home."

"Yeah." He held the boy's arms. "You love your Auntie Bliss, don't you?"

Bobby's nod was solemn. "Vic did it last night—after Auntie Bliss's mom left—and Auntie Bliss. Mom and Auntie Fab said they were sorry for Auntie Bliss. I was coming over to see her, but she'd left."

Sebastian let Bobby take his time telling his story. Bliss poured a glass of milk and gave it to him.

Bobby took a swallow. "First I thought it was Mom coming after me. I thought she saw me leave and come here. I hid." He grinned sheepishly. "I was gonna jump out at her. She hates it when I do that."

Neither Bliss nor Sebastian commented, but he saw her faint smile.

"It wasn't Mom, it was Vic—and Liberty. She was crying then, too."

"That's rotten," Sebastian said, out of his depth. "Grown-ups can be pretty mean, Bobby."

"I wanna get Liberty's fish back."

Sebastian met Bliss's gaze over the boy's head. "That's a deep hole, buddy. Dangerous. That's why it's being filled. Anything that's down there, is down there."

"Not far. I could almost get it."

Again Sebastian looked at Bliss.

"Bobby," she said, and he heard the sick fright in her voice. "You went inside the wire? You looked down there."

"Vic pulled up the stakes. They were loose afterward. But I stayed on my tummy." He held up a red, rubber flashlight. "You can't see the bottom."

"No," Bliss said, her mouth trembling. "It makes a turn—they think."

"I saw Liberty's fish. I thought I could have got it—if I was a bit bigger. The pieces. We could stick 'em together. Auntie Fab did that with the turkey plate. You didn't even know."

"No," Bliss said wryly. "I didn't know the turkey plate had been broken. We'll think of a way to make Liberty feel better. Forget the fish."

Sebastian bobbed to his feet. "Okay if I use your flashlight, Bobby?"

The boy gave it to him at once.

"You're not going near that hole!" Bliss stood in front of the door to the terrace. "Either of you. Not ever."

"You don't get to *allow* me to do anything," Sebastian said softly. "But I'll lie on my tummy." He grinned at Bliss. She didn't grin back.

"Come on, Bobby. Let's go fishing."

Two people had burned to death because of her. She'd almost died with them. And Sebastian was shining a flashlight down a terrible hole, looking for a broken fish she hadn't wanted in the first place. Could the world just stand still for a moment—please?

The entire barbed-wire barricade had been moved, and the concrete cover moved to one side. True to his word, Sebastian stretched out on his stomach, his head and arms out of sight. Bobby copied the man, but only his eyes cleared the rim of the hole. Spike tilted her head and whined.

Sebastian inched forward.

"Stop it!" Bliss ordered. She scrambled to sit astride his waist. "Come back now."

His left hand withdrew and he swiped at her. His voice echoed upward, "Get back. Stay back. I can see the thing."

"Liberty can make another fish, Sebastian. This is stupid."

"I don't think so." His shoulders eased over the edge.

Bliss clutched his shirt. "You're going to fall. Stop it! Bobby, get away from here." She pulled him to his feet and pushed him behind her. "We're interfering in a relationship. We can't fix it."

Sebastian grunted. He scooted backward and sat up. "It's there. Hit the side and rolled into a crevice. There's a million jagged rocks around the sides. God, you'd be torn to death before you got very far down."

Bliss clamped a hand over her heart.

"The clay she used is really thick. It only broke in half. Must have hit just right."

"It'll never be the same," she told him, plucking at his sleeve. "Come on. I'll talk to Liberty, make her feel better. I'll ask her to make me another one."

Sebastian wasn't listening. He picked up one of the stakes intended to secure the barbed wire to the ground, and grunted when he doubled himself into the hole again.

"Don't you go any nearer," Bliss ordered when she saw Bobby drop to his knees.

"I wanna see."

"Go back to bed before Polly misses you."

"She won't. She sings in the morning. Today's her 'dition."

How could she have forgotten that both Polly and Fab had appointments at Raptor today?

"You gotta hold this light for me." Sebastian's voice echoed. "Lean across me. Don't try to put your head down—there isn't room. Reach along my arm and take the flashlight."

Bliss didn't hesitate. The sooner she did what he wanted, the sooner she'd get his whole body back where she wanted it. She stretched out over Sebastian and sank her arm into the hole. He pressed the flashlight into her groping fingers.

He flexed and strained beneath her. Bliss rested her cheek on his shoulder and squeezed her eyes shut.

"Move beside me," he called. "Keep the light down here but don't touch me."

Reluctantly, she did as he asked. More and more of Sebastian disappeared.

The effort was futile, but Bliss hooked her free hand into the waistband of his jeans. She heard the grinding noise of pebbles sinking into dirt beneath some weight but couldn't turn her head.

An engine roared nearby, then died.

Metal scraped.

Heavy footsteps approached. A pair of hard hands grasped Bliss's waist and lifted her easily to her feet.

She looked into Vic's gray eyes. He took the flashlight from her. "You go on back to the lodge," he said. "Bobby, too. I'll help Sebastian."

"I'll help Sebastian," Vic's voice said above him.

Sebastian's head and upper body hung into the chute. Without the flashlight, with only the aid of weak, early sunshine, he saw the pointed edges of rocks protruding from all sides, but nothing more.

Instinct made him gain firm hold with both hands. He drove his toes more firmly into the gravelly earth around the hole and began to work his way back up.

The flashlight beam cut past him, pooled on the broken pottery fish. Sebastian held his breath, then called, "Hi, Vic. I'm coming up," and prayed he sounded a hell of a lot more relaxed than he felt.

"Geez," Vic said. "That's what I was hoping for. Liberty's really angry with me. You can get the fish, can't you? Maybe if I hold your legs."

Sebastian heard Bliss say, "No, Vic. Come on, Sebastian!"

"I feel like hell for upsetting Liberty," Vic said. "She pissed me off. I thought she was making a play for you, Plato. Jealousy does weird things to you."

"The only man she sees is you, Vic," Sebastian said, listening to his words bounce around the shaft, fly upward, fade out below. "I think we'd better let this go."

"You're there," Vic said. "A few more inches and you'll have it. Don't worry. I've got you."

The man's arm locked around Sebastian's thighs. A strong arm that lifted until Sebastian's toes left the ground. Lifted. Lifted. A few more inches and he'd be doing a handstand inside a crumbling tunnel to nowhere—nowhere he wanted to go.

"Vic!" Bliss cried. "He'll fall."

"I've got him. He's not going anywhere. Grab the fish, Plato."

In an instant of total clarity Sebastian knew exactly what Vic planned. "Can't do it," he said. "Ease me back a bit so I can move around." Blood pounded inside his skull. Each breath cost him too much.

"You can get it," Vic called. "Just take a piece in each hand and I'll pull you up."

Let go to take a hunk of pottery in each hand so Vic could "accidentally" drop him to death.

"Okay," Sebastian said. "But hold on."

"I'm holding."

Sebastian braced his weight on one arm, an arm that began to shake, and picked up a piece of the broken fish. "Got it!"

"Use your right hand for the other one."

"Bring me up with this first"—the innocent act shouldn't hurt—"I feel safer with a handhold."

"Get back, Bliss!" Vic said, his voice rising. "And send the kid home—and that damn dog. They make me nervous."

*He was nervous?*

Bobby said, "I wanna watch."

"Go on, Bobby," Bliss said. "Go on back, there's a good boy."

Sebastian jammed his elbow against rock and tried to steady his arm.

"Hey!" Vic shouted, shifting as if Sebastian were jerking his legs. "Relax, buddy. I'll haul you back up."

The piece of pottery Sebastian dropped shattered in the darkness. "Darn it," he said. "Vic, I dropped the thing. Geez, I can't believe it."

"Pull him up!" Bliss was beyond panic.

Vic waved Sebastian's legs wildly back and forth, pumped his ankles as if trying to hang on, but losing the battle.

"Don't look, Bliss," Vic almost screamed. *"Don't look."* He let go, but not without a final downward shove.

Bliss's scream tore through the blackness, and the pain that surrounded Sebastian.

His arms gave out, collapsed.

His back cracked against unyielding, clawing daggers of stone.

One shoulder, his left shoulder, slammed into the same ledge that had stopped Liberty's fish.

Consciousness wavered.

"Sebastian! Sebastian!"

Over the sound of Bliss's voice, he heard an engine roar to life.

With his one hand trapped beneath his shoulder, his other arm spanning the width of the chute, Sebastian hovered, then slid.

His head and body curled toward his legs.

He'd fall now.

"Sebastian!" Her tears distorted his name.

*Not yet. Not again. He would not leave her again.*

He jammed his knees to his chest and drove his feet against the wall. And stopped his sliding fall.

He hung upside down, his back and his feet and the power in his bent legs holding him above oblivion that wouldn't come soon enough.

The flashlight beam blinded him.

"Oh, my goodness," Bliss said. "Oh, please, don't let go."

He couldn't speak.

"Vic left. You fell, and he left!"

Sebastian put more pressure on his feet. Shifting millimeters at a time, he pushed his back upward, wincing at each fresh gouge into his flesh. He felt around for cracks, tested for any loose scree ready to foil him, and eased up some more.

Then he moved first one foot, and then the other.

The progress was slow, but the goal dimmed the pain.

*"Yes,"* Bliss said, shining the light to help as best she could. "You're fine, Sebastian. You're fine, sweetheart. Come on."

Inch by inch he groveled up the chimney.

"I love you, Sebastian," Bliss whispered, and her words whispered again and again, whispered around him, folded around him.

Every gain he made took too long, sapped too much energy.

Blood from somewhere trickled across his temple. He felt its warm stickiness.

One of his feet hooked over the rim of the hole.

Hope welled—and his right hand lost its grip.

He flailed, strained to reach upward.

A strong hand, two hands, caught his. More hands closed on his ankles

"We've got you."

"It isn't your time to go. Too soon."

Then he was hauled and enfolded and borne away, away from the yawning space.

Voices exploded.

Bliss wrapped him in her arms and held on, sobbing meaningless phrases, crooning.

Sebastian found the strength to hug her back. He removed what he'd carried in his mouth throughout his horror journey, and smiled over her head at William. "You've got great timing."

"Great self-preservation skills," William said, cracking a rare, wide grin that faltered just the slightest bit. "I need this job. You scared the hell out of me. Zoya's on a rampage. We've got pickets outside the building. I couldn't find you so I came here."

Sebastian couldn't make himself care about Zoya, or pickets right now.

"I felt your need." His other, and even more unlikely rescuer, was Venus Crow. Her sun yellow harem outfit fluttered in the wind. "But I was right. You are not good for Bliss or for Hole Point."

"No Point," Bliss said unevenly against his chest. "There isn't going to be a hole anymore."

"Thank you," Sebastian said, smoothing Bliss's hair with shredded fingers. "Thank you, William. Thank you, Venus, even if you do think I'm trouble, I think you're wonderful."

She lifted her chin, and her heavily penciled brows. A slight smile ruined the effect. "I'm glad I could help you."

A growl and a tug at his jeans destroyed any trace of warm unreality. Spike straightened her legs and pulled on one ankle of Sebastian's pants.

Bliss laughed and hauled her off. "Now she's protecting me instead of trying to scare me to death. Let him go, Spike. He's Beater's dad, remember?"

As if she understood, the dog released him and sat down with a thump. Her bared teeth let him know he'd better not step out of line.

Bliss frowned and worked strands of white from inside Sebastian's sleeve. "My scarf," she said, revealing what was left of the beautiful, lily-patterned silk. "Where was it?"

"Inside the fish, I think," he told her. "Pushed through its mouth and inside. I'm sure Liberty gave us the fish to bait—sorry about that—to scare Vic into taking notice of her."

Venus closed her eyes and said, "I feel evil here."

"You're probably very astute," Sebastian told her. "This was wrapped in the scarf. If we're lucky, it'll fill in the missing pieces." He held aloft the slightly damp canister of 35mm film he'd carried to safety inside his mouth.

# Twenty-seven

Taken with the aid of a special night lens, auras—magenta and green—fuzzed the edges of photographed images.

Bliss watched Sebastian spread the shots on his desk, and she watched blood-stained, tattered broadcloth stretch over his battered back.

"We've got to get you to a hospital," she told him. She'd told him the same things many times in the two hours since they'd left the Point. "You're bleeding from everywhere."

"I've bled. Past tense. I'm fine. Look at these."

"William?" Bliss pleaded. "Can you help me?"

"Thanks for everything, William," Sebastian said. "Now go back to work. I'll call if I need you."

William gave Bliss an apologetic shrug and left the office.

"Come and look at these."

"I can see them from here." She didn't want a closer look.

"No, you can't. The police are on their way over to pick them up. I want you to take a good look first."

Reluctantly, she did as he asked. "Poor Mr. Nose. Wrong place at the wrong time. He was too dedicated, wasn't he?"

"Yeah." Sebastian sounded as tired and empty as she felt. "He caught Vic draping pieces of your scarf on the wire around the hole and that was his death sentence."

Bliss did look closer then. One shot showed Vic hooking lengths of sparkling silk to the barbed wire. The next was of Vic looking directly at the camera. His face was folded in fury.

"Maybe Vic didn't mean to push Mr. Nose over the bluff, just get the camera away."

"Maybe. Could have been the same sort of accident I almost had today, huh?"

She rubbed the heels of her hands into her eyes. "Probably. I just can't figure out why he did it."

"We will. Look at this one."

Bliss stared and exclaimed. "Liberty. I didn't see her at first. She looks horrified."

"I'd say so. But she's there, and those aren't cookies in her hands."

Liberty held what was clearly a bell—no doubt Aunt Blanche's Steuben bell. Something white hung between her fingers. "I see the bell. What's the other thing, though?"

Sebastian shook his head and took a magnifying glass from the desk to study the photograph. "Didn't you tell me about a white mask that first night?"

"Yes. Inside my rooms."

"Well, here's your mask."

Bliss said, "Mmm," and pulled another photo toward her. "This was taken at the Wilmans'. At their party that night. In the conservatory." She'd never forget what had happened to her when those lights went out.

Sebastian leaned over her shoulder. "How the hell did he get in?"

"Nose?"

"Vic. Nose was a pro. His business was getting in wherever he needed to get in. That's Vic." He pointed to a figure in a white waiter's coat. The man's hair was pulled back and tucked beneath the jacket. "And that's you with your back to him. He posed as a waiter. Must have dealt with the lights, then dealt with you."

"The pieces come together," Bliss said. Each picture unraveled her composure a little more. "He wore rubber gloves. I felt them, and smelled them."

Sebastian used the magnifying glass again. "Yup. There they are."

"Oh, how awful." Bliss took her lower lip in her teeth. "He must have been the one who threw his coat into that closet. We were right there and we didn't know. If we had, Nose might not have had to die."

"Vic wouldn't have been easy to stop."

"But *why?*"

"We may never know. This is up to the police now. You're going to be my main job from here on."

"It isn't going to be that easy, Sebastian. You know that."

"I know nothing's going to scare me after what almost happened to you last night—and to me today."

"Liberty's gone, too."

"Are we surprised?"

"She wasn't with Vic when . . . I can't talk about that. I want to take care of you."

"All I need is a shower."

"Do you think Vic caused the fire?"

Sebastian shifted the photos around. "Maybe. I wonder how much longer it'll be before we find out more details about that."

"Like what?"

"I'm not sure."

The door opened to admit two police officers. "This is Officer Vegasan," the first man through the door said and added, "Miss Lovejoy already came in on her own." Evidently he didn't think he needed to remind them of his own name.

Sebastian told William to go home, locked the office doors, and faced Bliss. "Just you and me, kid," he said, and felt as jumpy as a teenager on his first date. "We've got a lot to do. All of it good."

"Now we know what happened with Vic it doesn't make any sense that he'd try to kill me in that trailer. I don't feel good about any of this."

Neither did Sebastian, but he wished he could protect Bliss from more anguish. "Liberty's blown the whistle on Vic. He was afraid if you and I got together, he's lose his cushy living situation—and his hopes of—"

*"Don't* say it. I heard what Ballard suggested."

"Avoiding the truth doesn't help. Vic wanted you to marry him. He wanted you to make him secure. I was a complication he never expected. And I do believe Liberty was right when she said he loves you."

"Poor Liberty." Bliss came to him and began unbuttoning his shirt. "Women don't do well when the men they love turn on them."

"I didn't turn on you, love." He waited patiently while she took off his shirt. "Bliss, I didn't—"

"I know you didn't turn on me."

"It was hell after I left." He winced as she pulled his shirt off. "I want to marry you, Bliss. As quickly as possible. Tonight, if possible."

"Well, it isn't possible. We'll have to go through the same official motions as everyone else."

He caught her wrists to his chest. "But you are saying you'll marry me?"

Her smile, the endearing tumble of her hair around her pointed face, the grimy sweatsuit she still wore—he loved everything about her.

Sebastian lowered his face to kiss her, but Bliss stepped away. "Yes, I'll marry you. If I don't, I'm a ruined woman."

He laughed. "Is that a fact? In that case I'd better call the jeweler I keep talking about."

"No need." Bliss shook her head. "You've still got the world's smallest condom in your wallet, don't you?"

"Uh-huh."

She reached beneath her sweatshirt. "I put this on again." The chain he'd bought so many years ago, with so much love and so much hope, glistened. On the chain hung the ring with its three small diamonds. Bliss undid the chain and gave him the ring. She extended her left hand. "It's about time I wore it permanently."

Sebastian turned the ring over and over in his palm. "You kept it."

"Did you ever doubt I would?"

Swallowing wasn't easy. "I didn't have the right to think you would."

"Put it on for me."

"Don't you want something more spectacular?"

"Never. It's amazing it isn't worn out from all the times I've looked at it."

The ring still fitted perfectly. He covered it on her hand and brought it to his mouth. "I'm a lucky man."

"Some men might not think so. I've brought you nothing but trouble."

"You didn't bring me that. I did." He looked into her eyes.

Bliss stroked his chest. "Are you going to let me get you to the hospital?"

"Nope. I'm scratched and scraped. I'll heal. I will let you wash my wounds—eventually."

She went to the wall of windows and trailed from one bank to another, closing out the light with vertical blinds.

When no more daylight showed, she wandered back, pulling her sweatshirt over her head as she came. She wore a creamy lace bra that barely covered her nipples.

He braced against a jolt of arousal.

The sweatshirt landed on top of his desk. "Those cuts have to be washed now. It'll be easier in the shower. Thank goodness you've got one here."

"Thank goodness," he agreed, reaching for her. She evaded him. "Bliss? Come here."

"You're an injured man. You may even have a concussion. You've got to take it easy."

"My brain never felt better. Come here."

"I'm in charge. Do you know what that means?"

Excitement contracted his belly. The force of his erection made his zipper a weapon of torture. "What does it mean, Bliss?"

"It means you're at my mercy." She smiled widely, showing

her pretty teeth. "Have I told you lately what your green, green eyes do to me?"

"You're enjoying this game, aren't you?"

"I'm discovering a whole new side to my personality. Chilly thaws. Hidden fires revealed. Watch out for hitherto unknown tendencies toward the kinky."

He'd laugh—if his pants didn't feel like an iron restraint. "Why don't you demonstrate?" Fast.

Her dark frown of concentration amused him. He crossed his arms.

She circled him. "You are a bit of a mess. I was considering pre-shower, during-shower, and after-shower."

Once more she ducked beyond the range of his grasp. "If we're going to manage all that, we'd better get started. Don't tell me you're all blow and no go, Chilly."

"Not at all," she told him. "But I think I'd better go easy on an injured man. I should wash that back and make you take a nap."

"No way," he said, out of breath. "I want the pre-shower."

Bliss's smile was beatific. "Really? Have you ever made love on a desk?"

He winced and broadened his stance. "No. You're killing me. Strip and get on that desk. Now."

"Uh-uh." Sauntering, slipping out of her sweatpants as she went, she approached the desk and pushed the zen garden to a corner. "You strip and get on the desk."

Amazingly, Sebastian felt color rise in his face. Excitement, nothing more. "You can't be serious." Clad in her wisp of a bra and matching panties—and nothing else, she sat in his chair and tapped her fingers on the arms. He said, "You are serious."

"I'm going to kiss you all over—to make you better, of course."

Above the bra, her rounded breasts rose and fell too fast to prove she was as cool as she sounded. Sebastian undid his jeans. "When you've kissed me all over, do I get to kiss you all over—to make you better?"

She crossed her legs. "We'll see." Her panties rode low on her hips. He could sweep her up in one arm and dispense with those panties, and the bra, in about two seconds. Then they'd see who was in control.

Sebastian kicked off his loafers and got rid of the rest of his clothes. "I don't think you'd better take too long with the kissing, do you?"

"Oh, yes," she told him. "A long, long time. On the desk."

"Bliss—"

*"On the desk.* Unless you're one of those men who prefer submissive women."

Sebastian walked around to stand in front of her and this time he didn't blush when she studied him from head to foot, with long, lingering moments on points between. From where he stood, her nipples were in clear view and the dark hair between her legs showed through her panties.

"The desk, Sebastian."

Sighing, he sat on the cool wood, swung up his legs and stretched out—and grimaced. "You're cruel. I'm a wounded man."

"Oh, good grief." She shot to her feet. "I got carried away. Get in the shower, darling. This can wait."

His back didn't feel too bad. "The pain's fading already. Kisses really work—when you place them just right."

"I know they do." Seriousness suited her blue eyes—pseudo-seriousness. And it suited her full, soft mouth. "Let me see. Where should I begin." She made another visual assessment of him.

"I'm all yours, my love. Start anywhere."

She turned her face, staring at his mouth before she covered it with her own. Holding his arms down when he would have reached for her, she parted his lips and slid her tongue inside. Moving gently back and forth, rocking their faces together, she kissed him deeply. She kissed him, and her soft breasts grazed his chest. And when she raised her head they were both out of breath.

Sebastian groaned.

Chilly Winters began to prove she had, indeed, thawed. She kissed his brow, his nose, his closed eyes, his jaw, the lobes of his ears before she licked inside and sent shivers to his toes.

"I can't handle this," he told her.

She caressed his shoulders and arms and said, "Yes, you can," before she placed more kisses where her hands had been.

Over his chest, rib-by-rib to his belly, she kissed. A nipping, delving foray into his navel brought his knees jackknifing up while she spread her hands over his hips and slipped them under him to find and follow every dip and crevice.

"Bliss," he moaned, arching his back. "Bliss, you're into torture. Who'd have thought it?' "

"You, if you'd been thinking at all."

"I'm thinking now."

"Thinking you don't like this?"

"Thinking I'll die if you stop."

"You won't be dying real soon."

Abandoning his belly, she shifted quickly to his feet and began her mouth map at his toes. No inch of his legs was allowed to feel neglected. When she parted his thighs to kiss the inner sides, he brought his hips off the table and she stood up.

"Devil," he told her. "Evil woman."

Without preamble, she cradled his balls and flipped the tip of her tongue over the tip of his penis.

Sebastian yelled. He had to. He yelled and sat up.

Bliss pushed him back, and took him into her mouth all the way to the hilt. She took him in, slowly sucked her way almost free of him—and promptly made another meal of his throbbing flesh.

He came. He couldn't stop himself. "Bliss! Hell, Bliss!"

Laughing, she buried her face in his crotch. "Don't swear. I don't like it."

"Oh, God! Nothing like that ever happened to me. Geez."

"You didn't like it?"

"Come here."

"That was the before-the-shower. Now we'll do the during-the-shower. As soon as you're up to it, that is."

"Enough." He spanned her waist and hauled her to sit astride his hips. "You'll see how long it takes me to be *up* to it, sweetheart. How about two before-showers, and two—"

The intercom buzzed.

Sebastian froze.

Bliss covered her mouth and giggled.

"I sent him home, dammit!" He reached above his head to press the button. "What? I told you to go home, William."

"I'm still catching up on what I missed today, Mr. Plato."

"You can call me Sebastian. You helped save my life, remember?"

The next sound was of William clearing his throat. "Thank you. A Ms. Polly Crow called."

Bliss opened her mouth but Sebastian put a finger over it. "I know Polly."

"She wants you and Ms. Winters to know she's been hired."

"That's Bliss to you," Sebastian said. "Thank you, William."

"Hired as what?" Bliss said, pushing his hand away.

He worked her panties down, gave up on the puzzle of how to get them off and disposed of them with a single, tearing tug.

William cleared his throat again. "According to Ms. Crow she's to be a sort of female Mr. Rogers on a children's TV show. She's very excited."

Sebastian nudged the very wet place between Bliss's legs and mouthed, "Very excited."

She lifted her bottom and braced herself on a hand each side of his chest. "That's great news, William. I'm going to thank Zoya myself."

"It was Mr.—I mean, it was Sebastian who arranged the interview."

"That's just fine, William," Sebastian said, grinding his teeth. "Thank you. You can go home now." He cut the connection.

Bliss's lips had parted. Her eyes glittered from the shadow of her mussed hair. "You're a dear man."

"They wouldn't have hired her if they didn't think she could do the job."

"I love you."

"I love you, too. I'm ready again. Sit on me."

Instead she played herself over his penis. Sebastian spied the cunning little fastening between her breasts and released it. She spilled free, her flesh white and full with pink nipples. The centers of her nipples stood out erect and too tempting—and wonderfully accessible above his face. Her breasts swung, just a little. He captured them, pressed them together, bobbed up to open his mouth over each crown, and grinned at her indrawn breath—and the way she forgot to keep her bottom just out of range.

His entry was sweet, slick, tight, a demanding contraction of clever muscles designed for moments like this.

Bliss's reaction was immediate. Her eyes closed. Her face became tense. Her lips flattened to her teeth and she panted. She panted, and pumped her pretty hips.

This time she cried out before he did, clamped down on him with a wild spasm before he ejaculated—but only instants before.

He couldn't keep still any longer. They rode out his climax together and Bliss fell on top of him, pressed wet kisses to his jaw and neck, to one of his nipples until he urged her face onto his shoulder. "Stop. Just for a moment, please. I'm older than you, remember?"

She sighed. "Two whole years. No excuse."

The intercom buzzed again.

"Oh, no," Bliss whispered. "What if he can hear us?"

"If he can, he's a very jealous man." Sebastian opened the line again. "Yes, William?"

"Ms. Fabiola Crow this time. She's now The Seattle Micro Breweries Woman."

Bliss raised her head and grinned.

"Great," Sebastian said, meaning it. "I thought she was exactly what they were looking for. She'll be all over town. Billboards, TV, everywhere."

"That's what Ms. Crow said. And she wanted to thank you. She wonders if now would be a good time."

Sebastian clamped Bliss's face to his chest. He was still buried inside her—and, wonder of wonders, he was getting hard again. "No, William, now would not be a good time. Tell her I'll be in touch, and congratulate her for me."

When they arrived, the Medina house was in darkness. Bliss ached deliciously. They'd enjoyed before, during, and after showering. For the rest of the afternoon and into the evening. When they'd finally left Raptor, she'd been surprised either of them could walk at all.

"I do want to get back to the Point and tell Polly and Fab how thrilled I am for them," she told Sebastian.

"You will. I've got to get into some clothes that aren't in shreds."

"How do you feel?"

He switched off the engine of the Ford. "Are you fishing for compliments?"

"You're injured."

"And you're the best antidote to pain on earth. Injured? Me? A scratch or two—nothing. Have you ever made love on the hood of a truck?"

"No! And I'm not going to now." She shot from the passenger seat to the driveway and slammed the door behind her.

Sebastian joined her and draped an arm around her shoulders as they walked into the house.

"Where the fuck have you been?" Maryan Plato swayed in the doorway to the living room. "You told me you'd be home hours ago."

Bliss tried to turn away but Sebastian kept her beside him. "You're drunk. Again."

"Fuck, yes, I'm drunk. What the fuck else would I be after waiting for you for hours."

Ron appeared behind her, an apologetic smile on his too pretty face. "Sorry, folks," he said smoothly. "We've had a bit of a shock. William told us he didn't know how to reach you."

Bliss heard Sebastian mutter, "I'll give him a raise."

"What?" Maryan asked, lurching toward them. "What d'you say?"

"I said, it's been one of those days."

Bliss almost chuckled.

"Where've you been?" Maryan's old pewter eyes strayed blearily to Bliss. "With her?"

"We've got bad news," Ron said quickly. "That Prue woman called. Bad and good news, actually. Seems we've waved bye-bye to our darling Zoya."

Sebastian held Bliss even tighter. "Spit this out, Ron. I'm not in the mood for games."

"Unless they're with her." Maryan pointed a wavering finger at Bliss. "That's gonna stop. You owe me."

Bliss's stomach revolved.

"Seems Zoya's flown the coop," Ron said, making a futile attempt to hold Maryan's arm. "That bitch O'Leary's been digging around and she found out Zoya was taking money from clients."

Sebastian stiffened. "Where is Zoya? I don't listen to stories about my people without giving them a chance to tell me their side."

"I told you," Ron said. "Gone. Cleared out."

"Good," Maryan said. "The bitch wanted you. She always wanted you."

"That's enough, love," Ron said, his smile fixed now. "Zoya was taking kickbacks, Sebastian. Simple as that. She'd been in big financial trouble even before she invested in the Bellevue operation. She didn't have the money to cover that investment, so she traded jobs for fees. Extra fees that never showed up on our books."

"*Our* books?" Sebastian said tightly.

Ron grinned. "Sorry. Your books. And it was Zoya who sent the kid to the guy who made the porn flicks. Another big kick-back, evidently."

Bliss's knees felt weak. "Sebastian?"

"Hell," he muttered. "If this is true, I've been a fool. A dangerous fool in this case. I'll have to speak to the WOT people. I owe it to them."

"You don't owe them anything," Maryan said. "Zoya screwed us all over. She's gone. End of story."

"If she caused a girl's death," Sebastian said. "I've got to address that."

"Get rid of her," Maryan said, indicating Bliss. "We've got to make plans to get out of here in one piece."

"I think Maryan's right," Ron said promptly. "Withdrawal is definitely in order. Whether or not you knew what she was doing, Zoya's activities will be linked to us. We could find ourselves fighting liability issues. We'll never be able to do business effectively here now."

Sebastian didn't correct the "we" this time. Instead he led Bliss past Maryan and Ron, into the room where the entertainment center shared space with exercise equipment. "Wait for me, my love." He kissed her lightly. "I've got to deal with those two. Then we'll go over to the Point."

"Maybe I should leave. I can call a cab."

"No, you can't." His smile tightened places she had excellent uses for now. "You're going to sit here and let me put my sister and her friend straight. I'm not going to be able to do anything about Zoya till the morning anyway. Not that I'm sure I believe what I'm being told."

"Why would they say such things if they aren't true?"

"Because they're scared their cushy lives may change with you around. A bit like Vic, maybe. Just not desperate or sick enough to commit crimes to get what they want."

Ron and Maryan waited for him in the vestibule. Sebastian closed Bliss inside the room and approached his sister. "You've got to go for treatment. You're an alcoholic. Among other things."

Her lips curled. "I'm the woman you've driven to drink. Give me what I've got a right to and I won't need the booze." She pointed to the door that separated them from Bliss. "She's dangerous. She's one of those ball-breaking feminists. Women's Studies prof? What else could she be but a ball-breaker? It's her friend who wants to ruin us. Send her away, Seb."

He turned and heard Maryan's cry. She'd seen the condition of his shirt—and his back. "It's nothing," he said, starting up the stairs. "I had a little fall and messed up my shirt. I'm going to change."

She followed him to his bedroom and inside. Ron was at her heels but she signaled for him to wait outside. His jaw tightened, but he did what she wanted.

"I've given my life to you," Maryan said.

When he went into his closet, she did the same and slid the sliding door over the entrance.

"Don't do this," he told her, selecting a clean shirt. "Get some sleep."

"I could have been anything I wanted to be."

"You're probably right." Sebastian's temper thinned. "I never stopped you."

"I had to look after you. Mom and Dad hated me for not being a boy, but they hated you for not being the son they wanted."

"I know that," Sebastian said softly. "What's the point of dragging it up now?"

"I always loved you."

He stared at her. "You've been a good sister."

"I've given everything up for you."

"You've enjoyed everything I've been able to give you."

Her eyelids lowered slowly. "Without me, you'd never have found start-up capital."

"What does that mean? I had to scrounge for that money."

"Forget it." She jerked her head up. "I never married."

"You've never been without a man. If you didn't choose to marry, it was your decision."

"Marry? *Marry?*" She advanced on him, her thin face white, the skin stretched tight over the bones. "How could I marry anyone else."

Sebastian stopped in the act of putting on his shirt. "How

could you marry anyone else? Are you saying I somehow stood in the way of you marrying someone?"

Without warning, she launched herself, wrapped her arms around his neck, fastened her mouth over his.

Sebastian stumbled backward, caught his heel and fell. Maryan was on top and all over him.

"I wanted you." She panted, and pawed at him—pushed his shirt aside and ran her hands over his chest. "I love you. I've always loved you. I want you."

He choked down the bile that rose to his throat. "You're my sister."

"I'm not your fucking sister," she told him through her teeth. "You were adopted by my parents."

"You're my sister," Sebastian repeated. He pushed her off with ease, but when he rose to his knees she dragged on his shirt. "You're drunk, or you wouldn't be saying these things."

"I'm drunk because they're true." She pulled him, tried to draw him down on top of her. "Make love to me, Seb. Don't waste time on her. Love me. Let's get rid of them all and be alone."

He opened his mouth to breathe and took in the sour scent of old alcohol. With a sense of disbelief, and disgust, he jerked her hands from his shirt and stood up. "Get out," he told her. "Get out and never come back."

"Seb—"

"And take that little freak of yours with you. Or is he planning to tell me he's in love with me next? His fawning makes me sick. He'd sleep with anything if it paid enough, Maryan. Don't tell me you haven't figured that out."

"Seb, *please.*" She fumbled for the waist of his jeans. "I can make you happy."

The weight of his horror galvanized him. "I never want to see you again," he said, pushing past her. "Send an address. I'll make sure you get your checks."

# Twenty-eight

Sebastian stood in the doorway, staring at her. Pallor showed through his tan. "Come on," he said. "I want you out of here."

Bliss went to him. "What's happened?"

He held her hand and headed for the front door.

"Sebastian! Wait!" Ron York ran down the stairs. "Wait, for God's sake, man. You can't leave her like this."

Sebastian's shudder shocked Bliss. He didn't turn toward Ron, but he did hesitate.

"She's had too much to drink," Ron said, hovering on the bottom step. "Why don't you let me drive Bliss home while you see what you can do to make Maryan feel better?"

Sebastian raised his face and looked down at Bliss. "Never. I'm never leaving you to anyone else again. Maryan knows what she's got to do, York. Make sure you're both out of here before I come back."

They left the house to be met by Beater. The dog shambled from a side path with the big, orange rubber spider in his mouth. He spared Sebastian and Bliss a baleful glance before leaping into the bed of the Ford.

"Smart dog," Sebastian muttered. "Even he knows when the air's hazardous to his health."

"*What* happened?" Bliss asked again. "Sebastian?"

"I'll tell you. Later. I've got to deal with this in my own way first. *Shit,* now what?"

Coming too fast, a car swung into the driveway. Rubber screamed as it stopped inches from the front of the truck.

With a sense of disorientation, Bliss watched her mother push open the door of her Mercedes and scramble out. At first she didn't notice Sebastian and Bliss. When she did, she burst into tears.

"Mom? What is it?" Bliss started forward, taking Sebastian with her. "Is it Daddy?"

"I've done everything wrong," Kitten said through her sobs. "I went to that place and you weren't there. Then I went to his—to Sebastian's offices. The doorman said you'd left but he didn't know where you'd gone. I never thought I'd say thank God for Prue O'Leary. She gave me Sebastian's address."

From now on Prue O'Leary was part of Bliss's past.

"You're upset, Mrs. Winters," Sebastian said, not entirely unkindly.

"Yes," Kitten agreed. "I've never been this upset in my life. What with all the terrible things in the papers. Bliss, why didn't you let us know you were involved in a fire. You might have died."

The fear in her mother's voice stunned Bliss.

"The papers say you went to meet Crystal Plato. She wasn't there. How could you do such a foolish thing?"

Sebastian made a noise that might well be sympathetic to Kitten.

"Crystal wasn't there?" Bliss said. "How do you know?"

"Oh, I don't remember how I know," Kitten said. She clung to the door of the Mercedes. "Yes. The papers. One victim. Male. You went into a trailer with that awful man."

"But I'm fine," Bliss pointed out, squeezing Sebastian's hand. "And I'm glad Crystal wasn't there."

"Even though she probably set you up?" Sebastian said.

"We don't know that."

"She called you. Then she wasn't there. She hated her father, she probably hated you—"

"Sebastian," Kitten said, her voice high and thin. "I won't

blame you if you refuse, but will you please come to our home and allow Bliss's father and me to show you both how glad we are she's all right? And how glad we are you two have finally found each other?"

Sebastian coughed into a fist.

"Oh, Mom," Bliss said softly. Why did it take a near disaster to bring out the best in some people? "You're so upset. Sebastian, I think I'd better drive my mother home. She shouldn't drive herself."

A fresh gale of tears erupted from Kitten. "I—want you both to come. Now! I don't want to waste another minute. How am I ever going to forgive myself? Bliss?"

Bliss pushed the nosepiece of her glasses. No previous experience had readied her to deal with her mother in this mood.

"Drive your mother," Sebastian said evenly. "I'll follow and take you on to your place."

"Oh, thank you!" Kitten rushed toward Bliss, her arms outstretched. "Thank you both."

Once Kitten was safely stowed in the passenger seat of her car, Bliss set off, taking the road across the Evergreen Point floating bridge over Lake Washington and exiting near the University of Washington to get to Laurelhurst. She checked the rearview mirror frequently to make sure Sebastian was still behind them.

Her mother huddled against the door and sniffled.

The drive to Laurelhurst and the Winters's lakefront home was made in near silence. Once Bliss pulled to a stop in the circular driveway in front of the house, Kitten got out and hurried inside.

Bliss waited for Sebastian. "Crystal wasn't killed," she said when he joined her.

He turned his face up to a star-encrusted sky. "Seems that way from what your mother says. Will you understand if we don't make this a long, fond homecoming?"

"Fond?" She smothered a cynical laugh. "There was never

any affection here, but if Mother wants to try for peace, I think we should let her. I want to get out of here as much as you do."

She led him into the house, into the elegantly Asian living room from which she could hear her parents' raised voices.

Conversation ceased the instant Morris Winters saw Sebastian and Bliss. He showed them his back and concentrated on the mirror-black windows overlooking the lake.

Kitten wound her fingers together. Her blue cotton sweater bagged at the bottom over a denim skirt with an unraveling hem. Without makeup, she was a tired-looking woman on the wrong side of middle-age. Her darting eyes showed she was also a desperate woman.

"Dad," Bliss said. "We're here because Mom told us you both wanted to see us."

After a long pause, Morris said, "Your mother is impulsive. I thought she'd learned the consequences of that. Evidently I was wrong."

"Okay," Sebastian said, pulling out his keys. "We're out of here, Bliss. Good night to you both."

"No!" Kitten said. "Morris, listen to me. This can all work out, I tell you. Just do what you said. Make sure they understand. Everything will work out."

The man spun to face them. He stared from Bliss to Sebastian and back, then prowled the room. "You aren't going to get in my way, do you understand?"

Bliss's hand went to her throat.

"Morris—"

"Shut your Goddamn mouth, woman," Morris said to his wife. "Shut up all of you."

"Come on," Sebastian said. "Time to go home."

"I told you to shut up!" Morris's eyes flamed. Nerves beside his eyes twitched. "Shut up!"

Sebastian moved toward him.

"Get over there," Morris yelled. He raised his right hand and pointed a gun at Sebastian. "Do as you're told. This is going to go one way—my way. I've fought too hard and put up with too much to fail because of this fool." He pointed the weapon at Kitten.

Bliss swallowed a scream. "Daddy!"

"Don't call me that," Morris Winters said. He inclined his head toward Kitten. "Ask her why you shouldn't call me that."

"Shit," Sebastian said under his breath. "Look, Winters. Let's all calm down. And let's not say or do things we're all likely to regret."

"My *wife* screwed around on me," Morris said, sneering at Kitten. "The little bastard she had was the result. But we've had an agreement. If she didn't do anything to mess with my career, I wouldn't do anything to mess with her precious reputation."

Bliss sat on the nearest chair.

"I said I'd get rid of it, Morris," Kitten said. Her mouth remained slack. "It was you who said I couldn't."

"Because the Goddamn quack you went to was a friend of my folks and he couldn't wait to congratulate them, or me."

"That's enough," Sebastian said quietly. "We're no part of any of this."

*It.* Her mother had offered to get rid of "it." Bliss closed her eyes.

"If the Moore girl had been there, this would all be over," Kitten wailed. "How was I to know she wouldn't be there?"

Bliss heard the words but they no longer made sense.

"Be quiet," Morris ordered. "Don't come any nearer, Plato."

"I did it for you," Kitten said. "As soon as Bliss told me where she was going, I knew what I was meant to do."

Morris laughed horribly. "But you screwed it up, didn't you? Again? Crystal wasn't there at all, and Bliss got out. All you got rid of was the old man, you stupid cow."

Bliss opened her eyes. Her mother? Her own mother had tried to burn her to death?

Her father wasn't her father?

Her mother had murdered a man?

"Bliss wasn't supposed to die," Kitten said. "Just that man and the girl. With them gone we'd be happy—"

"You're not taking me down," Morris said, too quietly. He waved the gun. "Get over here, Kitten. Beside me. She's finally going to do something useful." His eyes narrowed in Bliss's direction.

Kitten walked toward him like a woman asleep. "I did it for you," she said. "I did it for you, Morris. For us. And I've done what you wanted tonight. I've brought them here. Tell him. Tell Plato he's got to get out of Washington."

"Not good enough." Morris's face convulsed. "I'm going to kill them."

Bliss couldn't move. Sebastian stood quite still, but he stared at her, shook his head slightly.

She didn't know what he was trying to tell her.

"Him first," Morris said. "Then her. She'll have committed suicide. She was always unbalanced. She's always done things to hurt us. Tonight she came to laugh at me. This was celebration time because she'd publicly declared she was fucking the enemy. But she's going to crack up and kill him when he tries to stop her from killing herself."

"Morris!" Kitten fell to her knees and covered her head. "Please, Morris. They'll say we did it."

*"Bitch,"* Morris said, shaking with rage. "She's going to kill you, too. And wound me."

"No, she's not." Kitten turned her ashen, sweat-slick face up to his. "How would she do that?"

Morris laughed. He tipped back his head and laughed. *"No she's not,"* he mimicked. "Stupid cow! Of course she's not. But that's how it'll look. And the people will love me for my bravery in the face of family agony. My wife and child dead at my child's hands. The wound I suffer at my child's hands."

"Gunshots hurt," Sebastian said.

Silence fell.

"Tough to shoot yourself, Morris. What if you lose your nerve? How will you explain a pile of corpses in your living room then?"

Kitten surged upward. She surged upward, and screamed—and grabbed for the gun.

The shot jolted Bliss's spine all the way to her heels. She stood up and made fists in the air.

A second shot rang out.

One of Kitten's hands struck Morris's face, smeared blood from hairline to chin. She fell against him. Blood spattered his yellow polo shirt, and, as Kitten slid toward the floor, more blood soaked her husband's clothes. Streaks of blood running down his body, down his legs.

Bliss retched, and moaned.

"Keep still," Sebastian said in a harsh whisper. "Be quiet."

"Mom?" Bliss moaned. "Mom?"

Kitten slumped over Morris's feet. He stepped back, kicked free of her. Distaste curled his lips. "I caught my own wife when her daughter shot her," he said.

"Mad," Sebastian muttered. He took a step toward Morris but stopped when the gun barrel leveled in his direction. He said, "This isn't going to work. Why not quit while there's some hope you can come up with a story to explain why you'd kill your wife?"

"Never," Morris said. "I'm going to be President of the United States and no snot-nosed little bastard is getting in my way. I'm using you, Plato."

Footsteps in the foyer froze the scene. "Don't come in here," Bliss yelled, and shrank back when Morris's gun shifted in her direction. "Call the police! He's got a gun!"

Morris's face turned dull red. He backed toward the wall behind the door.

Maryan Plato appeared.

"Get out, Sis," Sebastian said. "He's behind the door and he's armed. Get the hell out while you can!"

She came into the room with dragging steps. Mascara trailed her thin cheeks. "Morris?" She peered around until she saw him. Swaying on sandaled feet, she gave the man a wobbling smile and waved. "Here we are again!"

"Welcome, Maryan. We're going to make things nice and tidy." Morris's voice was monotone. "Bliss Winters killed Plato's sister because she found out they had this sick thing. He was fucking his own sister."

Bliss flinched. They were going to die and Morris would tell disgusting lies about all of them.

Morris's attention was on Maryan. He approached her, shoved the gun down the front of her wrinkled dress—between her breasts. "She's going to take you out next. She already killed her mother."

Sebastian, stepping between Bliss and Morris, cut off her view. "Get down, Bliss! Now. On the floor. He can't shoot us all at once."

"Fuck you!" Morris yelled. "Next one to move dies first."

"Do it," Sebastian said.

Rather than follow his orders, she got up and flung her arms around his waist.

"Bliss," he ground out. "For God's sake."

"If you shoot him, you probably shoot me," Bliss told Morris. "Same bullet. Same trajectory. Explain that to the police."

"You were going to make sure everything was okay," Maryan said. "You promised, Morris. I tried to do what you wanted, and you promised. It almost worked, but Seb came back to the pool."

Bliss felt Sebastian grow even stiffer. "What the hell does that mean?"

Another gunshot exploded against Bliss's eardrums.

"Maryan," Sebastian said softly. "You shit, Winters. If you wanted me you could have had me. You didn't have to do that to her."

He lunged, and threw himself forward at the same time.

Bliss lost her hold on him, fell, rolled away. Her head hit a brass table. Blood had spattered the open, white-painted door—Maryan Plato's blood. Clutching her shoulder, she'd slumped against the wall.

Morris held the gun two-handed, his elbows locked, the barrel pointed at Sebastian's face. "I want you over there." He twitched the gun. "My ex-wife's bastard makes a good point. Trajectory's important. Face her. I like that. She's going to shoot you in the face, lover-boy."

"Don't move," Bliss told Sebastian. "Stay where you are."

She saw Maryan slip onto her side and inch toward Morris. Blood oozed between her fingers.

"Turn around, Plato," Morris said. Veins stood out at his temples. His color had turned a mottled purple. "Turn around, you little shit!"

Grimacing, crying out with pain, Maryan rolled into the backs of Morris's legs.

He flailed.

Another bullet sang, and buried itself in the ceiling. And Morris overbalanced across Maryan's back.

Sebastian threw himself on top of the other man, clamped one hand around his neck and reached for the gun.

The phone rang.

"Fuck!" Morris screamed. "I'm going to kill you. All of you."

Another ring, and another, and another.

The two men struggled, twisted. Maryan, wriggling from beneath Morris, tried to grab the gun just as Sebastian's fingers began to close.

Morris laughed. "Justice! She sold you out before. She'll kill you now."

Holding her head, feeling warm wetness in her hair, Bliss got to her feet.

The phone stopped ringing.

She crept toward the writhing mass.

Again, the gun went off, and again. Panels on the door splintered.

Sebastian grabbed Maryan's arm and pushed her aside. Her agonized moans tore at Bliss.

She went to her hands and knees.

Morris and Sebastian turned. The gun, their hands, pointed

toward Bliss. She scurried and made it to the phone, dialed 911, let the receiver trail from its cord.

More shots. Great sheets of window glass splintered, disintegrated.

"Seb," Maryan moaned. "Help me, Seb."

Bliss hesitated, but approached the two men from the opposite side. They revolved again. On top of Morris, astride his hips, Sebastian found the other man's throat once more and beat the clenched weapon hand against the rim of a low table.

Morris's lips stretched in a wide grimace.

His hand, bleeding now, jerked until the gun once more pointed at Sebastian. In slow motion, the trigger depressed.

A scarlet gash opened across Sebastian's left arm—and Bliss flung herself on top of Morris's face. She curled over his head, filled her hands with his hair, yanked. Her own sobs filled her ears, her own, and Morris's enraged cries of pain. His free hand found her ear and he twisted.

She felt blows land on his body.

Then she hit the floor again, face down.

And there was silence but for Maryan's wrenching gasps and the labored breathing of the two men—and her own pounding heart.

"You okay, Bliss?"

She raised her head to look at Sebastian through blood that had run from her scalp. "Yes." He had the gun. "I dialed the police."

"Good."

"They'll never believe you didn't do all this, Plato," Morris said. His eyes were swelling shut. "Maryan will help me. We'll tell them how it went. I'm going to be President Winters. I'll need you, Maryan."

She lay on her side, curled into a ball.

"They attacked us, Maryan," Morris said. "They killed Kitten and they tried to kill you."

"Fuck off," Maryan whispered.

"I'll take care of you," Morris said. "I'll—"

Bliss followed the direction of his gaze to a red-haired woman in the doorway. A red-haired woman with a gun of her own. Dressed in jeans and a grimy white sweatshirt, and tennis shoes, she came into the room. Slowly, she made a circuit of the gory scene. With one shoe, she turned Kitten onto her back.

Bliss saw her mother's staring eyes, her shattered neck, and turned away.

"It wasn't you, was it?" the woman said. "Bliss?"

Bliss looked at her and frowned.

"You didn't try to kill me in Dad's trailer?"

*Crystal.* "No," Bliss said, shaking her head. "No. I was inside when the fire started. I went because you asked me to."

"She did it, didn't she?" Crystal indicated Maryan. "She needed me, but she hated me. So she wanted to get rid of me."

Maryan remained on her side.

"My mother did it," Bliss said. She should be able to cry. "I told her I was going to meet you and she went up there to get rid of you. She said she didn't intend for me to die."

Crystal laughed. She laughed, but her violet eyes were sad when she looked at Sebastian. "Figures. She didn't want to risk you finding out the truth. Any of you. I tried to talk to you at the Wilmans', Sebastian. I wanted you to let me help you, but you just wanted to get rid of me."

"Shoot the bitch," Morris muttered through battered lips.

Crystal positioned herself with a clear view of the scene. "Get away from him, Sebastian."

He didn't move.

"Please," Crystal said.

"Killing him won't help anything," Sebastian told her. "The police will deal with him."

"It was all his fault," Crystal said, turning her face toward Bliss now. "Your dear daddy had quite a taste for young girls, you know."

Bliss held her stomach.

"He would come to his precious new ball field and watch the games. Actually, he watched the girls, the cheerleaders. He paid for my uniform. That was after he brought me to his little nest out there"—she inclined her head toward the building that housed Morris's study—"He brought me there and made me have sex with him. After the first time, it wasn't so bad. He bought me things. Promised me things. Until I got pregnant."

"Shoot her," Morris said. He jackknifed beneath Sebastian, but a blow to his jaw slammed him down again. "Shut her up," he whined.

A car engine sounded outside. There were no sirens, but a blue light cut the darkness beyond the windows.

"Let the police have him," Sebastian said.

"She sold you out," Crystal said. "Maryan. When she found out you were leaving with Bliss, she went to Morris. He pulled all the strings. He knew you'd been with me at a party. And the timing was about right. He said he'd make sure none of us ever wanted for anything as long as I said the baby was yours."

"Crystal," Sebastian said, with amazing gentleness. "That's all past now, all over. We've paid for it. Don't do anything that'll make us pay anymore."

Bliss blinked stinging eyes. All that, and the baby had died. All this.

Maryan squirmed until she could see them. Her mouth stretched in a grimacing smile. "And you weren't pregnant," she said, a croaking sound coming from her throat. "A phantom pregnancy. A fucking phantom pregnancy! But it worked. Kill him, Crystal. Kill Morris. He did it all."

"Please," Bliss said. "Please. No more."

"Give me the gun, Crystal," Sebastian said.

"He couldn't have done any of it without your help," Crystal said, approaching Maryan. "And all because you were in love with your brother."

"He's not my brother," Maryan said, holding a hand toward Crystal. "He's not."

"Don't," Sebastian said, getting to his feet. "Let's stop this. There's been too much suffering."

"Maryan wanted you, Sebastian. She ruined my life, and Bliss's—and yours—because she wanted you."

Behind Sebastian, Morris rose awkwardly to sit, then to reach for the gun.

Crystal rotated gradually, aimed, and shot Morris between the eyes.

Bliss was still screaming when a second shot found its mark. She screamed while Maryan's last breath left her body, and she screamed as Crystal turned the gun on herself.

"Oh, love," Sebastian said, holding out his arms. "Oh, my dear love."

Bliss flung herself at him, hugged him.

"Police," a voice called from the foyer. "Police! We're coming in."

Vaguely, Bliss felt another presence enter the room.

"Police!" the same voice announced. "Freeze. And drop your weapons."

Sebastian let the gun fall to the floor. "Be my guest," he said, turning to look at the law. "Welcome, Officer Ballard."

Followed by two more policemen, Beater slunk around the uniformed officers already in the room. He ambled to Sebastian and Bliss, sat down, and dropped his orange rubber spider at their feet.

# Epilogue

Sitting on the raised deck outside her rooms had been Bliss's choice. Sebastian knew he'd do anything as long as he could be with her. Their wooden chairs were side by side. The morning air was still chilly, but there was the promise of a beautiful day to come. Beater and his spider had found a puddle of sunshine beside a planter box filled with daisies.

They would overcome what had happened. Somehow they'd have to learn to make every day beautiful, and the past would make them stronger.

"What do you call a dachshund sitting on a rabbit?"

She raised her face slowly. "Hmm?" Her eyes didn't quite focus behind her glasses.

Sebastian ran a finger over the bones in the back of her hand. "In winter? In Minnesota?"

Bliss continued to stare at him.

"A chilly dog on a bun? Remember that, Chilly?"

The faintest of smiles crossed her lips. She turned her hand beneath his on the arm of her chair and laced their fingers together. "Just making conversation, again?" she asked.

"You've got it. You haven't spoken since we came out here."

They'd returned to the Point in the early hours of the morning, after a visit to the hospital, and a lengthy interrogation by the police. There would be more of that to come.

"How's your arm?"

He raised it gingerly. "Sore. It'll pass. How about the head?"

"Same. Seems trivial, somehow."

"None of it seems real to me," Sebastian told her.

"Not real at all," Bliss said. "I never loved my folks. No. I loved them in a way, a dependent way. That's the way it always is, I guess. Children are supposed to love parents, so I did. Probably because I thought they loved me and because they were all I had."

He studied her. The sun had risen and morning shadows spread phantom tree trunks across the grass beyond the kitchen garden. Her hair caught light in its red depths.

"I don't want to find out who my father was." The distance claimed her attention once more. "I'm curious. I'll always be curious. But not curious enough to go hunting. I don't want to dig around in Mom's past."

"Morris could have been your father, couldn't he? Your mother had . . . She was already married to Morris." He knew all the feelings Bliss was having. He'd been there, done that, as the flip saying went.

"Poor Mom. She was never happy, was she?"

"Maybe sometimes. We can't be sure what makes other people happy."

"She loved him. I know she did. She loved him too much and she never grew to be a person herself. I see that so clearly now. I should have tried to be closer to her."

Sebastian pulled her to her feet and settled her on his lap, against his naked chest. She rested her head on his shoulder and looped her hands around his neck. Her old terry-cloth robe was warm. Inside the robe, Bliss was soft.

He loved her so much it ached.

"Maryan didn't deserve to die like that," Bliss said. "She tried to save you. And Crystal. Oh, Sebastian, I keep thinking about her as a kid in high school. She never had any luck."

"Not really. And they almost took my luck from me." A certain kind of luck, the most important kind. "Without you, the rest didn't mean much."

"I just wish they could have another chance."

It was too soon to think about Maryan or Crystal. And he didn't feel like reminding Bliss that she'd been marked to die. "We're going to have children, aren't we?" he asked her.

Bliss leaned away to look into his face. She studied his eyes, then his mouth. She kissed him lightly, but evaded his attempt to pursue her lips. "Are we?" she asked. "Can we do it right?"

Sebastian had to smile. "Could we do it any other way? We're human. We'll make mistakes. But we're strong or we wouldn't be here, and relatively normal, so we'll be trying so damned hard we'll probably overdo it. They'll be spoiled."

The tears that filled her eyes caught him off guard. "Hey." he ducked his head and brought his face closer. "Don't melt on me now."

Her mouth trembled. "I had a sudden vision of our children. Of you with our children. You'll be wonderful. I've seen you with Bobby. He thinks you walk on water."

"He's a neat kid. He needs a dad of his own."

"Yeah. But he's got a great mom and a doting grandma and aunt. And we love him."

He stroked her jaw with a thumb. "Some people are ruined by their childhoods."

She smiled at him then. Smiled, and sniffed, and a tear overflowed to course down her cheek. "And some people are made stronger. That's us. You and me. I just wish no one had died while we were finding our way."

"*Because* we were finding our way," he told her seriously. "But we can't control the world, or the people in it. We can only do our best not to be destroyed by them."

"They tried," Bliss said. "But I'm not going to shake the guilt very easily. The goblin still lives inside me. The goblin who whispers, 'it's your fault they didn't love you.' "

Sebastian nodded. "I know that goblin well. He's part of it. And you'll grieve. We both will. But we'll do it together, right?" He rested his forehead on hers. "No suffering alone and in silence. We've both done too much of that."

"I can still hear their voices."

He caught her against him and hugged until he was afraid he would hurt her. "We're going to help each other, okay?"

"Okay." She hugged him back. "When they get Vic, there'll be a court case, won't there?"

"If they get him. Zoya, too, for different reasons."

She shifted on his lap and tilted her head. "You'd better think about getting ready for work."

"When I go, you're going with me."

"I've got work to do here," she protested.

"Then I'm staying here, too."

Her brow puckered. "We can't be joined at the hip, Sebastian."

"We can until we start feeling safe again. William's holding down the fort, but I'm going to have to fill Zoya's spot quickly—yesterday wouldn't have been too soon. I'm going to bring someone in from Los Angeles, I think."

She settled her head on his shoulder again but she wasn't relaxed.

"What's up?" Sebastian asked. "What's on your mind?"

"Nothing."

"Why do women do that? Say there's nothing wrong when everything's wrong?"

"It isn't. I don't like uncertainty, is all."

"There isn't any uncertainty!" He rocked her. "We know exactly what's going to happen."

"I don't."

The steps from the kitchen garden creaked. "Breakfast approacheth," Venus Crow's voice announced. "Are you decent?"

Sebastian laughed.

Bliss tried to struggle from his lap but he wouldn't let her go. "Decent as we're going to get, Venus," he called.

Bobby beat his grandmother up the steps and promptly scampered to Sebastian's side. Spike lolloped to Beater and flopped down in his patch of sunshine.

Venus arrived carrying a tray crowded with tall glasses of chunky, pale purple something. "A sad day," she said, her eyes doleful. "Mourning requires energy, my children. The living souls must be fed so that they may offer their strength to those departing."

The urge to laugh felt too hysterical for comfort. Sebastian stroked Bliss's hair and smiled at Bobby. "How's it going, Sport?"

"I don't wanna go," Bobby said. He hooked his hands on top of Sebastian's shoulder. "Mom's gonna be on TV. She said that's 'cause of you. But I don't wanna go."

"Go where?" Bliss asked.

"Somewhere new to live."

"Eggplant frappés," Venus said, swaying dreamily in a black, hooded caftan edged with gold braid. "The purple flesh heals ills. We must all heal. We must all prepare for change that may leave us bereft and cast adrift."

Sebastian frowned back at Bobby and said, "Who says you're going to need somewhere new to live?"

"Mom," Bobby told him. "She says Bliss and you will have your own home now."

"Not that I see harmony ahead in that," Venus intoned. "The gentle woman and the hawklike man. He will crush her, subjugate her. He has brought trouble in his wake. Disrupted the lives of the peaceful."

Sebastian clamped an arm firmly around Bliss's shoulders, holding her when she would have squirmed free. "Why don't you sit down, Venus," he said pleasantly. "We can all benefit from your wisdom." He put his other arm, the one that ached, around Bobby.

More footsteps came, more hesitantly, up the steps and Polly Crow's blond head came into view, followed by her sister's.

"A summit," Sebastian muttered, finally giving in to Bliss's insistent pushes against him. "The gang's all here. Let's talk."

Bliss resumed her seat beside him. Her place on his lap was promptly claimed by Bobby.

"Bliss and I are getting married," Sebastian announced, looking from face to face.

"A tragic mistake," Venus said, sinking to sit, cross-legged on the floor. "The stars have warned me. I have warned you. I cannot do more."

"Mom!" Polly and Fab said in unison.

Venus raised her hands, allowing her flowing sleeves to drip over her hands. "Take the eggplant. We shall all need our strength for the hard times to come. All driven from our home by strangers. But we must not dwell on our own misfortunes. The happiness of these two people, no matter how brief fate allows it to be, must take precedence over the misery of the rest of us."

Bliss hung her head. Sebastian peered at her and saw the smile on her lips.

"I haven't had a chance to thank you both for helping me get the job," Polly said. "I can hardly believe it."

"You got it because you're right for it," Bliss told her. "Sebastian will tell you that."

"Thank you." She cast her mother—who couldn't see—an annoyed glare. "And I think it's wonderful you're getting married. You're going to be very happy together. We'll soon find somewhere else to live."

"Yes," Fab said. "Thank you both for everything."

Bobby felt Sebastian's stubbly beard with his fingertips. Sebastian looked at Bliss.

"You're leaving the Point?" she asked Fab.

"Cast out," Venus said. "Cast out in the wake of a dangerous force. But do not concern yourself with us, Bliss. We have been alone and desperate before. We triumphed. We will triumph again. One can only hope you will not be the one to suffer."

Sebastian chuckled, he couldn't help himself.

Bliss poked him in the ribs—his bruised ribs—with a pointed finger, and he yowled.

"Animal sounds," Venus said. "The wolves approach."

Polly and Fab, both sitting on the deck now, smiled into their laps.

"I'm not closing Hole Point," Bliss said. "I'm not selling it—ever. We'd hoped you'd all stay on."

Sebastian didn't miss the "we."

"Of course," Bliss said. "You're going to be too busy to do what you have done, Polly. You, too, Fab. But we'd figured the two of you might keep on living here and overseeing things—at least until you had to go."

Bobby sat up to study each of the adults in turn.

Venus made unintelligible noises.

"Does that mean we don't have to move?" Bobby asked. He scooted to the deck and ran to his mother. "Can we stay, Mom? Can we?"

Polly studied first Bliss, then Sebastian. "We like it here. Bobby and me."

"So do I," Fab agreed. "But you're right. We can't manage without more help—especially not once you're gone."

"I'll be in and out," Bliss told them.

"I will never dance at this wedding," Venus said, bending farther forward over her crossed legs. "My soul is heavy. Not that you would allow me to dance at your wedding. I would be a reminder of the terrible risk you take in this union."

"Mom!" Fab and Polly moaned together.

"If you had someone you could trust as a manager, would you like to stay on then?" Bliss asked.

Sebastian reached for her hand again. He couldn't bear not to touch her. "Be the same as adding a third level of management. And we intend to pour some money in here. Not change things too much, just update and do repairs that have needed doing for a long time."

"Can we?" Bobby said, dancing a barefoot tattoo. "Can we stay."

"Well?" Polly looked at Fab.

"Possibly. Just yesterday Lennox was asking what was going to happen here once Bliss and Sebastian married."

"Lennox?" Bliss spread her hands. *"Lennox?"*

"We talk now and then," Fab said offhandedly. "He has his good points."

Sebastian said, "Back to the question of a manager to help out around here."

"I was thinking of asking Venus if she'd like the job," Bliss said, and she wouldn't meet Sebastian's eyes. "She knows about coping with difficult situations. Not that we plan to have any-more, but you never know."

Venus grew quite still.

The twins' heads turned in their mother's direction. "Mom?"

"What's the matter," she snapped, scowling at them. "Don't you think I could manage? I've managed more taxing situations than this little community."

"No, no," Fab said. "Of course we don't think you can't manage. We just wonder if you'll agree, that's all."

"You would live here in the lodge," Bliss said.

Sebastian added, "And be available when Bobby comes home from school, of course—and when Polly is working."

"The income would be good," Bliss told Venus. "And we'd certainly like to hear any ideas you have for maximizing occu-pancy. And increasing efficiency."

"We could provide you with additional help in that depart-ment," Sebastian said.

"That will not be necessary." Venus rose majestically to her feet and shook out the folds of her caftan. "I know how to make this the most sought-after facility in the country."

Sebastian leaned forward. So did Bliss.

"Do tell, Mom," Polly said.

Venus swayed inside her robes. "The premier belly dancing academy in the country." She pointed a toe and extended her arms. From beneath the robe, bells tinkled. "The *only* residen-tial belly dancing academy in the country."

"Sounds . . ."

"Interesting," Sebastian finished for Bliss.

"When is the wedding?" Venus asked, beginning to roll her hips. "I hope I have sufficient time to practice."

Turn the page for an exciting taste of
Stella Cameron's next book,
*GUILTY PLEASURES*
coming in March, 1997
from Zebra Books . . .

Don't miss Stella Cameron's previous
Zebra Books titles:

*PURE DELIGHTS*
*SHEER PLEASURES*

# One

The boy who scribbled, *"Least Likely to Succeed,"* beneath Polly Crow's high school yearbook photo had proudly signed his brilliant comment. He'd also laughed in her face when he handed back the book. Why not? After all, he had nothing to fear from a girl who came from nothing, and was going nowhere.

Polly folded her white cashmere cardigan tightly about her and breathed deeply of the stiff late summer breeze off Lake Washington. Back then she'd begun to believe Brad—she couldn't recall the other name—and his friends, were probably right. And if there'd been a least-likely-to-succeed award, she'd have won with no contest. She hadn't been eligible to win any other prizes.

But they were wrong. They were all wrong, including Polly, because she had amounted to something. And because she'd made good, someone was trying to frighten her to death.

As she liked to do at the end of each day's filming, she walked along the floating docks off the town of Kirkland's waterfront. Leggy impatiens, luminous pink, orange, purple, and white, slumped in wooden planters. Ivy geraniums faded by weeks in the sun trailed from baskets suspended on poles. Time for chrysanthemums and winter pansies.

The smell was coming-of-evening rich, sleepy-silk-sway-of water mysterious.

Polly's long cotton skirt whipped about her legs. Too bad she couldn't ignore the other, the menace she'd lived with for days.

Just some obsessive creep getting a cheap thrill from threatening a TV personality. It happened all the time.

And sometimes these freaks acted on their obsessions.

She wouldn't change her lifestyle, wouldn't start locking herself inside the condo, wouldn't tell anyone who didn't already know what was happening.

If she said aloud: "Someone leaves messages on my answering machine. No, I don't know who—he whispers. He says I only made one mistake in my life but he's forgiven that, that I used to be really good and I need him to make me good again," it would all become too real. Polly didn't want it to be real. She didn't want to voice, "I want you with me, or I want you dead." If she did, she'd have to admit she wasn't imagining the calls, imagining the worst threat of all: "I know you'll do what I want, what we both want, and get rid of anyone who stands in our way. Otherwise, I'll have to make sure you do."

Good?

Only one mistake?

Twenty-seven years old. Ex-addict. Never married. Single mother of a seven-year-old son. Daughter of a single mother.

Sam Dodge, the handsome rebel who'd wanted her because she made him look good, had taken her so low she should have been dead by now. But she hadn't died. Polly smiled at the wind, smiled at the watery sting in her eyes, smiled at the jumble of bittersweet memories.

Bobby had saved her. Of all things, rather than adding another stone to the weight dragging her down, getting pregnant at nineteen had stopped the fall.

*"I ain't gettin' slowed down by no brat. If you wanna keep on being my woman, get rid of it,"* Sam had demanded when she'd told him about the pregnancy. And when she'd refused he'd said, *"No account piece of trash. You'll never amount to anything without me."*

Even as she shuddered, Polly smiled. Sam had given her a choice between drink, drugs, abusive sex—and Bobby, dear, serious Bobby. No choice. Thank God what was left of herself had made the decision so easy.

The whisperer called Bobby a mistake. That had to be what he meant, and he threatened to get rid of him.

Bobby hadn't questioned being sent to stay with Venus Crow, Polly's mother who lived in nearby Bellevue. He'd accepted the story that the show was going into a production crunch and this was a great time for him to run free at the artists' colony that had once been his home. Venus ran Hole Point, and Bobby loved the place.

Venus hadn't questioned Bobby's visit either.

Some members of the cast of *Polly's Place* had been with her when she got the first message. She'd laughed it off and never mentioned the continuing calls.

The uncomfortable thud of her heart made Polly open her mouth to swallow. She ought to ask for help. The police wouldn't do anything unless something happened. Her heart leapt again. Unless she was hurt in some way—or someone she loved was hurt—they'd say there was nothing to be done.

She continued walking. Rafted boats jostled at moorages. Gusts of laughter and raised voices erupted from cabins and deckhousing. The wind was enough to send most of the messers-about-in-boats below for their happy hour.

These people weren't what drew Polly this way so often.

The real reason was something else she ought to pack away in her heap of shouldn't, and never-will-be's.

But a woman could look at a man, couldn't she? Especially when that's all she would ever do—look?

She strolled to the very end of the farthest dock from shore and searched about. No sign of the big, black rubber dinghy. No sign of the man in his wet suit doing whatever he did at the end of his day. Maybe he wouldn't come so regularly as fall and winter approached.

Polly rolled her eyes at the disappointment she felt; disappointment because she might not get more chances to take furtive glances at a man she didn't know.

He'd never looked her way—not deliberately. He didn't know her and she didn't know him. She'd never even heard him speak.

Polly stopped and narrowed her eyes to focus on the distant Olympic Mountains. She'd never heard the big man with his sun-bleached hair and curiously light brown eyes say a word, even to the black cat who rode with him in his dinghy filled with diving equipment.

She knew his eyes were brown, and that they were remote—cold even. She knew because he had met her gaze occasionally. Each time their glances had crossed for no more than a few seconds. Polly always looked away first.

Her walks weren't at exactly the same time each day.

Usually the dinghy appeared. It just appeared, floated into sight from shadows around the dock. No engine noise. The engine didn't burst to life until she'd retraced her steps to the park that edged the waterfront.

As if he waited for her to come, watched while he pretended not to watch, then left once she was gone.

Rubber fenders squeaked between the rafted boats.

Mooring lines creaked.

The man had strong teeth. She'd seen them between his parted lips as he pulled a mask from his lean face. And he chewed gum. Polly had always disliked watching someone chew gum. Not this time.

Gavin Tucker, an artist who appeared on the show with Polly, said the man ran a dive shop. Gavin had also questioned the diver's reason for hanging around this section of the waterfront when his shop was a mile away. Anyway, Gavin had pointed out, the scuba lessons advertised by Room Below—the dive shop—were held in Puget Sound, not here in Lake Washington.

Ferrito. She knew his name was Ferrito, that he chewed gum, and liked cats.

Kirkland wasn't a big town and the show pulled in people from the community. Polly and the rest of the cast were friendly and open. Finding out about any of them wouldn't be so hard—including their phone number.

Once more Polly searched about.

Finding out a person's habits wasn't so hard, either. But Ferrito wasn't here today.

He liked cats. He wouldn't make threatening phone calls. She didn't know what he would do, they'd never even exchanged a smile. Exasperated, by the power of a stranger to frighten her, by her own weakness, by the ridiculous leap in logic she was making, Polly turned back.

She'd never heard him speak . . . or whisper.

Startled, Polly couldn't move.

She hadn't heard the approach of his bare feet on the wooden planking of the dock.

"Hi," Nasty Ferrito said. "Nice evening."

Her blue eyes stretched wide open. Very blue eyes, but he already knew that from watching her TV show.

Apart from dropping her hands to her sides she didn't move. Polly Crow, bubbly singing star of *Polly's Place,* the most popular children's show to hit the box in a decade, stared at him with her mouth open. If he didn't know how ridiculous it would be, he'd say she was afraid of him.

"Getting colder." Talking about the weather. He'd finally decided to quit stalling and force a meeting with the woman, and he was talking about the weather.

She nodded, almost imperceptibly. On television her straight, thick hair appeared lighter. In person it was a dark honey blond. This evening she wore it pulled back into a band at her nape. Her skin was pale. He'd found out from watching her on the docks that she was thinner than she appeared on the screen. Average height, but small.

He preferred more substantial women—stronger women.

Or he had.

*Hell,* his legs felt shaky.

This wasn't close enough. Nothing would be close enough. He wanted to touch her.

"Are you cold?" he asked. Sounded too personal.

Polly Crow shook her head. Her neck was slender, the bones at its base delicate. He'd read about seeing people's pulses beat. This was the first time he'd ever noticed.

She bowed her head and looked up at him. Her dark lashes were tipped with gold.

And Nasty's heart stopped beating. He hadn't imagined the effect she had on him—no, he hadn't imagined that. A man shouldn't be able to feel protective and predatory at the same time. So? he was breaking new ground. He'd like to cover her up and protect her from the world—and be inside her while he did it.

Good thing he'd spent almost as much of his adult life wearing a wet suit as he had anything else. Wet suits were great. Short of armor, they were the best way he knew of masking an erection. The hard-on inside his suit felt as if it had the power to punch holes in concrete. He dropped to sit on his heels and stroke Seven who had, as usual, followed him up the steps from the side of the dock where he'd tied up the dinghy.

This wasn't the way he'd rehearsed this meeting but then, he was no expert at approaching women he thought he could fall in love with. In fact, he'd never done this before.

He'd never fallen in love. "Winter's coming." *Hell.*

"Yes," she said. Her voice wasn't breathy on television.

"Beautiful time of the year."

"Yes."

Oh, great. "Am I bothering you?"

Her shoulders rose. She gripped one of the standards that supported a hanging basket.

Nasty picked up Seven and bounced to his feet. "I wouldn't want to intrude." Yeah, he would. "Excuse me if—"

"No." She shook her head emphatically. "No. You excuse me, please. You took me by surprise, that's all. It's pretty quiet out here."

A nice voice. More than nice. Sometimes he closed his eyes to listen to her on TV. Laughter hung out somewhere in there.

And she could sing. All those kids' songs he listened to. He smothered a grin. Nasty Ferrito, ex-navy SEAL, tough veteran of more life-on-the-line covert operations than he could remember, made a point of tuning in *Polly's Place* and listening as if he was into *Down and Out the Main Monsters,* and watching *Gavin the Paint Man.* Ferrito's crusty partner, Dusty Miller, had plenty to say about that. Nasty passed it off as practice for when Junior, an old friend's little girl, came to visit. Dusty wasn't fooled.

"Nice black cat."

Her spontaneous comment surprised him. He stroked Seven's sinuous body and long tail. "Unlucky for some," he said. "We get along."

"That's thirteen."

Nasty squinted at her. "Seven."

"Thirteen—unlucky for some. Not black cats are unlucky for some—or seven."

Definitely not the way he'd rehearsed this encounter. "Communication gap," he said. Each time he looked into her face, that look lasted a little longer. He risked stepping closer and turning until the cat faced Polly Crow. "Her name's Seven."

"Ah, I see." Polly laughed. Her fingernails were short and devoid of polish. She smoothed Seven's head. "Why Seven?"

"Always liked the number and I found her—scratch that—she found me on a Sunday. Seventh day of the week. What are you afraid of?" He'd have to put that off-the-wall question down to rusty social skills.

"I'm not afraid of anything. What makes you think I am?"

He slung Seven into her favorite position, draped over his shoulder. "Hell, I don't know. Just a feeling." Another sense you developed when you lived largely on your instincts for a long time.

Her eyes became unblinking. She nailed him with that stare. "Why do you come by here each evening?"

"Do I come by each evening?"

"Yes, you know you do."

"Maybe I live on one of these boats."

"Do you?"

Triumph shouldn't be what he felt, but he did. She'd noticed him—noticed when he visited, and how often. "I live on a boat. But it's in front of my partner's house." He hooked a thumb over his shoulder. "Farther up the shore. I come in the evening because I like it here."

"Why?"

"I just told you why."

She crossed her arms. "No you didn't. The whole waterfront is lovely. But you always come right here." She pointed downward and crossed her arms again.

Not a big woman in any respect, but nice, very nice. Keeping his eyes above her breasts wasn't easy. "Why do you come here every evening?" he asked.

"Because . . ." Pink swept along her cheekbones, and the soft skin of her neck. "It's calm. Quiet. I like that."

"Calm and quiet on this dock rather than, say, that one?" He pointed south, then north, "Or that one?"

"I like this one."

"Know what I think?" Dusty always came out with the truth, swore he could live with letting the chips fall where they might. "I think you come here because I do. I think you come out here each evening hoping to see me."

Her lips formed a silent *Oh!*

Smugness didn't suit a man. Nasty felt smug anyway."You walked out here tonight expecting to see me. You were looking for me when I came up behind you."

"Ooh." She planted her feet in her flat brown sandals and her face worked through one expression after another. "Crumb! Well, I've never met a man with so much—*ego.* I certainly don't come out here to look for you. We just happen to come at the same time, that's all. It doesn't mean a thing. Not to me."

He wouldn't remark on *crumb* as an expletive—yet. "How old are you?"

"Twenty-seven." Another silent *Oh!* "Crumb! I can't believe it. You sashay up here, accuse me of taking walks because I want to see you, then ask me how old I am."

Nasty shifted Seven to his other shoulder and unzipped his wet suit to the waist. Despite the wind he was feeling increasingly hot.

Polly Crow looked at his chest.

"Sashay, huh? No one ever accused me of sashaying before. Sounds cute."

"There's nothing cute about you," she told him, glancing away, then back at his chest. "Nothing."

He'd swear she was responding to him. "Good. Cute wouldn't suit me." Maybe his thoughts were wishful, but he doubted it. "You're cute."

"You're pushy. How old are you?"

"Fair enough. Thirty-six. Is that too old?"

"Too old for what?"

"For you."

Polly Crow made a lot of silent, Oh's!

"You watch me, Polly Crow. You come out here and watch me in the dinghy almost every night."

"Crumb!" Again expressions washed over her features. "You know my name."

"Don't you think everyone in Kirkland knows your name?"

"No."

He spread the fingers of his right hand on his chest, inside the wet suit. "You're on TV every afternoon. Sing the song for me."

An amazed frown was all he got.

"Come on. *Everybody needs somebody. Everybody is somebody. Somebody needs everybody.* Sing it for me."

"No." She took a step backward. Her fascination with his chest was undeniable. "Are you telling me you watch *Polly's Place?* In the afternoon? A children's program?"

"Yep, yep, and yep. Quite often."

"Then you come over here to watch me in person."

"I come over here."

"Grown men don't make a habit of watching children's programs in the afternoon—probably almost never."

"Lots of grown men would if they knew they'd see you." He'd said it. No taking back the words. "You do hope to see me when you come here, don't you?"

Another pink rush rose up her neck. She spun away and gave a startled yelp as a scatter of seagulls came in for a landing.

"Don't you?" Nasty persisted. "I come to see you and you come to see me."

Their heads jerking, the gulls strutted across the decking. Seven spared them a glare but knew better than to take chase. "Hey," Nasty said softly. "I have scared you. Damn, I'm sorry. I didn't mean to do that. Would you like to see my boat?"

Polly turned to face him again. "You've got to be kidding. Would I like to see your boat? I guess it's more original than etchings."

He doubted she'd laugh if he told her he had some etchings on the boat. "Let me take you out on the dinghy, then. Peaceful out there."

"You think I'm going to get into a little rubber boat with a man I don't know?'

Smiling didn't come easily, never had, but he managed. "You might. Never any harm in asking."

"No, thank you."

"I'm good with boats. Safe. I'll take care of you."

Where there'd been a blush, pallor seeped in. "I don't need taking care of—by anyone."

This was not going well.

She said. "I can keep myself safe." But she didn't try to leave. "What do you think of answering machines?"

A flurry of activity passed between the gulls and they took off, crying and swooping, their wings battering the air.

"Did you ask me what I think of answering machines?"

"Simple enough question."

"Okay. I think answering machines are great."

"Because you can leave messages you'd be afraid to give in person?"

He couldn't begin to guess where this was going. "Because they make it possible to make sure you don't miss a call. And you don't have to be tethered to the damn phone all the time."

"I've got to get back."

"No you don't. You're through for the day."

Her hand went to her throat. "You don't know that?"

"Sure I do. When you leave here you'll go to your condo. Alone. Your boy's not with you at the moment."

A sharp breath made a scraping sound in her throat. "Good night."

Automatically, Nasty stepped aside. "Yeah, sure."

When she drew level, she paused and whispered, "Leave me alone, please. I haven't done anything to you."

By the time he rallied she was several yards away. He caught up easily. "Polly? Look, if I upset you, I'm sorry. Of course you haven't done anything to me. I thought it was time we talked. Nothing more complicated than that."

She stopped and stared toward the sky. "Time we talked? Now why on earth would it be time we talked?"

"I put that badly. I guess I haven't had a whole lot of practice at this"—he spread his arms—"and before you ask me what 'this' is, I mean coming on to women without at least asking them to dance or buying them a drink first."

"Charming," she said through her teeth. There was fire in those blue eyes now. "If some woman is stupid enough to dance with you, or let you buy her a drink, you think you can *come on* to her."

"Geez, not exactly. I mean, not—"

"She's supposed to understand you expect sex? Men like you are a menace."

"I do not—"

"Well, you and I haven't danced and you haven't bought me a drink."

"Would you like a drink?" He groaned aloud.

Polly wrinkled her nose. "That's disgusting."

"You looked at my chest."

She covered her mouth.

He should have stayed in the dinghy. "I mean, I think you find me attractive, too. I think I turn you . . ." *Great going, Ferrito.* "We may have a mutual appeal."

"You are absolutely unbelievable. And if you're doing what I think you're doing to me, stop it. I don't have any proof yet, but I'll get it."

He gaped at her.

"Oh, I know about scrambling numbers for anonymity, but sooner or later you'll make a mistake and get caught."

"Er, sure. Anything you say." Most people might be wholly confused by what she said. Nasty also knew about scrambling numbers—and a great many other covert procedures. "Polly, we've gotten off to a bad start."

Her laugh cut him. "We haven't started, period!" With that she set off at a brisk pace.

Nasty followed. "I guess I've said everything wrong. Will you give me another chance? Can I see you again?"

"Not if I see you first."

He strode along beside her. "That's a cliché."

"You ought to know. It's about the only one I haven't heard you use."

"If you knew me, you'd like me."

"I'd hate you. I already do."

The venom in her tone stopped him, but only for an instant. He fell into step as she turned to walk along another of the bobbing docks. "All I can say is sorry, again. I'll go away now."

"Good."

"You've very beautiful, you know."

When she looked sideways at him he could swear there were tears in her eyes. She said, "You just told me you were going away."

"I am. I wanted to tell you how beautiful you are, though."

"Thanks. I'll tell my husband you said so."

"You don't have a husband."

"Who are you?" Her voice rose. "Who *are* you?"

"Ferrito," he said quietly. "Nasty Ferrito. Nasty to my friends."

This time her voice was faint. "Nasty?"

"You can call me Nasty."

*"Nasty?"*

"Sure. And don't ask me why that's my name because I don't discuss it." He didn't even think about it. "Dusty Miller and I run Room Below. It's a dive shop. We're trustworthy people. I'm trustworthy."

A woman in red climbed from a motorcruiser and set off toward land. The flash of relief on Polly's face was impossible to miss. "You really are afraid of me, aren't you?" he asked.

"Good night, *Nasty."*

"Aren't you? Doesn't matter. I'll find out why."

"You'll leave me alone." Trotting now, Polly followed the woman.

"If you're scared, it isn't because of me. Let me help you."

"No!" She started to run.

"Lock your doors, Polly." Jesus Christ, she was terrified. Something had crawled inside her skull and ripped up her nerves. He'd just happened along when she was ready to break. "Do you hear me? Lock yourself in."

Her strides lengthened but he kept the same distance between them with no effort.

As she reached the grass verge at the shore end of the docks, Polly paused and looked back at him. Her eyes were dry but wild.

"It's okay," he told her. "Talk to me. Let me help you. Tell me what you need and I'll make sure you get it."

She didn't answer, but sped away once more.

Nasty threw up his hands and said, "Okay, you win. For now. But remember to lock those doors. A lovely woman alone is always vulnerable."

He let her leave him behind.

So he wasn't smooth. Maybe he'd handled things badly even.

But not badly enough to warrant her behavior. She was scared shitless about something and he wasn't through asking what it was. Next time he'd just have to be more forceful.

Yeah, next time he wouldn't take no for an answer.

When she ran, her long, white skirt flipped up around her knees. Even at a distance he noted how pretty her legs were. She had narrow feet. Nasty Ferrito was a foot man on occasion. Like now. He'd like to kiss Polly Crow's feet. He'd start with the toes, spend a lot of time on her instep, go slow, very slow—work his way up.

Bless the wet suit.

"Hello, Pretty Polly. Put the Kettle On."

The light on the answering machine still flashed, but a click came, then a buzz.

Polly felt so sick she had to sit down. That was it, the whole message. She pushed strands of hair from her forehead and felt moisture. She was sweating, but she'd been sweating since she left the hard-muscled, cold-eyed diver behind on the waterfront. ". . . remember to lock those doors. A lovely woman alone is always vulnerable."

Another click.

"Polly, where are you? It's your favorite super-model sister. I'm so sick of being an *object,* my love. All these pushy people *pawing* me. Can we meet? Puhleeze? Call me."

Fabiola. Polly smiled with relief at the sound of her twin's blessedly familiar voice and reached for the phone.

Click, buzz, click.

She peered at the counter on the answering machine. Six calls and she'd only heard two.

"Oh, Pretty Polly, you haven't been listening to me. I'm going to have to get very angry with you if you don't stop disobeying me."

Click.

She let her hand fall back into her lap. He as much hissed, as whispered. Who was he? The clock on the equipment no longer functioned. Why hadn't she fixed it or bought a new one?

Buzz. Click.

"Heavenly child, I feel you are in need of me. Come to Festus and to me. You are always so calm at Another Reality. I'll make you some of my latest tea. Soar to Serenity. It's a Belinda special, darling child."

Belinda and Festus of Another Reality, a crystals, incense, taro, tea, and wiccan-wannabe shop, had become good friends to Polly and Bobby.

Click.

"You should be there by now, Polly. You've had time to leave the studio and get home. Ah, but I mustn't be too harsh with you. Perhaps that dreadful man who writes the scripts has kept you late. Be very careful of him, pet, he wants you, you know. He wants your body, not your mind. I want your mind . . . and your body. Bye."

The scream Polly heard was her own. Shaking desperately she stared at the readout that should have given her the caller's identification. Blocked. Every time it was blocked.

Who could she ask for help? Venus was out of the question. Fabiola would panic, too. Belinda and Festus already knew and had suggested incense and a goddess to do something or other.

Once more the buzz on the line was followed by a click, and the whisperer said, "You have tried my patience, Pretty Polly. Why can't you understand that I, and only I am to see the woman you really are. That thin, white skirt"—he gave a grating moan—"with the light shining through. And the wind blowing. You know what that does. You do these things deliberately. Light and wind. Showing your legs. Oh, yes, your legs . . ."

The connection broke before the final message began. First there was only panting, then he said. "I've given you chances. I told you there is a connection between us. But you have denied me again. Others saw you on the dock, flaunting yourself. Disgusting. But don't worry, little Polly, I'm going to save you from yourself. . . ."

whispered. Who was he? The voice on the computer no longer threatened. Why had [illegible] begun a [illegible].

Buzz. Click.

"[illegible] that you are [illegible] to come [illegible]. You [illegible] Another Reality. I'll [illegible] you [illegible] tea. Now [illegible] it's a [illegible] cat, [illegible]."

[illegible] Another Reality [illegible] into [illegible] shop [illegible] become good friends [illegible] Polly and [illegible].

Click.

"You [illegible] Polly. You've had time to have [illegible] and get home. [illegible] the hand [illegible] that [illegible] who writes the [illegible] you [illegible] pen, he wants you to know [illegible] your [illegible] and [illegible] eye."

[illegible] Polly [illegible] was [illegible] desperately [illegible] she should [illegible] the [illegible] Every [illegible] was [illegible].

[illegible] ask [illegible]? [illegible] out of [illegible] question [illegible] would [illegible] had [illegible] something [illegible].

[illegible] the [illegible] was followed by [illegible] "You have [illegible] Polly. [illegible] can [illegible] the [illegible] that [illegible] have a [illegible] And the [illegible] [illegible] your legs [illegible]."

The [illegible] began, [illegible] said. "[illegible] you [illegible] between [illegible]. So you have [illegible] Others [illegible] Polly. I'm going to [illegible] you [illegible]."

*Stella Cameron loves to hear from her readers!*
*Contact her web page at:*
http://www.seanet.com/Vendors/bryan/stella.html